Light

Also by Margaret Elphinstone

The Incomer (1987)
A Sparrow's Flight (1987)
Islanders (1994)
The Sea Road (2000)
An Apple from a Tree (1990)
Outside Eden (1991)
Hy Brasil (2002)
Voyageurs (2003)
Gato (2005)

LIGHT

a novel

Margaret Elphinstone

CANONGATE
Edinburgh · New York · Melbourne

First published in Great Britain in 2006 by
Canongate Books Ltd., Edinburgh, Scotland

Printed in the United States of America

FIRST AMERICAN EDITION

ISBN-10: 1-84195-880-8
ISBN-13: 978-1-84195-880-4

Map on page viii created by Ian Berg

Canongate
841 Broadway
New York, NY 10003

Distributed by Publishers Group West

www.groveatlantic.com

07 08 09 10 11 10 9 8 7 6 5 4 3 2 1

For Ros and Katy, who were there

Acknowledgements

I would like to acknowledge the help of the following people, from north to south: Anne Sinclair, Fair Isle, and Simon Hall, Orkney, for taking Ben's part so well; MV *Halton* (Stromness) and her crew – Bob Anderson, Angus Budge and Mary Harris – for the epic voyages round the Scottish islands; the Sule Skerry Ringing Group, especially Mike Archer, Adrian Blackburn and Dave Budworth, for taking on a complete amateur; Fran Cree and Chris Barrett, Rua Reidh Lighthouse, for providing both setting and frequent retreat; Miriam McDonald at the library of the Royal Commission on the Ancient and Historical Monuments of Scotland; Ian Begg, for drawing Archie's map for him; Martin Hendry for the stars and planets; Jonathan Sawday for the sailing directions and David Kinloch for the voices. I also thank Ann Bardens, Mike Brown and Ros Elphinstone, and my editor at Canongate, Karen McCrossan.

I'd like to thank everyone on the Isle of Man who gave me ideas and hospitality, particularly those at the Centre for Manx Studies who so generously let me use their knowledge and research: Peter Davey, Kit Gawne, Jennifer Kewley Draskau, Breesha Maddrell and Philippa Tomlinson; also Roger Sims and the staff of the Manx National Heritage Library. I'm indebted to Eva Wilson, Castletown, for the benefit of her research, and Celia Salisbury Jones, Castletown, for much help and hospitality; Adrian Corkill, for his survey of Manx wrecks; and Alex Maddrell, Port St Mary, for sharing his deep knowledge and seamanship, and Ray Moore, University of York, for the weather data.

I wish to thank the people who generously shared their childhood memories of India: Kumkum Dabriwala, Cleodie Mackinnon, Helen Reid Thomas, Mira Shahani, Uma Shahani and Pete Stuart.

I could not have spent so much time on uninhabited islands without the hospitality of the Isle of May Bird Observatory Trust and the Calf of Man Bird Observatory Trust. I also wish to thank the University of Liverpool for hosting me at the Centre for Manx Studies while I researched this novel. A grant from the Carnegie Trust for the Universities of Scotland helped to finance my research. Finally, I'm indebted to the Bogliasco Foundation, Liguria, for awarding me a fellowship which enabled me to write the book in ideal conditions, which included an excellent view of the sea.

The old people said there was an enchanted island south-west of the Calf of Man, and it was seen once in seven years, when Old May Day was on Sunday. Some one of the name of Onny Vadrill was the last one that saw it; but it is often cloudy in the morning in May, and the people used to be looking for it for many years.

Manx Notes and Queries, *ed. C. Roeder*, 1904

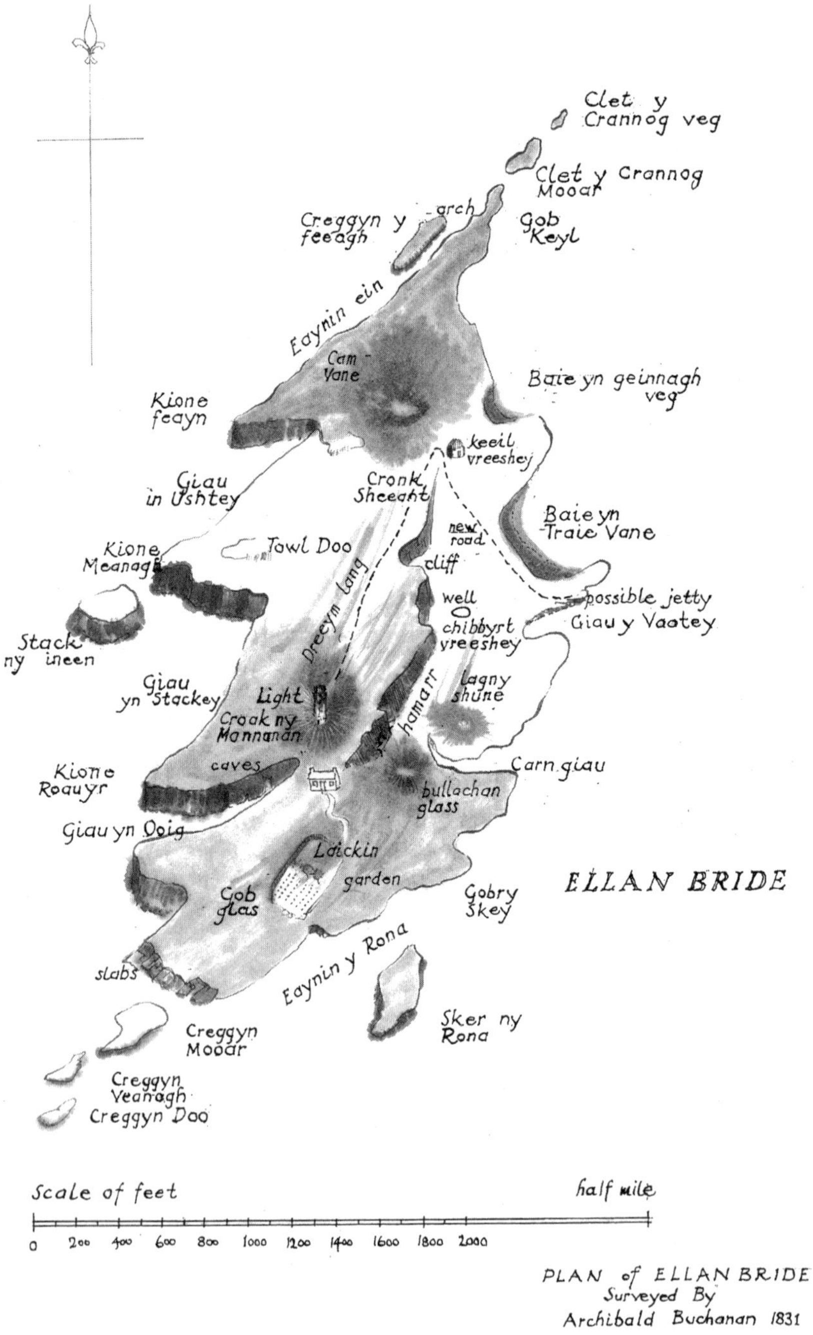

Clet y Crannog veg
Clet y Crannog Mooar
Creggyn y feeagh
arch
Gob Keyl
Eaynin ein
Cam Vane
Baie yn geinnagh veg
Kione feayn
keeil vreeshey
Cronk Sheeaght
Giau in Ushtey
Baie yn Traie Vane
new road
Kione Meanagh
Towl Doo
cliff
Dreeym lang
well
possible jetty
Giau y Vaotey
chibbyrt vreeshey
Stack ny ineen
lagny shune
Giau yn Stackey
Light
Croak ny Mannanan
hamarr
Kione Roauyr
caves
Carn giau
bullachan glass
Giau yn Ooig
Laickin
garden
ELLAN BRIDE
Gob glas
Gobry Skey
slabs
Eaynin y Rona
Sker ny Rona
Creggyn Mooar
Creggyn Veanagh
Creggyn Doo
Scale of feet
half mile
0 200 400 600 800 1000 1200 1400 1600 1800 2000
PLAN of ELLAN BRIDE
Surveyed By
Archibald Buchanan 1831

Chapter 1

INSIDE THE LANTERN THERE WAS ONLY LIGHT, AND THE hot rich smell of burning oil. Outside was blank dark. Close to, it was not one light, but twelve. Each lamp had its own reflector, a concave hemisphere lined with a mosaic of mirrors. Flame reflected flame across the curved surfaces until all the lights merged into a single beam directed outward into the surrounding sea. Looking into the light along the beam was like looking at the sun. If she did that she was left seeing only green spots with fiery edges swimming against her eyes, until they gradually faded away into nothing at all.

The trick was never to look into the light directly. She could look through the beam, at the floor, at the oil reservoirs, at the rectangular shapes of the six window frames surrounding her. Here at the top of the tower everything was sharp and bright, and outside this little hot space there was only emptiness.

If only that were true. If only they could have been left in peace, and overlooked, as they had been all these years.

If only it had never happened.

Lucy realised she was blaming herself yet again. But she couldn't stop wondering, even after five whole years, if she could have done anything to prevent it. Because now . . . If she'd managed to get down to the rocks that night . . . If she'd managed to reach Jim – then this other thing wouldn't be happening now.

On a day like today it was impossible to recapture the power of the wind. She of all people should know about the wind. She'd seen enough of what it could do to the sea. Of course she couldn't have stood up to it that night. Of course not. But she couldn't stop herself going over it again. She couldn't help re-living it over and over, wondering what she might have done differently.

That night she'd battled the wind with all the strength she had. She'd kept on staggering forward – she'd never dreamed of turning back – holding on to the rope. The wind kept knocking her over. Then the lantern had smashed on a rock. What more could she have done, when she couldn't even see? In the swirling dark she'd struggled on, feeling for familiar ground. The wind had eased. She'd realised she wasn't heading into it any more. Then she'd seen: down below there was white water where none should be. She'd been pushed too far to the south, almost into Cam Giau. The light never shone down there, so she'd not seen the edge through all the spray.

She'd fought her way back onto the grass, though somehow she'd lost the rope. Now the white water had gone she'd seen nothing at all. She hadn't been able to hear where the sea was, because the same wild roaring was everywhere. She'd seen the surf again just in time, right below her feet. But it was on the wrong side. Uphill had to be the way back. She'd got up high enough and there'd been grass underfoot. The wind hurled her off her feet. Her head banged on a rock. She'd been soaked already; she hadn't even noticed the blood. She'd nearly got to the top, as close as she could without being blown off. She kept being thrown down on sharp rocks. The sea was breaking right over the island. Right over the grass. She couldn't have gone closer. Only she'd had to keep close to the edge to know where she was. The wind had kept flinging her towards the water. Then she'd been crawling uphill, with the waves breaking right over her. The waves had broken right on top of the island. She *couldn't* have gone any further. It had been *impossible* to go any further.

But if only she'd managed it . . . If she'd only found the strength . . . If she'd *willed* herself not to be weak . . . If she'd not failed him that night – if she'd not failed all of them – then Jim would be alive now.

If Jim were still here, there would never have been the letter.

There was no point blaming herself, five years later. No one else blamed her. Diya had never spoken a word of blame. No one else supposed for one moment that she'd not done all that was possible.

She still thought – it was so hard now, to remember what that night had been like – that she should have tried again. Or gone with Jim in the first place. He'd said no, he could manage. He'd *told* her to stay in the house. That didn't mean she couldn't have thought for herself. She wasn't bound to do what Jim said. She knew what had to be done just as well as he did. She should have *known*.

But it was so hard to remember what it had been like. Not being able to stand against the wind. Not being able to see. Not being able to *think*.

Lucy put down the oil can, and unlatched the south window. She threw her shawl over her shoulders and sat, so that her silhouette didn't get in the way of the light, on the step of the metal platform that ringed the lantern. Now she could see out. She might feel she was suspended in a solitary bubble in the midst of chaos, but actually she was here, in this tower, in the middle of the world.

The light beamed out behind her. It made the stars very dim, but Mars shone red, low over the western horizon, and if she twisted round she could see the Plough just setting to the north of it. North-east, the two lights on the Calf flashed every two minutes. When she looked east she saw a thin pale line of light. The earth – Lucy sometimes allowed herself to be fanciful in her solitary moments – had survived the night. Somehow the thought calmed her. Human lives were so little: people did what they could in this world, and no one could do more. Lucy sighed, and rested her elbows on her knees.

The sea rose and fell against the shore like a dragon breathing gently in its sleep. As Lucy's eyes adjusted she could see pale lines of light that came and went: each rising wave caught for a moment in the beam of light before it broke. Then the next wave rose and broke, rose and broke, one white gleam for each, then nothing.

Shadows stretched away from the tower where the rocky outcrops caught the beam. There was no moon, so each elongated shadow was quite black, all of them reaching as far as they could away from Lucy, in a circle of which she was the centre. Only the tower on which she stood had no shadow. The night was almost done. She was thinking about Jim. What would he have done if the letter had come to him?

A pinprick of light appeared to the south-west about a quarter of a mile away, very pale in contrast to the thin stripe in the east, which was now tinged with orange.

Slowly the world turned grey, and then as white as ice. The water separated itself from the sky and became flat and bleak. Shapes humped out of the sea. The Calf of Man to the north-east was lightly etched in pencil, its lights dimmed by the growing dawn. Over the left shoulder of the Calf rose, faint and far away, Cronk ny Arrey Lea, and, in the far distance east of the Calf, she could just make out Snaefell. To the south, the little light went out, and turned into the ghost of a ship in full sail. Lucy fetched the telescope from the light room and held it to her eye, adjusting the focus. She saw a circle of magnified ripples, and then, after casting around for a moment, she found a brig with all sails set to catch as much of the fickle breeze as they could. No, it wasn't a brig – it had an extra mast – a ketch, perhaps? – a schooner? – no, it was a snow. It was too far away to make out her name. The ship was heading east against the tide, bound for Whitehaven probably, keeping a cautious quarter-mile clear of the tidal skerries that lay to the south of the lighthouse. Lucy saw the sails flap, and reluctantly fill again. It might be like that all day. The snow wouldn't be out of sight of the island for a good while yet. As Lucy watched, she saw the grey sails suddenly brighten, and the whole ship was bathed in yellow light.

Lucy went into the lantern, took the snuffer from its hook, and went clockwise round the twelve oil lamps, extinguishing each flame in turn. As each one was doused its mirrors all went blank. Smoke rose from the wicks, and vanished in the growing dawn.

The Calf lights were out. The sky was awash with orange and pink. The far lands turned purple. Now the sun was burning into the sea; she had to half-shut her eyes to look. A path of light shot from the heart of the dawn to the foot of the tower. The red sun was a line, a curve, a half circle. Lucy felt sunlight on her face. Down below on the island, the cock began to crow.

Chapter 2

HE'D BEEN DREAMING HE WAS BACK ON CAPE WRATH DOING the first survey. The wind howled over the headland. They could barely stand, let alone measure. At least the chain was too heavy to blow off . . . he hoped it was too heavy but it seemed to be floating somehow, and slippery like seaweed. Spray shot up three hundred feet and drenched them. Smith, junior to him though far more experienced, was shouting in his ear, 'Get down, sir! We must get down!' They were running – he and Smith and Ben Groat the apprentice – pummelled by the wind, east down the lee slope away from the cliffs. The land curved round to the jetty – there wasn't any track – and they crawled into a sheltered hollow under the rocks. It was all Archie's fault. He hadn't wanted to be defeated, not even by the weather. Now he was being punished. He'd made a mistake. Somehow he was back on the headland being blown seawards by an almighty wind. There was no withstanding it, and the edge was very close . . .

'You all right, sir?'

Archie opened his eyes. Daylight filtered into the room through the crack between heavy curtains. The boots was leaning over him, looking concerned.

'Half past five, sir. Were you wanting hot water, sir?'

'Yes, of course I do,' said Archie irritably. 'I ordered it last night.'

When the fellow had gone Archie lay for a moment looking at the cracks in the ceiling. Where had that dream come from? He'd eaten a dish of large Manx oysters last night, but all the same . . . all he'd had to wash it down was a single glass of port. And he had nothing to be nervous about; the present job was simple enough. Cape Wrath had been far harder.

This was no time for nightmares. He was lying, for once, in a comfortable bed in a decent inn. It was worth savouring the moment: from here on the travelling would be rough. The George Inn in Castletown was a respectable coaching establishment, quite unlike anything one would find in the Hebrides. There'd even been a discreet notice downstairs advertising Assemblies for members of the *ton* on Friday nights, and sure enough when he'd been looking for Benjamin Groat last night he'd stumbled into a spacious ballroom on the first floor. The polished floor stretched emptily to a little alcove at the end, and the whole room smelt overpoweringly of wilting lilies. High society was quite beyond his touch, and anyway by Friday night they would be on Ellan Bride, God willing, a far cry from genteel Castletown.

No, he had no ambitions in that direction. He could have come post from Douglas if he'd chosen; the turnpike road was excellent. He'd preferred to travel in the gig with Groat and Scott. Ben Groat could have been trusted to look after the gear, but Archie felt happier not letting it out of his sight. He knew nothing about these Manxmen. Hebrideans, however poverty-stricken, could usually be trusted to be honest, unless, of course, it was a matter of wreck.

'Half past five, you were saying, sir.'

Archie jerked awake. He must have drifted off again.

'It's twenty to six.' The boot boy was standing over him again. 'Your hot water's on the stand, sir. And your boots is done, sir. I left 'em on the mat there, sir, and . . .'

'Very good.'

The boots got breathlessly to the end of his message, '. . . and breakfast is serving in the coffee room, sir.'

When Archie sat up the room still swayed, although the *Mona's Isle* had been pretty stable, just a trifle choppy off the Mull of Galloway. So whatever had made him dream about Cape Wrath? It was all so long ago. The lighthouse on Cape Wrath had been finished three years since. He'd visited it once since it was lit, from the *Regent*.

If he saw Mr Quirk at nine . . . And now there was this other matter to settle. Yesterday evening, while Archie had been down to the harbour, where he'd discovered that it would be much simpler to keep the gig and travel overland to Port St Mary, his two chainmen had taken themselves off to a harbourside tavern. While Archie had been planning their onward journey, his henchmen had done their best to botch the whole job from the very start.

Damn Scott! What had he been thinking of? Nothing, of course. The man never thought. And there seemed to be more taverns to the square mile in this town than in Glasgow, even: naturally that had been too much for Scott. Archie glanced at his watch again. Ten to six. He flung back the blankets and strode over to the window.

When he pulled back the curtain sunlight flooded the room. Archie looked down from his second-floor window onto the market square. Opposite was the grey posterior of Castle Rushen, much less imposing from this angle than from the river side, which had been their first view of it from the Douglas road. He looked at the clock on the castle wall, thinking to check his watch, but it had only the hour hand. 'Eliz. Reg.' said the clock face: '1597'. And yet from all that he'd heard these Manxmen insisted that they weren't English.

Archie pulled up the window-sash and knelt to lean out. He could smell the sea, and the rich tang of seaweed. There was no wind, and the drought showed no signs of abating. They'd need a wind tomorrow, but there was nothing to be done about that save whistling for it. Otherwise the day was as fine as it could be, and from somewhere below him he could smell bacon frying.

The prosperity of this little town seemed English too. The market square was overlooked by douce three-storey houses, lining the narrow paved streets which went off in all directions. The cobbles were empty and newly swept, and to the right an imposing modern church blocked the view to the sea. Next door to the George a maid was on her knees scrubbing the half dozen steps up to a pleasant modern townhouse. After years of working in the benighted Highlands, Castletown seemed a most attractive little town.

Archie found himself thinking about his dream again while he shaved and dressed. His mother would have listened to no nonsense about port and oysters. She'd taught him to respect his dreams. *So why would all that come back to you, Archie? What haunts you still?* Well, there was last year's voyage on the *Regent*, for a start. He liked his employer's sons well enough. Young David Stevenson had been there, on his first tour of the lighthouses. It had been Archie's job as Assistant to teach the thirteen-year-old David as much of the work as he could. He'd seen David's elder brother Alan put through the same process. Alan was seven years younger than Archie. Alan would be made partner in the firm before this year was out, and then it would be Stevenson and Son.

Archie tied his starched cravat carefully, and put on his frock coat. He'd have to come back here and change before they left. More waste of time. He wasn't looking forward to this morning. He hated dealing with local officials, and in this case there was nothing to say anyway. He wanted to get out to the site. If only they could get away today they'd still have two clear working days before Sunday, which would have given him enough material to start drawing. Archie had no objection to breaking the Sabbath himself, but he couldn't ask the chainmen to do so: Ellan Bride was hardly in the same league as the Bell Rock. However, as matters stood they'd probably have to leave tomorrow – Friday – unless they went with the tide this evening . . . The boatman might be willing to stay on Ellan Bride overnight. So even if this Mr Quirk kept him waiting all morning it wouldn't actually make much difference. And now there was the extra man to be thought of . . . Damn Scott! Damn him!

No one else was breakfasting at half past six, so Archie had the table in the coffee room to himself. The fire hadn't been lit, but the sun was streaming in through the window. Wooden clogs clattered in the street as folk hurried to their work. A cart rattled by, its iron wheels grating on the cobbles. A fish-wife with full basket was crying her wares, and out of the window he saw the maid at the townhouse leave her clean doorstep to buy fresh herrings. The day beckoned.

But he wasn't left in peace for long. The landlord brought the coffee himself, and hovered round Archie while he ate his ham and eggs, obviously wanting to talk.

'Edinburgh,' Mr Kneen said cautiously. 'Now that was in the papers too. This terrible cholera! We were hearing the sickness had reached Edinburgh – I was reading that but two or three months back.' He glanced at Archie anxiously. 'You yourself will have encountered it, no doubt?'

'Oh ay, it was bad. But I wasn't in town then.' That seemed rather a short answer. Archie made an effort to be friendly. 'I was working up north when the cholera broke out. Dunnet Head. That's on the north coast of Scotland.'

'Ah, you'll have built some lighthouses up there too, no doubt?'

'Ay, I've worked up there quite a lot.'

'So you weren't in Edinburgh for the sickness? They say it's very catching. Very. You just need to breathe in someone's breath, that's all, and you've caught it. And then – just in an hour or two – that's you dead – finished!'

Archie shook his head. 'Oh no! It's not infectious. I mean, a traveller from London or Edinburgh, say, couldn't bring it here. It's not like that.'

'You're sure of that, sir? I heard that when it takes a hold, folk start dying like flies, in their hundreds. Thousands, even, all in the same place. Bodies lying in the streets rotting, and no one to bury them.'

'Ah, but that's the point.' As ever, Archie was drawn into conversation by the technical question. 'It spreads, but ay in the same place. It's not infectious – not like plague, for example – where one man could carry it across a continent. It spreads some other way. No one quite knows – they talk about a miasma – a contagion in the air. When the air is polluted, anyone who breathes it is at risk. But humans don't carry air around with them.'

Mr Kneen still looked worried. 'It's these big cities that's in now. Man wasn't made for to live in great cities. These city folk think we all want to be like them, but there's some of us would be happier left alone, and that's a fact.' He took a cloth, and began polishing the pewter tankards that lined the dresser. He obviously wasn't intending to go away yet. 'But you'll be a city man yourself, sir?'

'No.' Archie added, as Mr Kneen seemed to be waiting for him to speak. 'Not originally.'

There was a short silence. Mr Kneen adjusted the shining tankards on their shelf. 'You'll have been in the lighthouse trade a long time, then? But you've not been here before? You didn't work at the Calf or the Point of Ayre?'

'No.' After a short pause Archie volunteered, 'I worked at the Mull of Galloway, though. I've often seen the Isle of Man from there.'

'Ah yes, I was hearing about the grand new light they've put there. You can see it from Peel on a clear night, so a fellow was telling me the other day. So you built that light?'

'I was one of the engineers,' Archie corrected him. He became a little more expansive. 'I hadn't seen it from the sea since it was lit, though – not till yesterday. I came down on the *Mona's Isle*, and I got a good look at it when we rounded the Mull.' He relapsed into silence. He couldn't begin to explain the excitement he'd felt when he'd come on deck to see the Mull of Galloway lighthouse from the sea. Gleaming white in the rays of the rising sun, it had looked so familiar, and yet it was strange in its completed state. There was always something extra about the finished thing – something more substantial, a little more like itself, than even its designers had been able to imagine. Odd to think that folk would sail by the Mull light for centuries to come without giving the matter a thought. They'd see it now – as the scattering of folk on the deck of *Mona's Isle* had been doing yesterday morning – as if it had been there for ever. No one would even begin to imagine the sweat that had gone into the building of it.

'So you came down from Glasgow on the *Mona's Isle*? They're telling me all the time how these steamships are actually very comfortable, and quite safe too in all manner of weather. A fellow here was saying the cabins are as well appointed as this inn! Hard to believe, out at sea, but he swore to it. And they can make the passage just the same whatever airt the wind is in. It wasn't like that when I was a boy. Indeed it wasn't. But you'll know all about these great steam engines, sir?'

'I don't know anything about steamships. But they did let me into the engine room yesterday.'

'Now a fellow here was telling me all about that. He'd been talking to one of these steam engineers. A dirty job, and dangerous awful, down in the bottom of the ship with great machines clanking round you all day long. Pitch dark too. It's an awful big ship too, the *Mona's Isle*. And they go at a terrible speed, day and night, like there was no difference between the two! You'd never get out of that engine room if she was to sink, God forbid! I don't know how big she is, or how fast she goes, but it would make me anxious, and that's a fact.'

'Two hundred tons,' said Archie absently. 'And up to nine knots. No need to be anxious though: she was built at John Wood's in Glasgow.'

Someone was shouting from the hall, 'House! House I say! Is anyone there? Kneen, are you there?'

'I must go, sir. Will you excuse me?'

Thankful for the interruption, Archie buttered his toast, and seized the chance to look over the notes in his pocketbook.

He wrote underneath them in pencil: *Watterson. Betsey? Check draught.* And then again, as he sipped his coffee: *Scott*?

Scott was the very devil. Would Mr Stevenson expect him to stand bail for the fellow? They had their own laws out here. God-forsaken ones too, probably. So long as they didn't decide to transport the fellow: if it was as bad as that Archie would have to intervene. Though why should he? God knew what sort of sentence Scott would get. Maybe God cared; Archie didn't. He was inclined to leave Scott to rot. He'd brought it all on himself, after all, and Archie had a job to do. But Mr Stevenson might have other views about it. Bound to have, in fact. Did it matter? He didn't need to please Mr Stevenson any more. Archie had given everything to this job, and it had taken him this long to realise there were no more rewards for an ambitious young fellow unless his name was Stevenson. No, there was no need to worry about what Mr Stevenson would say about Scott.

Archie poured more coffee. While he sipped he unfolded a letter that was already limp with constant re-reading. It was sheer indulgence: he knew its contents by heart, but it gave him inordinate pleasure just to see the words again. That's why he'd brought the letter with him. It still said exactly the same, and it still thrilled him every time he looked at it. He was just beginning to realise that it was all true: this thing really was going to happen.

Dear Mr Buchanan,

Further to our meeting of the 17th inst, I am gratified to be able to inform you that your application for the post of surveyor to the Scientific Expedition of HMS Beagle *has been successful. You are required to report for duty at HMS* Beagle, *currently stationed at Greenwich, by September 1st, 1831.*

Following our illuminating discussion in London, I would highly recommend a perusal of Mr Lyell's new volume. Some of his arguments are unnecessarily ambiguous, and could even be interpreted as atheistical, but he is a man of sound observation, and, as far as I have yet read, he does allow a man the freedom to draw his own conclusions. You may find the work pertinent to our proposed expedition.

I should remind you that the Beagle *is a ninety-foot ten-gun brig, and will be carrying its full complement of sixteen officers. In addition there will be five supernumeraries, including yourself. Space for equipment and personal effects will therefore be severely limited.*

May I be the first to congratulate you on this splendid opportunity? I look forward to renewing our acquaintance.

Yours &c,
Robt. Fitzroy
Commander, HMS Beagle

Four months to go. Only four months. To hell with Scott. To hell with Quirk the Water Bailiff, and to hell with this God-forsaken Island. To hell with . . . no, never to hell with Robert Stevenson. Archie owed him too much, and liked him too well. It was going to be hard to tell the old man. But, even so, Archie had his letter. He could only begin to imagine how much this was going to change everything.

Chapter 3

THE COCK WAS CROWING IN THE YARD, OUT THERE WHERE the heat flattened the parched ground. It was so hot outdoors one could hardly draw a breath. In here it was cool. She could smell the tamarind tree that cast its shadow over the steps in a pattern of leaves that sometimes moved in the breeze. There was no breeze today. Today the tree shadows were as still as if they'd been carved in clay like the jali. Where she was standing, the sunlight made a sharply-etched latticework on the marble floor of the veranda, an exact echo of the intricate patterns of the jali through which it shone. When she shut her eyes the pattern was still there, emblazoned in green and gold. The marble was cool under her feet. Her sandals were on the step. She squatted down to shake them, and an enormous scorpion fell out. She screamed and dropped the sandal. And a voice called from inside the house: she was about to hear the comforting voice from inside the house: she could remember the different sounds, the very words, almost . . . almost . . .

The cock crowed again. Diya rolled over, and woke. A shaft of sun pierced the crack in the shutter. It fell right across the pillow where she'd been lying. The sea soughed against the rocks outside; she could hear it through the open window. At home in Grandmother's house Diya used to look out at the sea from her white bed under the rafters through the small square window of her top-floor room. She'd been able to see the whole of Castletown Bay over the top of the Garrison chapel. But that window, like all the windows in Grandmother's house, had been kept firmly closed. Here on Ellan Bride Lucy always kept the window open unless the wind was very strong. Diya had been forced to grow used to the unhealthy practice. Jim used to keep the window open too. In the beginning Diya had been frightened by the night air, laden with demons of the deep, smelling of salt and wind, stealing in through the perilous crack.

Diya didn't want the weather in her dreams, still less the sea. She could hear the sea now, and the sound of it seemed to brush her dream into oblivion. She tried to recapture the receding images, but they were dissolving in the relentless freshness of the island. She could smell salt all too plainly; in the dream it had been tamarind . . . the warm, spicy smell of the tamarind tree. What was gone, was gone for ever; only faint shadows might fall from the past into the present, and even those were merely an illusion.

Sometimes when Jim had been there he'd left the light burning by itself and come to her, briefly, in their curtained bed in the kitchen recess – his parents had slept in the bedroom then – but Diya knew that Jim was never unaware, even for a moment, of the steady beam of light outside the window. While the light was lit he would not sleep. He would come, on a calm night, and then, just as she was falling asleep, he would go again. She always woke with an empty place beside her. Now Lucy had Jim's half of the bed, and Jim was gone for ever.

They'd been so helpless. Exposed to all the fury of the elements, this island could – and too often did – turn itself in no time at all into a little hell on earth. That night five years ago had been worse than hell. In hell one despaired, and that was all. Hope was more cruel because it tantalised: it would seem to offer a glimmer of light, and then it would just blow itself away again in a night, leaving only destruction behind it. That was why the wind was the worst of all. Rain, mist, hail, fog, sleet: of all the elements that flung themselves against the island the wind was the real demon. It mocked you as it swept your strength away – you couldn't breathe, you couldn't balance, you couldn't even think. Diya hated the wind more than anything else in the world.

The wind that had swept Jim away that night had shaken the house so hard it made the stone walls shudder as if this were a house of cards. It had whined under the door, lifting the rag rug as if it were an animal come alive. When Diya had tried to look out for Jim's lantern, the shutter had jerked loose from her hand and been wrenched off its hinge. When the shutter banged against the wall, the cat had fled under the dresser, and the baby had woken up screaming.

Billy had screamed too; Diya could remember that: 'Mam! Mam!'

'Da!' Breesha had cried. 'I want my Da!'

'I'll go after him.' Lucy had jumped up and pulled on her cloak. She'd draped the heavy coil of rope over her shoulder, and lit the storm lantern from the candle.

Diya hadn't known whether to try to stop her or not. The truth was she'd wanted her to go. She'd *wanted* Lucy to risk her life, if it would bring back Jim. 'Take care!'

The door was snatched out of Diya's hand as soon as she'd raised the latch. The wind howled. Ashes flew up from the hearth, and the coals roared into a blaze. The candle had gone out. Both children had been sobbing as Lucy vanished into the swirling dark. What else could Diya have done but shove the door shut with all the strength she had? The wind groaned against it, protesting. But she'd managed to shut it out.

'Billy! Breesha!' She'd hung the nightgowns over the back of the wooden settle, just the same as usual. Why had she even bothered, when all the time . . .? But all she'd been able to think of was keeping things as ordinary as possible. 'What foolishness is this!' – that was more or less what she'd said – 'Silly children! On land there is nothing to fear. You should pray for the poor sailors, at sea on such a night as this!'

'I want my Da!'

Diya remembered how her hands had shaken as she'd unbuttoned their clothes, and pulled the warm nightgowns over their heads. She hadn't tried to make them go to bed. The whole house was shuddering. The roof beams groaned under the strain. The three of them had huddled in one blanket on the hearth while the coals blazed in the wind, and spray spattered down the chimney. Breesha was cuddling the cat tightly. All the time Diya had kept one hand on the cradle; the baby slept through everything.

At last the door had burst open. Jim!

No, not Jim. Lucy's hood had blown off. Her hair was soaked. She'd got blood on her face. She didn't have the rope or lantern. She'd tried to push the door to: Diya had run to help her. Together they'd managed it, while the wind battered on the outside with giant fists.

'Where's Jim?'

'I can't get down there! I can't get down!'

'Where's Jim?'

'I can't get down! The sea is right over the island!'

'But where's Jim?'

'I don't know, I tell you! I can't get down!' And then Lucy, who never cried – even now, Diya had never seen Lucy cry – had held her hands over her face, and drawn long shuddering breaths, as if the wind had done its best to suffocate her.

That was enough! No point going back to the past, any of it. Diya lay for a few moments watching dust motes dance in the thin shaft of sunlight. Lucy must have doused the light long ago. A harsh scraping sound started up in the room next door. Lucy was raking out the fire. Diya heard voices: Lucy's low and quiet, and Breesha's shrill treble. Diya pushed back the cover, and swung her legs out of bed.

Mally was like her mother in the mornings, slow to start. She was curled up like a dormouse under her flowered coverlet in the truckle bed in the corner. Mally had no jobs to do until after breakfast, so no one ever bothered to wake her. She didn't stir when Diya fastened the shutter back and the sunlight flooded in, chasing away the blue shadows, and turning the whitewashed walls the colour of pale honey. Apart from the sleeping child the room was empty. Diya pulled her nightgown over her head as she crossed to the washstand. She poured water from the blue jug into the matching basin, took a rough bar of soap and a flannel, and carefully washed and dried herself with a thread-bare towel.

The Gaffer had made this washstand. The table top was laid with blue and white Dutch tiles that came from a wreck at Langness in the year Jim was born. The ship was on its way from Lancaster to the West Indies, and all the crew had been lost, though bits of the cargo had been salvaged later. The tiles were found in a wooden box inside the broken hull when Jim's father and grandfather had sailed over to have a look at her. Diya loved the tiles, with their neat blue and white pictures of windmills, cattle and ships. There was so little man-made beauty here, such poverty of patterns and images; every little bit was like a drop of manna.

Diya, in her petticoat, stood at the oval looking glass above the chest of drawers and brushed her long hair. The swishing sound, Mally thought as she woke, was like the sea; in fact Mally could hear the sea now, echoing her mother's brushing, outside on the rocks.

Diya poured two drops of oil from a thick glass bottle on to her palm and rubbed her hands together. Then she ran them through her hair in long strokes, turning her head first one way and then the other, still watching herself dreamily in the looking glass. The gold studs in her ears flashed in the glass as she turned her head. Now this letter had come, Diya was thinking, something else would happen. She was frightened: she couldn't deny it. She had no money. Neither of them had any money. Lucy's salary was eighteen pounds a year, two-thirds of what Jim's had been. That was incomparably greater than Island wages. Lucy's salary was all they had to keep them.

They had no home but this. Diya could work, only who would have her? And what about Lucy? And how could Diya go into service when she had Breesha and Mally? No one would employ a housekeeper or a governess who brought two children with her. And whatever would Grandmother have said if she'd known Diya had sunk to that? What would either of her grandmothers have said, come to that? Better not to even begin to think of that, not to open the sealed door to that long-gone world.

Even so, the future would be easier for her than it could be for Lucy. There was no point in pretending otherwise. At least Diya knew how to live in other ways. That didn't mean she wasn't afraid. There had been so many changes, and she had learned exactly how much each change could hurt. *Liverpool dock: a grisly sea of faces. All the faces blank and white, like a picture not coloured in. And the appalling rain, the thin grey relentless rain. Was this sea of whiteness also people? The colour they made was terrible, thin and grey and utterly relentless. And there was no sun.*

Diya twisted her long coil of hair into a knot at the nape of her neck, and fastened it with hairpins. Mally, watching through half-closed eyes, loved the darkness of her mother's hair against the bleached whiteness of her petticoat. She was aware of the suppleness of her mother's body, and the way the petticoat extinguished it, even while it still showed what her mother looked like underneath by the folds in it, and the way it touched her body here and there.

Diya put on a blue print gown over the petticoat, and a white cap that hid her hair. Immediately she became her ordinary daytime self. Mally didn't quite realise that her mother now looked ten years older; she only knew that her mother was different when day came, and that her undressed self was Mam's own secret, which Mally only saw because she happened to be there. Aunt Lucy, unlike Mam, didn't bother to wear a cap. She said it would blow off in the wind, and who was there to see or care? Mally watched her mother slide her silver bangle onto her wrist, glance for one last time in the looking glass, and turn to face the day.

When Diya had left the room there was no need to pretend to be still asleep. Mally rolled on her back and stretched out luxuriously. She dimly remembered having Breesha in the bed as well. She remembered fighting for space and Breesha jerking the covers off her, but she could also remember waking curled up against her sister like two kittens in a box. Mally could not remember her Da. Sometimes Breesha or Billy mentioned him, and more often Mam would tell them stories about him. In Mally's mind the stories about her Da were as remote as India. Although he'd actually been there on the island with them all until Mally herself was almost two, in her mind Jim belonged to the happy times before she was born, the times which other people remembered, in which she'd had no share.

When Diya went through to the kitchen she left the door ajar behind her. The door used to creak, but Lucy had rubbed soap on the hinges and now it made no protesting noise. The sounds through the open door would wake Mally in due course, thought Diya, as they always did, and Mally would join them when she smelt breakfast.

Lucy was blowing last night's coals back into a blaze. Smokey the cat was rubbing against her arm, clearly hoping to be fed. Breesha was standing there in her nightgown, but when she saw her mother she grabbed her clothes from the back of a chair, and disappeared into the bedroom to wash and dress. The two women in the kitchen could hear her shouting at Mally. 'Get up, you lazy pig!'

'I'm not a pig!'

The bedroom door banged.

Billy emerged from behind the kitchen bed-curtain, knuckling his eyes. He was buttoning his shirt when his mother called from the hearth without turning round, 'Billy, are you getting washed? Remember to wash your neck! There's a tide mark there as big as the one on Stackey beach!'

Billy sighed as he poured water from an earthenware jug into an enamel bowl. No one was watching, so washing took him less than half a minute. He dragged the comb through his curly hair. He was darker than Lucy, but he'd inherited her thick curls and her freckles. His eyes were not like hers though; Lucy had grey-green eyes, but Billy's were bright blue and very wide open, giving him an air of startled innocence. Billy fastened his breeks with a wide leather belt that was much too long for him. Lucy had helped him cut an extra hole in it. The belt had been Uncle Jim's. Billy treasured every small item that he had inherited from Uncle Jim. A leather belt, a beaver hat for special occasions, both far too large for him, were small icons to Uncle Jim's memory and to Billy's status in a family of females. Jim's shirts had long ago been unpicked and remade for children's nightgowns and women's petticoats. Jim's Sunday blacks, seldom worn, were put away in camphor for when Billy was a man. Jim had been wearing his oilskin jacket on the night it had happened, so they didn't have that. Billy kept Uncle Jim's second-best knife in its leather sheath under his pillow, and wore it for fishing and other jobs. The telescope they all used, because they had to for the light. But Billy cared about that telescope more than any of them. It was more his than anyone else's, or so he reckoned.

Chapter 4

'For chrissake, Ben, is young Archibald no goin tae get me oot o here?'

Benjamin Groat shifted his feet uncomfortably, but he kept his face close to the barred grille in the door down to the dungeons. Ben was a big, gangling fellow, and he had to stoop to look through. The dungeon stank of excrement and foetid bodies. His gorge rose. At least he was on the right side of the door, standing in a chilly stone alley that led inwards from the old moat of Castle Rushen. The formidable keep, which was the main part of the prison, rose like a grey cliff behind him. It was surrounded by a great curtain wall, making the old moat into an enclosed prison yard. Ben couldn't meet Drew's eyes. He'd come here to help him if he could, but the plain fact was there was nothing he could do.

'He didna say so, Drew. That doesna mean he winna.'

'Bastard! Poxy whore's son! The bastard!' Drew Scott shook the bars of the grille, but the dungeon door was too solid to budge an inch.

A harsh voice came from the darkness below him. 'Stow that racket! And get out of the bloody light.'

Drew ground his teeth. 'Pack o bloody Manxmen. Give themsels airs. Think they own the bloody place. Dinnae want to be locked up with common felons! Common felon! That's whit the bastard called me . . . I'd knock his bloody brains oot but!'

'Ay well.' Ben sighed. He glanced swiftly down at Drew's face. 'Don't do onything, Drew, however much they rile you. You've no been charged yet, even. Turnkey telt me this was just the holding cell. It's no like they've put ye in the main prison bit. But if there's any more trouble now . . .'

''Tweren't nothing! You saw, Ben! The cully spat in my face! An I floored him. What of it? What kind a man wouldnae, if a cull spits in his face and calls him another thievin Scotchman? I never got called a thief. Never! I've no stolen aught!'

'That wasna what he said. Another of Atholl's thieving Scotchmen was what he said. He wasna saying you had your hand in another man's pocket. He meant the late Duke.'

'Dukes arena anythin to do wi me! Just as well. Young Archibald's more'n enough. For Chrissake, Ben, you mean he'll do naught? He's no goin to get me oot o here?'

'Well . . . what I mean is . . . he will, Drew. He must. What would Mr Stevenson say, supposing Young Archibald left you be?'

'Mr Stevenson isnae here though, is he? There isnae nae-body here but Mr Stuck-up Lick-yer-arse Fidget-face. And when did he ever give a damn? He'd let me swing an no lift a finger to save me, so he would. I tell you, Ben' – Drew's voice grew shrill, and Ben drew back involuntarily – 'he'll let these bastards hang me, an no give the snap of his fingers for't, so he will.'

'Who said onything about hanging, Drew? Your man's no deid nor like to be. They threw a bucket of water ower him and he came roon soon enough. '

Drew put his face close to the bars and whispered, so Ben had to come right up to the grille to hear him, ducking his head and putting his ear close to the metal. The stench from inside was appalling. 'Man in there says they transported a fellow who knocked oot a man just the same as what I did. Tavern fight. Just the same. Transported, Ben! Convict ships! They do a lot o that here. That's what they'll do to me if Young

Archibald doesnae go bail for me. Christ, man, I got tae get oot o here. Where *is* the bastard?'

'Young Archibald? He's away to see a fellow,' said Ben, not meeting Drew's eyes. 'Water Bailiff, he said. About the new light. Legal stuff. But Drew, they *kinna* transport you. They kinna! You've no done notheen hardly. Few days in here, that's what it'll be, just. Few days, couple o weeks maybe. That's all.'

'All! That'll lose me ma joab! Ben, I got to come wi you. I got my joab to do. You cannae go oot there wi'oot me. Whit'll ye dae wi but one chainman? Whit'll ye dae? He's got to get me oot but!'

Ben dropped his eyes. There were a few limpet shells among the refuse on the ground, and he clumsily ground them under his boot. 'Well . . . thing is, Drew . . . Young Archibald told me to see about hiring another man. Just for this job, like. Just if you couldna mak it this time roond.'

'Bastard!' Drew spat furiously, and Ben flinched. 'He'll bloody leave me here to rot! Throw me oot like yesterday's bones! He'll report me and lose me ma joab, so he will! He isnae even goin tae see the magistrate, you mean? You mean he isnae goin tae dae naught for me, Ben?'

Ben looked down at his feet. 'He's in a hurry, Drew. Waste of time, see, having to deal with this Water Bailiff. He wants to get off as soon as possible to this Port St Mary, and find this boatman. You know how he hates politics. He wants to get on with the job. He doesna want to lose another day.'

'The devil! Doesnae want to lose a day! An me like to lose ma life! There's no justice in it, Ben. The man's a murderer. He'll have ma blood oan his hands, sure as if he'd knifed me hissel. He's killt me, Ben!' Drew's voice grew shrill.

'Stow your noise, blast you!' The voice from inside the dungeon was as hoarse as a dying crow.

'That's no fair,' said Ben reasonably. 'It's no a hanging matter, I telt ye that. It wis just a brawl. And it was you that floored the cully. No one else. Young Archibald wasna in the tavern even. It's notheen to do with him really.'

'Christ, Ben—'

'You there!' The turnkey's voice sounded from the gatehouse up above. 'Five minutes, I said. That's ten minutes gone! You'll be losing me my place, with your ingoings and outgoings. Out you come there!'

'Outgoings is right,' muttered Ben. 'I got to go, Drew. I'll speak to Young Archibald, though. I swear I will. Don't give in to the doldrums, mate. I'll—'

'Get the hell out of there, I say!' The turnkey's boots clattered on the stone steps. 'Get the hell out or I'll charge you double!'

'I'm coming!' Ben leant towards the grille and whispered. 'Keep your hairt up, Drew. They kinna hang ye. They won't even keep you in here more'n a day or two, not if I can stop it. Here' – he reached into the pocket of his frieze jacket, and pulled out a greasy packet – 'It's bread and pickled onion. Fresh fae the baker. I thought you might be glad o it.'

Drew seized the bread, and thrust it into the bosom of his jacket. 'Ay well, thanks for that. And Ben . . .'

'Ay?'

'Would you have a bawbee about you? I dinnae get no grub in here withoot. I paid ma last sixpence and what did I get? Bloody stewed limpets. Limpets! Beggars' broth! He cannae leave me in here, Ben. You tell him . . .'

'You come on out o' that!'

Ben fumbled in his purse and drew out a shilling. After a moment's hesitation he passed it through the bars. Drew snatched at it, and feverishly pocketed the coin. 'Don't let them bloody debtors see! Thanks, Ben. True blue, that's you. But that Young . . .'

'I got to go, Drew.'

'Find oot!' Drew shouted after him, as Ben followed the turnkey away. Drew clung desperately to the bars. 'Find oot what they'll do! And tell Young Archibald . . . Ben, you'll come back, right?'

'Ay, I'll do that . . .'

'Like hell you will,' snarled the turnkey, grabbing Ben's arm and dragging him away. 'Out, you! And be thankful I wasn't taking another shilling. Five minutes indeed. I've a mind to be reporting you to—'

'Stow it,' said Ben. 'You got your shilling. I doubt you'll be reporting that. I'm off.'

As soon as he was outside the great gates Ben drew a deep breath of clean air, and stood up straight, blinking. He tended to slouch, which perhaps came from stooping down to get on a level with his fellows. For Ben was known to be good company, though steady with it. He'd drink with the others, but no one had ever seen him the worse for it, and it was reckoned to be impossible to provoke him to argument, let alone fight. He had an ugly freckled face, wiry reddish hair, and mild blue eyes. His father had been employed by Robert Stevenson as a stonemason at Pentland Skerries, and stayed with the firm thereafter. He was killed falling from the temporary bridge on the Bell Rock, just a week before the lighthouse was completed. That had happened two months before Ben's birth. The widow took her new-born infant home to Orkney. A small pension was forthcoming, supposedly anonymous, but Benjamin was aware very early on of the identity of his patron. Mr Stevenson had also offered John Groat's orphan an apprenticeship, to commence when he was fourteen. So Benjamin sailed for Edinburgh within a week of his fourteenth birthday, and was promptly directed to the Survey of Sutherland as 'prentice under the assistant chainman. What his mother thought about it no one knew; probably not even Benjamin had any idea. As for Benjamin himself, even those who worked with him closely knew rather less about him than that. He was a quiet fellow, and got on with folk, and Mr Stevenson thought very highly of him.

The sun hadn't reached into the hollow of the Castle Rushen moat. Out on the harbour quay the day was already bright. Ben shuddered, and walked round the castle, past a stone-breakers' yard, and on to the harbour quay at the front of the castle. Who'd have thought such an imposing building could house such stinking misery inside? Just like people really, thought Ben, and grinned to himself. He'd done his best, but it was good to be out of that place. Being a peaceable fellow himself, he'd had little enough to do with jails, thank the Lord.

The castle faced straight onto the harbour. The tide was coming in fast over flat slabs of rock and seaweed. A couple of herring smacks were moored at the Castle Quay, with the sea running in around their exposed keels. A schooner was unloading coal, and townsfolk with baskets and barrows were queuing up to buy, their boisterous banter drowning out the screams of the gulls. Further upriver a gaggle of farmyard ducks foraged in the exposed seaweed. Compared with Douglas harbour, where they'd berthed yesterday, with its fine new pier and good lighthouse, this place was a backwater – literally, one might say.

Ben wandered along the quay, and crossed a stone bridge over the river that flowed into the harbour. An old fellow was leaning on the bridge smoking a long clay pipe, watching the tide flooding in over the exposed mudflats.

'Morning,' said Ben cheerfully, stopping beside him.

'And a good morning to you.' The old man removed his pipe, and looked Ben over sideways. 'You'll be a stranger in these parts, then?'

'Ay.'

'English?'

'Not I!'

'Scotch?'

'No that either!'

'You're not sounding like an Irishman. Welsh?'

'No. Orkney,' said Ben, leaning on the rail beside his questioner. 'But I've been away fae home a long time. You'll ken this place pretty well, then?'

'I'm living here all my days.'

'Tell me, then – when we came last night, it was just gone high tide. It falls a good way, then?'

The old man looked at him sideways. 'More'n twenty feet just now. At low tide you'll not hardly be seeing a pint of water in the harbour, barring the river. Three-and-a-half hours after high tide the whole harbour'll be dry again.'

'That must make the fishing difficult.'

The old man sucked on his pipe deliberately; he seemed to be staring out to sea, but he was watching Ben out of the corner of his eye. Evidently he decided it was worth being communicative. 'Aye well, it's dangerous awful in the bay outside. But once your boat's in she's as snug as can be, as you're seeing indeed, here in the duck pond – that's the name we're putting on it here. When the herring are coming in, you see, the smacks are mooring off Derbyhaven mostly, and that's where they're beaching them in the winter.'

'Derbyhaven?'

'You are a stranger and no mistake!' The old man looked him over, but didn't ask any direct questions. Instead he jerked his pipe in an easterly direction. 'Over that way, a mile or two. That's Derbyhaven.'

'And there's a better harbour there?'

'Harbour?' the fellow repeated scornfully. 'Bless your heart, there's no harbour there at all. But you'd never be mooring in Castletown Bay, not when there's a westerly in. So it'll be the fishing that brings you here, no doubt?'

'No.' Ben leaned his elbows on the rail, and deliberately grew confidential. It was worth getting alongside the locals, though he was wary of the old fellow's sidelong glances. So far everything he'd said seemed true enough. 'I'm in the surveying business,' said Ben. 'Chainman. I work for the company that built the lighthouses on the Calf here. That'd be what? . . . ten, twelve year ago now?'

'So that's it, is it? Surveying? Is that making a map, like? There's a map of Castletown already, so they're telling, but I'm never seeing it.'

The air of benighted ignorance seemed genuine enough, but Ben wasn't at all sure. 'Ay well, we're no working in

Castletown. Like I say, you had our company here before, building the lights on the Calf. Lot of wrecks here before that,' remarked Ben casually, 'or so they say.'

'And plenty of wrecks since too! I'm not holding with all these lights everywhere. It sets folk thinking the coast is safe, and that's not so. Never was, never will be. There were wrecks before the lights – one or two wrecks along this coast every year, year in, year out – and wrecks just the same ever since. Listen, young fellow . . . but three months since there was a smack lost in Castletown Bay. Coming from Liverpool, she was. Smashed to pieces on the rocks out there in a storm, barely a mile from this harbour. Just out yonder, not a mile from where we're standing. Them lights on the Calf aren't stopping that sort of thing, now, are they?'

'No, but a light at that headland I saw across the bay might help.'

'Langness? And what would be the use of that? It's too low. A bit of spray on a wild night – a patch of fog – no, that would do no good at all. There's the Herring Tower there, anyway. What more would you be wanting? And how about the *Atalanta* was wrecked at Port St Mary last year? Now she was from Derbyhaven – John Watterson, he had knowledge of these waters – but that wasn't helping her, was it? And you won't never see them lights on the Calf near Port St Mary. And the *Atalanta* wasn't the only one at Port St Mary last year – there was that sloop from Scotland too. They were getting the cargo off – pig-iron, that's what it was – but the ship, she was finished. No, you can't tell me them lights have changed nothing.'

'I've kent places in Scotland where they've set up lights and barely had a wreck since.'

'Ah well now, you would have done, wouldn't you? That's how you'll be knowing all about what we're needing here. Well, well, isn't that fortunate now, that you're coming here to the Island to be putting us all right?'

'It's a busy route, then, along your coast here?' asked Ben innocently.

'Bless your soul, it's the busiest route in the Manx Sea. But a week or two now, and you'll be having them all here for the fishing. They'll be out west of the Island right now, but when the herring will be coming round the coast, the boats'll be following. Once the Cornishmen are coming along, that's when the season is really starting. And not just the fishing. Now it's all them steamers, going away to Liverpool, Whitehaven, Belfast, the Lord knows where . . . Oh yes, we don't do so bad, for poor ones who aren't knowing nothing at all. Not like you educated gentlemen from Edinburgh, of course.'

'I telt you: I'm fae Orkney. We don't have any steamer routes there yet. But we – me and my master – we came on the steamer from Glasgow yesterday.'

'Well, you won't get me onto one of them things. Blow up, like as not, and what will you be doing when the engine stops working? No sails, no oars. It's not nathural.'

'And no wrecks either. Or no so many. A steamer can get itself off a lee shore where a sailing ship wouldna have a hope.'

'Well, you're wrong there, young fellow. Weren't you hearing how the *George* was wrecked in Douglas Bay just last year? At least, they were getting her off in the end, but it wasn't steam that was the saving of her.'

Ben knew all about the *George*. He'd been told the whole story by a fellow he'd met on the *Mona's Isle*. He let the old man tell it again, but he was listening to the accent more than the words. The fellows in the tavern last night had been speaking their own language. That was really what had got Drew into a fight. Ben guessed they'd been talking pretty freely about the two strangers in their midst; certainly they had very obviously seemed to regard Drew and Ben as a source of amusement. Ben had tried to make out what they were saying – he'd listened to enough Gaelic when they were working at Cape Wrath to have a smattering – but he couldn't make out this Manx language. It didn't bother Ben what they might be saying, anyway, but it had bothered Drew all right.

Lot of nonsense this old fellow was talking, anyway, but it

was useful to know what folk were saying. Ben was used to prejudice against the lights. There was always a reason for it, and this Island had been a lawless country in the past by all accounts. There was no telling but what this chap knew a thing or two more than he'd say about wrecks. And there'd been some pretty fierce smuggling here by all accounts, but that was years ago, not since the war probably. The old fellow would mind all of that – probably he'd learned to sweet-talk the excise officers just the same way he was talking to Ben now. Anyway, it was just typical of these old fishermen, saying the lights had brought no benefit. You couldn't convince anyone who chose not to listen. You couldn't ever prove how it would have been without the lights, once they were there, and how the wrecks did get less, if you took into account that the shipping was growing and growing every year that passed.

It was true about the steamships though. They hardly ever got into difficulties the way the sailing ships did, because they could get themselves off the coast whatever airt the wind was in. Look at how they'd rounded the Mull yesterday morning in the *Mona's Isle*. With almost no wind at all they'd made about eight knots ever since they'd left the Clyde. They'd never have done that in a brig. It was a shame in a way. There was something about a brig, about the feel of the sea under the keel, and the sound of the wind and the tide, that you just didn't get on the *Mona's Isle* with her engines clattering away and her paddle wheels turning. Young as he was, Ben had been bred to a different world. No wonder these old fellows took it hard.

'You ken these waters pretty well,' he remarked, as the old man relapsed into silence and pulled at his pipe. 'You'll ken Ellan Bride? The island beyond the Calf?'

The old man took his pipe out of his mouth and deliberately spat into the river. 'Oh ay. Ellan Bride . . . it's surely not to Ellan Bride you're for going, young fellow? You're never going there? It's a dangerous journey, dangerous awful. More'n half a league south of the Calf itself, right out at sea. You're surely never wanting to go out there!'

'Ay. That's where we'll be working.'

'You will? There's a light at them there already, you know that? Been a light at them these fifty years. Fifty years and over it, even, or so they say. But you'll be knowing all about that?'

'I ken about the private light, ay. We're going to replace it. Build a new one.'

'Is that right? You'll be coming here to build us a new light on Ellan Bride? Well, well, you're coming along to do us all a favour. And you'll be bringing more Scotchmen over with you, and putting them on Ellan Bride, God help them? Well, well, whatever would we be doing without fellows like you coming along?'

'You don't think a new light's a good idea?'

The old fellow shifted his gaze from Ben's face, and seemed to deliberately change the subject. 'You're seeing that castle there?' He jerked his pipe towards the grey bulk of Castle Rushen above the quay.

'I could hardly miss it.' Ben decided not to mention his acquaintance with the jail. 'What of it?'

'Well, maybe I'll be telling you something about that castle. See the big it is?'

'I certainly do.'

'Well, I'll be telling you a story about that. That castle is old' – the old man's voice sank to a dramatic whisper '– older than the memory of man.'

'Then who built it?'

'That's what I'm telling you. Themselves it was, was building it, and I'll tell you, Themselves is keeping their rooms in it that no man can be entering. There's rooms in that castle no man is knowing of. There's folk gone in, now and then, over the years – young fellows, and a taste of Dutch courage taken at them – you'll know what that is? But never a one was ever coming back. And then a fellow was going in, but he took a skein of packthread, to be marking the way, like, and he was going in. Down and down he was going, down the long passages in the pitch dark, league after league . . .'

'A *very* big castle,' muttered Ben, under his breath.

'. . . until at last he was seeing just a flicker – just the smallest little flicker – of a glimmering of light. And that seemed to him the best thing he ever did see. So he was going on and on, right away up to the light, and he was looking in on the window. And inside that window he was seeing the buggane – it's the truth I'm telling you now, mind – seeing the buggane, and he lying asleep on a great stone table, laying his head on a book he was, and gripping a great sword in his hand, and breathing hard in his sleep. So the young fellow was running for it, away from the light and back along all the weary way, following his packthread, and out into the light of day at last. And so he was the one who was living to tell the tale.'

The old man was looking at him again through half-closed eyelids, apparently gauging the effect of his tale. Ben didn't like that look. He was fairly sure he was being made game of, but when he met the other's eyes, the old man broke into the blandest of smiles.

'Is that right?' said Ben cautiously. 'And what's that got to do with Ellan Bride?'

'Ay well, that'd be another story. But if it's my advice you're seeking, young fellow – and I daresay you're not, for without doubt there's more learning at yourself in a few years of life than at myself in all of threescore and ten, you with your Scotch education and all – but if asking you were, I'd say keep you away from that island, young fellow. Don't you be going near Ellan Bride!'

'There's an island where I come from,' said Ben, watching him closely, 'that's supposed to disappear on midsummer nights. So they say. My Auld Daa lived in sight of that island, and never once did it shift from its moorings, and you could see it any old time you liked, except when the mist was down.'

'Ah, but you weren't *on* that island, young fellow. Now were you? That's the thing. You might be seeing Ellan Bride any day of the year, but this time of year particular – May-time – you wouldn't want to be going too near the place then.'

'Well, that's a shame,' said Ben cheerfully. 'In fact it's a remarkable coincidence, since it's May-time now, and Ellan Bride is exactly where we're going to be.'

Ay well, so much for that, thought Ben, as he strolled along the other quay a few minutes later. The day's work was well under way. Warehouse doors stood wide open: he could see right into the chandler's and the ropeworks next to it. There was another schooner unloading blocks of sugar, each one carefully wrapped in sacking. Ben skirted the dockers and their carts, and crossed a wooden bridge back to the townward quay. And so much for Young Archibald telling him to sound out another chainman. If the old man he'd just spoken to was right, it seemed unlikely that they'd get anyone from Castletown willing to take on the job. Maybe they'd have better luck in Port St Mary. The boatman would surely have some ideas. Ben would have to explain to Archie that it would be better to wait until they got over there. Young Archibald always wanted everything sorted out yesterday; he never seemed to learn that the further you got from Edinburgh, the less life was going to be like that.

At the end of the quay a muddy lane led past a row of thatched cabins that faced onto the bay. There was a strong smell of woodsmoke, muck, rotting seaweed and drying fish. Barefoot children and prowling dogs tumbled in the glaur. Ben came out onto a shingle beach with one or two rowing boats drawn up close to the cottages. By this time he'd collected a little group of children who followed him curiously. He addressed the biggest girl: 'Will I get back to the market square this way?'

She shook her head uncomprehendingly, but now he could see the back of the big new church towering over the huddled cottages. The bell was ringing as he passed the school, and a noisy gaggle of latecomers pushed past him to the open door. Just as well, maybe, that he couldn't comprehend what they were calling as he passed. In no time at all Ben was back in the square with its fine town houses and the George facing the back walls of Castle Rushen. But it was quiet no longer. Even though there was no market today the fish-sellers had set out their wares on the slabs, and some brisk bargaining was under way. A group of red-coated officers on horseback clattered over the cobbles, narrowly missing a couple of girls bowling an iron hoop. Ben strolled across the square, enjoying the warmth of the sun. The morning was in full swing; it was time to find Young Archibald.

Chapter 5

BILLY OPENED THE OUTSIDE DOOR AND FASTENED IT BACK against the wall. The chickens scuttled forward, clucking for breakfast. Billy ignored them; they were not his job. He hooked the empty wooden buckets onto the yoke, swung it onto his shoulders, crossed the yard through a carpet of silverweed studded with papery yellow flowers, and headed along a narrow path among rushes and celandines. He stopped for a moment when he saw the snow, all sails set to catch the first whisper of a breeze. Even as he watched, the sails flapped. She was about quarter of a mile off the Creggyns, sailing directly against the tide. With so little wind she'd be there all morning. Later he'd look at her through the telescope and find out her name.

The spring flowed out from under a rock at the foot of a small cliff. It was built up at the back with an ancient stone wall. The wooden dipper was chained to a post. Billy knelt by the clear pool, and slowly lowered the dipper. He let the water swirl in over the rim, then lifted the dipper out as gently as he could. If the mud at the bottom of the pool got stirred up the water would be brown and murky, and he'd be in trouble. It was easy to be patient on a day like today, with the morning sun on his back, and the ground under his knees quite dry for once. An early dragonfly flittered above the pool, and buttercups, bogbean and forget-me-nots trembled at the edge.

Nine dippers made the buckets as full as he could manage

without spilling. Billy squatted with the yoke on his shoulders, and hooked on first one bucket, then the other. Slowly he stood up, taking the weight. Coming back along the muddy path was a heavy, careful job. He lowered the buckets just inside the kitchen door and put their lids on. Emptying the ash bucket was much easier. Billy tipped the hot ashes out over the rocks. When he came back the chickens were gobbling scraps from the trough. Breesha, still holding their empty bucket, was squinting at the sundial.

'It's nearly at V – I – I,' she said as he passed. 'I mean seven. Mrs Black's gone broody. She never lays anything. Just makes a fuss.'

'Put her in the pot,' said Billy.

'That's what your Mam says.'

'Good.'

'But not now. After the puffins have gone. It's a waste till then.'

'She'll eat her head off,' objected Billy.

'Well, that's what your Mam says, anyway.'

'Well, I don't care,' said Billy. 'I don't mind going for puffins today.'

'She didn't say today.'

'I might, anyway.'

The truth was that they both had to do what Lucy and Diya said, but Breesha didn't bother to say so, which was kind of her. Billy opened the door of the coal shed cautiously because there were rock pipits nesting under the roof inside. A bright eye watched over the edge of the nest as he shovelled the coal. The birds were used to the noise. Billy stopped and listened for a moment, but it was still too early in the season for any sound of cheeping.

Diya was stirring the porridge when he got back to the hearth. The porridge smelt good, and Billy hung around.

'You could put the bowls out.'

It would have been better to skulk in the yard. Billy laid out five wooden bowls, and five horn spoons.

'Milk, Billy.'

He took the cloth off the earthenware milk jug and reached it down from the stone shelf, holding it carefully in both hands. It was yesterday's milk, with thick lines of cream round the inside of the jug where it had stood at various stages since yesterday morning. Billy wiped away the top line of cream and licked his finger.

'Mally, you watch the porridge till Breesha comes back. Don't just stir the top. Scrape it off the bottom as well. Don't tip the pot or you'll burn yourself.' Diya took some corn and the milking pail, and followed the path where Billy's bare footprints showed clearly in the mud. She passed the well and the keeill, and trod carefully between the puffin burrows over spongy grass and mayweed. The puffins watched her through black-lined eyes, retreating a yard or so when she came close and flapping their wings in case they had to fly. The puffins in the burrows below protested with low guttural sounds like so many creaking gates. Diya stepped over a puffin's carcass – two wings and the desiccated outline of a body torn open by a blackbacked gull – and climbed up to the white cairn above Baie yn Geinnagh Veg. In a hollow just below the rock there was a wooden yoke. She scanned the green patches between the rocks, and rattled the corn in the bucket.

Hooves clattered on pebbles, and two goats came scrambling up from the bay. Turk still had a length of seaweed hanging from her mouth. Mappy was slower getting up the rocks because of her bulging stomach. Diya pushed Turk aside and let Mappy have first turn at the corn. Any day now Mappy would appear with a kid at her side; it was almost five months since she'd been put to the billy over at Meayll. Diya whisked the pail from under Mappy's nose and held it so that Turk stuck her head through the yoke. Diya put the bar across, and while Turk licked the pail clean she squatted beside her and began to milk. Turk was less docile than Mappy, and twice Diya had to shove her hind legs out of the way. Two jets of gleaming milk frothed into the bucket. Diya milked until both udders were empty, then released Turk, who went skittering away.

The children were scraping their porridge bowls when Diya got back. Diya dipped a jug into the milk pail, and gave each child half a mug of fresh warm milk.

Billy drained his mug noisily and wiped his mouth. 'PleasemayIleavethetable?'

'Whose turn is it to do the light?' asked Diya.

'Breesha's!'

'Mine,' said Breesha.

Diya glanced at Lucy, who shrugged. 'Off you go then. But Billy . . . *Billy!* . . . let me finish. Bring in some driftwood. And don't be too long.'

Billy grabbed the telescope, swung himself round the door-post, and ran.

It was one of the clearest days they'd had this year. Standing on Dreeym Lang, Billy focused the telescope on the Chickens Rock to the north-east, gradually emerging as the tide ebbed. Beyond it he could see the Calf lighthouses quite plainly, the high light on the left, and the low light on the right. The lights lined up exactly on the Chickens, so ships knew that when one light was right above the other they were in danger. Billy scanned the broken south coast of the Calf. Away east beyond the Burroo lay the low-lying coast of the Island. You couldn't see Castletown from Ellan Bride, but you could see the tower of Castle Rushen rising over the low land in between. Today Billy could even make out, when he got it right in focus, the Governor's flag flying over the keep. Mam said no one ever looked at Ellan Bride from the top of Castle Rushen because the castle was a prison, and you weren't allowed to go in. If you wanted to look at Ellan Bride from Castletown, Mam said, you had to walk out to Scarlett Point, and on a very clear day, there it would be, a tiny blue hump on the horizon.

At this time of year the west side of Ellan Bride belonged to the birds. All day long their cries echoed across the whole island, and as Billy got close to the cliffs the noise grew deafening. The birds had their own lives, but with the telescope Billy was able to see a lot that would otherwise have been secret. He trained the telescope on a place he knew at the top of Giau yn Ooig, and twisted it into focus.

The eider duck was still sitting plumply on her eggs. It was rare to find an eiders' nest on the island. She looked like another clump of moss amidst the hummocks of sea campion, sheltered in a little gully at the top of the cliff. Or, surrounded by the white flowers, she could have been one of the bare patches outside the puffin burrows, brown and mottled. Through the telescope her feathers were glossy, light brown and blackish on her back, and more delicately dappled on her neck. Her beady black eye seemed to look straight at Billy, but because of the telescope that was of course impossible. Her beak was grey, pale at the tip, and quietly tucked in. She paid no attention to the ooo-ooo, ooo-ooo of the raft of other eiders that floated below her. They might be the ones that were too young to nest this year. Eiders were allowed to ignore their relations, barring their own chicks. People had to go on knowing each other for ever. It must be very warm if you were an egg underneath that duck.

There was a flicker of movement beside him. Billy lowered his telescope as two razorbills skimmed the cliff top just a yard away. He'd been so still they'd stopped noticing him. Billy sat up, blinking. The puffins were still circling round and round the island; he could hear the whirring of their wings as they sped past. Even Mam didn't know why they circled and circled like that. There were always more of them doing it in the evening, but they were doing it now, and it was – he glanced up at the sun – nowhere near the middle of the morning. He still hadn't got the kindling. He'd climb into Giau yn Stackey before he went home and fetch an armful all at once. Diya thought you could only get wood from Giau yn Stackey by boat, but she was wrong: it was easy to climb down if you knew the right footholds. He'd stay out long enough to have walked over the slabs looking for little bits of wood that had drifted in during the last day or two. That would give him a bit more time to himself.

Billy sat turning the precious telescope round and round in his hands. Its leather case was scratched and battered, but the brass was polished until it shone. He wished it were really his own. It had been Uncle Jim's, and no one ever talked about which of them it belonged to now. Of course it was needed at the light, but even Mam just used it because it was there. She didn't care about the telescope itself. If Uncle Jim were still alive Billy wouldn't be allowed to take the telescope away from the light to look at other things. But he missed Uncle Jim. It would be better if Uncle Jim were alive and Billy didn't have the telescope.

Perhaps Uncle Jim was still alive somewhere. No one had ever found a body. Perhaps he'd been picked up by a passing ship and carried off to a far away country. Perhaps he was in India. The reason why he'd never written to say where he'd gone in five whole years was that perhaps he'd been shipwrecked on an uninhabited island, or somewhere where they were all cannibals and didn't write letters. No, not cannibals. Uncle Jim wouldn't have been eaten. Just normal savages. And one day a ship would land there to get water, and they'd find Uncle Jim, and then he'd come home again.

But Mam had said that wouldn't happen, and so Billy had never mentioned it again. Mam and Diya believed that the children didn't even think any more about Uncle Jim perhaps being alive. Mam and Diya were wrong. Mally didn't think much, but Billy and Breesha sometimes talked it over privately. Breesha said she was sure her Da wasn't dead. Sure of it. She just knew. Abruptly Billy clipped the telescope case shut, and stuffed it into his belt. He had the telescope anyway. Sometimes he thought Uncle Jim being drowned was all his fault because he'd been glad to get the telescope afterwards. But he'd never thought about having the telescope before Uncle Jim went away. He'd never, ever, wished that Uncle Jim was dead. He'd never even dreamed about having the telescope to himself before that night.

Billy stood up. It was better not even to think about all that. He'd been going to look at that snow again, see if he could make out her name. That was what to do next. That was a lot better than thinking.

Chapter 6

'A MOMENT, SIR, IF YOU PLEASE.'

It was Mr Kneen again. Archie turned back impatiently. 'Yes?'

'A message for you, sir. From Mr Quirk.'

'Mr Quirk? I was just stepping round to the Castle to see him now.'

'That's it, sir. He won't be at the Castle this morning. He'll meet you here at the George, in the usual parlour, at eleven o'clock. He sent a message.'

'Eleven!' Archie pulled his watch out of his waistcoat pocket and looked at it, as if that would somehow help. 'Doesn't he know we have to leave for Port St Mary this morning?'

'Ay well, sir, you won't be sailing today anyway, and it's less than six miles to Port St Mary. You're not needing to be away from here till this afternoon, I'm thinking.'

So they all knew his business, damn them, even down to the innkeeper. But that was only to be expected in a place like this. Archie tapped his watch impatiently. 'No doubt,' he said coldly.

He'd no sooner stepped out of the inn than he met Ben Groat in the Square. What with the cries of the fish-sellers, and the housewives hurrying to the bakery in their pattens, baskets on their arms, it was impossible to talk sensibly.

'Come round to the stables,' said Archie.

The stables were at the back of the inn, reached by a narrow lane full of dung. A solitary cow, newly milked, lumbered out from a stone-flagged passage leading into the nearest house, and picked her way towards the green at the end of the street. Ben explained why it would make more sense to look for another chainman in Port St Mary, and, to his relief, Young Archibald absentmindedly agreed. He seemed to have something else on his mind, which was all to the good. In the stableyard a boy was rubbing down a sweating hack, but there was no sign of the head groom. In the coachhouse their gear was still safely in the gig, untouched.

'Good,' said Archie, when he'd inspected everything. 'Ben, the devil of it is I willna be able to see this fellow afore eleven. I doubt we'll be away until well after noon.'

'Well, the horse'll no mind,' said Ben philosophically. 'In fact I could put the poor beast out to grass. There's a hobble in the gig. Then we could have a bite of dinner if we're still here at midday.' Ben followed Archie into the yard. 'I speired about getting to Port St Mary too. The road's no as good as the turnpike from Douglas, but it's dry enough in this weather, and flat all the way, the old fellow said.'

Archie was looking at the sky, biting his lip. Not a cloud in sight, and not a breath of wind. The drought seemed set to continue. There was no chance at all of setting sail today, and that meant that in all honesty there was no hurry. Five and a half miles in a gig along an indifferent road – say an hour and a half at the worst. It was – he glanced at his watch again – nearly eight now. Low water was at eighteen minutes past eleven. They had to sail to Ellan Bride on the ebb to have the current with them. If only they hadn't been held up by this business, they could have gone out on the ebb this morning. But they were missing this tide, damn it . . . and as for the next one, it was unlikely they'd persuade the boatman to leave this evening, as he'd then have to come home after dark, with no wind to help him either way. If they aimed at a dawn start tomorrow, he could send Ben to buy provisions now, while he saw this Mr Quirk . . . and now Ben was coming out of the stable, leading a depressed-looking roan, and was speaking to him again. 'What did you say, Ben?'

'About Drew, Mr Buchanan. What'll we do about Drew?'

'Nothing,' said Archie emphatically. 'Scott must fend for himself.'

'But Mr Buchanan . . .' Archie strode off down the street. Since the horse was in no hurry, Ben had to call after him. 'Sir!'

Archie turned round. He had to look up six inches to meet Ben's eyes; he always found that a disadvantage, but he said firmly, 'No, Ben. It was insane, what Drew did. Doesn't he realise we've got to keep these people on our side? He could have done us no end of damage. He must take what comes to him.'

Ben knew this mood of Young Archibald's. There was never any point pleading with him. They'd worked together since Ben had started out as apprentice chainman on the Sutherland survey – so long, in fact, that Archie very seldom gave Ben direct orders. They respected each other, and Ben hardly ever got the Young Archibald treatment which so infuriated Drew. Usually he deflected any signs of it, but in this case he'd promised Drew. 'But Mr Buchanan . . .'

'Well?'

'I saw Drew this morning, sir. Yon dungeon he's in is the filthiest hellhole . . . it makes the Tollbooth look like a palace! And he's no even been charged yet – they couldna find the constable – they may no even ken he's in there! If ye'd seen him, sir. We kinna leave Drew to rot!'

This time Archie did give him a civil answer, but all the same he shook his head. 'What would you have me do, Ben? If he's broken the law of the land, what *can* I do?'

'I'm sure you could, when you speak to this Bailiff today. A bailiff would be the right man, surely? Otherwise . . . what'll they do to him? D'you ken what the law is here? Because I don't. But seemingly they transported a fellow in like case.'

'They won't transport Scott! Doubtless they'll have him up before their magistrate, and let him cool his heels for a couple of weeks in jail. He brought it on himself; he'll have to thole it.'

'Then, sir . . .'

'What?'

'We might well gang hame afore that! What if he's in jail still?'

'Then he'll serve his sentence.'

'But if we don't take him back with us, Mr Stevenson's going to ken about it. And Drew willna have the money for the steam packet, I'm sure of that.'

'Is there any good reason why Mr Stevenson shouldn't ken about it?'

'It's Drew's job, Mr Archie,' said Ben firmly. 'I doubt he'd get another.'

'For good reason, it seems. Enough of this, Ben! We're a man short now, and there's work to do!'

'Ay well,' said Ben reluctantly, 'I think we could maybe hire one of the people at the lighthouse. At least they'd be getting some good out of us then.'

'There isn't anyone to hire at the lighthouse. Only women and bairns, Mr Stevenson said.'

'Ay well, a woman or a bairn can hold the end of a chain. One of them must be strong enough to carry the oil up the tower.'

'It wouldn't do,' said Archie decidedly. 'We'll have to ask Mr Watterson.'

'That'll be the boatman, will it?'

'Ay, he supplies the Ellan Bride light. They use him for the Calf as well sometimes.' Archie stared out past a row of thatched hovels to the empty sea. 'Five mouths to feed on eighteen pounds a year,' he added unexpectedly. 'Our lightkeepers get forty-five pounds a year. Did you know the Duke cut their wages by nine pounds when the proper lightkeeper drowned?'

'I'm no as surprised as I might be,' said Ben.

'No, and they don't love the Duke much hereabouts.'

'That was what did for poor Drew, sir. The Duke of Atholl being Scots. Once they found out we were Scots they started saying things in their own language. You could tell it wasna compliments exactly. They dinna love the Scots, for sure. The Duke wasna Drew's fault, and that's a fact.'

'Enough, Mr Groat! I don't want to hear another word about Scott!' When Young Archibald put on his Edinburgh English voice it was useless to say another word. Ben sighed to himself. 'No more about Scott! Is that understood?'

'Understood, sir.' Ben hesitated for a moment, as they strolled past the last cottages and on to the green above an open shingle beach. Ben bent to fasten the hobble. 'There you go, boy. Make the most of it while you can.' He straightened up, patted the horse on the rump as it hobbled away, and said casually, as he draped the leading rope over his arm, 'Seems it's a bit complicated, about this light on Ellan Bride? No just a matter of the Commissioners taking over from the private owner and building a new light, like I thought?'

'I wonder if this is the Port St Mary Road?' Archie sighed. 'No, Ben, it's not that simple. I wish we could just get on with the job and be done with it. It's like this, so far as Mr Stevenson explained it to me. Up until three years ago the whole Island – the whole of the Isle of Man, that is – belonged to the Duke of Atholl –'

'I thought he was just the Governor?'

'Before he was Governor he owned the whole place. The Crown bought him out, and made him Governor – a sort of Prince Regent if you like, but no so fat. But they're still arguing about what was sold to the Crown and what wasn't. The Duke kept the Ellan Bride light, anyway. It was a private light, and when the Duke sold all his lands on the Isle of Man, he didn't sell the light on Ellan Bride. The lawyers are still arguing about whether he sold the island the lighthouse stands on, along with all the other lands in his manor.'

'But what about the Calf lights? He sold the ground for those all right.'

'And a hell of a bargain he drove, too! Mr Stevenson showed me the letters. Sir William Rae kept writing from the Commissioners – half the time the Duke didn't even bother to answer.' Archie was getting really indignant now. 'And then he wanted to charge a ridiculous rent for the ground: fifty pounds a year for ten acres of gravel! Well, he didna get it, and the lights got built in spite of him. And this with wrecks off this coast awmaist every year! He couldna have done it under Scots law, Ben.'

'No a very public-spirited gentleman, seemingly. No wonder they don't like the Scots much around here.'

'It gets worse, Ben. For a hundred years the Atholls were favouring Scots here – everything from gentlemen's appointments down to the very house servants. And the auld Duke put a Scots family on Ellan Bride when he first built the light there.'

'Ay well. But at least he built a light. That was something.'

'For profit, Ben, profit! I'm telling ye, these private gentlemen – so-called – are just in it for what they can make! They dinna care about the lights, or the shipping, or the wrecks, or the good o the country. The Atholls have probably made half a million out of this damn light, over the fifty years it's been there. We only got the light on Ellan Bride at last when the old Duke died. And d'ye ken what we paid for it – just last year this was – *£130,000*! What's more, the Commissioners dinna tak ony extra dues from the Manx lights at all. No a penny. If a ship's paid its dues for the Scottish lights, that covers the Manx lights too.'

'Ay well, even if the old Duke had got the price he wanted he couldna have taken it with him. And the light itself isna much good, I'm thinking, if we're about to build a new one.'

'Och, to be fair, the light was good in its time. But it's been there fifty year. It's obsolete.'

Ben strolled along, deep in thought, adapting his stride to Archie's, then asked presently, 'So why have you got to see this other fellow this morning? That's nothing to do with the new Duke, surely? He doesna come into it any more?'

'Och, there's politics on this damn Island as well. The new Lieutenant Governor – that's Colonel Smelt – wrote to the Commissioners to say that the harbour dues ought to be coming back to the Isle of Man. They feel sore here because their taxes all get spent in London, and nothing comes back to the Island. That seems to be the gist of it.'

'There's others who could say the same as that.'

Archie wasn't listening. 'Anyway, no one's taking extra harbour dues from Ellan Bride now it comes under the Commissioners. Don't ask me, Ben. Mr Stevenson said I was to steer clear o all that. My job – and I'm no relishing it overmuch – is to meet this Water Bailiff and just keep repeating that I don't know, I'm just the surveyor. But I'm to keep him informed, and tell him my conclusions when we've done the work. I just have to keep the waters smooth, Ben, and no say anything.'

Then I'm surprised Mr Stevenson picked you for the job. Naturally Ben didn't speak that thought aloud, but merely said, 'So who's the Water Bailiff, sir? Is it no the Governor you should be talking to?'

'No, thank God. I've been told to liaise with the Water Bailiff, and keep him fully informed of all developments. They have their own sort of Parliament here, Mr Stevenson said – and the Water Bailiff is part of that.'

'Fair enough,' said Ben equably. He had to admit, hard though it was for Drew, that it was going to be much easier without him. Drew and Young Archibald brought out the very worst in each other. When it was just himself and Archie, Archie seemed to relax. Their backgrounds were not so very different after all. When Archie forgot that he had become an Edinburgh surveyor, Ben noticed that he lapsed into the accents of his early years. Today Young Archibald had been harder to handle. It was always the case when he was nervous. Probably he'd been worrying about today's interview ever since they left Edinburgh. That was why he'd been so prickly. Drew would never understand that, any more than Archie would understand how Drew had got into that fight. And what Drew could never see was that Archie was good at his job. When he was roused you could see that he cared about it passionately. Too much, perhaps. He wanted more than Mr Stevenson was prepared to give. Maybe Robert Stevenson knew that, and maybe he didn't. It was no business of Ben's, and it was quite certain that no one would ever ask Ben what he thought about it.

Chapter 7

AS THE TIDE EBBED THE CREGGYNS SLOWLY GREW. WHEN IT was as calm as this, at high tide there were only empty circles rippling outwards to show that the Creggyns were there at all. Once Creggyn Doo had revealed all its shining shelves of seaweed, you knew that Finn's yawl could come alongside the landing rock at Gob y Vaatey. It was too soon yet. The seaweed on the Creggyns rose and fell gently with the waves, gleaming like the hair of an underwater giant. Maybe the golden weed was the thick curls of the sea king who stirred his cauldron at the bottom of the sea and made the storms rise, but he wasn't cooking anything down there today. Maybe his storm-pot was empty. Today the sea was rippling silver so that when you half-shut your eyes you saw all the sparkles at once like stars falling.

A brig was becalmed south of the Creggyns. Mally was fairly sure it was a brig, though it seemed to have an extra mast. Mally could recognise nearly all the ships that passed. The others knew them all, except for Mam, who was the only one who couldn't read these things without thinking about it. But other sorts of reading Mam did best of all. Like words. Mam could read words much more than Lucy, but Lucy could read ships like no one else ever born.

This was a good sitting place if the wind was at all easterly. Today there was hardly any breeze, just the warm smells of the island. Mally had done the jobs Mam had given her this morning. She always had to wash and put away the porridge dishes after breakfast because she didn't work in the lighthouse yet. But when she was eight she would take her turn doing the light and not have to help with the dishes every single day. That would be better than the way it was now.

She could see the horizon all the way round, which meant that this was a very good day. Sky and sea didn't meet everywhere because of the far lands. The far lands, when you could see them, were always on the horizon, even though Billy said they weren't all the same distance away. Mally would never have wondered about that if Billy hadn't mentioned it, but now it was lodged in her mind as another of those inexplicable things, shadowy shapes on the edge of what she knew for certain.

Today the far lands had come very close, more like real earth than blue clouds, which is what they looked like most often. The Gaffer had come from the far lands when he was young. He came from Scotland, which was north. That was so long ago that Da and Aunt Lucy hadn't yet been born. Today you could see as much of the Island as was ever possible. The Island with a big 'I' was the Isle of Man. Ellan Bride had a small 'i' because it was little. Last year Mally had been herself in Finn's boat, and actually stood on the Island. It was as firm underfoot as Ellan Bride. She'd told Mam that, and Mam said the phrase she wanted was *terra firma*.

Ellan Bride was *terra firma*, and occasionally the Island was *terra firma* too. The far lands were just names, and with the names came stories. There were stories from each place, but more stories from India, because India was the mother of all stories, and in the other countries the stories were fine, but just not quite like the India ones. But India was as far from here as any place could be, and never even so much as a very faint line on the horizon which might be a passing cloud, and no one was likely to get that far, unless they were grown up. For grown-ups all things were possible, though often they didn't seem to bother.

Mally was sitting in a sheltered crevice between two angled rocks. At eye level, about six inches away, there was a little clump of pink sedums growing out of a crack in the rock. This was nearly the highest place on the island, but not as high as the light tower. The tower had been built high enough for the light to shine out to sea on all sides, because that was what it was for. The light was the reason for everything. In the dark or in the fog the light must never go out. That was their job – hers and Breesha's and Billy's and Lucy's and Mam's. All the ships that sailed the seas were safe, because when it was dark or foggy the light would never, ever, go out.

At the top of the tower, Lucy opened the window to let out the heat and the smell of oil. She and Breesha paused on the platform to look at the becalmed ship.

'. . . that's how you're knowing it's a snow, not a brig,' Lucy was saying. 'See, there's another mast next to the mainmast.'

'Maybe she's come from the West Indies,' said Breesha, enjoying the sound of the name. 'Bringing sugar and rum and tobacco to Liverpool or Whitehaven.'

'Maybe.'

'If we had the telescope we could see her name.'

'Dratted boy. He must have taken it straight after breakfast.'

'He always wants to look at things,' explained Breesha.

Aunt Lucy replied, astonishingly, 'The telescope doesn't belong to the light. The Gaffer bought it in Douglas. That would make it Billy's.'

'But you said before it had to go with the light!'

'Things change,' said Lucy.

Breesha opened her mouth to speak, but Aunt Lucy had turned her back. There is *something*, thought Breesha. She felt a pang of fear. No one had spoken, but *something* had happened, and Lucy and Mam knew what it was. Billy didn't know. Mally might have heard something, as she slept in the bedroom. Mally did sometimes hear Mam and Lucy talk when they thought she was asleep. Mally wasn't quite as young and stupid as they thought. At least, not always. Anyway, whatever it was, Aunt Lucy would know what to do. Breesha watched Lucy trim the burnt ends off the four wicks in the lowest tier of lamps, and draw them out so they were just the right length. This was a job that had to be done just right: Breesha wasn't allowed to trim the wicks yet.

'There you are. You can be making a start on those.'

Breesha always did the lowest row of lamps, and Lucy did the top two tiers. No one else could work as fast as Aunt Lucy. Breesha took a handful of tow and started cleaning her south-facing reflector. Now it was nearly summer the black film over it wasn't nearly so thick. Last night the lamps had burned for barely eight hours; in winter it was sometimes sixteen. But the summer oil was worse to clean off because it was much stickier than the winter oil. The whale oil they had now was quite good. Last winter's oil had been horrible. Sometimes they'd found bits of skin and blubber floating in it. They'd creamed off the worst bits when they opened the barrels, because usually that kind of stuff was floating on the top. When they'd first opened those barrels they'd smelt like rotting fish. The oil they were using now just smelt as if a hot animal had been sleeping in the lantern.

At last the reflector was as clean as Breesha could make it. She fetched one of the linen rags from the basket and some chalk white, and started polishing. In summer she always started with the south reflector because as the morning went on the sun got so fierce. In winter she saved south until last. Because each of the numerous mirrors inside the reflector was at a different angle to the sun, each one was a different colour. Breesha could make the colours change by moving her head around and squinting at them. She had to do that anyway to make sure there wasn't a single smear, but if she half-shut her eyes it was like Aladdin's chest of jewels gleaming in the light of the magic lamp. Then if she opened her eyes and looked straight into one of the little pieces of glass, what she saw was herself, and if she looked into more than one at a time there were many Breeshas, all at slightly different angles, like the jigsaw puzzle Diya had bought for them all from Douglas, when all the pieces were laid out and not yet put together.

The jigsaw puzzle was another matter altogether. Breesha saw her many reflected selves smile and sit back. It was almost like not being herself, seeing that girl with an oily scarf wrapped round her head so it hid her hair, and a dirty smear on her brown cheek, sitting there in the reflectors with a white sky behind her. But she was inside that girl's head, because that girl was remembering about the jigsaw puzzle, and only she, inside her own mind, knew that.

'Aunt Lucy?'

'Uh-huh?' Lucy didn't look up; she was squinting to see if her reflector was done.

'Remember how we did the jigsaw map?'

'Did what?'

'The jigsaw map that Mam got on the Island.'

'Oh that. Yes.'

'And it had the whole of Europe and Asia on it. It had India and everything, but it didn't have the Island.'

Lucy didn't answer. Breesha went on thinking about the jigsaw map as she polished. She and Billy had put it together so often they knew it by heart. Most of the land in the world was very large. India was far larger than England. England was far larger than the Isle of Man. The Isle of Man was far larger than Ellan Bride. Ellan Bride was about the smallest place in the world, and yet it was the largest, if you happened to live on it and had hardly ever been anywhere else. Breesha had been to Port St Mary, and she had twice been to Castletown, only that was so long ago she couldn't remember it. From the top of the lighthouse you could see five different countries. Six, Mam always said, if you counted the kingdom of heaven. But you might as well not count that, because you couldn't go there unless you were dead. It was good doing the jigsaw puzzle. It would be better to have another one, one day. She and Billy had got to the point when they knew their jigsaw puzzle almost too well.

'That jigsaw puzzle,' said Lucy presently. 'Never again. It was nearly driving me mad. All over the kitchen table.'

'But we always remember to do it on the tray now! We just didn't know to do that the first time until it was too late.'

'Pointless, anyway,' said Lucy.

They worked on in silence. The sun shone fiercely, until it grew so hot inside the lantern that Breesha could feel the sweat running down her back. Lucy wedged the window wide open, and that brought in a whiff of cooler air. Sunlight winked on glass and made Breesha's eyes water. Outside the island basked in the spring light. Pale tide streaks made long lines off the Creggyns. Breesha shut one eye, and squinted across the last reflector. The mosaic of mirrors gleamed without blemish, every piece.

When Breesha worked with Aunt Lucy there was almost no talking; it was quite different from being with Mam. Aunt Lucy liked it that Breesha never had to be told anything twice. So when all the reflectors were done Breesha went back to the house without being told, jumping down from rock to rock instead of following the zigzag path. Mam wasn't in the kitchen, but the broth was simmering in the iron pot. Breesha lifted the big kettle from the chain, and half-filled the bucket. The kettle was very heavy. She poured the boiling water carefully. Billy had once scalded himself doing this job, and he'd had to sit with his feet in cold water all morning.

In the yard the chickens were foraging round the ditch where Diya had thrown out the night slops. Flies clouded thickly over the empty feeding trough. When Mrs Black saw Breesha with another bucket in her hand she scuttled over, clucking excitedly, even though she knew just as well as the other chickens that breakfast came only once. Even Mally, who could be silly about chickens, wouldn't fuss when Mrs Black appeared on the dinner table. Breesha clambered up to the light again, following the path this time and using two hands for the bucket.

She topped up the bucket with cold water from the butt outside the storeroom. This side of the lighthouse gleamed in its fresh coat of white. Every summer they had to work their way round the fifteen-foot tower until all the outside was whitewashed. Only yesterday morning Aunt Lucy had touched up the lettering on the carved scroll over the door in black paint: *Et in Arcadia ego.* The Latin words meant that even though Ellan Bride was the best place in the world men would still get drowned here.

In the workroom at the bottom of the tower Aunt Lucy poured some of the water into a second bucket, and added soap to one and vinegar to the other. Aunt Lucy had already put the oil cans away; the first rule was that the clean things and the oily things must never, ever, get mixed. Even Mally knew that. Breesha took a clean rag for her soap bucket, and a crackly dry leather for the vinegar bucket, where it immediately turned soft and slippery in the hot water.

She enjoyed cleaning the windows on a sunny day. She liked the smell of soap and vinegar. At first the water was so hot she could barely put her hands in it to wring out the cloth. It made her skin red and raw, but it soon cooled. First she washed each pane with hot soapy water until it was clean, then she rubbed it with the leather until it shone. She took care to get right into every corner; Lucy always noticed if a corner got missed. That took a long time. Even after a short summer night there was a greasy film all over the glass. The light chamber had six glass windows facing all round, because shipping could come from any direction. Each of the six windows was made up of six small panes. Aunt Lucy always did the top four, and Billy or Breesha, whichever it was, had to do the bottom two. Cleaning the glass was the longest job, and in winter it could take the rest of the morning. At first the soapy water just made the glass even blurrier, and then as Breesha rubbed and rubbed it gradually got clear again. It was hardest on sunny days because she could see every single smear, and she had to go on until the whole pane was shining bright.

'Clean water,' said Lucy.

Breesha sighed; they could have made it last just one pane longer. When she came back up the ladder with the heavy bucket, she glanced out of the cleaned north-west window. A small black speck was detaching itself from the Calf. 'There's a boat coming from the Island.'

Lucy stopped cleaning and looked out of the window. 'So there is.' There was something in her voice Breesha hadn't heard before. She felt that same quick pang of fear. There is *something*, but they're not telling us. Lucy cut across her thoughts. 'That window's still mucky, Breesha.'

'It's on the outside.'

'We'll see.' Lucy stood upright and shook out her leather. 'I should be doing the outside today anyway, while the weather's so good . . .' She looked at the distant speck, and seemed to hesitate.

'Can I help?' Doing the outside meant getting onto the balcony and moving the rope ladder round that was fixed to the iron weathercock on the top of the tower, and climbing three steps off the parapet, with a leather bucket on a rope beside you, then leaning on the wooden ribs between the panes, with your face against the roof of the tower, higher than anything else in the world, while you rubbed away at the outside glass, right into the very topmost corners. On a day like this there would be just the blue arch of sky above you. In stormy weather it was different, but those were the very times that the lantern got most salted up. That was when Lucy tied the rope round her waist, and Mam and Billy both went up and held the end of the rope looped round the rail, and the job had to be done one-handed because Lucy always had to have one hand to cling onto the hooks when the wind was wild. Aunt Lucy was the strongest person in the world, and afraid of nothing.

'No,' said Lucy.

'But you let Billy!'

'Billy's a boy.'

'But *you're* not a boy!' cried Breesha.

'You can be doing the bottom panes, same as inside.'

Breesha stood between her aunt and the top of the ladder. 'Aunt Lucy. You let Billy do the top ones outside and you don't let me. I'm three months older than he is. When you were young you did all the jobs. You told us. But you weren't a boy.'

Lucy relented, and gave her an answer. 'My Da was only ever letting me do outside when Jim was away. I was older than you when I was starting boy's work. And I only did it all the time after your Grandda couldn't manage it any more.'

'So if Billy goes away one day, I could then?'

A shadow seemed to cross her aunt's face. 'God knows what you'll be needing to do, Breesha veen, before we're done. Now then, I'll fill up the oil cans while you're getting some more water. Did you refill the kettle?'

'Of course I did!' It was lazy and thoughtless not to leave the kettle full. Only Billy sometimes forgot. Indignantly Breesha seized the bucket and tipped the dirty water over the rail. There was no wind today; it fell straight down. On windy days you had to throw the water downwind, and it flew up in a shower of spray and vanished. Breesha went backwards down the ladder to the platform floor, then ran down the spiral steps, bare feet pattering on the stone, the empty bucket swinging.

When she came back Aunt Lucy was leaning over the rail, looking north towards the boat they'd seen. Just looking at her from behind, Breesha could see how Lucy's shoulders had suddenly relaxed. 'It's just a smack. It'll be slow going for them today. Poor weather for fishing, too.'

The relief in Lucy's voice was palpable. So everything was all right again; the unknown threat had passed. But Breesha knew she was right: there was *something*. And if Lucy and Diya didn't mean to tell them, she and Billy were going to have to find out what it was.

Chapter 8

ARCHIE SAT IN THE PARLOUR OF THE GEORGE, IMPATIENTLY skimming the latest copy of *The Manx Advertiser*. The Water Bailiff was late. On the second page of the paper there was an outspoken article on Reform, reprinted from the *Westminster Review*, severely trouncing the recalcitrant Tories. For a few minutes Archie forgot the time altogether. That the Tories could do this! In the face of the will of the people so uncompromisingly expressed! In the face of a government majority, the Prime Minister, the whole law and constitution, let alone justice, progress, industry and equality! The Tories had forced a dissolution of parliament rather than let the Reform Bill go through, and now, after all the excitement, a landless lighthouse surveyor still had no right to vote unless he took ship to America and started life all over again. If the coming election didn't bring the Whigs back, and Reform along with them, there'd be barricades up in London as well as Paris, and what's more, if it wasn't for the *Beagle*, he'd be tempted to join the revolution himself. It was all a man without a vote could possibly do. Archie threw down the newspaper, and strode over to the window.

Twenty-five past eleven. There was no real reason for him to meet this Water Bailiff at all. The Commissioners had referred to it as a 'courtesy visit'. Mr Stevenson had been more forthright. 'The Isle of Man Tynwald has no rights in the matter at all, but they like to think they have. We'll need them to co-operate later, when we're building. In fact we'll probably have to ask for favours. So just do your best to turn them up sweet, Buchanan. There's nothing else you can do; it's up to the Commissioners really. These Manxmen haven't a leg to stand on, but don't for God's sake say so to their faces.'

'Ah, Mr Stevenson?'

Archie turned round. He'd been told that Quirk was a lawyer, and had imagined a shark-like adversary moving in for the kill. There were plenty of those in Edinburgh. In fact the Water Bailiff was a stout, genial fellow in an old-fashioned embroidered waistcoat and broadcloth suit. 'Quirk, sir, George Quirk, at your service.'

Archie shook the outstretched hand. 'Buchanan, sir. I'm not Mr Stevenson. I'm one of the Company's surveyors.'

'Buchanan. Yes, indeed. My father had the pleasure of meeting Mr Stevenson. That must have been, what . . . thirty years ago? I was a mere boy, but I remember much discussion concerning the lighthouses. Yes, there was a lot of talk about Mr Stevenson's visit – but that's thirty years since. Long before your time, sir, but I remember it well.'

Archie flushed. Just because thirty years ago he'd not yet been weaned he had no need to feel at a disadvantage now, but if that had been Mr Quirk's object it had not been unsuccessful.

'A difficult business this, sir, a difficult business,' went on Mr Quirk. 'Shall we sit down? What can I order for you? A pint of porter?'

'Nothing for me, I thank you, sir. I hope our business isn't going to be difficult.'

They sat at the window. Mr Quirk retained his kindly smile, but the way he took out a pocket book filled with papers, and laid them open on the table in front of him seemed alarmingly business-like. Archie recognised the familiar seal of the Commissioners of Northern Lights. 'Well, well, we may as well come straight to the point, Mr Buchanan. It's this matter of harbour dues.'

That was what Archie had expected him to say. 'Mr Stevenson told me there'd been questions asked about harbour dues.' He did his best to emulate Mr Quirk's urbanity. 'But it doesn't apply to us. The Commissioners of Northern Lights have never had any extra revenue from their Manx lights. The Manx dues have always been included in the charge for Scottish lights – it says so in the Act of '15.'

'For the new lights built by the Commissioners at the Calf and Point of Ayre that is correct – what you say is perfectly true so far as it goes. But the Ellan Bride light raised a very considerable income from harbour dues while it was in private hands. And that income is still going – always has gone – straight out of this country. In short, sir, all profits have gone to Scotland, to the owner's estates.'

'But the Ellan Bride lighthouse belongs to the Crown now. That means the new light will be built and maintained by the Commissioners of Northern Lights, in the same way as the ones on the Calf of Man.'

'And the revenue will go back to Edinburgh, collected by the Commissioners. I should remind you, sir, that Ellan Bride is part of the Isle of Man, and any income arising therefrom should be administered by our own government.'

'But there won't *be* an income! It's quite the opposite – the purchase of the old light, and the building of the new one, is going to be an enormous expense. It'll take the Commissioners years to recover the money! And your government isn't paying a penny for that, is it?' He'd been too forthright. For a moment he had a vision of Mr Stevenson at his elbow, shaking his finger reprovingly. 'What I mean to say is,' added Archie, as mildly as he could, 'if there are any harbour dues they'd have to be used to recoup the expense of purchasing and building the light, just like in Scotland.'

'*If* there are any dues, you say. I abhor casuistry, Mr Buchanan.' The Water Bailiff was no longer smiling benignly. 'What I think you mean to say is that the Commissioners have every intention of collecting dues for Ellan Bride, and they have every intention, that being so, of retaining all monies in Scotland, overriding the claims of the Manx government. It's all one with Crown policy on our ports and harbours, sir. We make the investment, and maintain the properties, and not a penny of the income do we recover.'

'But, sir, in this case you're *not* making the investment. The Commissioners – I mean the Crown – bought the light from the Duke of Atholl, and if there *is* any income in the future – and as to that I simply don't know – I'm just the surveyor – but *if* there is, it would have to go first to recoup the expense – the *huge* expense – of taking over the light in the first place.'

'The Duke of Atholl,' remarked Mr Quirk, 'was much inclined to promote a Scotch connection, for which, saving your presence, sir, there is no historical precedent. In 1815 it was the Duke who allowed the care of Manx lights to be devolved upon the Scottish lighthouse authority.'

'Well,' said Archie, 'it was going to be that or England, wasn't it? But the Liverpool merchants wouldn't have Trinity House here, and so you got us. I thought your Manx Parliament was pleased to have lights at Point of Ayre and Calf of Man. Now we're going to improve the light on Ellan Bride. There's no change of policy in that.'

'Allow me to correct you, sir. The light on Ellan Bride is a very different matter. It already exists – has existed for fifty years – as a Manx lighthouse.'

They seemed to be going round and round in circles. Archie looked out at the canvas awnings over the shambles opposite, and tried to work out if there was any wind at all. Even if there were, it was no use to them here. They should be in Port St Mary, standing by the boat . . . Quirk was still ranting about how much the Duke of Atholl had filched from the Isle of Man. He seemed to be implying that the Crown should have paid the Manx government, rather than the Duke of Atholl, when they bought the lighthouse. That was nonsense. In fact – Archie recollected himself with a start – perhaps it was his job to point this out.

'But Ellan Bride was a private light! It belonged to the Duke and it was his to sell!' Archie did his best not to sound exasperated.

'Are you aware, sir, of the distinction between the manorial lands, which included the island of Ellan Bride, and the lighthouse itself, which is a public service in the same category as ports and harbours?'

'Yes – I mean – I know – Mr Stevenson told me – that there was a lot of trouble over ports and harbours. But that's nothing to do with the Ellan Bride lighthouse! It was a private light, always, and the people here – your government, I mean – never had any interest in it.'

'Interest, sir! If you knew of the "interest" which the late Duke appropriated from the people of this island! But as his countryman you would no doubt wish to defend him.'

'Not at all, sir.' He was *not* going to lose his temper. He owed Mr Stevenson that much, at least. 'I keep saying: the Duke sold the lighthouse to the Crown. The Act makes it all quite clear: the Crown then handed it over to the Commissioners of Northern Lights, because they look after all the lighthouses on this Island. What I mean to say, sir, with all due respect, is that the lighthouse on Ellan Bride does not, and never has, belonged to your government.'

'But the revenue from it, if revenue is being collected, should come to the Island. After all, it is the Island which provides the light, so it should get the revenue from the ports who pay the harbour dues.'

Archie knew that if the Manx Parliament had owned it, the Ellan Bride light would have brought them a fortune. But surely he could cut this interview short? He'd been told to make this so-called courtesy visit, but he was, after all, only the surveyor. He wasn't even employed by the Commissioners, or the government. If he'd wanted to be a politician he'd have gone into politics.

'Well, sir, I'm just the surveyor. I work for the lighthouse engineers. We have a contract to rebuild the Ellan Bride light.

I've just come to do my job, sir.' He could hardly be more tactful that that; even Mr Stevenson would have admitted that his manner was conciliatory.

'Very well.' Mr Quirk suddenly seemed to abandon the question, as if he could no longer be bothered to argue about it. He wasn't smiling any more. Archie watched him shuffle through his papers again. 'There is a secondary question, of course. It's debatable whether it is in fact necessary to rebuild the Ellan Bride light.'

'That's why I'm here, sir,' said Archie. At least this was a matter he did know something about. 'The particulars we hold in Edinburgh suggest that the Ellan Bride light – which was built, as I say, fifty years ago – is no longer up to modern requirements. The beam isn't powerful enough, and also there's been confusion because in poor visibility Ellan Bride is ay mistaken for one of the Calf lights. The merchants of Liverpool have petitioned us to give Ellan Bride a revolving light too, showing a red sector as well as a white – just like at Cape Wrath – so as to differentiate the signal.'

'You say all this, sir, but I don't think you're familiar with any of our lights on the Island. You've never been here before? You've not looked at the present light on Ellan Bride?'

'No,' said Archie. 'That's why I'm going over there as soon as I can.' He thought of taking his watch from his waistcoat pocket and pointedly looking at it, but decided against it. 'The range of the present light is no more than four leagues, even in optimum conditions. In view of the vastly increased traffic to and from the ports of Liverpool, Whitehaven, Glasgow, Dublin and Belfast – to say nothing of all the minor ports – and the way the herring fishing is expanding – a more adequate light on Ellan Bride must be a priority.' Absorbed in the technical question, Archie forgot for a moment that he was dealing with an adversary. 'We'll have tae build a higher tower and design a better lighting system.'

'But the light has already been improved! The range is far greater than it was fifty years ago. In fact I've seen it from here!

Over at St Bees they only replaced the coal-burning light a few years ago! Ellan Bride has always been kept up-to-date with oil lamps.'

'I must beg to differ, sir. The lamps on Ellan Bride were installed in 1790. I agree the Duke was ahead of his time when he bought them – they were the latest invention back then – but that's more than forty years since. St Bees was an anomaly. I can't comment on that. I don't work for Trinity House.'

'But I understand the Ellan Bride light to have modern glass reflectors!'

'Have you seen them?' asked Archie.

'No, in fact I have not.'

'Have you ever been on Ellan Bride yourself, sir?'

'No, sir, I have not. But I am reliably informed that the reflectors are of the latest modern design.'

'No sir,' said Archie firmly. He was on his own ground now. 'The reflectors were modern when they were built, but the science of lens design has developed greatly since then. The lights on the Calf can be seen six or seven leagues away in clear weather. The Ellan Bride light is only visible for just over half that distance. And, as I explained, we need tae devise a signal that will differentiate Ellan Bride more clearly from the Calf. We'll probably use the latest French lenses on the new light. At the verra least we'll use modern Argand burners.'

'So, if everything is already decided by your employers,' said Mr Quirk testily, 'I fail to see the object of this consultation.'

'I came here because your Governor requested it,' said Archie. 'His letter said that you wanted to discuss technical questions with the surveyor before he went to the site. I've come to survey the island. That's my job, sir. I survey the site in detail, and take my plans back to Mr Stevenson.' Archie glanced at the bright sky outside the window and made to rise from his chair.

'I take it, then, that you'll report to me on your findings before you leave the Island.'

That meant he must be free to go. With any luck there'd be

no further official obstruction. Let them argue about the bloody harbour dues for the next twenty years if they liked. It was nothing to do with him. 'Certainly sir,' said Archie. He stood up and held out his hand. 'Good day to you, sir.'

Mr Quirk pursed his lips and looked at his papers again. 'There is just one other matter.'

'Sir?'

'The keeper of the new light. There is at present, as I mentioned earlier, a Scotch connection. The Duke was inclined to favour his own countrymen in all spheres, and that has been a cause of considerable dissatisfaction. But times, as you will note, have changed.'

'Sir?'

'Presumably you'll be making a new appointment. I can suggest a reliable, deserving man who would make a satisfactory employee.'

'You want the Commissioners of Northern Lights to evict the present keepers because they're Scots? All our employees are Scots, of course!' Archie couldn't quite keep the anger out of his voice.

'Indeed no, sir. You quite misunderstand me. In any case, the Ellan Bride light has been kept by the same family since it was built. It was one of the late Duke's appointments from his Scotch estates. Perhaps the present keepers no longer regard themselves as foreigners. I wouldn't know. But that is not to the purpose. My point is, it is unlikely, is it not, that the Commissioners of Northern Lights would employ women?'

Archie frowned. He didn't want to give way, but the ground had shifted. Besides, it was no business of his. 'That is correct, sir. The Commissioners don't generally employ women.'

'Then I may have a suitable name to suggest, sir, when you return. I take it that the policy of the Commissioners would be to employ a local man?'

'I think you'd have to approach the Commissioners about that. I'm just the surveyor.'

Chapter 9

FLINT RASPED ON QUARTZ: STRIKE . . . STRIKE . . . STRIKE . . . A spark shot up, vanished. Stone on stone: strike . . . strike . . . strike . . . Sparks flew. A spark fell in the tin. Moss smouldered. A tiny fire sprang up, red as blood. Brown fingers picked up the flaming moss, held it to the wick, which sprouted a bead of blue, and then a proper flame, yellow and steady.

The huge dark retreated. The keeill was round them, close and solid, corbelled up to the slabbed roof. The roof was five big slabs like an upside down floor; the floor where they squatted was cold earth. The altar was a single rock with shining white pebbles scattered at its feet. The cross was propped against the east wall beside the altar. You could hardly tell it was a cross: its outline followed the curves of long-ago water over the stone from which it was carved. It looked like a giant gingerbread man with no eyes. You had to look closer to see the faint markings etched on its surface. An abandoned starling's nest filled the aumbry on the south wall; the stones below were streaked with white. There was a faint chattering from within the walls.

'Hark to that,' said Billy, and held up his hand to make Breesha and Mally hush. 'It's the *kirreeyn varrey*. They've come back.'

'Just,' said Breesha, pleased. 'It was all quiet two days ago.'

The warbling chatter stopped for a moment, and then started again. 'That means it's proper summer now. Not just spring.'

Sure enough, over the reek of earth there was a musky smell like ancient hay: that was Mother Carey's chickens: the *kirreeyn varrey*, silent in the daytime, huddled on their invisible nests within the honeycomb of thick stone walls.

Breesha put the lamp carefully in its hollow on the green rock. The green rock was hard as iron and slippery-smooth, and in the lamplight it had a strange dark glow of its own. It had taken the strength of all three of them, a year ago, to roll the green rock from its place on the right-hand side of the altar into the centre of the keeill. You could still see the hollow in the earth where it had lain since the saint left it there. Billy hadn't wanted to move it, but Breesha had said it was important to have the holy rock in the middle, so they could sit in a triangle round it with the lamp burning in the hollow in its centre.

Breesha held a sprig of bog myrtle in the flame, and watched it shrivel. The scent of myrtle mingled with the smell of singeing. Breesha laid the blackened twig on the green rock, next to the lamp. She made the sign against the evil eye, and Billy and Mally followed suit.

'Now we can begin.' Breesha always sat in what Mally thought of as the central place, with her back to the altar, facing west towards the low door. Mally sat on Breesha's left and Billy on her right. If Mally turned her head to the left she could see a line of bright sunshine at ground level, just above where they sat, and she could hear the cries of the kittiwakes circling above the cliffs. It was reassuring to look at daylight. Once you'd crawled in through the entrance the ordinary world could begin to seem too far away. Breesha said that was all right, because the saint herself had lived here and so this was holy ground. Nothing could touch them, said Breesha; they were as safe as a goat kid inside its mother, always snug whatever storms raged outside. Mam said the same thing when she tucked them up in their beds on stormy nights, but that was in the warm house with the fire burning in the grate and the proper kitchen lamp shining brightly. Mally had never been inside the cold, earthy keeill when there was a storm. She never wanted to, either, saint or no.

'I'll tell you what the matter is,' Breesha was saying. 'Bad things are happening. There are bad things happening in the far lands, and the trouble for us is that they're coming here. They could come any day, and once they do everything is going to change very fast.'

'Yes, well,' grumbled Billy. 'There's no point talking like a fairy story. You don't really know any more than we do. What bad things? There isn't a war on, is there? Finn would have told us about it if there was.'

'Is it a buggane?' whispered Mally, glancing towards the door. She wished the sun would start to reach in and touch her reassuringly where she sat. But it was still too early, and there was only the thin line of clear white light, as far away as the sky.

'No, it's not either of those things.'

'Well, spit it out then,' said Billy.

Breesha leaned forward. Her face glowed in the lamplight. Her shadow grew huge and flickered across the gingerbread cross so that its arms seemed to move. Mally looked firmly back at the doorway. 'I found the letter,' whispered Breesha, so they had to lean forward to the light to hear her.

'*What* letter?'

'I knew there was something. *Something* was wrong. There was *something* they weren't telling us . . .'

'Well, we both knew that. In fact first off, it was *me* that told *you*.'

'Yes, but you didn't guess it was a letter! But the thing is, it *had* to be. Because whatever it was happened *after* Finn went away last time. They were all right when Finn came with the coal last month. They were happy then.'

'They were laughing,' said Mally. 'And Mam made a pudding with currants in it, boiled in the broth, and Finn stopped for a whole tide and had dinner with us, and they were laughing.'

'Exactly! And nothing has gone wrong with the light, or the island, since then. We'd have known about anything like that. So what must have happened is Finn brought the letter and they didn't read it till he'd gone. They read it after he went away.'

'That's silly,' objected Billy. 'They'd open it first thing, soon as they got it. *I* would. They always do, if there's a letter. Mind when the letter came from the Duke's agent about getting the new handcart? Mam opened that the minute it came, and talked to Finn all about it. Stands to reason she'd do that with any letter, because Finn would have to do the arranging about bringing anything.'

'Ah but, I don't think Finn gave her the letter when he *came*. I think he handed it over when he *went*.'

'Why?' asked Mally.

'Because he'd know what was in it, of course, and didn't want to talk about it. So he gave it when he was just leaving'

'I don't like that!' cried Billy. 'That makes Finn a coward, and he *isn't*.'

'Don't blame me. I'm only telling it how it was – how it must have been. Anyway,' added Breesha, 'there are different sorts of coward. Don't you want to know what was *in* the letter?'

'Course we do. I told you before to spit it out! But I don't reckon you can! You don't know what was in it, and I bet they haven't told you.' And if they have, thought Billy, it will be very unfair, because I'm the man here, not Breesha. He sighed. Thoughts like that worried him: he and Breesha never used to try to get the better of each other like this. All their lives they'd thought as one, and lived as one. Everything was going wrong between them suddenly, and he didn't like it. Maybe it was because of this horrible letter. But he didn't *know* that. Where was the proof? Breesha could have made up the whole story about the letter. But she never told lies. Not unless she believed them herself, that was. Billy shook his head. It was all too complicated. The sun was shining outside. He dragged his eyes back to the little flame floating in its pool of oil. 'Anyway, if you *do* know, just spit it out and be done with it.'

'That's what I'm trying to do! But you have to *listen*! I *knew* there must be a letter. And a letter would go to Aunt Lucy, not to Mam, if it was important, because she's the lightkeeper. So if Aunt Lucy had hidden it, it would be with her things. In her chest. And I looked, and it was. It was folded in with her clean petticoat, halfway down her sea chest. It was addressed to the Light Keeper, Ellan Bride, and there was a red seal on it.'

'A *seal*?' repeated Mally. 'There can't have been! Not wrapped in a petticoat! It would be much too big and wet. Do you mean dead?'

'Not that sort of seal. A seal,' said Breesha mysteriously, 'is like putting a lock on a letter. If you break the seal everyone knows that someone has read the letter who shouldn't have. But this seal was broken already.'

Mally tried to imagine the broken red seal. It was still seal-shaped in her mind, like a little slug, or a drop of blood-coloured water sliding down the window.

'What was on the seal?' demanded Billy.

'I didn't look—'

'Well, you should have. That way you'd know exactly who you were up against.'

'How . . .' began Mally.

'—because it was more important to read the letter,' went on Breesha as if neither of them had spoken. 'Besides, I didn't know how much time I had. And it was all in script so it was very hard to read.'

'But you always say you can read script!'

'There's script and script. And this was a hard sort, so I couldn't work out all of it. But listen! The important bit—'

'We *are* listening. We've been listening for *ages*! Just spit it out for goodness sake!'

'All right, I *will.* They're going to build a new lighthouse on Ellan Bride, and they don't want us!'

For a long moment they were all struck dumb. Breesha, having spoken the terrible words out loud for the first time, was as stricken as any of them. She felt guilty, as if by having said the thing, she'd made it real. They all stared at the little yellow flame as it burned unflinchingly, untouched by their troubles. Which might be a good thing or a bad thing, thought Breesha. Callous, and yet reassuring.

'*What?*' Billy tried to gather his thoughts. 'What? I mean who? Who says this?'

'A man called Wm Rae says it. I think it's Wm. He writes from the Commissioners of Northern Lights.' Those words had been easy to read because people talked about them so often. The Calf Lights were Commissioners of Northern Lights. St Bees and Skerries were Trinity House. The South Rock and Haulbowline were the Ballast Board in Dublin. But Ellan Bride was none of these things. Ellan Bride was a Private Light, and belonged to the Duke of Atholl. But the Duke had never come to claim his light and now he was dead. Ellan Bride was *their* Private Light. It was Private because no one else ever came, except Finn with the supplies. Ellan Bride was the safest place in the whole world, or had been, up till now.

'But they can't come here!' said Mally, echoing Breesha's thought. 'They wouldn't know how to land! Finn wouldn't bring horrible people to Ellan Bride. No one else *could.*'

'Wm is short for William,' said Billy numbly. 'I could write Wm for me if I liked.'

'Is *that* all you've got to say?'

'No,' said Billy. 'I need to think, though.'

'Think about what?'

'What we're going to do, of course.'

'What does it mean, they don't want us?' asked Mally. 'Does he mean because we're children?'

'Not *us*, silly. He means they don't want *any* of us. They don't want Aunt Lucy to be the lightkeeper any more.'

'Is that what the letter said?' demanded Billy, 'Or did you just think it from what was in the letter?'

'The letter said an . . . an . . . alternat-ing arrangement.'

'Altern-at-ing? Maybe he means a revolving light like the ones on the Calf. But that would be silly, because the whole point of the Calf lights being flashing, and ours not, is that the ships know which is which. Anyway, Mam would still be able to work that. Maybe they don't know yet how good she is at working things. But my Mam could work any machine they chose to invent, I reckon. And I could help her, anyway.'

'She could do it anyway, without any help. But that's why it'll be,' said Breesha. 'They'll think she can't work the lights because girls don't. If you were grown up –' she flung at Billy, '– I bet they'd keep *you* on!'

'It's hardly my fault I'm not grown up!'

'I didn't say it was!'

But Breesha had been accusing him of *something*. Billy stared unhappily at the lamp, willing himself not to get into a fight with her. This news was far too important to squabble over. 'What *exactly* did the letter say?' he asked her. It crossed his mind he'd never have dared to look for a letter, even if he'd been the one to guess it was there. Certainly he wouldn't have had the courage to read it, even if he had been able to read script, which was not the case. No one had ever had a secret letter on Ellan Bride before, but Billy knew very well that they were supposed to steer clear of one another's secrets in other ways. Breesha, he felt, had not only been clever but also brave enough to be bad. He had to hand it to her. 'Anyway,' he added, because it was only fair to say so, 'it was something that you read that letter. Otherwise we wouldn't even *know*. And we need to know, so that was pretty good, you doing all that.'

Breesha's face lit up like the sun coming out; her moods changed so suddenly these days that Billy was bewildered. He hadn't said anything that special, only what was true.

'But *why* are they going to build a new lighthouse?' asked Mally. 'I don't see why, when we've got one already.'

'I expect they want a better one,' said Billy. 'Ours is quite old. Finn says the ones on the Calf are much more modern than ours, and even those are quite old already. They have Argand burners and we don't. And now there are new sorts of lenses too. They're better than reflectors. You can see them much further away, specially in bad weather. I don't mind if they build a lighthouse with a new revolving lens. But it's the bit about *us*. Are you *sure* the letter said that about not wanting us?'

'They don't want us,' Breesha repeated dully. 'That's what the letter said.' The light that had swept across her face when Billy praised her had vanished as fast as it came. Suddenly she clenched her fists, and tossed her head. 'If anyone comes to Ellan Bride and tries to make us go away, I'll *kill* them.'

Mally gasped. The lamp never flickered, but she was sure there was a small movement in the shadows above the altar. The gingerbread cross loomed behind Breesha, listening balefully. For the first time in her life Mally made the sign against evil without Breesha telling her she must do it.

'Don't be so silly,' said Billy crossly. 'You don't know *how* to kill anyone. And you wouldn't if you did, because you'd be hanged, and you're not silly enough for that. If this is a proper meeting, we ought to be talking about what we're *really* going to do if anyone comes to change everything. We ought to be making a proper *plan*.'

Chapter 10

THE CALF LAY ON THE STARBOARD BOW AS THE YAWL SURGED forward with the ebbing tide into the choppy waters east of Calf Sound. They were into open water now, leaving the cliffs of Spanish Head astern. Since they'd left Port St Mary the little yawl had opened up one inhospitable bay to starboard, and then another. The cliffs were shattered by wind and weather, or some earlier convulsion of nature which a man could only begin to guess at. The rocks looked like grey slate for the most part, streaked here and there with shining quartz, but slate broken and fractured into huge blocks. Mr Lyell, in his revolutionary book, argued that aeons of unending change had created the rock formations one saw today, but in Archie's experience the sea cliffs often looked deceptively like the results of a sudden, unimaginable cataclysm, and perhaps nowhere so much as here. God knew how this Island – or any island, come to that – had actually been created. Mr Watterson had been telling Ben some tale about Finn McCuill hurling stones at a marauding giant from the Scottish hills: curious how even the most unenlightened folk required an explanation of some sort. It must be part of the human condition. And the plain fact was that Archie, and possibly even Mr Lyell, didn't know the whole truth any more than this simple Manx fisherman.

But Mr Watterson knew a lot of things that were useful, and it was Archie's job to get as much information from him as he could. Mr Watterson was the only man who did this run regularly. He'd brought his son Juan along as crew, a sulky boy who wouldn't meet the eyes of the two strangers, and who'd barely grunted a greeting when they met. Today they'd also brought along a sack of oatmeal wrapped in oilskin, a heavy wooden box from the grocer in Port St Mary, and Ben was sitting forward on a crate containing two piglets. There were occasional squeals and scufflings from within the crate, and each time Ben addressed the piglets beneath him with soothing blandishments, which, as far as Archie could tell, were having no effect at all.

This young fellow Buchanan wasn't yet realising how lucky he was, Finn Watterson was thinking. Usually there was hardly a single day in the month that you were getting out to Ellan Bride and back again. The tide was right just now to be going out there on the ebb and back on the flood in full daylight, and although there hadn't been a breath of wind for days, with this drought-like weather, just last night this easterly breeze had sprung up. They could hardly have wished for better. It was the best time of year, of course, but this Master Buchanan would soon be finding out what sort of undertaking it was to get a new lighthouse built on Ellan Bride. They'd need Finn Watterson, that was for sure. No one else landed regularly on the island, and Finn was aiming to be there once a month or so all through the summer. But these young fellows from Scotland – they'd not seen what it could be like getting the barrels of oil ashore on a difficult day. The sacks of coal could be heaved over the side and fetched by the keepers at low tide, but you couldn't be doing that with the precious oil. No, when they were building this new light they'd be needing him for sure. It would be just a question of naming his price. No doubt but his family could be using the money, with half a dozen places at least to put every penny.

It was no loss to him to tell these lighthouse surveyors as much as he could. They certainly couldn't be using the knowledge without him. Master Buchanan had been asking him about a bigger boat, but they'd never be working with anything as big as a smack going into Ellan Bride. No, they'd be coming back to him, and his yawl, that would be able to make a landing if anything could at all. In any case a smack, he'd explained to Archie patiently, would be stuck fast ashore in Port St Mary until the tide was covering the rocks at Gansey. They'd be losing too many hours that way, even with the long summer days ahead, for a smack to do the journey in a day. Finn had shown them the shore marks that gave them the only safe route out of Port St Mary harbour. And there was the Carrick – another treacherous outcrop right in the middle of the bay. When the Carrick is covered, he'd explained to them, that's when the bay goes slack. But once you could see white water over the top of the Carrick you'd have water enough to get into harbour again, but none to spare. And if there was too big a sea breaking over the Carrick, you'd not be putting to put to sea for Ellan Bride, because you wouldn't be able to land when you got there.

'What sort of rock is it on Ellan Bride?' asked Archie suddenly.

'The same thing as the Calf. Same as Spanish Head that you were looking on to starboard just now, that's the truth. The cliffs you're looking on now – Ellan Bride is made out of the very same stuff.'

Hard slate, thought Archie. On the Calf they'd built the lighthouses with stone quarried from the future lighthouse cellars. Ellan Bride was only sixteen acres to the Calf's six hundred and fifty, but if it had the same high quality slate as the Calf they'd be able to do the same thing. Unlike a rock lighthouse, the tower on Ellan Bride only had to stand up to the weather, not to the sea itself.

Yet on the drive from Castletown Archie and Ben had passed great pavements of limestone, exposed by the sea. Where did the limestone give way to slate, deep under the seabed? And what had caused the change? Mr Lyell said in his book that some rocks had been formed by the endless drift of matter down to the sea bed, others by great convulsions in the earth's crust aeons ago. What had set the whole process in motion? How had it happened? And to what end? Ah, if one knew that, perhaps one would know all.

'If the wind was fair,' said Archie aloud, 'you could sail from the Calf to Ellan Bride in an hour or so, couldn't you?'

'It's all of half a league, I'm thinking. That's far enough in bad weather. Many a day you wouldn't be sailing from one to the other at all. In fact most days, I'd say, if you wanted to be landing anything. Now, to starboard: that's the Calf Sound opening up.'

A piece of the Island detached itself and formed a separate entity. In between a thin strip of water gleamed. 'We are putting the name Baie ny Breechyn on that bay there – breechyn is breeches, indeed – if you'll look on it from the Ligghers – that cliff up there – the water will be looking the same shape as a pair of breeks.'

Finn smiled at Ben, sitting up there in the bows, and getting a bit wet too, by the look of it. Ben grinned back. Finn's boy Juan stared resolutely out to sea.

'There's a landing place at the Island there. We are putting the name Cabbyl Giau on it – that means Horse Inlet – the giau is what you'd be calling an inlet, I'm thinking.'

'Ay. We have the same word too, where I come from,' said Ben.

A pleasant fellow, this Benjamin Groat, Finn was thinking, and a good man in a boat too. The other one didn't do much to help us get off – maybe he was thinking himself too much the gentleman – but this fellow Groat wasn't above giving a hand when it was needed. Maybe I'll be working with Groat again, thought Finn – we'll see. He's a big strong fellow too, and I'd be trusting him in a hard place – more than the other. The other's a bit uncertain, I'd say. Tough enough, but you couldn't be sure what he'd be doing. I'd be taking the one without the nerves, Finn decided. The piglets were kicking against the side of their crate. 'There, there, boy,' Ben was saying through the slats in the crate. 'It'll no be long now. And ye'll no be dinner for a long time yet. And in the meantime, ye'll be living in clover!'

'What's Cow Harbour like?' Archie asked abruptly, still staring into the Calf Sound. 'On the north side of the Calf? How easy is it to land there?'

'Ah, there's a place or two you can be landing in fair weather. But the Sound's no place for what you're wanting. No place at all. Why, at full flood or ebb you'll be getting the water coming through there at seven – eight – nine knots even. And when wind meets tide – ah, you'd not want to be anywhere near the place. Now – look – just where we're at now – this is where the ebb is splitting – see how we're coming into the choppy water, even on a day as fair as this. A bit further to starboard, and we'd be swept into the Sound. And if the sea gets up at all – where we are now – well, it'll be getting a lot rougher than you'll be wanting to see.'

Sure enough there was a surge of darker water just a few feet from them, with spiralling whirlpools along its edge. The yawl seemed to hesitate, then was swept forward with the tide.

'I see. You'd not want to be working against that.'

'You would not, sir. This is bad water. Even on a day like this – you'll be keeping an eye on things. You'll never be at ease – or you oughtn't to be – not in these waters. These seas are powerful awful any day in the year. You know what they say: "Those who live by the sea sometimes die by it." You're not seeing what it can be today, sir. Not at all.'

They watched the currents swirl, and the water breaking on the distant rocks that guarded the Sound. They all knew what the sea could do. Danger was less than a hand's breadth away, even on a day like this: just one small change and everything could alter, all in a moment. There was no space for mistakes. The bright sun, the sparkling waters, the helpful breeze – these were precious gifts, but all the more chancy because of that. You never forgot the other face of the sea. You dared not. It wasn't fear you felt exactly: it was a fine tension that you'd let go of at your peril. You just didn't forget that all time out here was borrowed. A good day was a glorious gift, but you never trusted the giver, not for a moment. You took what you could get, and you always kept your eyes open.

They were leaving the Sound behind, and the wild east coast of the Calf was sweeping by them. 'I can see why you'd not want to work against the tide, whatever airt the wind was in,' remarked Archie.

'You would not. So where the tide is splitting, you see now how we're needing it to be taking us south of the Calf. So when you're coming down on the ebb, like we're doing, you want to be standing well out to sea once Spanish Head is lying astern.'

'And at the flood it'll be running through the other way?'

'That'll be right. The ebb is taking you out and the flood is taking you back. The ebb starts about an hour and a half before high water in the Sound. That's how you need to be planning it. But sometimes that's hard to get right with the daylight – no one would be doing the trip in winter anyhow, I'm thinking.'

'So the lightkeepers have to be supplied for a whole winter?'

'Yes indeed, sir. And there's many a day at any time of year you'd not be wanting to be out here.'

'Well, at least it'll be better than the Bell Rock,' called Ben cheerfully from the bows.

'At least at the Bell Rock they had a decent port to go back to.'

'I wouldna ken, sir. I only drink ale myself.'

Mr Watterson grinned, and the boy Juan stifled a snort which might have been the beginnings of a laugh.

'Now you have to be watching the cletts off the Burroo. See ahead there?' – Finn pointed out a great stone stack at the southern tip of the Calf – 'We're steering well clear of her just now. You see that arch opening up just now? That's the Eye. You can see that from just by Castletown. The Burroo's a dangerous place, dangerous awful. If you're ever bringing a ship into these waters, you'll be wanting to keep full clear of the Burroo, if you're valuing your lives, especially at the spring tides. And if there's any southerly wind you get the waves coming very steep. There's seven or eight cletts – you'll know what cletts are, Master Benjamin, seeing you're an Orkney man – so you'll be keeping well clear. With a flood tide taking you the other way, you could be finding yourselves on the rocks before you're knowing it, and that's the end of you. Oh, it's a fiendish place. Some of the trickiest waters in the world, off the Calf here, indeed.'

In his leather case with his notebooks, Archie had a tracing of the 1815 map of the Calf made by his predecessors when they'd surveyed that island in preparation for the new lights. The Burroo and the cletts around it had been named and marked with great emphasis. Archie would have liked to look at the map again now, but he could see choppy water ahead: this wasn't the place to unfold a plan. He knew the map of the Calf by heart now anyway. No one had ever surveyed Ellan Bride before. He'd be the first.

'Ay well. Some say that about Orkney too,' said Ben.

'Ah, but this is a trickier sea. Waves thirty feet high, and the current going about ten knots, when the sea gets up, in no time at all. And no distance at all between the crests: they'll be coming in so close together a ship will be having no time to make a recover. And once you're driven close to these islands, and you're finding yourselves on a lee shore . . . well, Master Benjamin, you just don't want to be there.'

'Ay well, they say the Irish Sea is a tricky spot. We were working at the Mull of Galloway. I saw some big seas there.'

'Ay. It's the whole of the Atlantic you're getting, pouring into the Manx Sea twice every day, and nowhere to be putting itself. So it's tricky water. The keepers on the Calf, now – Scotch, like yourselves – they're saying they've never seen such desperate seas as they're seeing here, in these waters.'

'And for better for worse, we've got to work in them,' said Ben cheerfully.

It was choppy off the Burroo. Ben pulled his boat cloak tightly round him as gouts of water came flying over the bows. The boy beside him turned his back to the bows and hunched his shoulders. With the wind on the port beam they were making good time. They steered well clear of the stacks, and the wicked cletts, which showed long trails of white where the tide parted around them. Ben had seen what the Irish Sea could do from the Mull of Galloway. Finn was right, he thought: this was indeed a fearsome place.

They rounded the Burroo at a respectful distance. A new stretch of water opened up ahead.

'I can see the lighthouse on Ellan Bride, sir,' called Ben.

About ten points to starboard, Archie saw an obstinately vertical mark in the distance, as if someone had jabbed a lead pencil against the horizon.

'Those rocks yonder,' Finn was saying, 'we're putting the name Chickens on them. That's because you'll be seeing the stormy petrels flying about here – what they call Mother Carey's chickens. Now the Chickens'll be the most desperate rocks in the Island. The ships are thinking they're well clear of the Calf, and they're running straight onto the Chickens. There's no mercy for them then. It was because of the Chickens they were building the Calf lights. You'll see, if you'll line up the two towers yonder, on the Calf: from the Chickens the one light is straight above the other – you keep them well apart and you'll not be in any danger. Before them lights this was a terrible place for wrecks, dangerous awful. I was going out there with my father after the *Sally* was lost – twenty years that'll be now – smashed to bits she was. And she was a Whitehaven ship that was knowing these waters as well as anyone. She was headed for Ireland, but the Chickens out there was as far as ever she was getting. Now if anyone could be building a lighthouse *there* . . .'

White water was breaking over the Chickens rocks. Archie thought of Dulsic, off Cape Wrath, which had the same configuration: a wicked skerry, right in the path of any unsuspecting ship that thought itself well clear of the headland. Like the Chickens, many a ship had been wrecked there for the lack of a light. Hard to imagine a wreck on a day like this: the noise, the terror, the chaos, the sheer power of the sea when it was roused. On rocks like these, no man or ship could withstand a big sea for more than a moment once they were caught.

The first time Archie had seen the Dulsic skerries was from the Cape Wrath headland. He'd stood with Mr Ritson – Archie had only been the under-surveyor then – looking down on a furious sea. Huge plumes of spray broke over them, nearly three hundred feet up. When he'd come back to Cape Wrath by sea a week later, Mr Ritson had gone ashore at Sandwood Bay, and sent Archie ahead in the ship to take sightings from the sea.

Archie had found the Cape transformed. They'd sailed out of Loch Laxford and edged their way north. When dawn came the sea was calm and milky. The sun slowly rose and tinged everything pink. All day he'd stood in the bows, watching that wild coastline unfold. At the Cape there was only an easy swell. The skipper said he'd never seen it as calm as this. A little crown of breaking waves, barely tinged with white, marked the fearful skerries. On a sudden impulse he'd strolled aft and told the skipper what he wanted to do. Perhaps the man was too surprised to say no; in any case he'd had the boat lowered, and sent three of the crew along with Archie.

Down in the boat the swell seemed a lot bigger. They'd come close in to the skerry. McGill was at the tiller. He couldn't time it right; a wave caught them, threw them forward, then pulled them back, a yard short of the rock. Then Angus took over. If Angus couldn't do it, no one could.

'Now!' They came in on the top of the wave. Water churned in the two-inch gap between boat and rock. 'Now, sir, now!' Archie scrambled over the gunwale. He was standing on the biggest Dulsic skerry. It was just a rock, flat and wet, ringed with seaweed. Only a sailor, or a lighthouse surveyor, could have any idea what it meant to stand here. He'd stood for fully two minutes, half-scared that Angus wouldn't be able to get him off. When the boat came in with the next wave, he'd launched himself clumsily headfirst over the gunwale, and had had to scramble up through the legs of the oarsmen. But he'd done it. He'd stood on the notorious Dulsic. He'd been a young fellow then. The skipper had not reported him to Mr Stevenson. It was all of five years ago.

Finn Watterson altered course, so that the Ellan Bride lighthouse was directly on the bow, leaving the Chickens half a mile to starboard. He watched this Master Buchanan thoughtfully. There was something he was needing to say, but he hadn't quite got the man's measure yet. Master Buchanan looked pleasant enough, dark-haired and dark-eyed – the girls would be wild after a well set-up young fellow like that – but Finn was guessing at an austerity in Archie that might be stopping him taking full advantage. So much the better for him, if that were so! But the lad had an absentmindedness about him. He'd be asking the right questions, showing a fair bit of sense, in fact, and then he'd be going off in a dream again, like he was doing now. Something on his mind, seemingly. Whether that was a good thing or a bad thing for the question Finn had in mind, he wasn't sure. Master Buchanan was a bit stand-offish, not easy in his ways, but maybe it was just shyness. Finn's own father had once met Robert Stevenson, when that gentleman had been coming to look at the Calf thirty years ago. Nothing stand-offish about *him* – a very easy gentleman to work with. Finn was wishing it were Mr Stevenson here himself, so he could be speaking to him about the matter that was troubling him. Mr Stevenson would be able to do something about it too; Finn wasn't sure this young fellow Buchanan had the power. Finn had been hearing yesterday how Master Buchanan had been seeing Master Quirk at Castletown yesterday, and seemingly Master Quirk had been saying afterwards this Master Buchanan was just a sprat, and it was the bigger fish he was after – waste of time talking to him in fact. But that was surely not fair. The lad was just the surveyor, doing his job: he'd not be coming here to be dealing in the politics.

Slowly Ellan Bride took on a third dimension. There was very little of it. It lay low and green, the lighthouse standing in the centre like an unlit candle. The sun winked on the lighthouse lantern. The island was hardly more than a rock with a strip of green, surrounded by the silvery sea. Archie and Ben had seen hundreds of islands like it, but there was still something about a new island, a sense of possible discovery. Archie felt his impatience draining away. The east wind that had brought them here might not take them back so easily, but after all, what did it matter? He had no urgent appointment until September. If he were forced to spend the halcyon days of May becalmed on Ellan Bride, wasn't that simply a foretaste of all the unknown islands yet to come?

He'd spent too many years trying to hurry along and achieve things. There had been so much work to be done, and what greater work could there be – so it had seemed, at least until last year – than the immense task of lighting up the seas? What could be more humane, more advantageous, more audacious, and more conducive to the greater good of all, than illuminating the coasts of Scotland for all the shipping that had to pass, now and in the future?

He'd only worked with Robert Stevenson a week when the old man had taken him out to the Isle of May. That was ten years ago. Archie had never been to sea before in his life. They'd had a wild crossing, the little boat ploughing doggedly through turbulent seas before a rising wind. They weren't even sure that they were going to be able to land when they got there. Somehow the boat had managed to slip through the rocks into the east landing, and then they'd struggled up to the lighthouse, which stood right at the summit of the island, against gusts of icy rain. Indoors the lighthouse was quiet and spacious, the workrooms and keepers' quarters a model of naval orderliness. Archie had been deeply impressed. The sheer elegance of the new lighthouse, the opulent restraint of the Council Chamber where the Commissioners had their annual meeting, the clean lines of the tower itself, the scale and precision of the new lighting system . . . all that had been such a contrast, not only to the wild weather, but also to the squat little tower that stood in the lee of Robert Stevenson's light. This was the ruin of the old coal-burning light, out of date and unregretted, preserved merely because of a passing poet's whimsical desire for the picturesque. For it was Walter Scott himself who'd asked for it to be kept, back in 1814 when he'd been on the May with Mr Stevenson.

Ten years ago Archie had stood on the flat roof of the new Isle of May lighthouse, leaning into the wind, while the sea crashed on the rocks below. Though he hadn't said a word, he'd been drunk with sheer happiness. Mr Stevenson's new lighthouse was not only functionally perfect, but also an outpost of civilisation, a little piece of Edinburgh illuminating the chaos and the wilderness. It seemed like the embodiment of an ideal; this, it had seemed, was what his new job was all to be about.

Even now, Ellan Bride might hold its atom of discovery. It was always like this: as soon as he got away from Edinburgh Archie began to wake up. It wasn't that he didn't like the world he lived in; it was just that he preferred to be on the very edges of it, and yet somehow bring with him everything that was good about the civilised world. In his experience that was how new ideas were most likely to happen.

'No one bides on the island but the lighthouse people?' Ben was asking. Archie brought his attention back with a start. He should be making the most of every minute with Mr Watterson, finding out as much as he could. Where had his wits gone a-begging?

'Not now.'

'So there were others?'

'There were one time. But that was a long time ago.'

'And the lightkeepers? They telt us in Edinburgh that the keeper was a woman.'

'That's right. The sister to the last keeper, him that was getting drowned. And a little family with her.'

'Have they got a boat?'

'A fourteen-foot yawl. Nothing much. But they're not going offshore but for a bit of fishing usually. I'm bringing in the oil for the light, and the coals for winter, and anything else they're asking.'

'What about mail?'

'Mail? They're not getting none of that. A few times a year, maybe. If there's a letter and I'm passing, I'll take it. I'll be calling by sometimes when I'm at the fishing. Sometimes I'll be taking a bit of extra fish.'

'Otherwise they do their own fishing?'

'They do,' said Finn, and added presently. 'They'll be putting out baulks – long lines, that is – when it's fair weather. Plenty of cod offshore – callig – ling – they'll be getting that.'

The island drew nearer. The lines of rock were tilted at an angle of thirty degrees or so, as if the island was a layered cake slowly sliding off a tilted plate. Archie wondered if the layers below extended right across the sea bed. If only one could look down into the sea as through a glass . . . but the waters kept their secrets, and it was hard to see how it could ever be otherwise.

A cloud of birds hung over the island, and as they got closer they could see that they were ceaselessly circling round it.

'Puffins,' said Ben.

'Tommy Noddies – Ellan Bride puffins,' corrected Finn. 'It was always the Tommy Noddies on Ellan Bride, and Manx puffins on the Calf. But back when my father was a boy, there were long-tails got ashore from a wreck on the Calf, and there's not hardly no puffins to be found on the Calf these days at all, for all they would be getting a good living out of them for many a year before that.' Finn glanced at the surf breaking over the Chickens. 'Wind's freshening. I'm hoping we'll be making a landing, for all.'

'You think we might not?' Archie broke in sharply.

'We mightn't be getting into Giau y Vaatey. Or if we are

getting in, I mightn't be getting out again. I was hoping the wind wouldn't be freshening. It's too late with the tide now to be putting you ashore on the slabs.'

Archie bit his lip. But there was no point saying anything. The very wind that had brought them here so easily might now be their undoing. Having got so far, it would be maddening to have to go all the way back, beating into the wind. Nothing he could do about it. Nothing anyone could do about it, but wait and see.

There were puffins in the water, and puffins flying past the boat, some with beaks full of little fish. If it wasn't for the tower at the top of the hill the island could have been primeval; the rocks and the birds belonged to . . . what? . . . the third day of Creation? The fourth? But now it was the sixth at least, because when Archie looked up he could see the lighthouse tower.

A crack appeared in the northern cliffs. They passed a stack with a pinpoint of light in its heart that gradually grew until the stack turned into an arch, and they could see the sea shining on the other side. Beyond the stack was a fissure full of tumbled boulders, and the dark mouth of a cave. Sea and sky were suddenly full of birds. A wild clamour rose from the crack, and a plume of kittiwakes, far more graceful than the puffins, soared above the headland, riding the air currents. A thin ribbon of white fringed the rocks ahead. A scatter of rounded boulders suddenly turned into seals, which humped their way down to the water and dived in a series of neat splashes. A minute later half a dozen heads surfaced close to the boat, watching the new arrivals with dark, dog-like eyes.

'If you'll be taking the second pair of oars, Master Benjamin. Juan, stand by the sail!'

The boat rounded the point, and immediately a gentler coastline opened up before them. A colony of shags watched the boat uneasily as it slipped past their skerry, then one by one the birds shambled into flight, or flopped into the sea to emerge yards away.

Now they could see the long green back of the land. The light tower wasn't built on the very highest point: a little rocky knoll rose before it, but the fifteen-foot tower out-topped the summit. A line of low cliffs ran, parallel to the shore, from the highest point of the island down to the northern promontory. Below the cliffs green turf sloped to the sea. They saw the line of a turf-covered dyke above first a small sandy beach, and then a bigger one. A rowing boat lay on the beach. 'That's good enough, they'll be getting her pulled up right now,' said Finn. 'The two of them, just – they couldn't always be managing it. But there's the boy now. That'll be helping.' Finn Watterson glanced up and looked Archie straight in the eye for the first time. 'The boy's been brought up to it, sir. His Granddad it was, was the first keeper. The family's been brought up to it, is what I'm wanting to say. Everyone wouldn't be wanting that life, but they've been brought up to it, you see. All of them.'

Abruptly Finn shifted his gaze as they passed the beach. 'Ready, boy. *Now!*' The sail came down in a series of jerks. Ben and Juan unshipped the oars. 'Keep her going as she is.' Finn was standing at the tiller, scanning the rocks. 'That's the landing place, you see? All right, we'll be taking a look.'

White water was breaking on the rocks at the entrance to a narrow giau. The water in the inlet looked smooth and green, but there were sharp waves breaking on the shingle. The yawl rocked in the swell where the sea began to funnel in. The oars dipped. 'As she is! Keep her as she is. Let's be taking a look . . . Ay, we'll be getting in all right . . . it's whether we'll be getting out again . . .'

Archie stopped himself biting his knuckles. No point worrying, or willing them to go in. It was Finn's decision, and Archie's job to abide by it. It might be days before they got so near again. Finn was looking out to sea again, testing the wind.

'Right, we're going in! Soon as we're alongside, you two get ashore. I'll be offloading the things – fast! All right! Hard a-starboard! Master Ben, take the painter. Juan, don't be shipping your oars. We'll need to be rowing out fast. All right, Master Buchanan: you're seeing that black rock up above there? And the streak of white across the cliff below it? We're lining 'em up, right? Ready then! *Now!*'

Seaweed-covered rocks guarded the dark giau. Shags nested on the rocky sides; they jabbed the air menacingly as the yawl slid in on the top of a wave. The tide was at its lowest, and the rocks were thick with seaweed. Between the fronds there were patches of barnacles and baby mussels where boots could get a grip. A yard to go – Ben stood ready on the gunwale. He glanced up, and saw three figures above him on the rock, silhouetted black shapes with the sun behind them. All female – the solid outlines of their dresses made them look as if they'd grown out of the shadowed rocks – but each one a different size. Just for a second they seemed tall and menacing, dark shadows between him and the sun.

The next wave rose. Ben threw the painter ashore, and the tallest woman caught it and tied it to a rusty iron ring in the rock. The boat fell back and rose again. Ben leapt ashore with the next wave. Then Archie jumped too, and landed on the rock beside him.

Chapter 11

THROUGH THE CLOSED SHUTTERS THE SUN MADE STRIPED patterns against the bedroom wall. Between the shutter and the glass a trapped bee buzzed and buzzed against the pane. The wind murmured in the chimney, rustling the dried-out rushes in the grate. Mally's truckle bed was made, the flowered coverlet pulled up over the pillow. The floor had been swept, the rag rug freshly shaken. Lucy's print gown and petticoat lay across the rocking chair, where the cat had made itself a comfortable nest out of them, and curled up on top. The framed text above the bed was embroidered in blue and white, with a border of forget-me-nots in matching threads: *This is the day which the Lord hath made. We rejoice and be glad in it (Psalm 118: 24)*

Lucy lay sprawled across the bed in her nightgown, half-covered by the sheet. She wore no nightcap, and she'd thrown off the blanket. She was sound asleep, having gone to bed as usual after noonday dinner, and no dreams had come to trouble her.

There was no time to think; they had to help. As Finn and Juan swung the cargo across, the two strangers Finn had brought with him caught each piece and heaved it up the rock. Automatically Diya, Breesha and Mally grabbed the bundles as they were dumped on the seaweed and carried them over the slippery rocks. And what extraordinary gear it was: a long wooden box, a roll of chain, a stack of poles roped together, a heavy wooden box with a lid. 'Take care with that one!' the big fellow called as Breesha and Diya lifted the box between them. A portmanteau came up, and a canvas haversack. Mally picked up a black leather case. It was heavy, but she managed to heave it up onto the grass. Then came a sack of meal: that was more normal. And last of all: 'It's the piglings!' screamed Mally, the strangers momentarily forgotten. 'Finn, you've brought the piglings!'

'I have that, Mally, I have that!'

The crate with the piglets was heavy. Finn and Juan got it onto the gunwale. The next wave rose. Archie and Ben grabbed it by its rope and swung it across. On the slippery weed they managed to get their hands under the crate, and together they manhandled it up to dry rock. The piglets squealed furiously, and scrabbled about so the weight kept shifting. The woman was going to try to take the crate from them, but Archie brushed her off. 'S'all right. This one's heavy.' There were shouts from below. Archie and Ben shoved the crate up the last awkward step and dumped it on the grass.

When they looked round the *Betsey* was already halfway out of the giau. Two pairs of oars were working furiously against wind and tide. The yawl was barely moving. It was going to be a damn close thing. Archie straightened up, brushing his coat sleeves, as he willed the boat to get off: Finn had done the job and got them ashore – he deserved not to be stuck here. They hadn't had time to discuss the likelihood of him getting back to collect them on Monday or Tuesday. Well, Finn knew what they wanted, and he'd come back when he could. Anyway, he still had another two shillings to collect. And there were so many more things to ask him . . .

The *Betsey* fought the swell at the mouth of the giau, hung in the balance, and came up into the wind. A minute later she hoisted her sail and headed off on the port tack. 'That's it,' said Ben. 'They'll make it now. They'll get round the island while it's slack water, and beat back with the flood on the windward side.'

Once the boat was under way Diya reluctantly turned inland. The two intruders were on the grass just above them, staring out to sea. They'd still be able to see the *Betsey* from up there. A moment later the boat must have vanished from their sight, because now the men were looking down at them.

Breesha pulled urgently at her mother's sleeve. 'Shall I go and wake Lucy?' she whispered.

'Yes, go now. Quickly! And Breesha . . . put the broth back over the fire, so it'll be hot.'

'We're not going to *give* them anything?'

'Indeed we are, Breesha veen. You must always be civil to the stranger at your door. You know that!'

'But not *these* . . .' Breesha remembered she wasn't supposed to know who they were. Better warn Mally not to give anything away either. But Mally, now that the flurry of activity was over, was clinging close to Mam, clutching a corner of Diya's old gardening pinafore, thumb in mouth, like a great baby. Mally had clung to Mam like that once before, when they'd gone ashore at Port St Mary last year and Mally had been so upset by the strange people. She'd kept saying, 'Who's that, who's that?' and Mam had kept on answering, 'I don't *know* who it is, Mally veen. We don't know everybody!' Mally's voice had sounded so small and frightened, quite unlike her usual self, as she'd gripped her mother's cloak tightly in both hands. 'But *why* don't we know them? *Why?*'

How *dare* these people come here now and frighten her sister? How *dare* they step ashore as if they had the right?

I want my Da!

Breesha's fists clenched tight with rage. Rage at Finn, for betraying them – bringing their enemies to the island, as if he didn't *know*! Rage at her Da, for not being here any more when they needed him. If her Da were here this couldn't be happening. How dare you! *How dare you not be here now! I hate you, Da! I hate you!* Breesha caught her breath with a shiver.

'Mam!' She tugged her mother's sleeve again. 'Mam, will I go and find Billy?'

Diya was still staring numbly at the strangers standing up there on the island. She gave herself a little shake. 'For what, Breesha veen?' she said. 'Billy'll come soon enough. I told you to go and wake Lucy – and put the pot back on. Go on. I mean it, Breesha! *Now!*'

Breesha scowled, and suddenly ran, dodging past the invaders without a word of acknowledgement, and disappearing behind the Tullachan.

Diya came slowly up the rocks, holding Mally's hand so hard that it hurt. Her throat felt tight. She was trembling, but she willed herself to stop, or Mally would feel it through their clasped hands.

The time has come, Diya beti. Koi hai – is anyone there? He's waiting for you on the veranda. Your father is here! Usually Father comes and sits on the veranda for a short time only. He brings presents – a doll, ribbons, bangles, metai. He asks what Diya has learned, has she been good, is she happy, is she well, is she clever? Yes, his little Diya is all of these things, and he smiles, and smiles again, and in a little while he takes his leave, as always. But not this time. This time Diya is going too. Her small square box is packed and tied with a strap. A label in English writing is tied to the strap. Because now Diya is leaving the safe place, the cool house, the hot garden with its enclosing walls and swept paths, the tank, the courtyard, the tamarisk tree, the borders filled with marigolds and Mittu the parrot. Goodbye, Aji, goodbye, my very own Ajoba. I never saw Aji weep before. Goodbye to all of you. Goodbye, Diya beti! But I didn't know then that it was goodbye for ever.

She looked so mournful, stepping over the slippery rocks, clasping her child's hand in hers. For the little girl was clearly hers. The child had the same brown skin, same delicate features. And when the two of them looked up at him, they had the same dark, unhappy eyes. Was it his fault? Was it their presence here that caused such sorrow? Archie stepped forward uncomfortably, and held out his hand to help the woman over the difficult rock step.

She ignored the outstretched hand, and jumped up easily on to the grass, the child following. When she stood facing him, her eyes were on a level with his own. Both woman and child gazed at him unwinkingly, and their eyes seemed to hold all the reproach in the world. 'You will be the Commissioners of Northern Lights, I think?'

'Not in person,' stammered Archie. She spoke like a gentlewoman. He hadn't expected that. She seemed perfectly collected, not nervous of him at all. It was just that her eyes were saying something so very different. He cleared his throat. 'Archibald Buchanan, ma'am, at your service. We're the surveyors employed by Mr Stevenson, the engineer. I believe you've been notified . . . you had a letter, I mean. You were expecting our arrival?' He hated himself for sounding so hesitant, but then, he was used to dealing with men, not beautiful women with dark eyes that looked at him as if he were a murderer.

'My sister had a letter.'

'You're not . . .' He'd been about to say, 'Miss Geddes', but a woman with a child in her hand who was so clearly a replica of herself should obviously not be addressed as Miss.

'I am Mrs Geddes. My late husband was the lightkeeper.'

Every word she spoke made it seem the more extraordinary that she was here. She was a lady. She spoke the King's English. Her skin was as brown as a hazelnut. She wore gold studs in her ears, and a sacking apron stained with soil. He saw that her hands were dirty, covered with earth in fact. She didn't take her eyes off him. Ben was standing right beside him, but she didn't even glance in his direction. She was steadfastly watching Archie.

She saw Archie looking at her hands. 'You must excuse us, Mr Buchanan. We were working in the garden when my daughter saw the *Betsey*.'

'Not at all.' Everything she said somehow put Archie at a disadvantage. He pulled himself together. 'I'm very sorry if our presence on the island inconveniences you at all, ma'am. We're here to do the preliminary survey for the new lighthouse on Ellan Bride. We'll be staying for a couple of days. I believe the letter from the Commissioners asked you if you would be so kind as to accommodate us during our stay?'

'We've brought our own provisions,' put in Ben suddenly. He smiled at the lightkeeper's widow. Trust Young Archibald to get on his high horse, just when you could see the poor woman, and her bairn too, were simply terrified. They weren't exactly the sort of people he'd been expecting, but that probably made it worse for them. Foreigners – that was obvious. He wondered how on earth they got to be here – how the hell had the Ellan Bride lightkeeeper managed to pick up anything this exotic? But that was of no consequence just now. Brown-skinned Mrs Geddes might be, but she'd turn men's heads in the Canongate. The effect in this remote place, and with the child clinging like a little elf at her side, was quite unnerving. But Ben felt sorry for her more than anything. 'We'll try not to get in your way too much, missus. We'll be out all day. But a roof over our heads at night – that's all we'll be needing, and I hope we'll no be a trouble to you.'

The big, ugly man was much the nicer, thought Mally. She sneaked a look up at Ben, who caught her eye and winked. Mally looked down, shrinking back against her mother's skirts.

And yet Ben had seen the wee lass jumping up and down, squealing with delight at the boatman when he offloaded the pigs. Ben grinned at Mally and said, 'Should we no be letting the grice – the pigs – out of that box, don't you think? They've been cooped up in there a long time.'

Mally glanced at the crate, and looked wide-eyed up at Ben.

'If you tell me where to take them, I can carry them up for you.'

Mally looked at Mam. Mam said, 'You show him, Mally.'

It was too hard to speak to a person Mally had never seen

before in her life. He wasn't like anyone she knew. But Billy had freckles too, in the summer, and when the man smiled it seemed to remind her just a bit of another smiling face she'd once known well, but couldn't quite remember. Mally, still holding Mam's hand, but not so hard now, pointed dumbly towards the house. Ben followed her pointing finger. You couldn't see the house from here; it was hidden behind the Tullachan, a low green knoll between the jetty and the garden. Mally would have liked to explain that to Ben, but it would have meant speaking to him, and that she couldn't quite do. Not yet.

'Come up to the house, gentlemen,' said Diya. 'You'll be hungry, and there's broth on the fire. You won't have had any dinner. Mally, show the kind man where the piglings are to go.'

'Ben,' said Ben, introducing himself. 'Benjamin Groat, missus. And what's your name, young lady?'

Mally opened her mouth to whisper, but the obstinate words wouldn't come out.

'This is my daughter Mary,' Diya said. 'We call her Mally. You must forgive her, Mr Groat. We don't usually see strangers here.'

Diya gave Mally a little push, and watched her silently lead Ben away. She turned to pick up one of the sacks.

'Will I take that for you?'

'I can manage it, thank you.' Diya swung the sack of oatmeal onto her shoulder. 'Perhaps you should bring that case of yours; you don't want your papers to get wet.'

How did she know the black leather case held his drawing materials? And where did she get the strength to heave a sack like that, apparently without any effort at all? Archie, temporarily as bereft of speech as Mally, picked up his drawing-case and portmanteau, and let Diya lead the way. He noticed as he followed her that her feet were bare, and begrimed with garden soil, as was the hem of her old print gown. The path wound between rushes and cotton grass. She left her bare footprints firmly imprinted in the mud as she walked. Archie trod over them in his heavy boots; the path was narrow and there was no avoiding them.

They skirted the green knoll, and there was the gable-end of a low stone cottage right in front of them. At the front, the slate roof hung down over two small windows and a central door, so the house looked like a face with beetling eyebrows frowning out to sea. The door stood wide open, and a couple of chickens were pecking at invisible scraps on the threshold. A cockerel and some more chickens – and a motley flock they were – foraged on the green turf outside the door. The pig-pen, re-fashioned from ship's timbers, had been built up against the garden wall. Ben was leaning over the fence and Mally was jumping around inside the pen, clutching a pan of scraps. Either the child or the piglets – it was impossible to tell which – were squealing wildly. Of the other girl – the one who'd run away as soon as they'd landed – there was no sign at all.

Diya stopped in front of the door, and motioned Archie to go in. 'If you please to come in, sir.'

'After you, ma'am.'

He had to duck under the lintel. A stuffy warmth met him, and the smell of broth. It took a moment for his eyes to adjust. Diya dumped the sack of oatmeal by the door. 'If you'd like to sit down, Mr Buchanan, the lightkeeper will be here shortly.'

But the lightkeeper's been dead five years! Stupid thought – the lightkeeper now was the dead man's sister – hard to think of a lightkeeper as a woman though. Archie didn't really want to sit down; he wanted to look about and get on with the job, but somehow the woman's civil clarity was impossible to withstand. In short, she made him nervous, and that irritated him. It was hard to take his eyes off her. She was not what Archie had expected at all. He sat down gingerly at the end of a bench.

Diya unfastened her gardening pinafore and hung it on the back of the door. Then she took an earthenware jug from a shelf, poured water into a bowl, and washed her grimy hands with soap. She dried them carefully on a bleach-white towel.

Only then did she add more water to the broth pot, and begin to stir it briskly. She was dressed like a peasant, but no peasant Archie knew – and he knew many, none better – poured water and stirred broth as if every gesture were part of an invisible dance. Graceful – that was the word that came to mind – she moved with grace. He felt instinctively that she lived her whole life with grace. But her eyes were so sorrowful. Was that for the death of the lightkeeper, or was it because he, Archie, had arrived on the island? And was silence natural to her, or was it occasioned by his unwanted presence? He swallowed, and spoke to her.

'This is kind of you. The lightkeeper isn't here just now?' Silly question: there was only half a mile of land altogether, so the lightkeeper could hardly have gone far.

'She has to sleep, of course.'

Once again the woman seemed to be reproaching him. But he'd done nothing! And perhaps he was imagining it. 'Of course.' Archie fidgeted on his bench. 'Well, we'll start work as soon as we've brought up our gear. It'll be light until eight or thereabouts, so we should get well started this evening. I hope we'll not be imposing on you for long.'

'Sunset will be at one minute past eight.'

Of course, they'd have the times of sunset and sunrise tabled exactly, because of the light. But there was no need for her to correct him like that.

The room darkened as Ben's big frame blocked the door. He came in, blinking, Mally at his heels. 'Ay well, the piglings are settling in, at all events, and there's nothing wrong with their appetites. Is there, Miss Mally? The piglings are fed and watered, and Miss Mally is offering me the same, which is right kind of her.'

Mally giggled and swung the empty scrap bucket. Ben must have induced her to speak to him at last, but now she suddenly saw Archie, sitting at Billy's place at the table, and she stopped still, silent as a stock.

'Will you sit down, Mr Ben?' Diya said to him. 'Mally, give

the gentlemen spoons for their broth, and come and take the bowls for them.'

'I can take those.' Ben took two wooden bowls full of steaming broth. Mally put a horn spoon in front of him, and skittered another across the table towards Archie, as if scared of coming too close. She brought the heel of a loaf, and a crock of butter, put them quickly on the table, and then hung back, watching the strangers eat. She seemed to find their behaviour at table even more intriguing than the piglings'. Ben, fully engaged with his broth, took no notice of Mally, but Archie found her wide-eyed gaze disconcerting.

The broth was good, and very welcome after the long hours in an open boat. When Archie looked up again, Diya and Mally had gone. The door stood open, and the sun was pouring in silently across the swept earth floor.

'Good Lord,' said Ben in a stage whisper. 'It's like being in a bloody fairy story!'

Archie's rare smile made him look years younger. You could see the boy in him, but who that boy had been, Ben had little idea, even after all these years. 'Which story were you thinking of, Ben? The three little pigs?'

'One little pig sailed away without landing,' said Ben. 'I reckon that leaves two.'

'No,' said Archie. 'Scheherazade.'

'Sheer what?'

'*The Thousand and One Nights*, Ben. You ken what that is?'

'I hope not, Mister Archie! No in May-time! Give yon Finn a couple of days, like we said, and he'll be back for us.'

'Meanwhile we've got some real work to do, and there's no fairy tale about that. We're a man short still. Finn said there was a boy. I should have asked her about the boy.'

'What about yon one who ran off so quick? That was another lass. Mally's sister, so she said.'

'She telt you that, did she?'

'Well, she nodded when I asked if it were so. But I didna think to ask about the boy. The lass could do the job, I suppose, if we could catch her – the bigger one, I mean.'

'No. We're no using a girl to do our work, Ben. You should have asked that peerie one about the boy.'

'Well, you could have done that, sir. Asked the mother, I mean.' Ben scraped his bowl. 'I reckon the lightkeeper's lightsome widow had us both pretty well tongue-tied, sir. But no matter. She can cook all right, no doubt about that, and that's the main thing.'

CHAPTER 12

ALREADY THEIR PLAN HAD GONE COMPLETELY WRONG.

Lying hidden below the horizon on the edge of Hamarr, Billy trained the telescope on Giau y Vaatey. He'd seen the *Betsey* before any of the others because as soon as dinner was finished he'd gone to watch the seals on the Cronnags. He'd just had time to count twenty-three seals basking in the sun on the west side of the cletts. The seals, full of fish, had barely been bothering to raise their heads to look about, and Billy, up on the cliff, had been lolling in similar after-dinner contentment, enjoying the heat of the sun on his back. The seals sang softly across the sound. Sleepily Billy had scanned the shining seas beyond the cletts. Suddenly he'd caught sight of the *Betsey*'s brown sail. Everything Breesha had said in the keeill yesterday had come flooding back to him. In a moment he'd clamped the telescope to his eye, and had focused it on the *Betsey*.

The *Betsey* drew nearer. She was quite definitely coming to the island, and fast: the wind was about as favourable as it could be. Soon Billy could make out a figure up in the bows. Juan? He couldn't see who else was there because the sail was in the way. But when the *Betsey* was just off the cletts he'd been able to see her broadside on. He'd counted four figures in the boat. Four! So it was all true! Breesha had been right about that letter. Even now the enemy were on their way. He'd only half-believed it until that very minute. He'd had no time to warn

Breesha. He'd run up the Dreeym Lang, keeping pace with the *Betsey* out at sea, until he'd been on top of the cliff just above the well. Then he'd wriggled into a cleft where he couldn't be seen from below, and focused the telescope.

Someone had shouted up by the lighthouse. Billy sat up and peered over the edge of his little hollow. Someone had been up at the light – they must have seen the *Betsey* – but no one was there now.

'Breesha! *Breesha!*' No answer. Had it been Breesha? He couldn't leave his vantage point to go and look. Billy wriggled into position again, and focused on the boat.

The *Betsey* was coming round the point. Now she was opposite Giau y Vaatey. The sail came down. The oars were unshipped. Two people were rowing: Juan and someone bigger than Juan. The *Betsey* was hanging around, not coming in. There was a fair bit of white water on the cletts. This east wind would be funnelling straight into Giau y Vaatey. Maybe they daren't come in. Maybe they'd just go away again.

He heard shouts below. Breesha came running full-tilt past the Tullachan. A minute later Aunt Diya and Mally appeared behind her. They were – they *couldn't* be – this was no part of the plan – but they were – they were heading straight for Giau y Vaatey. Billy was furious. Trust Mally to forget what they'd decided – but *Breesha* – had Breesha lost her mind completely?

There was nothing he could do without giving himself away as well. And maybe the *Betsey* would just go away again. She was still hanging about out there. Maybe they'd just go away . . .

But they didn't. Suddenly the *Betsey* swung to starboard, forged into the Giau on the crest of a wave, and was lost to sight below the cliff.

Minutes passed. Billy was tempted to climb down and creep in closer. But that was bad tactics. Supposing he was a smuggler, and they were excise men . . . he'd know to wait. This wasn't a game. This was just as important as the old days of the Running Trade. An old-time smuggler would tell him to wait. Uncle Jim, if he'd had to plan this, would have known to wait.

Someone moved at the top of the rocks. Aunt Diya. Then Mally. Carrying stuff. Just as usual. If it were just as usual he ought to be down there, helping. If he were, he'd see Finn and be able to find out about the strangers. Suddenly Billy longed to see Finn and be able to ask him all about it, but of course he couldn't without giving himself away. The two extra figures hadn't been his imagination. The enemy were absolutely real, and he must stick to the plan, even if no one else did. There was Breesha. She was helping Aunt Diya. They were carrying what looked like a bundle of long poles. What did Breesha think she was *doing*? But all he could do was wait.

The strangers came next. Two strangers, struggling under the weight of a big crate. They dumped it at the top of the rocks.

Breesha suddenly appeared again, pushed past the enemy and rushed back towards the house. Billy couldn't call to her because those men were standing there. What did she think she was *doing*? He'd just have to keep the enemy in sight without her help.

Although . . . if those men went on up to the house he could maybe slip down to the boat and catch Finn and Juan while they were still down there. Because once Finn came up to the house, Billy wouldn't be able to get him alone. Whereas now . . . but no – it was too late. The *Betsey* was in sight again, slipping away from the island. Through the telescope Billy saw Finn and Juan straining at the oars. For a moment it looked as though they'd be driven back in . . . but no . . . they were making way . . . they were almost there . . . the *Betsey* was out of the giau. They were well offshore . . . the sail was going up again . . . Billy couldn't speak to Finn after all. It was just themselves now: he and Mam and Breesha and Aunt Diya and Mally, on their own against the enemy.

The enemy didn't look so very formidable from here. Billy twisted the focus so that one after the other the strange faces appeared in full detail inside his circle of vision. The shorter one wore a wide-awake hat, and a thick sea jacket. He didn't look as dangerous as the tall one. The tall one had a face like a pirate. He ought to have carried pistols and a cutlass, but he didn't; instead he had a battered carpet bag and a large parcel done up in oilskin. As Billy watched he laid both of these on the turf, and picked up the big crate instead. And now he was heading off towards the house, staggering a bit under the weight of the crate, and Mally was running ahead of him, evidently showing him the way. Had Mally forgotten the meeting at the keeill? And what was in that crate?

The shorter man was following Aunt Diya. She had a sack on her shoulder and he was carrying a portmanteau and a black leather case. I'd like to know what's in that case, thought Billy. I bet that would tell us something. Maybe Breesha will get the chance to look.

Diya and the stranger disappeared behind the Tullachan. Billy thought for a moment, and then ran, stooping low to keep below the horizon, in the opposite direction. Then he scrambled down to the keeill, and cut cautiously across open ground to the top of Giau y Vaatey. No one was about. He kept his eye open for attack, while he examined the stuff they'd offloaded from the boat. It was all piled up together. The oddest thing was a great length of chain tied up in a bundle. It had mysterious tags hanging off it, all different shapes. Then there was a long wooden box with a broad carrying-strap of battered leather. And a much smaller box, padlocked. Billy tested it for weight. Whatever was inside was pretty heavy. Next to it were three metal legs joined together at the top, all tied together. There was also a bundle of thick wires like arrows, but they looked too top-heavy to shoot with. And there were a couple of painted poles. Billy couldn't see how anyone could build a lighthouse with tools like these. Perhaps Breesha had read the hard script wrong. He couldn't make sense out of any of this stuff, anyway.

All the time Billy kept glancing back towards the Tullachan.

He hadn't reckoned on an approach from the north. When someone whistled from up by the keeill, he jerked round, and froze. But it was all right. The whistle came again. He knew that signal.

Billy whistled back, and doubled back to the keeill. Breesha was standing with her back to the turf wall, watching the path behind him. He dropped back against the wall beside her.

'What were you *doing*? I thought we'd agreed we'd hide if anyone came, and spy on them before they knew we were there!'

'Ah, but I found out *much* more this way!'

'But it wasn't the *plan*!'

'Well, that doesn't matter now,' said Breesha impatiently. 'Your Mam went up to the light – I ran ahead to warn her – because she wants to speak to you first.'

'First before what? Did you speak to those men?'

'Before we have to go and meet them of course. No, but I *saw* them, close to. And I saw their stuff that they brought.'

'So did I,' said Billy. 'But it didn't make any sense.'

'Ah, but it does! It's what we knew would happen. They've come to measure!'

Measuring meant standing still while Aunt Diya decided how much he'd grown, and watching her cut up cloth for shirts and trousers. Billy frowned, but decided not to admit his ignorance.

But Breesha knew he didn't know. 'Measure the *island*, silly. That's what Mam said the stuff was for. But they mustn't. We have to stop them.'

Billy didn't answer at once. Things were clicking into place inside his head. That chain . . . poles with numbers on . . . In the lighthouse there was a chart of the Manx Sea, with all the far lands a white blank, and the sea covered with lines to show how many fathoms deep it was in each place. They had no map of Ellan Bride. There never had been a map of Ellan Bride, of course, but that didn't mean there never *could* be. And oh, thought Billy, how grand it would be to have a map of the island! They could put the names of all the different places on it. He'd like a map of Ellan Bride more than anything in the world, except for the telescope and Uncle Jim's knife. But *how*? Just for a moment he wanted, to the exclusion of every other desire in life, to see the map of the island in the making.

'. . . *whatever* it takes, Billy, we have to stop them!'

'Why?' The dream dissolved. Billy remembered that the enemy wanted to turn them out of Ellan Bride, and felt a pang of deep disappointment. It could have been so much more glorious, he thought dimly, even while vaguely conscious of his disloyalty, if the dark man, and the man with the pirate's face, had not been enemies at all, but bringers of gifts from unknown far horizons. Supposing they were friends, and would let him see how to make that map! And he couldn't go on hiding from them much longer anyway, now that they'd gone into the house, because eventually he'd miss his supper.

'Did you say Mam was at the lighthouse?'

'Yes. I went back to wake her, see. And when she woke up properly she said, "Oh God, oh no. Not already", and then she said, "I have to think." And she got up and put her gown on, and she was doing up the buttons as fast as she could, and I helped her, and she said, "Are they coming here now?" and I said "Yes" and she said "I'm going up to the light, Breesha. Do you know where Billy is?" And I said "No", because I didn't. And Aunt Lucy said to find you and tell you to come back to the light. She said "I have to think" and she ran out of the house before they got there, and went straight up to the light. I guessed you'd be watching them with the telescope, so I came along Dreeym Lang looking for you. Then I saw you down at the giau, and so I came down here and signalled, in case they were about.'

Billy rubbed his head. What Breesha was saying made him feel anxious in a way he didn't like. But his Mam was never anxious. 'Let's go up to the light then,' he said.

* * *

Lucy had known this would happen, but somehow she'd not quite believed it. The strangers had come. They were on the island. They were here, and with them came all the old terrors. The last strangers were the men who'd come five years ago, asking about Jim. Those two cold-faced men who'd asked all the questions . . . the endless dreadful questions: 'Where did he go?' 'When did you see him last?' 'Why did he go outside?' 'A block and tackle – why hadn't it been brought up already?' 'Why did he leave it until so late?' They'd never met Jim; they hadn't known who he was. They hadn't known anything about him. They'd believed he was careless, which was never the case. They wouldn't understand that the block and tackle had been left on the rocks because they'd still been bringing the barrels up. They wouldn't believe the storm had blown up so quickly. They refused to realise there just hadn't been time . . . They didn't care about Jim, and there was no kindness in their relentless questioning.

It had been like those other terrible questions before Billy was born. Lucy hadn't been able to answer those either. That hadn't been because there was no answer, but because she'd refused to tell. She didn't know which was worse, to be pressed for some answer that didn't exist, or for one that did. She just knew how much she'd hated the strange men asking, as if they'd had a right to know: the master of the house – 'sir' – speaking to her for the first time since she'd been in his employ . . . the doctor, the drunken vicar . . . 'Who is the man?' 'Who is the man?' 'You know who he was, you must tell us.' 'You have to tell us.' 'We need to find the man.' She hadn't told. She'd been punished for that as much as for what she'd done in the first place, and even now she wasn't sure why she'd been so desperate not to tell. To protect him? Had she felt she owed him that? But he wouldn't have got punished in any case, only her.

The one safe place was the island, but they were going to be cast out. What would happen to her and Billy now? I can't go back to Castletown, Lucy thought. I can't. But the strangers were already on Ellan Bride, and she knew there was no longer any choice.

No one still alive had ever seen Lucy cry. That must not change, whatever else did. Lucy sat up, shaking, blew her nose hard on a piece of tow, and rubbed her wet cheeks. They mustn't know that she'd been crying.

The sun still shone, winking against the glass of the lantern. The arch of sky was still azure. The island still basked in the brightness of a spring afternoon. The only sign of the strangers was the little pile of cargo at the top of Giau y Vaatey. Otherwise it was just like any other lovely afternoon, except that everything had changed.

It was foolish to think she could control their lives, even on the island. Lucy had felt so strong all the time she'd been the breadwinner for them all. She'd kept the light burning. Her faith in herself had never faltered. Yet even on the island there had been times when she couldn't make everything right. A memory flitted past: her mother's face, the face she'd known all her life, only completely changed. Lucy had long buried that memory. Usually, if she thought about the past at all, her mind's eye focused on the Mummig she'd had when she was little: a powerful figure, enduring as the island itself, firm-voiced, solid and rosy-cheeked. Only in those last months had the familiar face been grey and skeletal, lines etched where none had been before, and huge eyes avidly watching Lucy, Jim, and Jim's baby Breesha, as if trying to take them in for ever more. There had been a terrible beauty in that dying face, but until this moment Lucy had buried the memory along with the pain. Mummig was dead and buried, far away at Rushen Church. Twice Lucy had walked that long mile from Port St Mary behind a coffin. Since the day her Da had followed that road Lucy had never set foot on the Island again. Lucy and Diya were the only ones on Ellan Bride who could remember Mummig. There'd been no anger in her mother's face as Lucy remembered it – the anger had been all Lucy's – only a heart-breaking resignation. But the acceptance was

Mummig's, not Lucy's. Lucy didn't have any resignation inside herself. She tried now to search herself for some borrowed store of silent suffering, but her chest was empty.

But how could she fight? She had no way of protecting herself against that other world. She had no way of protecting any of them. She'd tried not to tell the children – perhaps that was wrong – but when Breesha came running to wake her, it was clear Breesha already knew . . . never mind how; it didn't matter now. Lucy had put all her trust in the sundering seas that kept them safe, just as long ago the islanders had been enveloped in the cloak of the sea-god himself, hidden in the mists and storms against all comers. Mummig used to tell them that story, and all her life Lucy had trusted in it. She'd been right to do so: the sea had kept them safe from everything but Death, because Death had his own way in to every place on earth, and even Mannanan in the olden days had not been able to conquer Death. But now something worse than Death had got through. No – Lucy gave herself a small shake – it could not be worse than Death. That was stupid. Lucy had always found a way through everything that had happened. Things were better than they had been eleven years ago, and she'd got through that. Then she'd been stuck, terrified, in the other world and she'd had to find her own way of getting back. Now, at least she was still on her own ground: for the moment anyway.

The door opened at the foot of the tower. Lucy stood up, rubbing her eyes. She must not look as if she'd cried. This was no time for tears: no time for fear either. It was her job to play the man's part, and she mustn't give in to her own weakness again, whatever happened.

'Mam?' Billy's voice sounded cautious, as if some unseen enemy might be lurking in the tower.

'I'm up here, Billy.' Her voice sounded perfectly normal. 'Come on up.'

Bare footsteps pattered up the stairs – two pairs of feet – then came up the ladder. Billy and Breesha erupted into the lantern. 'Mam!' cried Billy, and she see could at once that under the bravado he was scared too. 'What are we going to do?'

'Take them by surprise and throw them off the cliffs?' said Breesha. 'We *could*, you know.'

'Breesha, don't be silly! Billy – Breesha – you're understanding what these men have come for?'

'They want to build a new lighthouse,' said Billy. 'They want to send us away. But, Mam . . . we *can't*. We don't want to go anywhere!'

'Aunt Lucy, how are we going to stop them? What do you want us to do?'

Lucy pulled herself together. 'Billy, Breesha . . . I'm not wanting you to do anything. Certainly not anything foolish. These men are just the surveyors. It wasn't their decision. We can't stop them doing their job, and if we're making it difficult for them it'll be worse for us in the end. So what we do – your mother and I are agreeing on this, Breesha – what we do is we treat them as we would any other guest that was coming to our door. If they're telling the men who sent them that we're good people, then we have a better chance of being allowed to stay. And if they are forcing us to go, they'll have to give us compensation. But they won't if we do anything stupid. Are you understanding me?'

The children looked unconvinced, which was no wonder, because Lucy herself had no faith at all in what she was saying. It was all she could do to speak the words. But if she had no faith herself, she was managing to keep faith with Diya, as she'd promised to do when this time came. The plan – in fact the very words she'd just spoken – was all Diya's. When the letter came it was Lucy who hadn't been able to think straight, although until then she'd always thought of herself as the one who was really in charge. It was Diya who'd been able to think it out and have a plan ready, not Lucy.

'Mam said we had to give them broth. I think she should *poison* them.'

'Oh stow it, Breesha. Mam's right. If we kill them we'll be

hanged. Won't we, Mam? We can't go around doing things like that, can we, Mam?'

The world-weariness in Billy's voice shocked Lucy more than Breesha's histrionics. 'Children, *of course* we wouldn't *dream* of hurting them. We're living in a civilised country! We'll be all right – no one can *really* hurt us – and of course we won't be doing anything to hurt these men either.'

'We're *not* in a civilised country. We're on the island! And the island's *ours*, and these people have no right to be here!'

'Yes they do, Breesha. The island isn't ours. It's belonging to –' Lucy hesitated. Since the Duke had died she wasn't exactly sure who the island did belong to – 'Well, it's up to the Governor, or Tynwald, or the Commissioners of Northern Lights. It's not *ours*.'

Breesha looked at her aghast. 'Aunt Lucy, what do you *mean*? Of course it's ours! You call it our island! You know you do! Always! And we're here, aren't we? How can you *say* that?'

'Because it's true,' snapped Lucy. Had the child no notion what was real? She seemed to be saying it was Lucy's fault. Always her fault . . . But that was true too, because every irrational word the child spoke so wildly met its exact echo in Lucy's own mind. Breesha knew nothing of the real world they lived in, but she knew what was inside her aunt's mind all too well. And those things must never be voiced, never. 'I'm not wanting to hear any more of this nonsense! It's *not* our island. We know that perfectly well! And we'll behave like civilised beings. However we're feeling. Are you understanding me, Breesha?'

Breesha stared at her. Then she spat. The spit went nowhere, but Billy and Lucy were frozen in shock. 'Traitor!' The scream was high and wild as the gulls above the tower. '*You!* No! No! No! *Traitor!*'

Breesha slid down the ladder. They heard her bare feet smacking down the stone steps. The door slammed. To his utter shame, Billy found himself sobbing, still hugging the telescope to his chest. He let his mother put her arms round him.

Neither of them ever cried. It was all getting too difficult to bear. He sniffed, and dragged his shirt sleeve across his eyes.

'Oh, Billy veen, it's not as bad as that!' Lucy was herself again in an instant, now that her own Billy, who was always so equable, was upset. 'I've lived through worse. We'll manage all right. Of course we will. We always do, Billy veen, you and me, and we always will. True blue, Billy! That's us. True blue!'

He swallowed, and gave her a watery smile. 'True blue!'

'That's my boy. We'll be finding our way through this.'

'Shake on it?'

'Shake on it!' Lucy spat in her palm, as Billy spat in his. They solemnly shook hands. 'Now then, let's be going down to your poor aunt, and giving her a hand.'

He smiled at her a little shyly. After all, he was the man of the family. 'Like civilised beings, Mam?'

'Like civilised beings, Master William. We'll show them what we can do. Forward now!'

Chapter 13

ARCHIE AND BEN WERE AT THE SUNDIAL. THE SHADOW ON the dial fell exactly halfway between two and three. The east wind had moderated, and sunlight flooded the island. Archie was checking the sundial against his watch and pocket compass when Ben said, 'I think this must be the lightkeeper, sir.'

Archie looked up. The lightkeeper was coming down the zigzag path from the lighthouse. She was bareheaded and barefoot, and she wore a blue print gown, rather short – it barely reached her ankles – and a tattered apron. Of course, they hardly needed to dress for company in this place. She was followed by a boy in a threadbare shirt and patched nankeen trousers, with a leather telescope case slung across his shoulder.

'Ah,' said Ben in an undertone. 'Yon'll be the boy.'

'He's verra young.'

'So were we all – once. I wasna much older than that when I started this job.'

Archie smiled fleetingly. 'I mind it well.' He raised his voice and stepped forward as the lightkeeper approached. 'Miss Geddes?'

'Yes, sir.' Lucy had thought at first that the one dressed like a gentleman seemed quite friendly. But when he turned towards her he stopped smiling and looked remote and forbidding. She was an obstacle in his way, and he didn't like her. Lucy felt cold inside, and wished Diya were here. But she had Billy with her, and she was fighting for the whole family. She had to: there was no one else. Lucy walked straight over to the invaders, and faced them firmly.

The lightkeeper didn't curtsey. Instead she stood there sturdily, looking them over. This woman was much more what Archie had expected. She was quite pretty – though that was not to the purpose – with thick curly hair and a fair, open face marred only by the weathering of an outdoor life, and too many freckles. She looked tough. It wouldn't surprise him to see this one swing a sack of oatmeal onto her shoulder and stride away. She wasn't as tall as the other; in fact in every way she was less disconcerting than her sister-in-law. Also, she couldn't quite hide her nervousness, although she held out her hand like a man, and shook Archie's hand firmly. Then she turned to Ben.

Ben shook hands with her too, and smiled. 'I'm Benjamin Groat,' he said. 'And this'll be Billy, will it?'

Billy's mouth dropped open in surprise.

'Your friend Finn telt us about you.' Ben held out his hand to the boy. It was like edging a halter towards an unbroken colt, and for a moment he thought the lad would shy away.

Billy had never shaken a stranger's hand before. He slowly held out his hand, staring wide-eyed at Ben's face. Ben shook hands with him heartily. Billy couldn't take his gaze off this tall man, who was not like Finn, and not at all like Uncle Jim had been, but who met Billy's eyes as if he knew him already, or might wish to make his acquaintance. 'How do you do?' said Ben easily.

Billy tried to reply, but somehow the words got stuck in his throat.

'The letter said you'd come,' Lucy said to Archie. Her voice shook a little. 'You're the surveyors sent by Mr Stevenson?'

It wasn't Ben's place to discuss matters with the lightkeeper, but as always it was hard to restrain himself. When he'd suggested once to Drew that Young Archibald suffered from acute shyness Drew had snorted into his pint pot and ended up in a choking fit. Not for the first time, Ben found himself wondering if Archie ever talked to any women at all. He had ten years' advantage over Ben – though Ben hadn't altogether wasted his twenty-one years as far as pretty girls were concerned – so why on earth couldn't Young Archibald set this poor Miss Geddes at her ease by showing her that, painful though their errand might be, they were friendly creatures who'd do their best to repay the enforced hospitality of her little family by being as pleasant as they could? Archie was talking to her now as if she were a committee of elderly Commissioners. And as for the lightkeeper herself: the other woman had been something out of a fairy story, but this one was a real, honest-to-God, healthy woman, and none the worse for that. She didn't look much older than Ben himself. If the boy was hers – and he looked as if he was – he must be ten or eleven – then she'd have to be – what? – twenty-five – twenty-six maybe – at the very least. It would be good to see her smile, but in the nature of things, given what they'd come here to do, that was hardly likely. Ben felt a faint twinge of disappointment. But when the subject of Billy came up, he broke his silence. Young Archibald would make such a mull of it, he had to intervene.

'The fact is,' Ben broke in, smiling reassuringly at Billy, 'we lost our second chainman in Castletown. Never mind how – that doesna matter. But we're a man short. And your friend Finn said there was a strong boy here who might be glad of a job. Finn thought very highly of you, Master Billy – that was clear – so we were hoping we might be able to take you on to help us. What would be we paying, now, sir?'

Archie had forgotten to mention that; in fact he'd forgotten even to think of it. 'Twopence,' he said hastily. 'Twopence a day. For two or three days' work, probably.'

'There you are, young sir. Would you be so kind as to join the crew, while we're here? Is tuppence a day acceptable to you?'

Billy stared at him, his eyes wider than ever. 'Tuppence?' he whispered. 'For me?'

'Tuppence a day. That might be a groat, or even a whole sixpence, by the time we're done. Sixpence, Master Billy, if you do well! We'll have to train you, mind,' said Ben. 'Show you the ropes and that. Maybe you'll end up a surveyor yourself. You never know. I was fourteen when I started. You're no fourteen yet?'

Billy shook his head, overwhelmed. He'd never had a farthing of his own in his life – had never even dreamed of such a thing. It was Mam who earned money. Sometimes he'd seen her counting coins, and giving them to Finn, but he'd never thought of having anything to do with that. And this strange man thought he might be fourteen! A man, in fact, as far as doing a job of work was concerned. He cleared his throat, and met Ben's eyes squarely. 'I'm ten.' This time his voice came out properly. 'But soon I'll be eleven. And . . .' He looked doubtfully at Lucy. 'If my Mam says . . . I don't know . . .'

'That's a man's wage, Billy,' said Lucy, her voice very firm and clear. 'And you'll be learning too.'

Billy looked at Ben, and slowly nodded. He didn't so much as glance at Archie. 'All right.'

Billy was following the men about like a tantony pig. He'd changed sides within five minutes of making their acquaintance. Billy was a traitor. No, that wasn't fair. Billy hadn't had a choice, and anyway, he was in the best position now to spy on them. So far as that went he was in a much better position than Breesha was.

Breesha lay on her stomach on the lighthouse parapet, and cautiously edged the telescope forward between two of the iron railings. They couldn't possibly see it from below, unless they looked up at the exact spot. The two men wouldn't think of doing that, and Billy wouldn't give her away. Billy knew she was here. He'd lent her the telescope. She'd whistled from behind the keeill when she'd seen him going down to Giau y

Vaatey with those two men, and he'd run back to speak to her. He wouldn't stay, but he told her the tall man was called Benjamin and he was nice, and not an enemy. And Billy was working for him, and he was going to get twopence for each day that the men were here. Benjamin had arranged all that. It was the other one who might be an enemy, but not to worry: Billy had his eye on him.

Breesha was in no way reassured by anything Billy said, but at least Billy had lent her the telescope. That showed he was still on Breesha's side. She knew he wouldn't give her away by looking up to the tower. From here she could watch exactly what those men did, almost wherever they went on the island. Billy could have said to the men, 'Breesha must come too.' No he couldn't. It was Aunt Lucy who'd said the men could take Billy. Billy had told her that much. Aunt Lucy never listened if anyone argued. That meant Billy had had no choice. But he could choose not to be pleased about it, and Breesha had seen very clearly that he was as glad as anything to go with those two men and pretend to be like one of them.

Breesha focused the telescope. The men and Billy were standing on Dreeym Lang, at the very top of the island. They'd finished carting all their strange gear up from the jetty, and the tall one had wheeled the handcart back to its place by the outhouse. When they got to the garden wall they stopped. Breesha twisted the focus so she could see better. The tall man had a pot and a brush. She watched him make a white mark on the corner of the garden wall. Whatever for? She felt it was taking a liberty; after all, it wasn't *his* garden wall. Now the two men were following Billy past the garden towards the slabs. In a few minutes they were out of sight.

So why had they gone down to the slabs? They wouldn't be building their lighthouse there. Anyway, Breesha knew where they were, and if she waited long enough she knew exactly where they'd reappear, whichever way they came back. She sat up, cradling the telescope in her lap. She wondered where Mally was. It was lonely doing all the spying by herself.

That was a new thought: she was lonely. She didn't like it. All her life up until now, either she was with the others or on her own, but neither of those states had ever troubled her. She'd never really thought about the change from one to the other. But Billy wasn't just somewhere else today; it was more as if he'd left her behind completely. That had never happened before. Those men could have picked her to go with them. She was the eldest. It didn't occur to Breesha that she hadn't given them much chance; she knew that no amount of chances would have changed the way things were. It was because she was a girl. Breesha turned the telescope round and round in her hands, and stared out to sea, frowning.

What made it even more confusing was that it didn't make sense to be angry about both things at once. The most terrible thing of all was that they would be made to leave the island. Nothing could make a person angrier than that. Breesha wouldn't leave Ellan Bride unless they dragged her. She just wouldn't get on the boat. They'd have to carry her, and if they tried to pick her up she'd bite them. But she was beginning to realise even that wouldn't work. Mam wouldn't fight. Aunt Lucy wouldn't fight. Mam had taken the enemy into the house and given them broth. If Breesha bit anyone Mam would probably slap her, and apologise for her to the enemy. You couldn't resist properly if all your allies deserted you. The real thing to be angry about was having everything taken away from them, but no one else was *being* angry. Even Breesha herself was unfaithful to the real cause: she was also angry because the men had ignored her, and taken Billy with them. But she couldn't *want* to go with them, because if she did she'd be a traitor. And yet she *did* want to, because she could show them that, girl or not, she was just as much use as Billy. If they were measuring, in fact, she was better than Billy, because Billy was much more careless at sums than Breesha was. He still didn't know all his tables, even though Mam insisted on both children reciting them by heart at every lesson.

But there were the men again! They were coming up Gob

Glas, following the coast round to the deep-cut inlet of Giau yn Ooig. Breesha lay down on the parapet and focused the telescope.

Billy was leading the way. They all stopped at the edge of the giau. The short man had a big notebook – Breesha twisted the focus to make the outline sharper – and he was writing things down in it very quickly. Billy seemed to be talking. He had his back to the lighthouse, but Breesha could tell from the way he waved his arms about that he was telling them things. *Telling* them things – about the island, no doubt! How *dare* he! Breesha gave a little hiss, and shifted her sights onto the tall man. He was looking down at the shore below, where Billy was pointing. He carried a big canvas knapsack on his back, and the bundle of metal arrows slung over his shoulder. He said something. Maybe it was something funny, because he smiled. And the other man stopped writing, looked up, and laughed. Breesha caught the shorter man's face full on, framed by the lens. It wasn't villainous. On the contrary, it was a vivid, merry face, lit up by laughter. He looked like Ali Baba after the Forty Thieves were all vanquished, not that Breesha had ever seen Ali Baba, but the stranger looked just the way Breesha always pictured him when Mam told them the story. It was the way the man looked up from his busy writing, and suddenly laughed – he looked *happy*. Somehow that compounded Breesha's confusion. She didn't know what to think about it, so instead she concentrated on following the three figures as they skirted Giau yn Ooig, following the coastline.

'And the stack out there?' Ben was asking, raising his voice above the screams of the kittiwakes. He added, in unconscious imitation of Finn: 'What name would you be putting on yon?'

Billy drew breath. No one in his life had ever asked him so many questions. The strangest thing was, he was beginning to realise that these men didn't know any of the answers. When the children did their lessons with Aunt Diya, she asked much more difficult questions than Mr Benjamin Groat or the

Writing Man were doing, but Aunt Diya knew the answers all the time anyway. That was why Billy didn't like lessons very much: the ignorance that lessons exposed always seemed to be his. Somehow Breesha seemed to know things without being told, and even if the facts were new to her she always had an opinion about them. Billy avoided lessons when he could. Even Mally never seemed to get caught out the way he did, and now she could read almost as well as Billy. But these grown men weren't pretending; they truly didn't know anything at all about the island.

'You mean Stack ny Ineen?' said Billy wonderingly. 'Because that's the Maiden's Stack, of course.'

'And who was the maiden who gave her name to a bit of old rock like yon?'

'Keep to the point, Ben,' muttered Archie. His eyes darted here and there across Giau yn Stackey, and the pencil flew across the paper. He was standing a few feet from the edge, where half a dozen puffins were eyeing him warily, ready to fly if he came any closer. The racket and smells of thousands of nesting birds came wafting up from the giau. Tier upon tier of birds lined the cliffs opposite: kittiwakes above, razorbills and guillemots perched on the precarious ledges below, barely out of reach of the high-tide mark. The dark swell below the cliffs was dotted with stray feathers, and scattered rafts of guillemots. Unseen waves washed in and out of a hidden cleft beneath their feet.

Billy watched Archie in awe. The Writing Man could walk and look and write and draw and talk all at the same time. It would be exciting to see what was in that notebook. Breesha would want him to find out in any case. He cast an involuntary glance back to the lighthouse, but Breesha was keeping well out of sight. 'The maiden lived on the Calf and she wanted to marry a man who came across the sea from the Island and her father didn't want her to so he brought her here and put her up on the stack so she'd die and no one could get her only the man climbed up and got her and took her off and they went away and the father never saw either of them ever again,' said Billy. 'Did you *really* not know that story?'

'Actually I did,' said Ben, following Billy's glance up to the lighthouse tower. There was a little flash: something had moved and caught the westering sun just for a second. Ben had heard the whistle from the keeill, and recognised it at once as an oyster catcher that had never sprouted feathers in its life. Nor had it escaped his notice that when Billy had come running back from the keeill his telescope was no longer slung across his shoulder. He was equally certain that Archie had totally forgotten that one of the children was still unaccounted for. 'I heard just the same story about another Maiden Stack when I was a boy. There must have been a hell of a lot of stranded maidens in those days, don't you think?'

Mr Benjamin had said 'hell', but there was no one here to scold him. Billy grinned back a little doubtfully.

The Writing Man said, 'We'll put another station at the top of the Giau.' He climbed a few yards to higher ground, so he could look back to the last station. Billy followed his gaze to the little red flag fluttering by the lonely boulder at the top of the slabs. They'd also put a white paint mark on the garden wall at Gob Glas. Ben carried the paint, the brush, some measuring twine, and other undivulged mysteries in his big canvas knapsack, as well as all the arrows. The Writing Man only carried his notebooks; Billy wondered if he was weaker than he looked. Just then the Writing Man stopped and looked up to Cronk Sheeant. 'Ay, you can see that summit from here too. That's fine.'

Billy watched as Ben took another of the long metal arrows, and twisted it neatly into the crumbly soil by the Writing Man's foot. The tattered red flag caught the breeze, and began to flutter as if it were a big butterfly just come alive.

'I'd reckon the cliff's two hundred feet,' remarked Archie. 'Maybe a bit less. We'll find out. But the boy's right. Nocht could land on the west side. I doubt there's even a way down.'

'There's *lots* of ways down!'

'Into this giau?'

Billy hesitated. The climb down into Giau yn Stackey was his own closely-guarded secret. 'I reckon you *could*,' he said cautiously.

'I doubt it,' said Ben. 'Mr Buchanan can climb a bit, but he hasna been practising. Which way do *you* go?' He caught Billy's doubtful glance and said. 'We won't split on you. I swear it. Cross my heart and hope to die. And so does Mr Buchanan. Is that no right, sir?'

The Writing Man didn't seem to be listening. After a moment's hesitation Billy pointed across the turf. 'You start *there*,' he whispered to Ben. 'It gets a bit sliddery, specially now 'cos the birds shit all over the place. You have to kind of wind your way across, past where the kittiwakes are. Then you lower yourself backwards down into the gully and go down over the big rocks. There's lots of shags' nests in there. Coming up is easier 'cos you can see where you're going.'

'Maybe we can cross that off our list of landing places.'

'But the landing place is where you came in! No one *ever* landed on the west side!'

The Writing Man suddenly gave Billy his attention again. Whereas Ben was friendly all the time, the Writing Man took no notice of anyone unless he wanted to know something at that moment. Billy didn't mind that. His Mam was a bit the same, and there was nothing muddling about her. 'So where does Finn Watterson land, if it's too rough for the slabs, and he canna get into Giau y Vaatey?' asked the Writing Man, as he led them uphill. Away from the cliff edge, the noise from the giau was immediately deadened, so they could talk in ordinary voices again.

'There's Geinnagh Veg and Traie Vane,' explained Billy. 'But Finn wouldn't be running ashore there except on a rising tide because of getting beached. Except just sometimes he stays a whole tide. He puts the coal off at Traie Vane on a high tide, and at low tide we barrow it up. And now we roll the oil barrels up at Traie Vane too.'

‘Traie Vane will be White Beach?’ asked Ben. ‘That’s the one we passed on our way in? North of Giau y Vaatey?’

‘You said “now”?’ asked Archie sharply. ‘You used to bring the barrels ashore somewhere else?’

It was hard to tell them. Billy looked out to sea unhappily, while they waited for him to speak. The puffins had started their evening circuit, thousands and thousands of them whirling round the island, silent but for the endless whirring of their wings. ‘At Giau y Vaatey,’ Billy said at last. ‘But not after Uncle Jim . . . my Uncle Jim isn’t here any more. We used to have a block and tackle at Giau y Vaatey, only that night . . . it was the same night, you see . . . that’s what he went down for . . . to move it . . . And the block and tackle was swept away as well. In the morning it was gone. It was a long time ago now. And we can’t get the barrels up the rocks by ourselves. So there was no point getting another block and tackle. So now there isn’t one any more.’

‘That’s a shame,’ said Ben, watching him. *It was a long time ago now* . . . five years, thought Ben. In his mind’s eye he was seeing another boy, just about Billy’s age, walking the banks at Woodwick, watching the horizon . . . always watching and still hoping, long after all hope was gone. Tam had been Ben’s friend. When no one could persuade Tam to leave the shore Ben had stayed and walked with him, up and down, up and down, with the spray flying in their faces, looking out over the great grey rollers into the storm-tossed sea. There could be no funeral because there were no bodies. Tam’s father and brothers had never come home again.

‘Two sandy beaches, and the landing place, all facing east,’ muttered Archie. ‘And the slabs, of course. Fine in a westerly, but . . . Well, we’ll have a look at the rest of the west side in any case. Lead on, Billy!’

Mally found out where the strangers were by going up onto Dreeym Lang and watching the birds. A cloud of black-backs had risen over Gob Keyl. Mally ran to the top of Cronk Sheeant. The turf where she stood was studded with thrift and eyebright, and the shadows of the circling puffins made the ground shimmer like the sea. In the west the sky was turning gold, and a cold little breeze was coming off the sea. The gulls at Gob Keyl were settling again, but now the terns beyond Geinnagh Veg were rising into the air with cries of fury like a sudden snowstorm. Sure enough, a moment later Mally saw three figures skirting the nesting grounds. Billy was leading the way, taking the strangers by the higher path. They were almost above the beach. Mally hitched up her skirt and started to run, leaping from rock to rock as she skirted the tumbled edge of Hamarr, down towards Geinnagh Veg.

She met them, as she had planned, right beside the keeill.

'Well, well, Miss Mally. So you've abandoned the piglings?'

'This is the keeill,' Billy was explaining.

Archie laid down his notebook, weighted it with a stone, and walked round the keeill, examining it carefully. He found the entrance. They watched him get down on his hands and knees to peer in. Then, without a word, he disappeared inside.

Mally and Billy looked at each other, nonplussed. The strange man wouldn't have walked into their house without asking. Was the keeill different? It was difficult to tell; nothing like this had ever happened before. But it was a relief when Archie came out. He stood up, dusting the earth off his knees.

'Interesting,' said Archie. 'I wish I had a light.' He turned to the two children. 'Was this once a chapel, dae ye ken?'

They stared at him, puzzled. 'That's the keeill,' said Billy again.

'Breesha's keeill,' added Mally, suddenly finding her voice.

'Breesha?'

'Not my *sister*, I don't mean. I mean the real one.'

'She means the Saint,' said Billy.

'Saint?' asked Ben. 'So this is the saint's chapel?'

'This is the saint's *island*,' said Mally. Now she'd actually managed to speak to them, ordinary talking didn't seem difficult any more. 'She lived here. That's why the island has her name.'

'St *Bride*, you mean?' asked Archie, his attention quickening. 'Breesha is Bride?'

'Of *course*,' said Billy. How could they be so ignorant? He wondered for a moment if they were making it up.

'So you do know her?' Mally asked Archie seriously.

It was the first time one of the children had addressed Archie directly. He couldn't smile at her easily as Ben did, but he could answer this particular question. 'Oh ay. I grew up by one of her chapels too.'

'Where?' demanded Mally, frowning over the possibility of other islands, other keeills. 'On another island?'

'It wasna an island at all,' said Archie. 'It was by a muckle great river, and St Bride's chapel was just upriver, jist aboot as far as your keeill is from your house.'

'Did you have a house like ours then?'

'No.' Mally opened her mouth to ask another question, but Archie went on suddenly without being prompted. 'It was a mill. St Bride's Mill above Kilmahog. We didna have an island, but we had the river, and we had a grand mountain. And the mill too, of course. And all the places we kent had their own names, jist like here.'

Ask him some more, thought Ben, willing Mally to go on. She'd just elicited more information from Young Archibald than any of his colleagues had managed to do in ten years. Perhaps he'd had a young sister of his own – would Mally ask him that? Ben willed her to do so, but Mally had no idea she'd rushed in where none had dared to tread.

'Our chapel is bigger nor yours,' said Archie, speaking to Mally as if she were just as old as he was, 'but it's a ruin. Just a few peerie stanes left, that's all.' He walked round the keeill again, and glanced at his watch. 'Very well. We'll take a look at the bigger beach, and then we'll be back where we started. Billy, can you show us the highest tide mark? The height of your highest spring tide?'

'Course I can. It's marked anyway, above the giau. My Gaffer marked the place. I can show you where. And I know how far down the ebb goes too, but you can't see that now, of course.'

'I'm coming with you,' said Mally.

No one answered, or took any notice of her. She followed the three of them doggedly, down to the sands at Traie Vane, where the seals flopped into the water at their approach, leaving only the scuff-marks of their bodies where they had lain basking, undisturbed, on their primeval sands.

Chapter 14

DIYA AND LUCY WORKED THEIR WAY ALONG THE ROWS, earthing up young potato plants. If this drought went on much longer the garden would be seriously short of water. They ought to keep a close eye on the well too. It was many years since they'd been reduced to fetching water all the way from Towl Doo for every purpose except drinking. Diya realised, as she hoed the dusty soil, that it was the hot weather that was triggering so many recollections in her mind, both waking and sleeping. At this time of year India sometimes seemed to come almost close enough to touch, if only one could simply stretch one's hand out across the intervening years.

As the sun dropped, the garden wall cast a long shadow over the potato patch. They'd nearly finished when Lucy straightened up and wiped the sweat out of her eyes, leaving streaks of mud across her forehead. 'Mind you,' she said, as if they'd been in the middle of a conversation, 'I don't know why we're doing this. We'll not even be here to eat them.'

Diya said nothing until she got to the end of the row. Of course she'd thought of that, but unlike Lucy she hadn't said anything. Eleven years Diya had worked in this garden. The first year she'd worked with Jim's mother when Lucy hadn't been there. From Mummig, Diya had learned the times to dig and the times to sow in this particular place. She'd learned to cart up seaweed from Traie Vane, and to mix it with the winter's muck from the midden. She'd learned about the soil and the wind and the weather: things that were unique to each garden. When Diya first came, Mummig had grown potatoes for the whole year, and a few rows of kale, beans and onions. Like Diya, Mummig had loved flowers, and her rows of vegetables were bordered with marigolds, heart's-ease and stocks. She'd put in lavender that attracted clouds of small blue butterflies, and a patch of mint in one corner. That was all. When Diya, who'd known such very different gardens, suggested other things, Mummig would shake her head and say, 'No, no, Diya veen. You'll never be getting that to grow *here*.'

Mummig had been wrong. Mummig had not been off Ellan Bride for twenty-five years. She used to say, what was there to go for, when she had all she needed where she was? But Diya couldn't be like that. Back then, she used to sail over to Port St Mary with Jim, and think nothing of it. When Breesha was a baby she'd twice taken her to stay with old friends in Castletown for a few weeks. It had been a breath of another life. She hadn't been in touch with Sally for at least two years. She must write to her today so Finn could take the letter when he came back. Sally would take them in for a month or so, surely, when they had to leave, and give Diya time to look about while she worked out what to do next.

It would be hard to leave the garden. Diya had planned this garden as if they'd been going to stay for ever. That was the only way one *could* work in a garden. Some things would take twenty years or more to mature, like the apple trees along the south wall. Last year's apples had given them pies and puddings until the end of October. In another ten years they'd probably have apples to store all winter. Mummig had scoffed when Diya had brought the infant trees home. She'd been suspicious of the currants and gooseberries too, though she'd conceded that the raspberries might do all right. Mummig had never thought of building rectangular shelters out of driftwood, and setting honeysuckle, briars and dog roses to climb over them until they were like hedges, protecting each little square of ground.

Mummig had never even seen some of the plants that Diya brought back from Castletown. The fuchsia hedge that grew so thick it had to be cut right back every year – that hadn't even been known in this country when Mummig was young. Diya knew that you could transplant some plants but not others, and the only way to find out was to try. Now they grew carrots, turnips, leeks, radishes and lettuces, as well as a whole variety of flowers that Mummig had never even dreamed of.

Flowers were holy. Mummig would never have put it like that – she was shocked, in fact, when Diya once said so – but her feeling for them was the same as Diya's. Now, in the most sheltered south-west corner of the Ellan Bride garden, hedged about with phlox and moon daisies, the white jasmine grew. There were already buds on it; in June it would flower. On still summer nights you could smell it from the house. It came from Grandmother's garden at Castletown. Once when Diya had been staying with Sally she'd asked the new tenants if she could go in and take cuttings from her old favourites. They hadn't minded; the walled garden was nothing to them. They hadn't looked after it as Grandmother had done. When Diya went back the lawn was straggly and unkempt, the borders full of weeds, the apple tree unpruned. Some of the old plants had vanished, while others flourished untended. Breesha had been a toddling infant then, playing on the unscythed lawn while Diya slowly filled her trug with cuttings. Breesha wouldn't remember that day now. Did she remember those visits to Castletown at all? Probably not. They'd never been back after the child turned three.

But jasmine – as Diya hoed up the dry earth against the small potato plants she saw it clearly in her mind's eye – jasmine was one of her earliest memories. Jasmine and roses had grown tall in the shade of the garden wall; the air was loaded with their scent. Aji used to bring swathes of flowers into the house each day, and arrange them before morning puja: *tulsi* – that was basil, which only grew under glass in this country – and *hava dhania* – what would that be in English?

Diya wasn't sure. Aji would give people flowers to wear when they came to the house. She'd put bright flowers in Diya's hair in the morning. Then at Diwali she'd make wreaths of marigold and mango leaves to hang on the door. The Indian garden hadn't been like a Manx garden at all. The colours had been so bright, and every tiny patch of shade was a benediction. The trees had towered over her. Bluebirds and little green parrots flashed to and fro among the branches. The wall was flaky stone and stretched away into the burning sky. Diya kept away from the wall because snakes and scorpions liked to crawl into the cracks. There was only one way to see out of the garden, and that was to scramble up by the tank until she was almost as high as the wall and she could peep over. The white road lay below. She seldom walked on the road because she never set foot outside the gate without an adult. The road was a strange world. When the rickshaw coolies came pattering past, she hated the sound of their bare feet on the dusty road. When she did walk outside the garden gate she always came home covered with dust. The dust got into her eyes and she felt it gritty between her teeth. She hated dust, but in the garden, with its brick paths watered from the tank at dawn every day, there was no dust at all.

Diya carefully earthed up the last potato plant, and straightened up. 'Even if we're not here to eat them,' she said calmly, as if Lucy had only just spoken, 'it's worth doing. In fact – you know what – if the world were going to end tomorrow it might as well find us in the garden.'

'Diya,' Lucy burst out, as if she could contain the thought no longer. 'What are we going to *do*?'

'Something,' said Diya calmly. 'Have the surveyors said anything to you about when we must go?'

'Nothing at all. But the letter was telling us!'

'The letter didn't say when. We need to ask them when. In fact we should ask them all about it. Mr Buchanan's probably got all their future plans with him, written down in that notebook of his, no doubt. I wish I could have a look at it.'

Lucy shuddered. 'And when they are telling us? What then? I don't want to ask!'

'*I'll* ask them, if you like. And then – we need to have a plan of our own.'

'What sort of plan?' Lucy had never felt so helpless. She hated herself for not being able to think straight. She was the one who'd never been afraid of anything, all the time they'd been together. But elsewhere – that was another thing. 'How can we be making a plan?'

'First we need to know when we have to leave. I'm going to write to Sally – my friend in Castletown when I was a girl. And to the vicar at Malew. Finn says the new vicar is a good man, and my friend Sally knows his wife. He doesn't know us, but after all I was christened and married in Malew Church, and my grandparents are both buried there. He'll recognise a duty to us, I'm sure. When we get there—'

'Castletown?' Lucy looked at her in horror. 'We're not going *there*?'

'Where else?' Diya hid her impatience. Of course it was harder for Lucy. 'It's the only place where I know anybody. You don't know anybody anywhere else, do you?'

Lucy looked at her with frightened eyes. 'I don't know anyone anywhere! Except Finn.'

Diya knew that wasn't true, but Lucy never talked about that part of her life, and Diya knew better than to pry. All she said was, 'We can't go to Finn. Not with all those children in a cottage smaller than ours!'

'I'm not saying we should. I'm just saying he's the only person over there I know.' Lucy brushed her hand across her hot forehead. 'Diya, I don't know what to *do*.'

Sometimes Diya forgot how vulnerable Lucy could be. It was eleven years since Diya had seen what the outside world could do to her. 'Listen,' said Diya. 'We'll find a way. Why don't you leave me to think of something? I promise you I will.'

'That's not fair on you!'

'Yes, it is. It's the sort of thing I know about. Making changes. Having to start again. I'm good at that. You're still the light-keeper, Lucy. Keep your mind on that – that's what you must do. I'll work out what to do afterwards. I'll write my letters, and Finn will take them when he fetches the surveyors. The only thing is . . .'

'What?'

'Money,' said Diya. 'We have to think about money. I told you before: you need to write a letter to the Commissioners of Northern Lights and ask if they're going to give you a pension. That's what they ought to do. It won't be much. It can't mean anything to them, but it'll mean a lot to you.'

'To us,' said Lucy, looking dazed. 'Not just me.'

'Well, we'll see.' It had clearly never crossed Lucy's mind that the family might have to separate. This was hardly the moment to suggest it to her. 'But you need to write the letter before the surveyors leave, so they can take it with them.'

Lucy looked panic-stricken. 'Now? Write it *now*? But I don't know what to say!'

'Then I'll write it. They won't know my hand from yours. Do you want me to do it?' There was no point saying to Lucy that the letter might be useless. Neither Lucy nor Jim had been employed by the Commissioners of Northern Lights. It was the Duke of Atholl who'd paid them. If the Commissioners won't be responsible, thought Diya, I'll write a letter to the new Duke over in Scotland. But there was no need to worry Lucy with that idea now.

Diya's task would have been easier if she'd been sure that what was right for the family was also what she wanted for herself. She knew that Jim would expect her to look after his family – not just his children, but also his sister and his nephew – as willingly as he would have done himself. Jim would never have been disloyal to Diya. She'd always known that; perhaps that was why she'd married him: she'd been certain she could trust him, and she'd been right. She'd also known what she was giving up, but she hadn't realised, in the turmoil of those days following Grandmother's death, how much those things would matter to her. It wasn't the material things she missed, although she did like to have beautiful things around her. In any case, Ellan Bride had its own sort of beauty, when the weather was good, and she'd reluctantly learned to love that too, in a way – but no, it wasn't possessions. It wasn't status either. If you lived on Ellan Bride there was no one above you, and no one below. You were a whole society, rich and poor, mistress and servant, all on your own. Sometimes when Diya started work in the kitchen in the morning, she pretended to be her own servant, doing the daily tasks to satisfy an exacting mistress who was herself.

It was easier now she was her own mistress than it had been at the beginning, working for Mummig. That was a wicked thought. She mustn't think it, even to herself. But when Diya first came to Ellan Bride it was always Mummig who said how things should be done. Diya had to admit now she'd learned more useful things from Mummig than she had from all her expensive education in Castletown, but it had gone against the grain, however well she'd hidden her resentment. The cook's sister! Diya could never admit to a soul how much easier her life on Ellan Bride had been after Jim and Lucy's beloved Mummig was dead.

But at least Diya didn't have to feel guilty about Jim. There was nothing to hide about that. She'd missed Jim every day since the night he'd gone. And even more she missed their broken nights. The light had come first, of course: the light must always come first. But the other part of Jim's nights had been Diya's, and no one else's. She'd married him because she trusted him, it was true, but also because – though she'd never admitted to it until the day before Grandmother's funeral, when he'd found her in the kitchen – every time she'd laid eyes on him she'd been aware of an attraction. Of course such a thing could never have been dreamed of while Grandmother was alive, and Diya was still Miss Wells. But even now Diya could remember the day – she couldn't have been more than fifteen

– when she'd gone down to the kitchen and first found a rough-looking young man standing before the chidlagh, gobbling – there was no other word for it – one of Annie's hot scones. His patched jacket was stained with salt, and he smelt of the sea. He looked at her so directly, while he stuffed the rest of the scone into his mouth, that in anyone else she'd have thought it impudence. His eyes were the same colour as the sea. Diya had only been fifteen, after all: a mere child, and one, moreover, who read far too many novels from the Circulating Library. In her fancy this strange young man was like a gust of wind blowing off the sea – it must have been one of the first gales of September – forcing itself right into the basement of Grandmother's stuffy house. It was shocking, like the northern weather when she'd never been used to it, but curiously exhilarating too. Diya hadn't really understood what she'd felt, at the time.

Then, four years later, what else could she have done but marry him? No one from the Castletown world – the world she still missed more than she dared to acknowledge – had come to help her after the bailiffs came. Grandmother was dead. Her father was dead. Only Jim had come, and offered himself. He'd saved her. What would have become of her, if it wasn't for Jim?

But even when he was alive she'd had ungrateful thoughts. She'd never told Jim what she missed. What would have been the point? He wouldn't have understood. He didn't know what it was like to sit at dinner, with the white cloth spread, and the silver dishes sparkling in the candlelight, and talk of matters that made the world grow larger, as if the bounds of thought were infinite . . . No one opened up subjects like that on Ellan Bride. The world they all thought about was as small as the island itself. Diya had felt wicked, even when Jim was alive, because in the depths of her heart she was ungrateful. And now, when Jim's sister was so helpless, and relying on Diya completely – *trusting* her, as Diya had once trusted Jim – Diya was, in her secret heart, feeling more disloyal than Lucy would ever dream of.

Diya came to the end of the row, looked up, and found Lucy on the other side, looking into her eyes. 'I'm a fool,' Lucy whispered. 'I'm sorry, Diya. I'm sorry to be no use.'

'Don't be ridiculous.' What Diya had successfully hidden from Jim could be much more easily kept from his sister. Faced by the immediate task, Diya was quite capable of hiding her inmost thoughts even from herself; there was no point doing otherwise. She and Jim's family – after all, her own children were Jim's family – were bound together for ever. Hadn't she promised him that, when she married him? 'You're the light-keeper,' said Diya aloud. 'I couldn't be that. We all do what we can. Will you leave the letters to me, and stop worrying? Just keep your mind on what we have to do here, and deal with the surveyors. All right?'

There were eggs for supper, as well as broth and bread. 'You missed your dinner, being at sea,' Diya said to the two surveyors. 'You'll be hungry, no doubt.'

That was an understatement. Archie was thankful when Ben brought out some ships' biscuit from their own supplies and added it to the food on the table, somehow without causing offence to anybody.

'Has it got weevils in?' Breesha asked her mother. She still hadn't addressed a word to the two strangers, but nevertheless contrived to take her fair share of biscuit without acknowledging Ben's presence.

'Shouldna have,' said Ben cheerfully, though Breesha was pointedly not looking at him. 'It was fresh from the chandlers in Castletown yesterday morning. You'd have to take it to sea for a few months to give the weevils a chance to hatch.'

'But it might have their eggs in,' remarked Billy with his mouth full.

'Mally, don't spit your food out like that!'

'But Billy said—'

Breesha ignored them, and tapped her biscuit on the table like a proper sailor, but no weevils fell out. 'Were there weevils on the India ship?' she asked her mother, when everyone was quiet.

'Not that I remember,' Diya replied. 'But the food wasn't very good. Salt beef and salt pork – I couldn't touch it. Mind you, I'd never seen meat on the table in my life. Luckily there was rice aboard, and I remember they used to give me a bowl of that. But that was all – no vegetables, which was what I'd always been used to. They said the meat was bad. It certainly looked very bad to me. Everyone complained to the captain. When we went ashore at Cape Town we bought lots of fresh fruit to take back on board.'

'And a goat,' put in Mally. 'Tell them about the goat.'

'Oh, the goat! Yes, my father and Mr Grant – he was bringing his family to England too – they clubbed together and bought a goat. After that we children had fresh milk as far as St Helena, but I think the goat was left behind there for some reason. Or maybe it died. I can't recall.' She turned to Archie and said politely, 'But you'll have travelled yourself, sir, no doubt.'

'Me?' said Archie. 'Only in Scotland really, although I visited London recently. I've never been anywhere else.'

'Mrs Grant had the goat's milk too,' corrected Mally. 'You told us so before. And you couldn't guess why, because no one explained. But all of a sudden when you were crossing the Equator she had a baby. It was a boy, and your Da said she ought to call him Meridian. Only she didn't. She called him Henry George.'

Diya ignored this addition to her tale, and went on talking to Archie. 'But you know the sea. All Scotchmen know the sea.'

'Not really,' said Archie. 'My father never laid eyes on the sea in his life. I never saw it myself until I left home.'

Even Breesha looked at him then. Archie found six pairs of eyes fixed upon him, expressing varying degrees of pity and amazement, and to his annoyance he felt himself flush. He seldom thought of home these days – of the still pond above the mill, and the great wheel turning, and the water racing back into the river, down into the Falls of Leny where the river fell tumbling through the pass to the green meadows below. On an evening like this the sun would have set behind Ben Ledi, and the glen be all in shadow, but if you climbed up to the ridge you'd see the red sky and, below it, ridge upon ridge of Highland hills stretched out in the last rays of the sun. That was where he belonged, and he wasn't ashamed of it either. Archie looked away from the group at the table, almost hating them for their ignorance, over Breesha and Billy's heads to the gable-end above the fire. There was a shelf above the hearth, with a piece of whitened driftwood curved like an antler, a couple of sea urchin shells, and – 'What's that?' asked Archie sharply, forgetting to be polite.

Breesha and Billy swung round to see what he was looking at. 'Which?' asked Diya, staring at the gable wall, as she held the broth ladle poised over the pot.

'At the end there.' It was all Archie could do not to jump up from his bench to see. 'A fossil of some kind, I do believe. A very fine specimen, too.'

'That's the goniatite!'

'That's our goniatite!'

'That's Master Forbes' goniatite!'

The children all chorused at once, even Breesha. Lucy, who hadn't said a word since everyone came in, got up and fetched the lump of limestone from the shelf, and laid it on the table in front of Archie. 'Have a look at it, if you like,' she said to him.

Archie picked up the goniatite and turned it over, examining it closely. It was made of solid limestone, but its form was that of a coiled shell. It fitted snugly in the palm of his hand. He could see every ripple in the shell, every delicate convolution. It wasn't hard to imagine that a quivering creature huddled inside, alive as anyone in the room. But the shell had turned to solid stone.

'Master Forbes said it was once a live snail-thing,' said Mally. 'But now it's turned to stone.'

'He didn't know why,' said Billy.

'There's a standing stone at Meayll,' remarked Breesha suddenly, to no one in particular. 'It used to be a troll. It ought to have gone home before the sun rose but it didn't. As soon as the light struck it turned to solid stone. That's true, because I've seen it – the stone, I mean.'

It was the first time Breesha had entered a conversation that included the visitors, but Archie wasn't listening. It was Ben who answered, keeping his tone deliberately casual, 'Sometimes you get whole rings of stones like that. You'd think those trolls would be more careful, would you no?'

'It belongs to Master Forbes, you say?' said Archie.

'No,' said Billy. 'He gave it to us.'

'Really? Did he find it here?' asked Ben.

'He couldn't have,' said Archie absently, examining the goniatite. 'There's no limestone here.' He turned suddenly to Lucy. 'Is there? At low ebb, perhaps? Certainly there's none on the surface.'

'No,' said Lucy doubtfully. 'I don't think so.'

'He brought it on the boat with him,' Billy said. 'It comes from Langness. He'd been looking at rocks all along from there to Port St Mary, so he had it with him. Finn brought him, and left him here for three days to look at our island.'

'He was the first stranger who ever came,' said Mally.

'That's not true,' said Lucy. 'When I was little the engineers came from Liverpool to put in the extra reflectors. They brought toffee in a brown paper bag. Jim and I hadn't ever had toffee before – we didn't know what it was. But we tried some, and it was first rate.' She didn't mention the other visitors who'd come five years ago, and she hoped neither Breesha nor Billy would decide to remind her. Luckily they were absorbed in watching Mr Buchanan examine the goniatite.

'What's toffee?' asked Mally. 'Can *we* have some?'

'But Master Forbes was the last visitor we had,' went on Diya. 'And that was the summer before last. A very interesting young man, Master Forbes. He was only sixteen, but he'd studied rocks all over the Island – the Isle of Man, I mean – he'd been looking at the rock formations at Langness. Then he walked along to Port St Mary, and met Finn on the shore, just loading the boat to come out here. So he asked if he could come along with him.'

'Finn liked him too,' said Billy.

'I knew Langness well when I was a girl,' remarked Diya, making conversation, 'but I'd never thought of the different kinds of rock all being piled up in layers before. Or about the fern-patterns on the rocks being fossils. Master Forbes had been making drawings of them – he'd taught himself all about them. I should think that young man will go far.'

'Where is he?' asked Archie abruptly. 'This Master Forbes? Is he in Castletown?'

'Oh no, he's left the Island now. He went away to college, Finn said. London, or Edinburgh – somewhere like that,' said Diya vaguely.

Archie pushed his bowl away, and took a magnifying glass from an inner pocket. He'd obviously forgotten the family were at table. He examined the goniatite, oblivious to them all, even though Billy and Mally were craning over his shoulder, trying to see through the thick lens as well.

'Master Forbes stayed here for two nights,' Diya told Ben. 'He went all over the island, studying everything.'

'We saw a minke whale while he was here,' said Billy, without looking up.

'We liked him,' said Mally.

The goniatite would have lived in the shallows of the sea. It had once been a gastropod like a whelk or a winkle, or more like a sea snail really, but much larger. There was no living creature left in the world, so far as anyone knew, that exactly corresponded to it. Or not in these seas. Perhaps when he was on the *Beagle* they'd find living examples of species long thought to be lost . . . Captain Fitzroy had thought so: why, he'd argued, would anything have been created, only to be extinguished long before the end? Archie wasn't sure about

Captain Fitzroy, though . . . he hadn't told him everything he'd been thinking about. There'd been a painful scene at home, last time Archie had visited his parents, when his father had called him a blasphemer, and his mother had ended up sobbing into her handkerchief. Archie's parents were not untypical; perhaps on the *Beagle* he'd be able to discuss these matters in a true spirit of philosophical inquiry. But what else had lived in that primeval sea where the goniatite had once flourished? And how long ago? It was long before the Sixth Day dawned – metaphorically speaking, of course – and there could have been no eyes to see. No rational eyes, anyway. No consciousness, no thought. *Why?* That was the question Mr Lyell – and this young Forbes, whoever he might be – found written on the rocks all round them.

The rocks . . . but perhaps the real answer lay in the sea. The eternal sea, untrammelled by thought or reason, where perhaps nothing had changed . . . These good people thought Archie had been deprived, never setting eyes on the sea until he was four years older than the unknown Forbes had been when he came to Ellan Bride. They were wrong. It was a gift to come first to an unknown element long after one had attained the age of reason, and to be able to perceive it with a clear mind. And yet it hadn't been quite like that.

Archie's yearning for unknown horizons had already been whetted on the banks of the Clyde, where he'd seen the great sailing ships from all around the world moored at anchor, and the steamers docked at the new piers. Sometimes he'd watched a brig or a schooner unfurl its sails, and glide silently downriver towards that world he'd never seen: the open sea . . . And then, that first week in Edinburgh, standing on the summit of Arthur's Seat – for his instinct in any new place was to get an overview as soon as he could – he'd looked out on an expanse of blue, and found no horizon, only a distant haze where sky and sea merged into indefinable brightness. That was before he'd ever heard the waves breaking on the shore, or felt the salt spray on his skin. But even then, watching the light play across the distant waters, he'd felt a quickening of the heart that had had – if he were totally honest with himself – nothing to do with reason. Rather, it was a sense of awe as overwhelming as the element that inspired it. And now, sitting in the lighthouse kitchen on Ellan Bride, if he shut out their voices, and listened only to the sound of the waves outside, and the cries of the circling gulls, the same sense was with him still, accompanied by an infinite number of questions. Only the answers remained as unfathomable as ever.

Chapter 15

OF COURSE LUCY SHOULD HAVE KNOWN THAT THE SURVEYORS would want to come into the lighthouse. Ever since they'd arrived she'd been longing for the evening, when she could leave everyone behind, as she always did, and return to her real work. So much had happened since dinner-time she'd started to feel as if her head would burst. Talking to two complete strangers was exhausting, and Diya's words in the garden had brought back too many memories. She was tired, too, because she'd been woken less than an hour into her afternoon's sleep. She wanted to get back to the simplicity of darkness, her own company, and the familiar light.

That was why she'd come up to the lantern early. She sat on the parapet with the window open behind her, watching the sun slowly set in a glow of pink and orange behind the dark blue hills of Ireland. To the north-west, a dozen or so herring smacks were coming in to fish off the Calf. High in the sky above the boats, streaks of cloud, purple in the evening sun, were moving slowly westward. The Creggyns were under water, and only the long tails of the changing tide showed where they were. It was one of those evenings when the far lands moved in closer, while the sea seemed like a silvery lake. The speck out to sea between here and Wales was the steamship on its way from Liverpool to Dublin. It was earlier than usual because of the calm weather.

She'd walked out on the tussle between Diya and Breesha.

She never had that sort of trouble with Billy. Maybe he'd get more difficult too. Lucy hoped not. She had a certain sympathy with Breesha – when Lucy had been a child she'd resisted the girl's part, too – but this particular fight was merely stupid. No, not stupid – Breesha had more wit than most – it was more a desperate sort of innocence. Didn't the child *realise*? Obviously not, and someone ought to tell her, before – before they had to leave the island, anyway. Lucy caught her breath at this sudden new light on the reality of their departure.

The fight had started because Lucy and Diya had made up the kitchen bed, where Breesha and Billy usually slept, with clean sheets for the guests. They'd done the same for Master Forbes two years ago. Lucy had laid out a bolster and blanket for Billy by the hearth. Then Breesha and Mally had come in from feeding the pigs, and Diya had told Breesha to move her nightgown through to the bedroom. Luckily the surveyors had been out – painting marks all over the island without a by-your-leave, no doubt – so at least they hadn't heard the row. But what did Breesha *expect*, at her age? It was time, Lucy thought grimly, that her mother explained a few things to her. Lucy had had to learn the hard way, but she wouldn't wish that on Breesha, especially with no island to go home to.

The sun was almost touching the mountains of Mourne. Lucy got up and went into the lantern, ducking under the lintel of the open window. She'd just picked up the taper and tinderbox, and laid them out, ready to light, when she heard the door open at the foot of the tower. Men's voices echoed up the spiral stair. Damn them! *Damn* them! They were taking their time, evidently having a good look round down there. Well, they'd find nothing amiss. Shod feet stamped up the steps. They probably thought of the lighthouse as theirs already. Certainly they hadn't hesitated to paint a great black stripe on the north side of it. No doubt they had their reasons, but they might have asked.

Lucy was standing by the light, holding the unlit taper,

when Archie, and then Ben, appeared at the top of the ladder.

'Can we have a look at the light?'

At least Mr Buchanan had *asked*. Lucy had been ridiculously afraid he might not. After all, what difference did it make now?

'Of course.'

It was irrational, but Lucy couldn't help hoping they were noticing how well-maintained the lights were. She'd realised that what Ben Groat thought of her wouldn't change the Commissioners' minds, and even Mr Buchanan probably had very little influence. It wasn't that she hoped for anything; it was simply because the lights were these men's work, as they were Lucy's, and she wanted them to see that she was good at her job. Even though she didn't want them here and didn't care what they thought. No, that wasn't true. She *did* care, and wished she didn't, because she was going to lose all this anyway.

'It's a fine example of a primitive catoptric system,' said Archie, when he'd walked twice around the light. 'These must be some of the earliest parabolic reflectors in a Scottish light. And these are early Argand burners – dae ye ken where they came from? They're no the original lights, obviously, but Atholl's records dinna mention any replacements.'

'This isn't a Scottish light,' said Lucy coldly. 'These lights were installed in 1790. My grandparents had cresset lights here before that.'

'In 1790? But no all three tiers,' said Archie, peering into the shining reflectors. 'I think masel that the top tier was installed a little later.'

Maddeningly, he was quite right. 'Yes, they started with eight reflectors. But the Liverpool merchants petitioned the Duke – that's what my father told me – to make the light brighter. So he had the other four put in later.'

'When?'

Lucy did a quick sum in her head. *When I was four* was much too personal to say to the ice-cold Mr Buchanan. 'In 1808,' she told him.

'So now you can see it from four leagues away?' Ben asked her.

Lucy nodded. 'In very clear weather you can see it from Scarlett Point, just by Castletown.'

'The Duke was abreast of the times,' said Archie. 'The first Argand light like this in Scotland was in '87 – that's when they built the light at Kinnaird Head. These are gey fine examples – I've no seen so many facets in a single reflector. Look, Ben, it's a superb piece of craftsmanship.'

'They were made in Liverpool,' said Lucy to Archie's back.

'I wish we'd seen it from the sea,' Archie said to Ben. 'Mind you, a dioptric system should increase visibility to eight leagues. Wi the new lenses you'll see this light a lot further away than Castletown. You might even see it frae Ireland.' He turned abruptly to Lucy. 'Can you ever see the South Rock light from here?'

'No.'

'Have *you* ever seen this light from just by Castletown?' Ben asked her.

'Yes.' Lucy looked past him. The sun had almost dipped behind the mountains. 'Excuse me, sirs. I must light the lamps.'

She knelt down with her back to them. They heard the scrape of the strike-a-light. Lucy blew out the tinder, and stood up with the lit taper in her hand. She began to go carefully round the lights, tier by tier: west, south, east, north. Slowly the lantern filled with light. The surveyors stopped talking and watched the lightkeeper. Through the open window the waves breaking on the shore sounded like the breath of the sea itself, bringing the lantern alive with its light. Gradually the sunset dimmed as the light inside grew stronger. When all twelve lights were lit, they merged into one strong circular beam, reflecting outward into sudden night.

Ben sat down on the top step of the stair, below the beam of light, and considered the lightkeeper, while Archie made notes on the light.

'Sir,' said Lucy, from behind Archie, 'would you mind not standing in the way of the beam?'

Archie squatted on his heels, still writing, apparently oblivious to her tone.

The lightkeeper obviously wanted them to go away. When they didn't, she sat on the floor, out of the path of the light, and evidently prepared to wait. Ben watched her, wondering when she'd been to Castletown, and what had happened to her there. He was willing to bet it must be about eleven years ago. Only one male stranger ever seemed to have stayed on Ellan Bride since she was a toddling bairn, and that was the youthful Master Forbes, two years ago. So Lucy had been to Castletown, had she? Clearly she wasn't willing to talk about it. Living here all her life, with just one brother, must have been a curious life for a lass. Maybe it had made her too straightforward. When she was sure of herself she treated a man as if she were another man herself. Then suddenly she'd turn as prickly as a hedgehog – much more like a lass – but Ben reckoned that was only because she was scared. The other one – Aunt Deer, was it, Billy called her? – she'd survive leaving Ellan Bride all right. Ben had a feeling she mightn't be entirely sorry to go, either. Ellan Bride was a far cry from India, and Aunt Deer seemed to be a woman who knew the world, perhaps better than anyone currently on this island. But the lightkeeper – that was another kettle of fish – a fellow could only hope she'd manage to make her way in the world. Would she put a ring on her finger when she left here? He had a feeling she wouldn't want to, and by the time she realised that she must, it would be too late, for her, and for the boy too. But there wouldn't be anyone to tell her that.

'Are you going to replace these lights then?' asked Lucy suddenly.

Archie, absorbed in his writing, seemed to have no notion how hard it had been for Lucy to ask that question. He replied at once, 'Oh ay. We'll probably use the new Fresnel lenses.'

Lucy looked blank.

'Fresnel lenses?' Archie looked up at her. 'You don't know? Och, they've been using them in France for near on ten years. Fresnel designed the first for the lighthouse at Cordouan. The way it works – instead of having a single dioptric lens, you have a central lens, and concentric rings built up round it. That way you refract far more light back into a single beam – nearly a third more than you'd get from any catoptric system. Here –' he held his notebook so she could see '– like this.'

She reluctantly moved near enough to look. As Lucy watched Archie draw, Ben watched Lucy. She frowned in just the same way as Billy when she was concentrating. It was Aunt Deer who taught the children their lessons. Did that mean that the lightkeeper was not used to book-learning? Ben suspected that might be the case. Who would have taught her, anyway? Archie was explaining to her about the necessary refractive index of the glass to be used in the widening concentric lenses, and Ben was fairly sure that she wasn't taking in one word. But there was absolutely no doubt that she knew her job. Ben had seen more than a dozen lighthouses in operation over the last seven years, and this was the best-maintained light he'd come across yet. All was in perfect order – the tower, the store room, the log book, the tools, and not least the lights themselves. The standard of the Ellan Bride light would be hard to beat, and the chances were it would never be as good as this again. It was a crying shame. And however many concentric lenses they put in the new tower, something good would have gone for ever.

'You see?' said Archie to Lucy, putting his pencil back in its case.

'Mmm,' said Lucy, heartily wishing that they'd go. They'd been in the tower the best part of an hour, and she wanted to see the planets appearing. The night was as clear as could be, and just now Saturn, Mars, Venus and Mercury – from south declining to north – were all lined up in the western sky in a most unusual fashion. Tomorrow, if it stayed clear, the new moon would join them, almost due west between Mars and

Saturn. Lucy wanted to watch, on her own, and have a chance to think in peace.

'I'm thinking we should leave the lightkeeper in peace now, sir,' said Ben, uncannily echoing her thought. 'That's if we're going to look at the light from outside, and get a good night's sleep, and you're wanting an early start.' He smiled at Lucy. 'Thank you for showing us your lights. They're in the best condition I've ever seen, if you don't mind me saying so. And I've seen a few.'

She gave Ben a fleeting, troubled smile, but clearly her mind was elsewhere. Archie closed his notebook. 'Thank you, Miss Geddes,' he said curtly, and followed Ben down the ladder.

Chapter 16

CLEANING THE LANTERN NEXT MORNING WAS JUST THE SAME as usual, except for what was happening on Dreeym Lang. The puffins were circling the lighthouse tower as they had done since the day it was built. Through the open window of the lantern Breesha and Lucy could hear the cries of the kittiwakes from Giau yn Stackey. The basking shark was back offshore, close to Stack yn Ineen: they could see the big triangular fin, and the tail fin about fifteen feet behind it, cruising slowly along the wide entrance of the giau, as the great fish grazed among the seaweed forests. All these things had been there since long before the lighthouse, from before the keeill even, perhaps from the very beginning of time itself. When you thought about the island in that way, the lighthouse, and with it the arrival of Gaffer and Gammer fifty years ago, had sprung into existence just in the very last second of the island's history. Lucy's whole life – nearly – had been spent here, but as far as the island was concerned that was of no more moment than this year's eggs incubating in the puffin burrows. Less, in fact, because the eggs, if you considered them as a whole, and not as each one separate from the others, had been here for ever. But then, Lucy's mind was able to imagine the island – as she was doing at this very moment – lying here uninhabited ever since the world was made. Everything the island was, and ever had been, existed inside her head, like the idea of a bird in the yolk of an egg. But nothing was more easily broken than one little egg.

Whatever it was the surveyors were doing down at the foot of the tower, it marked the beginning of an ending that neither Breesha nor Lucy could quite fathom. Two days ago it had seemed as if nothing would ever change – no, that wasn't true: the letter had already come. Lucy just hadn't fully taken it in. Whereas Breesha, Lucy thought, sighing, had grasped their plight immediately. Perhaps the child's crazy defiance had arisen out of a clear-sightedness that Lucy lacked. Lucy wasn't sure. But neither of them was able to concentrate this morning, and, after all, there was no hurry. The day stretched ahead; it didn't matter if they were up here until dinner-time. It was easier than being in the garden, sowing vegetables that might never be harvested, or only by unimaginable strangers. Of all the family, unlike each other though Lucy and Breesha were, they were probably the most vulnerable to what might happen. Obscurely aware of all this, Lucy made no attempt to stop Breesha leaving her work to watch what was going on. On the contrary, where Breesha led, she was occasionally willing to follow.

'Aunt Lucy, you have to look!' Breesha wriggled further along so Lucy could crouch beside her on the parapet. 'They've hammered an iron peg into the crack on the high rock of Hamarr. *That's* what all the hammering was. See? Over there! But they can't put a new lighthouse *there*. It'd fall down the cliff!'

'They've got to do all the measuring first,' said Lucy. 'It'll be to do with that.' She went back to her polishing, but she didn't call Breesha away.

'They've got another of those arrows with the red flags at the top of Cronk Sheeant,' reported Breesha, loud enough for Lucy to hear, but not the men. If the surveyors knew they were being watched they gave no sign of it. 'And now Mr Groat's given Billy one of the long poles. Look, they're right down below us. He's making Billy hold the pole right by the lighthouse . . . Now the Writing Man is walking away . . . He's going in a straight line towards Cronk Sheeant . . . He's measuring, like for planting potatoes.'

Lucy stopped polishing the top reflectors and glanced down to Dreeym Lang. Archie was pacing with a peculiar long stride. 'Yards,' said Lucy. 'He'll be pacing how many yards.'

They could see the top of Billy's head down below, where he stood holding the pole, which was a good deal taller than he was. Breesha and Lucy watched Archie stop pacing when he reached the top of Cronk Sheeant, and look back towards Billy. He made a note in his book.

'Well, well,' Lucy sighed. 'We've work of our own to do, Breesha veen.'

'Aunt Lucy?' said Breesha presently, rubbing away at the many little mirrors as they winked in the morning sun.

'Mmm?'

'If they're building a new light . . . if there's going to be a new lighthouse . . .'

'Mmm?'

'What's going to happen to all these?' Breesha stopped polishing, and squinted across her reflector to check there were no smears. An infinite number of Breeshas, all at slightly different angles, squinted back. The glass was perfect. Breesha sat back so she could breathe out without misting it up. 'To our lights? Will they cast them all away?'

Lucy stopped polishing and stared at her. Outside, they heard the rattle of a metal chain.

'What's *that*?'

Back on watch, they saw the big chain had been undone. Ben was holding each end of it by a brass handle. They watched him pull both ends until the chain was lying in a double row stretched across the turf. Then he took one end of the chain. 'Right, stay by your mark, Billy!' they heard Mr Buchanan say.

Mr Buchanan was beside Billy now, out of sight below the lighthouse tower. Breesha stood up and leaned over the iron parapet so she could see where he'd gone. 'He's down there,' she hissed to Lucy. 'That's where they painted that line yesterday, right on the tower.'

Ben was walking backwards very slowly towards the arrow on Cronk Sheeant. He laid out the chain as he went, and he kept looking back to the place where Archie must be standing just below them.

'Mr Buchanan's pointing,' whispered Breesha, leaning as far over the parapet as she dared. 'Left, and left. Right. What's he doing that for?'

Lucy stood up cautiously, and leaned over beside Breesha. Archie had no idea they were directly above him. 'I could spit on his hat,' whispered Breesha beside her.

'You will not!'

Being directly above Archie, Lucy saw that a straight line from the circle of his hat would go through Billy's pole and the summit of Cronk Sheeant. Ben was laying out the chain along the line; whenever it deviated from the line Archie signalled him back into position. Gradually the unfolding chain revealed a pattern. Through the telescope Lucy could see how the markers along its length all had different outlines, though the same ones were repeated regularly, like the varying wings of different birds. She didn't worry about Archie looking up and seeing her. If ever a man were absorbed in a particular task – and Lucy knew very well what that was like – Mr Buchanan was absorbed in his. When the chain reached the arrow on Cronk Sheeant, he hurried over to Ben, and wrote in his book. He had his big book with the leather cover, and a small green notebook. At the moment he was using the green notebook. There was something innocent, thought Lucy, as she focused the telescope directly on his face, about his complete concentration. That's why he takes no notice of us, she realised. Diya said last night she wondered what he was writing: well, I don't wonder. I *know*. Not how to do the measuring – I don't know that – but I know *how* he's thinking about the measuring and not about us. It'll be like doing the lighthouse records – the dates each new barrel is opened, lists of supplies and notes on the ships and the weather. Anyone would be allowed to read that notebook. It would all be very carefully recorded and quite transparent, so nobody could get it wrong. Sometimes Diya wrote things down in a notebook of her own which no one else ever saw. Lucy didn't see the point of that. Maybe that was why Diya thought Mr Buchanan's book would tell them something they didn't know. Well, thought Lucy, it wouldn't. It would be too straightforward for that. That meant that Mr Buchanan was not the enemy, however rude he might be. He was just the surveyor. Lucy wondered if she could explain all this to Breesha, and whether it would help the child if she did. She sighed, and went back to polish the south-facing reflectors, which was as far away from the surveyors as she could get.

'The Writing Man's going back to the high rock mark,' reported Breesha from the parapet. 'What's he going to do now? Mr Groat's coiled up the chain again. He's taking it back to the first mark and laying it out double like it was the first time. Now he's pulling it out. Aunt Lucy, you have to come and *look*. Look there! See – now they're measuring between Billy's pole and the high rock mark.'

'They'll be at it all day,' said Lucy presently, and went inside again.

There was silence for a while except for the waves breaking and the distant clamour of birds, punctuated by voices from below. Presently Lucy heard the chain rattle once more. The sound was followed by a long pause.

'They've coiled it up,' called Breesha. 'But they've left arrows in each place they measured to. Now they've gone back to the high rock mark. What's the Writing Man doing now? He's standing on the rock, right on the mark they painted. Aunt Lucy, you *have* to come and look!'

Lucy came out with the telescope. No one was looking up at the tower. She quietly raised the glass to her eye and focused on Archie again. 'It's a compass,' she said. 'He's taking bearings, like we do on the ships.'

'Three three eight,' Archie said, loud enough for them to hear. He wrote something in his notebook. Then he took another bearing on Billy's mark. 'Two four three.'

He put the compass away, and Lucy went back into the lantern with the telescope. Breesha stayed where she was. She watched the men gather up the chain and arrows, and move away towards Cronk Sheeant, where they seemed to be starting off with the poles and chain all over again. Billy had to stand in a different place holding the pole, and once the Writing Man spoke sharply to him for not keeping it straight. It was all taking a long time. Breesha sighed, and followed Lucy back to the reflectors.

'Oh look,' said Billy to Ben Groat, as soon as he was allowed to put the pole down again. 'There's the basking shark!'

Archie and Ben followed his pointing finger. They could see the shark cruising slowly off Giau yn Stackey. The Writing Man immediately took a miniature telescope from his pocket. Billy watched him clip the covers back from the lens, and pull out two brass sections until the telescope was three times as long. Archie trained it on the shark, and twisted the smallest brass section until the focus was right. Torn between wanting to see how a telescope that folded in on itself like that could possibly work, and wanting to show that he knew all about the basking shark, Billy said to Ben, 'It comes in the spring and autumn mostly. We think it's the same one. I've looked at it through *my* telescope. If it turns over you can see its white belly under water. It does that when it's eating, I think. But it doesn't eat people or anything. A killer whale might, though. Sometimes we have *lots* of killer whales. They go round and round the island looking for seals. But the basking shark is always just by itself, and it only eats fishes.'

'Hardly even that,' said Archie absently, still looking through the telescope. 'It eats very small creatures – plants and animals – that float below the surface of the sea.'

'How do you ken *that*?' asked Ben. 'You've looked inside its mouth?'

'Yes.'

Billy gazed at him, his own mouth dropping open. 'In the *sea*?'

Archie lowered the telescope and smiled. Billy hadn't noticed him smile before; he looked quite friendly. 'No. I was once working on an island called Islay, and there was a basking shark washed up in Laggan Bay. I went over and had a look very early one Sunday morning. It was the only day we had off – though unfortunately somebody saw me, even at that hour. It was worth it, but smelly. I cut through its gills with my knife, and I could see – it has great huge bristles inside its throat and gills, like filters. It couldna swallow anything big.'

'But it's got a huge mouth!' cried Billy, forgetting to be shy. 'I've seen it!'

'Ah, but it's like this.' Archie squatted beside Billy, and opened his notebook at the back. One side was already filled with the drawing of the goniatite, and some very neat script underneath. Archie was making a rapid sketch on the blank page. It looked more like a fat worm than a fish. Archie drew a big gaping mouth, a little eye, and five big grooves along the side. 'Those are the gills, see. So if it cruises around like that one out there is doing, wi its mouth open, it picks up all the wee plants and animals floating in the surface water, and then it spurts out the water through its gills. Like that – see?'

'You mean like spitting through its nose.' Billy considered, and then said, 'Why?'

'What do you mean, *why*? The beast must eat.'

'But why like that? *Why* does it have bristles? *Why* does it spit through its gills? Why doesn't it have teeth? Other fishes have teeth.'

An image of the goniatite flashed through Archie's mind. The limestone beds by Castletown were crammed with inexplicable creatures. In the hard slate of Ellan Bride there were probably none. *Why?* The boy was right: that was the question one had to ask. Mr Lyell must have asked himself the very same thing, and now his book was boldly suggesting some possible answers. Had Archie himself known, when he was ten years old, with the same certainty as Billy, the correct question to ask? And if so, who had led him astray? He was certain there were more answers lurking, like an unseen presence, here on Ellan Bride and in all the other places he'd observed in one short life-time. Archie gazed out at the basking shark. The sea around it was bubbling like a pot on the boil, with all the little fishes jumping to the surface in turmoil as the great black shadow swam over them. Evidently they didn't know the huge fish had no teeth. *Why* didn't they know? What atavistic instinct told them what to fear, even if it was all illusion? But the answer eluded him: slippery as a will o' the wisp, the unknowable seemed to mock him – to mock the whole world he came from – because he'd only been taught how to ask questions that already had an answer.

Billy was still looking at the drawing of the basking shark. He evidently abandoned the larger question for something that Archie could reply to. 'Can you draw *anything*? Can you draw a killer whale?'

'Ay.' Archie stood up, shaking off his reverie. 'But we've work to do. If you want, I'll draw you one later.'

'Tonight?' Billy looked at the Writing Man with a new respect. 'I mean, I've seen *lots* of killer whales, of course. And when they jump you can see them all right. But I've never seen one except in the sea.'

'Nor have I. But there are illustrations.'

'Illus – rashuns?'

'Illustrations – engravings – in books.' Archie closed his own notebook dismissively, but then he seemed to think of something else. He suddenly turned his attention to Billy, as if he were a specimen laid out for observation. 'Has anyone taught you to read and write?'

'We do lessons with Aunt Diya,' said Billy a little sulkily. He wanted to talk about whales, not lessons. 'I can read print. And I can write a bit. And we do sums and things.'

'You have opportunities for field observation here that few

boys have,' remarked Archie. 'If you can write, you should keep a record of what you observe.'

Ben caught Billy's puzzled glance. 'He means you see lots of animals and birds that boys in other places canna see. You could have a notebook like his and write down what you see. And the date you saw it on. Your Aunt Deer hasna telt you about whales? You havena got any pictures of sea creatures in books?'

Billy wriggled. He preferred the sort of questions they'd been asking before, which he could answer with easy authority. And he didn't want a notebook in the least, though he wouldn't mind having a pocket telescope with folding-up sections. 'Stories,' he mumbled. 'Like Jonah.'

'Ay well,' said Ben. 'I doubt you'll be wanting to observe your whales from the inside.'

Billy grinned. Archie had turned away from them. He was looking across at Towl Doo, and writing something in his notebook. 'We used to play Jonah in the keeill,' Billy told Ben, quietly so Archie couldn't hear. 'Breesha said we could pretend it was the whale's belly. We covered the entrance with a blanket to block out the light. But Mally had nightmares and Aunt Diya said we had to stop.'

'I think I'd have had nightmares too. Does your cousin often think of games like that?'

Billy thought it over. 'She's the best at thinking of games. But she doesn't like just looking – I mean *observing* – observing things much. She could write it down all right, but she gets bored with just looking.'

Through the telescope Breesha was looking at the fish jumping all round the shark in Giau yn Stackey. It was just like on the island, she thought. They all had to stop what they were doing and get into a great turmoil because the enemy had come. From the top of the tower she was beginning to see a pattern in what the men down below were doing. Bit by bit they were moving across the top of the island, measuring between the red-flagged arrows they'd put in yesterday. That must be what the Writing Man was putting in his notebook. She couldn't work out why they were doing it, but they must be getting the shape of the island from the way all the arrows connected up to one another, like writing invisible lines between the stars to make pictures of men and animals. If they weren't enemies she could ask them. Lucy had gone, but Breesha went on observing the enemy, waiting to see what they did next.

When they got to Carn Vane they used the Carn itself to measure from. When Breesha focused on the heap of white stones on the bare turf she saw they hadn't bothered to mark it; obviously it was enough of a marker in itself. That was what it was for: when you were out in the boat in late summer, if you lined up Carn Vane with the Saint's cell below the keeill, you could get right over the best place for mackerel. Breesha wondered if Billy had told the enemy that. Surely he wouldn't! Finn said you should never tell anyone your fishing marks. They hadn't even told Master Forbes, and he'd been a friend. Even if it didn't matter any more – even if they were sent away and never went fishing again – Billy wouldn't betray them all like that.

All of a sudden Mally appeared below the tower. Breesha watched her running her fastest along the ridge to Carn Vane. It was too far away to hear what she was saying to the men, but Ben Groat laid the gear in a neat pile by the cairn, and the Writing Man put his notebook away. As they strolled back towards the tower Breesha could see they were talking. Billy walked beside them. When Breesha set the sights on Billy's face she saw he was smiling.

Mally ran ahead, vanished out of Breesha's line of sight below the tower, and a moment later Breesha heard the patter of footsteps on the stone stair. 'Breesha? Are you up there? Mam says dinner-time!'

Chapter 17

DIYA SQUATTED BY THE WELL, DIPPED HER CUPPED HANDS into the cool water, and drank. When she'd finished she didn't get up at once. Under the lee of Hamarr, the sun, trapped in the hollow of the cliff, was actually hot. The air smelt of clover. The long crescent of sand at Traie Vane shone white as the moon. Small waders were running up and down the receding tideline, where little waves curled and broke. If she half-closed her eyes and looked at the sea, it turned into an endless pattern of shifting sparkles, almost too brilliant to bear. The blue hills of Cumberland were three-dimensional today, they'd come so close. But nothing was quite as it seemed. As soon as she left the shelter of the cliff she'd feel the wind. The pattern of the waves was not just reflections; there were little white-caps out there as well. Lucy would write in the log book 'a light easterly breeze'. None of them – not even her own children – had any notion of what Diya meant by 'cold'.

Cold had been her enemy for more than twenty years. Did one ever become accustomed? Cold was a metallic shade of grey. Sailing north, twenty-two years ago, the sky had vanished, and gradually a lowering greyness had crept into its place. Even to look at the grey had made her heart turn cold. When she went on deck the wind had blown its ice-laden breath right into her face. It was like being gradually pushed down a deep well. One had to get out into the light, but even the light was cold. The garden at Castletown had been enclosed by high walls, and there were places where Diya could turn her face to the sun and actually feel its warmth. That's how she'd first become friends with the cat. The cat sought out just the same places, and in her first loneliness Diya felt she'd found a friend.

But that was long ago. Diya jumped up, slung her knapsack over her shoulder, and ran down the hill to Traie Vane.

The sea was cold too. She walked along at the edge of the breaking waves. The waders ran ahead, keeping out of her way, then took to their wings in a flash of white, and settled back to their feeding a few yards behind her. Traie Vane was one of the best places on the island. In India there'd been a white beach too, fringed by coconut palms. The sea was so warm they could walk right into it. She remembered walking with her cousins in their bright saris, the colour reflecting on the blue water as the cousins walked in, waist-high – almost up to Diya's neck. She remembered clutching their hands, jumping up and down in the sea and being able to jump so much higher than on land, like magic . . . and then when they came out their clothes were dry in a moment. Not like here – now – with her wet gown flapping round her ankles. She could no more walk into this sea than fly over it. Traie Vane was made for the waders, not for human beings.

She made a quick gesture of reverence as she passed the keeill. It was curious how the weather – and the letter, perhaps – had brought so many memories back . . . it was the future she ought to be thinking about, not the long-ago past. The future was in her hands – all their futures – because she was the only one capable of making any sensible plans. But it wasn't just plans that had to be thought of. It was also a question of being honest with oneself.

As Diya skirted the top of Baie yn Geinnagh Veg, half a dozen seals humped their way down to the water when her shadow fell across them. It was a help to be alone so that she could think things over. Unlike Lucy, Diya had been able to take in what the letter said when it first came, and she'd considered the matter from all angles before the surveyors ever set foot on the island. But now that the surveyors were here, somehow, in an odd way, they'd allayed some of Diya's fears. Not by anything they'd said or done, but simply by *being*. They came from the outside world, and they reminded her that that world was not a huge and overwhelming mass, but simply another set of places, another set of people. You didn't encounter them all in a lump, but one by one. Few were wholly unpleasant. Some were not only well-disposed but also intelligent. One could talk to them, and that was what made life interesting.

That goniatite . . . There'd once been a clergyman, on his holidays, who'd come from across. He'd sat in Grandmother's drawing-room – he must have brought an introduction from somebody – and spoken enthusiastically about the fossils he'd been finding in the limestone beds between Castletown and Port St Mary. Diya – would she have been ten then? eleven? – had thought him yet another tedious old man. So many people visited Grandmother. They were all old, and they all talked a great deal. Diya hadn't realised, when she was a child imprisoned in that drawing-room while the sun shone beckoningly against the windows, that she was gradually learning to talk like that too. Even less had she realised how much she would miss discussing the sorts of things one found in books, when there was no one who was interested. It had been a real pleasure to meet young Master Forbes two years ago, but he'd gone away now, into the wider world. He was a young man, and free. Of course he'd gone.

This Mr Buchanan was neither an elderly clergyman nor a hobbledehoy. On the contrary, he was a very personable young man. He was a gentleman, if not by birth – Diya had no way of judging that – then certainly by education. His profession was respectable enough, although Diya had never actually heard of a gentleman being employed as a surveyor. If Grandmother had still been in Castletown, it was unlikely that Mr Buchanan would have had an introduction to the Wells' house. But if he *had* had an introduction, he wouldn't have disgraced himself. Jim had never been invited Upstairs – of course he had not – any more than Mr Groat would have been. But Mr Buchanan would have been as at home Upstairs as in the kitchen, and he and that long-ago clergyman could have talked quite happily about the goniatite.

Diya was not worried about a change of place, or new people. In fact she'd been thinking about it for a long time. She did worry that Breesha was far too clever to live for ever in a world of her own imaginings. Breesha was already growing unruly, in thought if not in deed. It was one thing for her mother to teach Breesha all she could, but some things one could not learn in solitary lessons. Breesha needed more than a little sister and a stolid boy. She needed a friend as quicksilver as she was herself. She needed what Diya had found when she met Sally. If only Breesha could realise it, Mr Buchanan was not her arch-enemy but the embodiment of opportunity – a messenger from the world outside. But Diya was the only one of the family to recognise that Mr Buchanan was not an enemy. Their real problem was, much less straightforwardly, money.

Diya had had no money when she married Jim. He'd never have come near her if she'd had an income. He could only think of her as being within in his touch when he heard that she was destitute. And if Grandmother had still been alive, Diya would never have been allowed to consider his offer for a moment. If Diya had had money when Grandmother died, there'd have been no Jim, no Breesha, no Mally . . . she'd never have been here on Ellan Bride. So life went on, even without money. Perhaps she was wrong to be so afraid of poverty. Had she not learned better, twelve years ago? For twelve years money had not been important. Diya almost feared that she wouldn't know how to use it any more. Going to market in Castletown, haggling with the fishers, the butcher, the baker, the farmers with their carts of vegetables . . . She never used to go to market with Grandmother, of course, but with Annie. Annie ruled the big kitchen in the basement of the house at Castletown. The kitchen had always been warm. Annie used to let the little cold eight-year-old waif from India sit in the big rocking chair with the cat, right up close to the iron range that took up the whole of the south wall. If only Annie were still in Castletown – she was Breesha and Mally's great-aunt, after all – she'd have done what she could to help them now. But Annie was far away in America, and they probably wouldn't ever see her again.

That had been a shock too, when Diya first arrived: having white servants. Even on the ship, being waited on at table by a white man . . . and then the docks at Liverpool . . . the white porter wheeling their trunks ahead of them on a handcart . . . she'd never seen a white man doing anything like that before. She hadn't even realised that they *could*. Well, one possible solution – Diya had thought about this quite a lot – was to become a servant herself. Not in a private house . . . no private employer would take Breesha and Mally as well . . . but a school, perhaps, or an orphanage . . . something like that. One asset Diya had in abundance was what Lucy called book-learning. Grandmother had seen to that. That was the only thing Diya really did know about – from both angles – how to teach girls. God knew, most girls, whatever their background, knew little enough. She'd be quite capable of running a school of her own, but for that she needed money. Money. Always money.

Diya trod from tussock to tussock between the puffin burrows. Murmurs of disapproval came from underground, while the puffins on the surface waddled grudgingly out of reach. Diya stopped just above Gob Keyl. Someone had stuck a red-flagged arrow in the ground above the arch. Everything else was just the same as usual: the shags clustered on the rocks, the crowded tenements of guillemots and razorbills on Creeggyn y Feeagh. This was the height of the nesting season, and the racket was deafening. By the time the birds left again, so might they – the human inhabitants – have gone too. Where did the birds go to when they left the island? Nobody knew. All one could say was that one day the ledges were filled, and the air filled with the raucous screams of avian family life, and then, within a week, the little ones would be enticed down to the water in the safety of the dark, and one morning they would all be gone. Unlike the human species of Ellan Bride, the birds must know where they were going. Some inner certainty must take them – for surely a puffin or a guillemot was not capable of rational thought – to . . . to *somewhere*. Did puffins *remember*? Or did some blind instinct lead them, old and young alike, over the horizon, none knowing whither? It was a waste of time to speculate. Unless one came back into the world as a puffin the question must remain forever unanswerable. At least if that happened one would never need to know what 'cold' meant.

Diya knelt among the burrows, and took a pair of thick leather gloves from the knapsack. They were big enough to come almost to her elbows. She lay prone on the sandy ground and reached into the nearest burrow. It was empty to the length of her arm. The next burrow was more fruitful. Her hand closed on solid flesh, and even through the tough leather she felt the nip of a powerful bill. The puffin came out struggling and jabbing furiously. With a violent twist Diya wrung its neck, and dropped it, warm and lifeless, into the knapsack. Nothing in the next burrow, and a single egg in the one after that. The fifth burrow yielded another adult, not quite as plump as the first, but good enough. Soon the knapsack was weighed down with five fat puffins. Five puffins – seven people – those surveyors would bring hearty appetites to their Sunday dinner. The birds wouldn't be properly hung – they were best left for up to a week – but if she hung them up this morning, and put them in the pot first thing tomorrow, they could simmer until dinnertime. They should be tender enough. So that was tomorrow taken care of . . . today they'd have to make do with fish stew. It would only be dried fish, but there was no chance of getting the boat out while the men were here, what with everyone having to do extra work. The surveyors hoped to leave on Monday or Tuesday. They were not alone in their hope. Diya prayed that the weather would hold and Finn would be able to come.

Coming back past the keeill, Diya saw Mally on her own, paddling in the shallows of Traie Vane. There wasn't anyone to play with this morning. Billy was working with the surveyors, and it was Breesha's turn to do the light – she'd have to do it every day, in fact, while Billy was working. This might be the moment . . . Diya left the knapsack on the shady side of the keeill, and ran down to the sands.

Diya and Mally met about halfway along the beach. 'Mam,' said Mally, pleased, as Diya fell into step beside her.

They walked along in silence for a bit. It was a good way of thinking, going to and fro while the waves broke and swirled round their feet. On the firm sand they didn't have to be distracted by finding places to tread. When they got to the end of the beach they turned round and started again.

'Did you see what the surveyors were doing today?' asked Diya presently.

'They didn't want me. But the piglings did. I scratched their backs.'

'The piglings' backs? Or the surveyors?'

Mally thought that was very funny. 'I couldn't scratch *their* backs anyway. They'd be *much* too high.'

'You know why the surveyors are here?'

'They're going to build a new lighthouse, Breesha said. It was all in the letter.'

'Breesha?' asked Diya sharply. 'What did *Breesha* know about that letter?'

Too late, Mally realised her mistake. 'Nothing,' she mumbled.

I *see*, thought Diya. Breesha was growing up too fast; sometimes Diya felt she hardly knew her any more. And yet hadn't she just been thinking about Breesha, and her education, and future opportunity? The part of Breesha that was like herself was the very part that alarmed Diya. It was the part that could not rest content, but must always seek to know more, and do more . . . but there was no point pursuing the point with Mally.

'You know, Mally, that when they build the new lighthouse, we're going to have to leave the island?'

It was quite different when Mam said it. When Breesha had told them about the letter in the keeill, it was like a game. It was the sort of game that Breesha *did* think of: a bit frightening and only half-comprehensible, but not exactly real. But when Mam said the same thing, it sounded real, like something that was actually going to happen. That was much more frightening: so frightening, in fact, that Mally couldn't make it mean anything.

Leave the island? Leave the *island*? However hard she tried Mally couldn't make the thought add up to anything at all. 'You mean, go away on the boat with Finn? Like when we went to Port St Mary?' Mally shook her head. 'I don't want to do that any more,' she said decidedly.

'Yes, we'll go on the boat with Finn. And I'm afraid we will have to go to Port St Mary. But we won't stay there. We'll go on to somewhere else.'

Mally looked across the sea to the mountains of the far lands. They were looking quite close today, but they were still blue and unreal. She thought about 'somewhere else', and tried to make it into a real place. 'Castletown?'

'Maybe Castletown. That's where we'll start by going, anyway.' Diya looked down at Mally, who'd begun stamping big splashes into the sea with each footstep, wetting both their skirts. Mally was Jim's daughter, much more than Breesha was; what Mally felt was what Jim would have been feeling. Impossible even to hint to the child that her mother's own feelings were mixed . . . 'It won't be like when we went to Port St Mary, Mally. That was just for a day or two. This will be for good. We're going to live over there. We aren't going to be coming back.'

'What?' said Mally, and jumped very hard, landing on two feet so water splashed all over them. 'See that? I'm a gannet, diving!'

'Mally,' said Diya. 'We're going to go away from Ellan Bride. We've got to. And we won't be coming back.'

Mally stopped jumping. She stood still, staring at her mother, while the next wave broke around her. Her hand crept to her mouth.

'That's what the letter said,' said Diya. 'We have to leave here, and go and live somewhere else.'

Mally bit her fingers so hard that it hurt. But that didn't make Mam say she didn't mean it. She could see the cliffs of Hamarr behind her mother's head, and the tower of the lighthouse, and the blue sky arching over all. She knew, for absolute certain, that she'd remember this moment – the shining sky, the dark outline of her mother's head, the sun-touched cliffs of Hamarr, the circling puffins and the gleaming tower – she would remember this exact moment for ever. She knew that, but this other thing – what Mam was saying – she couldn't grasp it. She felt as if the whole island was wheeling round and round them, like the puffins. Nothing was firm any more, except for the moment they were in, that was suddenly turning everything ordinary into something else.

'You mean . . . leave Ellan Bride . . . leave it for *ever*?'

'Yes.'

Mally looked down as a bigger wave swirled around their feet. It made white lace-like patterns on the sand. Then it went away, and the lace-marks soaked away and vanished.

Diya looked down onto Mally's dark head. She couldn't see her face. 'I'm sorry, Mally,' she said gently. 'But we have to face it.'

'No.'

'What did you say, Mally veen? I can't hear you. Look at me!' Diya took Mally's hand.

'No!' Mally wrenched her hand away. She screamed at Mam, louder than she'd ever screamed in her life. 'No! No! No! Go away! I hate you! I hate you! I won't go away! I won't! No! No! No!' She rushed up the beach and flung herself face down on the sand, screaming. 'No! No! No!'

But when Mam sat down beside her, Mally soon let Mam pick her up, and hold her on her knee and rock her. Mally's screams subsided into desperate sobbing. Diya didn't tell her to hush. She didn't say anything at all. She just rocked Mally in her arms the way she did when she was a baby.

At last the sobs subsided into hiccups. Diya said, 'Mally veen, I think you've cried enough. It won't be all bad. Some of it will be good. None of us wanted it. But it's happening, and now we have to face it.'

'I won't!' Mally didn't sound defiant any more, just exhausted.

After a while Diya said, 'I was a bit older than you when the same thing happened to me. I didn't want to leave my home any more than you want to leave yours. But I had to, all by myself. You won't be all by yourself. We'll all be together.'

'You had your Da,' said Mally, reluctant to be drawn into conversation, but still having to point this out. 'I haven't got a Da.'

'Ah, but I didn't really know him. I'd never lived with him. He just came to visit sometimes, but we always sat outside on the veranda. My Da never came into the house. I'd never eaten with him. He wasn't of our religion, so he never ate with us. The first night I was with him, in Bombay, I couldn't touch the food. I didn't know how to eat, away from my family. I thought I would die, being taken away. But I didn't. Sometimes on the ship I was even happy, although I was sad. And after a while I got used to everything being different.'

'But you didn't like the weather,' murmured Mally in spite of herself.

'No, I hated that. But I'll tell you what I did like. Shall I?' Surely, young as Mally was, she'd begin to see, even if she couldn't admit it yet, that there were other possibilities. Breesha would understand better if only she could be brought to listen. That wasn't going to be easy either: Breesha could be much more obstinate than Mally.

There was a pause. 'All right,' said Mally reluctantly.

'The thing I liked best about the new life,' said Diya, 'was being allowed to go out without a grown-up. In Castletown I was allowed to go out to play. I could go out of the front door and down the steps into the market square all by myself. In India I never went outside the garden on my own. Imagine if you could only go into the garden here, and not go anywhere else on the island! That was what it was like for me at Ajoba's house in India. I used to climb up by the tank in the Indian garden and look over the wall. I could see the road, but I couldn't go out on it even if I wanted to. I could see the people going past down below. The only time I ever saw them on a level was if an elephant went by. I can remember being up on the wall when some white people came riding by on top of an elephant. I could see their faces, right on a level with my own. I was so scared I jumped down and hid.

'But in Castletown I could go out and play with other girls. I'd never had anyone exactly my own age to play with before. My cousins were all much older than me. My Mam had been the youngest, you see, so all my cousins were older. I was the baby, and I'd never had a friend who was my own age and didn't think I was just the little one –' Diya shot a glance at Mally's face when she said that, then went on, staring out to sea while she talked '– but then Annie – I told you about your great-aunt Annie – she was Grandmother's cook – when she was tired of me being in her kitchen "getting under her feet" – that was what she used to say – she used to tell me to go out. "Why don't you go out to play, Miss Diya? There's Miss Sally and Miss Diana, just gone across the square. Why don't you take your hoop and run after them?"

'At first I wouldn't. I was too scared, and it was all too different. But soon Sally was my best friend. She was just the same age as me; our birthdays were the same month. She'd come and knock at our front door, and say, "Can Diya come out?" And I was allowed to go. We could run around the square, or down to the harbour, or out to the fields and the beach. It was the *freedom*, Mally. I'd never felt free like that before.'

'We're free here,' said Mally, sniffing. She smeared the back of her hand across her nose, and wiped her hand on her skirt.

'Another thing I liked was playing with Sally at her house. Sally's Mam was always nice to me. I think she was sorry for me because I'd never had a mother of my own.'

'You did,' pointed out Mally. 'You said everyone has a Mam, only yours died when you were born so you can't remember her.'

'True. The other thing I liked was doing lessons,' went on Diya. 'Mrs Grant taught me to read when we were on the ship. I didn't like it at first. Then I realised it meant I could read books if I wanted to, by myself, whenever I liked. When I got to Castletown I had different teachers for different lessons. Grandmother saw to that. Most of them were nice. I had music lessons with Miss Quayle, and Sally and I had French lessons with a French lady – Mademoiselle Dupin. Later she married a Mr Cunningham. When I was older we had dancing lessons in the ballroom at the George. That was fun, Mally! We did country dances, and quadrilles, and when I was eighteen I was allowed to learn the waltz. But what I always liked doing best was reading. Grandmother had a lot of books, but the books I liked best came from the library. I was allowed to go by myself to the Circulating Library – that's a place with lots of books and you can choose whichever one you want to borrow – I could choose any book I liked, Mally, and take it home to read! All by myself! I'd never have been able to do that in India, even if I had learned to read there.'

'I don't like books with lots of writing in.'

'Yes, you do. You liked *Robinson Crusoe*, and *The Thousand and One Nights* and *Gulliver's Travels*! You liked all of those!'

'But I wouldn't have if *I'd* had to do the reading bit.'

'Ah well, that part gets easier. And when you don't need someone else to read to you, you can do all the choosing. You can read whatever you like!'

'Well, I don't want to,' said Mally. 'I'd rather *do* whatever I like and stay at home on Ellan Bride. I don't want to go away, and you'll never make me want to! You didn't want to go away from India. You told us so! You can't pretend different now!'

'I'm not pretending anything. I'm just saying when you have to do something that seems horrible, you can still look at it from another angle.'

'I don't want to look at it from *any* angle!' Mally began to sob afresh. 'I just want to stay at home on Ellan Bride. I don't want to go *anywhere*!'

Chapter 18

WHEN DIYA AND MALLY CAME INTO THE KITCHEN THEY FOUND Lucy unpacking the box of provisions brought by the surveyors.

'Mr Groat said to unpack them all and help ourselves,' said Lucy, 'seeing as how we're feeding them entirely. Look, they're bringing *three* different sorts of cheese. Three! Look, what do you think this is? It's looking a bit mouldy, isn't it?'

'No,' said Diya. She picked up the cat, who was trying to climb into the box, and dumped her on the floor. 'Get out, Smokey! That's Stilton. What a huge slice, and fancy bringing Stilton cheese on a trip like this! Grandmother used to buy half a Stilton at Christmas. By the time we'd finished it, it was always practically walking. But it's *good*. Here –' she cut a piece off, and crumbled it into three '– try that.'

'Ugh!' said Mally.

'Don't spit! Well?'

'It's a bit strong,' said Lucy. 'I think I like it. I don't know.'

'What's in there?' asked Mally, tugging at an unopened brown paper parcel.

Mally had been crying, but Lucy didn't remark on it. She just said, 'Why don't you open it and see?'

'Salt pork.' Diya was delving in the box. 'More ships' biscuit. Couldn't they have brought fresh bread? What's this? Butter! He should have told us! It's been sitting in the warm kitchen all night – never mind, it'll be fine. Look, Mally, yellow butter made from cows' milk! It'll be *good*. Potatoes, onions . . . what's this? A pie! I know where he bought this! If only we'd known . . . we can heat it up for dinner today. Look, Mally, a real bought meat pie! It was made by the butcher in Castletown. I haven't had one of these since Grandmother died.'

'What are these?' asked Mally, looking at her opened parcel.

'Let's see . . . Oh Mally, he's brought sugar plums! We used to have them for treats when I was a little girl. See, it's a preserved plum on the inside, all coated in sugar. Six sugar plums! Who'd have thought it!'

'So that's what engineers live on!'

It was the first time they'd laughed together since the strangers had come.

'Actually,' said Diya more soberly, 'I think it's what engineers buy when they've heard they're staying on an island that has children.'

'It was Mr Groat who did the shopping,' Lucy said. 'He told us so.'

'What's this big book?' asked Mally, picking up a large blue volume from the other end of the table.

'Be careful with that! That's Mr Buchanan's book,' said Lucy. 'I found him in the yard reading it when I was coming in this morning. Everyone else was still asleep.'

'I don't suppose he slept very well,' said Diya, turning the book round so she could see it. 'The kitchen bed isn't that big.'

'And Mr Groat would have to sort of lie across to fit in it,' pointed out Mally. 'The Writing Man probably got squashed out.'

'*Principles of Geology*,' read Diya, looking at the title page, '*Being an attempt to explain the former changes of the earth's surface by reference to causes now in operation.*' There was a marker about a third of the way through. Diya turned to the first page and started reading.

'What's it about?' asked Lucy, as she put the ships' biscuit on the shelf.

'Geology,' said Diya absently. '*Geology is the science which investigates the successive changes which have taken place in the organic and inorganic kingdom of nature* . . . that means things like rocks and water – how islands like Ellan Bride got made, Mally – and things like plants and birds and animals – creatures like us.'

'You mean things that aren't alive and things that are?' asked Lucy. 'Just so you know – I'm putting the pork in the meat safe.'

'Everything's *alive*,' said Diya. 'At least, it's all part of the same thing.'

'Part of the whole world?' said Mally.

'Listen to this . . . *We trace the long series of events which have gradually led to the actual posture of affairs; and by connecting events with their sources, we are enabled to classify and retain in the memory a multitude of complicated relations* . . .'

'I'm surprised he couldn't sleep if he was reading that,' said Lucy. 'Shall I put the pie in the bread oven?'

'Oh, the pie! Yes, do.' Diya went on reading. 'But it's *interesting*, Lucy,' she said presently. 'What he's saying is, whether you're talking about the rocks that make an island, or people living their lives in history, it's the same thing happening . . . an impulse . . . no, not an impulse . . . more of a *process*. What I mean is – what I think he means – everything is always changing, and you can't understand why properly if you don't work out what happened before, and how everything got to be how it is now: *the state of the natural world is the result of a long succession of events* . . . And that's *true* – I mean, Ajoba taught me that. Everything in the world has come and gone before, more times and through more ages than we can ever imagine. In India we knew that. That's why when I had to be christened and go to church with Grandmother it all seemed so *silly*.'

Silly, reflected Diya, as she went on unpacking the box, and yet oddly reassuring. She could remember going to the temple with Aji – had it been once, or many times? – and being slowly pushed forward in a hot crowd of all castes until they were past the courtyard. They'd queued to be anointed with kumkum, then laid their wreath at the foot of the wonderful, frightening, life-size image of Aji's beloved Ganesha. The Temple had been full of the smell of incense, flowers and sweaty bodies. The parish church at Malew could hardly have been more different, but one thing Diya had learned from Aji and Ajoba was that difference was unimportant. Grandmother, on the other hand, had been convinced that it mattered greatly. Diya and Grandmother had worshipped sedately from their enclosed pew in the new wing of Malew church, where the come-overs sat. Sally sat out of sight with her family in the old part of the church where the landed families had their hereditary pews. Strangers and servants sat upstairs in the gallery. Everything was carefully ordered and in its correct place.

There were so many different ways of looking at things. There was no single principle that made sense – however much the vicar of Malew preached that there was – or at least, no principle that a mere mortal could comprehend. There was no point saying any of this to Lucy. It wasn't that Lucy had no comprehension – it would be unfair to suppose that – but that she wouldn't want to discuss it. Mr Buchanan, now, who'd brought *Principles of Geology* with him to read: *he* might be interested. On the other hand, he might be shocked. Diya had learned in Grandmother's house not to talk too much about the Indian part of her life, because it was too upsetting for people. Diya had kept so many thoughts secret since she was eight years old. It was like keeping the fire doused all the time, never letting it flare up, never letting anyone *see*. But a man who carried *Principles of Geology* around with him . . . she had a notion *he* wouldn't mind seeing what she had to say, if he had the chance.

'There's something else in the box.' Mally was standing on a chair so she could reach right in. She unwrapped the little parcel. 'It's got another bag inside with writing on. What does that say, Mam?'

Diya glanced up and read the label. 'Coffee. Lucy, they've brought *coffee*! They must live like kings!' She put Archie's book down and sniffed the little parcel. 'Oh, how wonderful – it's actually *coffee*! Lucy, smell that. Coffee!'

Lucy laid the bread oven in the grate, and raked hot ashes up all round it. Then she came over and sniffed the bag of coffee. 'Not bad.' She passed it to Mally. 'We could make some after dinner. Can we make it in the teapot?'

'I don't see why not. Mally, sniff that!'

'Ugh! The sugar plums smell a lot nicer than that.'

Later on, when the pie was hot, Lucy sent Mally to call everyone home for dinner. As soon as Mally had left the kitchen she said to Diya, 'You were talking to her, then? Is that what was upsetting her?'

'Of course.' Diya sighed, and laid *Principles of Geology* on the kitchen bed so there was room to lay the table. 'In a way I wish I hadn't. But she has to know. Better to hear it from me and be done with it.'

'You had to be honest.' Lucy frowned as she cut a slab off the big block of butter. She wrapped the rest of the block in a clean cloth, and put it in the water bucket by the door to keep cool. 'Mr Groat understands what it's like for us,' she remarked. 'At least, I think he does. Is there any point asking him . . . I mean . . . he might know if the Commissioners might change their minds. I mean, these surveyors . . . they've seen now that we do know how to look after the light.'

'No one will listen to Mr Groat.'

'I don't know: this Mr Stevenson, who runs it all . . . Mr Groat likes him, you can tell. He *might* be able to have a word with him.'

Diya shook her head. 'No, he wouldn't. Put that out of your head, Lucy. The one who could put in a word is Mr Buchanan. You'd need to talk to him.'

'Why?' Lucy put the bread down on the table, and looked directly at Diya. 'Because he's the right class, you mean?'

'Exactly.'

Lucy sighed again. 'It's the sort of thing I'm never knowing. Mr Groat . . . being a chainman is not so important, really?'

'No. But the surveyor – he could talk to Mr Stevenson.'

'Ah, but can *I* talk to *him*? I'm not sure that I can.'

'Well, I'll try to have a word with him if I get the chance. And you do the same. But Lucy . . .'

'What?'

'I wouldn't hold out too much hope. Better to make other plans.'

Lucy clattered the horn spoons in a heap on the table, and went outside.

When she came back everyone was sitting at the table, and Diya was helping them all to hot meat pie with kale. No one remarked on Lucy's lateness as she took her place at the head of the table, or on the fact that she was out of breath from running furiously twice round the garden wall as the simplest antidote to too much emotion.

'I *like* this pie,' Billy said, with his mouth full.

Breesha glowered at him.

'So what's all this about a road?' asked Diya, as they settled down to eat. She was much more skilled than the rest of them at talking and eating at the same time, and it was a moment before anyone was able to answer her.

'We'll be building a track up from the jetty to the light,' Archie said thickly. He swallowed, and went on more clearly, 'To bring up the materials. And afterwards it'll serve the light.'

'*What* jetty?' asked Breesha suspiciously, glaring at him.

'The one we're going to build. We—'

'Not for big boats?' broke in Lucy in alarm. 'You're not never doing that! They'll be bringing long-tails, like on the Calf! The long-tails destroy everything – the birds – the puffins – the *Kirreeyn varrey* – They'll be eating the lot! You can't never be bringing big boats here!'

'Bring what? Och, you mean—'

'Don't say that! I'm talking about long-tails.'

'There'll be nothing bigger than a smack,' said Archie. 'There couldn't be. We'll make sure there are no . . . long-tails.

But there'll have to be a jetty at Giau y Vaatey. We'll need to bring the heavy supplies in alongside. We'll put in . . .' Archie's voice trailed away.

. . . *a block and tackle*. No one spoke for long moments.

Presently Ben said easily, 'So we'll start levelling this afternoon between the lighthouse and Giau y Vaatey. That means we'll measure all the heights. This morning we were doing the surface work. The chaining doesna show the difference in heights. But once you know the heights, you can work out the surface measurements so they come out right on a flat plan.' He saw that Mally and Billy were looking puzzled. 'Your island isna flat, is it? But a map has to be. So on a map you have to find other ways of showing how high the land is. And you have to measure along the ground *as if* it were flat. That means you have to do a sum.'

'Ugh!' said Mally.

'Do you no like sums?'

'Not much. I like doing stories though.'

'I like sums,' said Breesha suddenly. She was breaking her vow not to chat to the enemy, but it was unbearable to be excluded when they were talking about things that she was good at.

'There were lots of sums this morning,' said Billy loftily. 'Measuring triangles.' He shot a sideways glance at his aunt and cousins. 'The angles of a triangle add up to a hundred and eighty degrees. And if you know one angle and the length of two sides you can find out what the third side is. Or if you know how long all the sides are you can know what the angles are. And then you can do offsets and make sure you've done it right. *Ow!*' He glared at Breesha. 'What . . .?' He stopped himself in time, even though she'd caught him just on the ankle bone where it hurt most.

'That's very good, Billy,' said Diya calmly. She turned to Ben. 'So how do you measure the height of the land?'

'They have a level,' interrupted Billy, who was getting above himself for once, and enjoying the sensation. 'It's a telescope, except what you see comes out upside down. Because yesterday at low tide we made a mark halfway between the flood and the ebb which is the mean-tide mark. So this morning we went down there and put the measuring staff on it and took a reading. And after that Mr Groat had the staff up at the keeill, and we looked through the level again – I mean Mr Buchanan looked through it – and we measured up as far as the keeill where Mr Groat was. And after dinner we're going to set the level up by the keeill, because that's the next station, and I'm going to have a look through it myself, Mr Groat says, just so's I know what we're doing.'

'That's very interesting,' said Diya. She held Ben's gaze and said, 'I teach the children arithmetic, but my daughter here is getting beyond me. She has a natural aptitude, you see, and she often wants to know things I can't tell her. I'm sure Breesha would like to have a look at your level too. I believe she was watching you this morning from the lighthouse when she was doing her work. Of course, one has a bird's-eye view from up there. She saw how you measured the distances and the angles between the points. In fact, I'd be quite interested to look through your levelling telescope myself, if you can spare the time.'

Trust Ben to bring this on them! They had other things to do on Ellan Bride than to give elementary surveying lessons to a parcel of women and bairns! Naturally Archie didn't say so. Instead he flushed, and said, 'Och well, ay . . . ay well . . . of course, ma'am, if you wish it.'

'Thank you,' said Diya gently. 'Now, sir, may I offer you more of this excellent pie?'

Lucy couldn't think how Diya managed it. She herself knew of only one way to conceal her feelings, and that was to remain silent. Probably even silence was ineffective. In all the years they'd lived together Lucy had never found Diya as remote as now. She almost mistrusted her; Diya's cool politeness to the two surveyors seemed so false, although Diya was only behaving as she and Lucy had agreed beforehand. Diya had insisted, and Lucy quite agreed, that there was no point alienating the surveyors, or indeed any representative of the Commissioners of Northern Lights. Probably no tactic would gain them any advantage in the end. Diya had told Lucy not to imagine that she'd be allowed to work at the new lighthouse, and yet Lucy, who didn't know how to be strategic, was the one who kept hoping against hope that she might, even now, be able to stay on as lightkeeper. Perhaps it was easier for Diya because she didn't share that hope. Behind that thought lay the awful suspicion that Diya not only didn't hope to stay, but actively hoped to leave. She'd never said so. Could Lucy accuse her of treachery if she secretly longed for the life she'd left behind when she married Jim? Diya couldn't help it if that's what she really wanted. However that might be, Diya had also told Lucy that there was no going back to her old life anyway. When she'd married Jim she'd lost caste – Lucy wasn't familiar with the term, but she'd been in service long enough to understand what Diya meant – and once that was gone, Diya said, it could never be got back.

The meat pie was good, but for once Lucy had no appetite. She toyed with the helping on her plate and longed for the meal to be over so she could retire to bed. It was all too confusing. Diya had turned into a stranger, and the one who met her eyes across the table with something like sympathy in his own was the big, ugly surveyor, Benjamin Groat. Mr Buchanan had no time for her, that was clear enough, but Mr Groat seemed to have an inkling of what they might all be feeling . . . *if* they were all feeling the same. Perhaps they weren't any more. Mally was upset, of course, but she was too little: she couldn't really understand what was happening. Lucy's own Billy was so easy-going, and at the moment he was so seduced by his twopence a day, and being treated seriously by two men – and no wonder, when he'd hardly met anyone of his own sex since he was five – that he seemed to have temporarily forgotten the family's plight. Only Breesha felt as Lucy did, and that was odd, because Lucy had always had to hide her impatience with her volatile niece, who seemed to have inherited a character totally alien to her father's Scottish forebears. Lucy knew she mustn't regard Breesha as any kind of ally. Breesha needed to be guided, not encouraged. She faithfully reflected Lucy's most dangerous thoughts. Poor Breesha; she little knew.

And now Diya was talking to Mr Buchanan as if they were old friends, which was ridiculous. No, that was unfair. She was talking to him as if he were paying a social call at her Grandmother's house in Castletown. Lucy recognised that kind of talk from her own disastrous encounter with gentlefolks. She couldn't help hearing it now as the discourse of deceit. Scenting danger, she dropped her eyes to her plate, and tried to imagine herself alone at the table, nothing to do with what was going on at all.

'I understand,' Diya was saying to Archie, 'Mr Lyell is saying in his book that in order to understand the present conformation of the land, we have to understand its history. So what you mean is: thousands of years ago there wouldn't have been any island that we'd recognise as Ellan Bride – in fact, the materials that make up this land wouldn't even have come together, let alone be a recognisable entity – and if we want to know how Ellan Bride came to be here, we have to read the rocks, and in that way we might be able to discover the story of its past.'

To hell with the island's past, my lass, Ben was thinking. What *I'd* really like to know is how *you* came to be here. I'd give me granny to ken the story of *your* past. He wondered if Young Archibald had found his tongue all at once because someone was actually interested in discussing what he was really thinking about, or whether it was because he'd suddenly noticed that Mrs Geddes was a raging beauty. Ben reckoned it was probably the former. The only way he'd ever seen Archie show any awareness of the female sex was by relapsing either into painful shyness or a daunting formality.

Ay well, this new departure was all very entertaining, but Ben couldn't see that anything would come of it. The whole thing would be a grand joke, in fact, if it weren't that the lightkeeper was in such a state of vexation. Ben looked thoughtfully across at Lucy's downbent head. She hadn't eaten her dinner either. What was she thinking about? The future? Maybe she was realising her sister-in-law didn't belong here and would be glad to get away. The bairns would be all right, no doubt. Bairns could adapt. But the lightkeeper was old enough to be set in her ways, and from what Ben could make out she'd made a right mull of mainland life so far. It was all a sad coil, and no mistake.

'Not only read the rocks, ma'am,' Archie was saying, 'but also correct all the false readings men have made before. You see, what's really *unimaginable* is the time scale. Not just thousands of years: *millions*. Two hundred years ago men were trying to explain the sequence of events – right through from the debris of early volcanic activity to the evidence of previous life we find in fossils – and fit it into the four thousand years calculated by theologians. That meant they *had* to think it was a miracle. For example, if you were convinced that mankind hadn't inhabited the Nile delta until the nineteenth century, you'd look at the pyramids, and the Sphinx and all the rest of it, and you'd *have* to believe that there'd been an unnatural cataclysm – a miraculous intervention in the course of human history. If you thought the pyramids had been raised in a day you'd have no choice but to think it was done by supernatural agency. But once you admit that the whole thing took thousands of years, you give yourself permission to believe that the laws of history, or of nature, as we know them have *never* been violated. They've held since the beginning of time. Take Ellan Bride, for example: if this island had been conceived in a single night, and no through millennia, that would indeed be no sma' marvel. In other words, when you accept the true time scale, and measure the history of the natural world accordingly, the verra idea of a miracle becomes simply *unnecessary*.'

'It's a fascinating theory, Mr Buchanan. What gods do you worship?'

Archie stopped short, and gaped at her. What gods? In his country a question like that would have been a hanging matter not so many years since. Although he was lucky enough to live in more enlightened times, the shadows still fell long across the generations. His father had called him an atheist the last time he went home, in that painful episode which he preferred not to recollect. He didn't think he was an atheist. But what did this woman mean? What *gods*? *What* gods? She showed neither shock nor incomprehension. She merely looked at him with civil interest, and all the certain ground of Natural Philosophy on which he stood seemed suddenly to shift under his feet. A cataclysm – an intervention in the inviolable laws of nature – Archie struggled to recapture the thread of his argument. 'I dinna think I do worship,' he stammered. 'I was taught, of course . . . I was brocht up in the Scottish Kirk . . . But we were speaking of geology, I think.'

Diya nodded gravely over the children's heads as they noisily scraped their bowls. The way she addressed him, she and Archie could have been alone in her Grandmother's drawing room. 'Of the immutable laws of nature,' she agreed, 'as exhibited in the conformation of the earth. In that context our lives become so small, Mr Buchanan, do they not? What can one do in the face of that but turn to one's own gods?'

'I'm sure I don't know, ma'am.' Archie tried to make a recover. 'The whole trend of Natural Philosophy, as I understand it . . .'

Lucy pushed her chair back and stood up abruptly. 'I must go. I have work to do tonight.'

'Goodnight, Mam,' said Billy. 'Aunt Diya, is there any more pie?'

Ben just got a glimpse of the bedroom before Lucy slammed the door shut behind her. He saw a double bed with a patchwork quilt, and a text on the whitewashed wall above it. He didn't think the lightkeeper would sleep very well today. It was her bad luck to be born a woman, and there was nothing anybody could do about that. But he was sorry for her; there was no denying that. Aunt Deer wasn't going to do much to comfort her from what he could see. For two pins, if it wasn't against the immutable laws of society – Ben gave a wry grin – he'd go after the lightkeeper himself, and tell her that he for one was on her side. But he couldn't do that, not without an unnatural cataclysm of some sort, and they didn't need that while they were stuck on this island; indeed they did not.

Chapter 19

'SO THIS IS ONE OF THE BENCH MARKS,' EXPLAINED ARCHIE. 'Once ye've fixed your bench marks, you can measure the height of everythin else in relation to them.'

'Why here?' asked Breesha, looking round. They were all standing in the hollow that sheltered the keeill. Out of the wind the thrift was coming into bloom, a pink carpet with threadbare patches where the bedrock broke through. There were white splashes on the rock where a gull had been feeding; it had left behind a blue-grey pile of half-digested mussel shells. On the south side the keeill was covered with orange lichen, except that on the biggest rock the lichen had been scraped away and a rough cross newly painted on the stone.

'Because the track'll go past here on its way from sea level to the lighthouse.' Now they were back at work Archie was listening to sensible questions. 'We're calculating the height of each fixed mark above sea level, until we get to the summit of the island.'

'A fixed mark?' said Diya, looking from the keeill down to Baie yn Traie Vane, where a mallard with three chicks at her tail breasted the gentle swell just beyond the breaking waves. 'So you know exactly where you start from?'

'That's it. The bench marks will never change, so we have to make sure they're there for whoever needs to read them in the future. That's why I picked the Celtic chapel for one of them.'

'That's not a Salty Apple! That's the keeill!'

'Ay, so you said yesterday. *What* is it you call it?' asked Ben curiously.

Mally felt as if Mr Groat was challenging her. She shrank back against her mother. Her thumb went to her mouth.

'Keeill is the Manx word for chapel,' explained Diya. 'Legend has it that Saint Bride lived as a solitary on this island for many years. She was – how would you put it? – awaiting enlightenment. This is her keeill. And the turf wall there was her garden, and over there her cell. Here she prayed, and this is a holy place, where you've set up your mark.'

'You don't mind?' That was so unexpected, coming from Mr Buchanan, that Diya wasn't sure she'd heard him aright.

'Mind?'

'It's common practice to put bench marks on kirks,' said Archie abruptly. 'Although I hadn't thought of this one as still in use. You dinna mind?'

'How we use it is no matter,' said Diya. 'Nothing we do now will change this place.' She caught Archie's puzzlement. 'No,' she added simply. 'I don't mind. For your fixed point you could do worse.'

'*And* she was the lightkeeper!' put in Breesha, challenging them.

'She?'

'Saint Bride, of course. She was the *first* lightkeeper. And nobody stopped *her*! *I* should know. I've got her name.'

'My daughter is referring to the legend that when Saint Bride lived here, sailors would watch for her light burning inside the keeill, and know to steer clear of Ellan Bride on dark nights. When Bride heard of this, she used to set her lamp above the keeill so all the ships would be able to see it, and keep safely away from the rocks. The miracle was that although she only had a tiny oil lamp, the sailors could see the light from far away, in all weathers and seasons, whenever they needed it. This was a great crossroads of the sea even then, and many ships sailed between the far lands.'

Mr Buchanan nodded, but he didn't answer. Diya would have liked to know what he was thinking. He'd been shocked by the question she'd asked him at dinner. That had been disappointing, because she'd somehow deluded herself she could speak her mind to him. That had been foolish: she'd known for long enough that her real thoughts must always be held back. But did he half-believe the legend about Saint Bride? Did he think there was some sort of truth in it? It was pointless to think he'd even be interested.

'So that's what Finn Watterson meant, when he said "And long before that, too",' remarked Ben. He was watching the duck with her chicks in the bay. She'd probably started out with more than three; it was more than one duck could do to fight off all the black-backs. Mrs Geddes grew no less formidable on closer acquaintance. She would be very attractive if she were not so alarming.

'Did he?' replied Diya. 'I expect that's what he meant. Everyone knows about Saint Bride's light.'

'That's why it's called Ellan Bride, of course,' said Breesha, who was watching Ben and Billy as they unfastened the long wooden box. 'What's *that*?'

Once Ben had dismantled the box, they could see that it wasn't a box at all, but a long flat pole in three five-foot sections, with numbers boldly marked on it like an outsize ruler.

'It's for measuring the level,' said Ben. 'We set it against the bench mark here, and then we measure the difference in height from the next station. We're following the line of the road – the one we'll build – up to the top of the island.'

'But you're putting it upside down!' Breesha protested.

'Ah now,' said Ben, winking at Billy, who knew the secret. 'You wait and see! Now we'll go up to the next station.'

The next station was halfway between the keeill and Dreeym Lang. As they followed Archie uphill, Ben said, 'From halfway, you see, we can take a backsight – a measurement back the way – onto the benchmark on the keeill, and a foresight – a measurement further on – up to Dreeym Lang. Then we do one more along Dreeym Lang to the highest point. Then we'll ken the exact height of the highest point on the island. We can work out any more heights we need from that.'

When they reached the next station Archie swung a square wooden box off his shoulder, and laid it on the ground. Meanwhile Ben untied the legs of the tripod, and set it up so it stood firmly in the short grass. The children crowded round as Archie opened the box.

The instrument inside looked like a short fat telescope mounted on a metal frame. They watched Archie lift it tenderly out of its travelling box, mount it on the tripod, and screw it into place. He adjusted the legs of the tripod until the instrument seemed to be level. It was much more complicated than their telescope. It had lots of brass wheels of different sizes, and knobs in different places. The biggest wheel had degrees marked on it like the compass in the lighthouse, but there was no arrow to point north, only the strange telescope fixed on the top of it.

'What's it all *for*?' asked Breesha. She couldn't help showing that she was interested.

Now that they were on site Archie's irritation melted away. The first apprentice he'd taught had been Benjamin Groat, seven years ago when they did the Sutherland survey. He forgot that he was talking to women, to whom the information would be useless because they could never do anything with it. He wasn't looking at them, but at the level, so it seemed quite natural to explain its intricate science as precisely as he could, just as he would have done to a potential engineer.

'All right. The first thing you have to do is get it completely level. You see this glass, here on the side of the telescope. That's the level. That's right, look closely. What do you see?'

'Numbers on it, like a ruler.'

'A bubble at the end.'

'Right. So that's an air bubble, floating in oil. So if you want to make sure that the instrument is absolutely level . . .'

'I know,' cried Breesha. 'You have to get the bubble exactly in the middle.'

'That's it. It'll float into the middle when you've got it completely level. So you've got these wheels, see –' Archie showed them the brass wheels under the big circle with the degrees 'These are all for levellin the instrument. You calibrate – I mean, you set it – by turning the wheels very slowly – ken, like this – so you get the wee bubble in the right place by levellin the whole machine. Here, do you want to try?'

Breesha was quicker than Billy, and got in first. Archie was unable to remonstrate, with her mother standing there. To his surprise the girl was quick to get the feel of the instrument. Keeping her eyes on the bubble in the tube, Breesha turned the wheels. 'The bubble keeps wriggling about. There – no, it's gone again – wait, wait, I can do it . . . It keeps *wriggling* . . . Like that? Is that better, look? Is that it?'

'Good,' said Archie. He bent down and looked through the level, and rapidly adjusted the four brass screws below it with his thumbs. 'That's fine.' He'd forgotten the child standing next to him wasn't his apprentice, let alone a boy, so he said without thinking, 'All right. Now, have a look through the glass. What dae ye see?'

Breesha put her eye to the glass and looked through it. 'Nothing,' she said. 'It's all grey. Oh . . . I can see a grey line . . . Two grey lines . . . three. One going up and two next to each other going across. I can't see anything else, just grey.'

'Turn the wheel at the top. Slowly . . . slower than that.'

Breesha turned the little brass wheel. 'I can see . . . it looks like bobbles . . . like raindrops on a window pane . . . no, more like seals on a very foggy beach. That's what it looks like.'

'Keep turnin the focus.'

'No, it isn't! It's the sea! And there *are* blobs . . . I think it's birds. It's those eiders! It's focused much too far out! It needs to go down. Oh no – it's turned into the sky. Let me try again

. . . Now I've got land as well as sea. No, it isn't, it's the measuring pole. I want to get the pole into focus . . . it's gone! I can't do it!'

'Ye're movin it the wrong way. Move it the opposite way.'

'But it's *that* way.'

'No, it's in reverse.'

'He means like a tiller,' said Billy. 'Let *me* do it!'

'No! Wait. Ah,' cried Breesha. '*Backwards!* Like that. You have to do everything the way you don't think . . . Now I've got the pole in it again! I can see the writing!'

'Can you read it? Bring it into focus. Here, turn this wheel. Slowly now, until you can see.'

'I can! I can see it! I can see 4 . . . 5 . . .' Breesha looked up, startled. 'But, but – it's the *right* way up. Only when I look with just my own eyes it isn't! The pole's upside down and the telescope turns it back over! How can it? *Why* does it do that?'

'Because it's no jist a telescope. It's like a telescope – there's a lens in there which collects the light rays from the object, jist like a telescope, and the refraction from the lens forms an inverted image . . .'

'He means the lens turns everything upside down and back to front,' put in Ben quietly.

'But in a telescope you have an extra lens to correct the inversion. That's no necessary in the level, because the function isna the same . . .'

'He means it would be no good looking at the world upside down through a telescope, but it's all right for making a map.'

'If you like, I'll make you a drawing of it tonight, and show you how the refraction works. But noo ye ken you have to see everything through the level in reverse. So: what you need to dae next is get the vertical line lined up wi the pole. Can ye dae that?'

'Wait. No . . . It's going backwards again . . . There . . . wait . . . Yes, all right, I've got it in a straight line now.'

'So is there a number between the two horizontal lines?'

Breesha told him without hesitation. 'Six.'

'When can I have a turn?' interrupted Billy.

The question brought Archie back to his senses in a flash. This wasn't a young Ben Groat he'd been instructing; these children – two of them girls at that – were nothing to do with the job. They'd wasted quite enough time already. And did their mother damn well expect to have a shot at the level too? They'd be here all afternoon, getting under his feet. Archie frowned, and opened his mouth to speak, but Ben got his word in first.

'Everyone can have a turn,' said Ben firmly. 'Billy, then Mally, and then Mrs Geddes. After that we must get on. It's Mr Buchanan who really does the levellin. It's very skilled. When he's taken all the readings he has to add up all the foresights and all the backsights and tak them away from each other, and the result is the difference in height from the first fixed point to the last.'

'Ugh,' said Mally. 'I hate sums.'

'So I just keep the levellin pole absolutely straight, and Billy will help me with that. But this evening Mr Buchanan will do a drawing of the optics for Miss Breesha so she understands how they work. After supper. Will you no, sir?'

'Eh?' said Archie, startled. He looked out to sea but there was nothing there but a mallard with some chicks bobbing about near the breaking waves, and that was no help at all. 'Ay well . . . I mean, yes. Yes, quite.'

Only in dreams can time ever go backwards. In the dream Jim was alive and young, but even that was no good, because it was too late. The boat was pulled up above the tide line at Traie Vane, and Lucy and Jim had to haul it down to the water before the sea began to ebb. The boat was so heavy, and there was so little time. If they didn't get the boat down they wouldn't be able to cross. Only it wasn't Traie Vane after all; it must be somewhere else because the island was on the other side, far across the sea. If they were properly on Ellan Bride they would be able to see the keeill from here, just above the shore. But if the keeill had gone then they were in the other place, and they had to launch the boat in time because otherwise they'd never get back. Lucy stopped hauling and looked up to see if the keeill was there. It wasn't. Instead it was Mummig standing there, smiling and waving to them. She thought at first Mummig was her familiar self, with her plump red cheeks, and her grey gown stretched tight around her comfortable waist, just the way it used to do. But when Lucy looked again she realised that her mother was dead because now she could see how her skin fell off her bones in ribbon-like shreds, and the grey gown was hanging loose in mouldering tatters. And Mummig was laughing because Lucy and Jim weren't strong enough to launch the boat by themselves, and the tide was ebbing, and there was nothing the two of them could do to stop it. They were only children after all, and anyway no one could ever stop the tide and that meant that they wouldn't be able to get home after all . . .

The only way out was to wake herself up. Lucy rolled over, and forced herself to open her eyes. Her fists unclenched themselves; slowly her breathing fell into rhythm with the waves on the shore outside. Listening to the sea, the nightmare in her chest gradually dissolved. There was the white ceiling above her head, with the familiar cracks running across it. There was *This is the day that the Lord hath made* hanging on its nail as it had done for the last fifty years. There was the tiled washstand, and Lucy's – no, not Lucy's any more: Lucy was grown up now – Mally's – truckle bed in the corner. All these things were the same. Yet the dream could not be entirely banished, because so many other things had changed.

Lucy always saw Jim's face much more easily in dreams than in waking life. It was harder to remember his voice, even in dreams. Voices were more difficult to hold on to: she couldn't recapture any of their voices, however hard she tried. It was horrible to dream about Mummig like that. In real life Mummig had never mocked Lucy or condemned her. All she'd said, when Lucy had come home, was 'I'll take in any child of our family, and not never be ashamed, wherever it came from. If you'd been coming home with another woman's man, you'd be finding the door shut on you. But a child – no, I'm not shutting the door on any child of ours. You know I wouldn't do that, Lucy veen.'

But her mother had insisted on knowing the truth. She'd made Lucy tell her most of what had happened in Castletown. Probably she'd told Lucy's Da as well. That was such an appalling idea that Lucy couldn't even think about it. Some things were private. Mummig had never understood that. Lucy had managed not to name the man, but she'd been forced to tell almost everything else. It had felt like a second violation, and, like the first, it came cloaked in treacherous kindness. Both times it had been somebody wanting something, and getting it by pretending to be kind. It felt very wrong to couple her mother with that other treachery, but in her heart Lucy felt it was true. There was no one now who wanted to take anything from her at all, fairly or unfairly. Was that better? Lucy frowned at the text on the wall. She honestly didn't know the answer to that.

When Jim was alive he'd treated Billy and Breesha alike, as if they'd been twins, and both of them his own. When Lucy first came home she'd been nervous of Diya. She hadn't seen her sister-in-law since Jim's wedding, because Jim and Diya had come straight back to the island. Of course she hadn't known Diya before that. Servant girls were not acquainted with the daughters of East India Company officials. Diya's grandmother was a Captain's lady, and she'd belonged to the Quality of Castletown.

The first time Lucy had ever seen Diya, Diya hadn't seen her. Lucy had been visiting Aunt Annie, her mother's sister, who was the cook at Mrs Wells' house. Mrs Wells lived in one of the most imposing houses in Castletown. Three storeys of big windows faced onto the market square, but of course Lucy didn't go upstairs. The way to the kitchen was through the back door. The front kitchen was one of the biggest rooms Lucy had ever seen. It was half-underground, and when you looked up through the windows, which gave onto a narrow area, you could see the skirts of the women as they passed on the pavement above, and the thin black legs of the gentlemen. It was very snug in Aunt Annie's kitchen, and for a homesick girl who'd never been in a town before it was sanctuary. Aunt Annie's rocking chair was drawn up close to the big iron range in the south wall. Lucy never saw Aunt Annie sitting in that chair, because she was always bustling about. Lucy and the over-fed grey cat always had the chair to themselves. The kitchen at Mrs Wells' house seemed so comforting and secure: if Lucy had known, in those first days at Castletown, that within two years all this would be gone, and her own high hopes for the future all gone too, she'd never have believed it. Perhaps that was just as well.

Lucy had only been able to visit Aunt Annie on alternate Thursday afternoons, because that was her day off. Mrs Wells had given Annie permission to entertain her niece in the kitchen on those precious days. The big house where Lucy worked was about a mile from Castletown. On her days off, Lucy walked to Scarlett Point if the weather was good, and then along the shore into town, where she had her dinner with Aunt Annie. She never went anywhere else; she didn't know anyone else in Castletown except the other servants where she worked, and of course they never had time off on the same day. Lucy had never met Aunt Annie before either, because Aunt Annie couldn't stand the sea and was never likely to come to Ellan Bride. (And yet when Annie emigrated with her new husband, she was willing to brave the whole Atlantic. Perhaps, thought Lucy, that's what love can do for a woman. But I don't know anything about that kind of love.)

But Aunt Annie – who can't have been so very old after all, though she'd seemed so to the fifteen-year-old Lucy – hadn't yet become engaged to her Johnny when Lucy first arrived in Castletown. Aunt Annie took it upon herself to bring Lucy up to snuff, and did so by telling her as much of the local gossip as she could. That was how Lucy first heard about Mrs Wells' scandalous granddaughter.

'Oh no, they're not Manx,' Aunt Annie had said, in answer to Lucy's question. 'No, no, you're more Manx than they are, though your Da's as Scotch as they come; at least there was enough sense at him to pick a woman from the Island. But that's by-the-by. No, no, the way it was, the Captain was losing his leg at Trafalgar, and after that he took a terrible fever, and was never the same again. So they were discharging him on half pay, and like many another half-pay officer he came to the Island. Oh, there's a good few on the Island fought at Trafalgar. There's Captain Quilliam for one – lives next door – he's a local man, though of course he married well above his station. I think it was maybe himself was suggesting to Captain Wells he should settle here in Castletown. Cheaper for these English half-pay officers to come here, when there's not a living wage left to them. But the Captain wasn't like some. He was a respectable man with a lady wife. No drinking or dicing for him. Not that he'd have had the health for it even if he was showing a bent that way, which I'm thankful to say he wasn't.

'No, no, the Captain was a respectable man, and well into middle age. He must have had an income from somewhere, because how else could they be renting a house as grand as this? His widow was able to stay on in it too, and she's not one to pinch and scrape, indeed she isn't. I don't mind. It's better to be working for a woman that isn't asking a lot of questions, but is knowing that if you're wanting good food you must pay the price. Though her health's not good – not that she admits to it – she never says nothing about it, but if you're working in a house, you can't help but know . . . But where was I? Yes, indeed, they weren't spring chickens any more, the Captain and his lady, when they came to Castletown. We never saw the boy. He was already gone away to India. They'd got him a berth in the East India Company, seemingly, and off he'd gone to heathen lands as soon as he turned eighteen, long before ever his Mama and Papa landed on the Island.

'Oh, when I was first here as scullery maid – fifteen years ago, that was – and myself about your own age then – there was always talk Downstairs of the Young Master out in Bombay. That boy was the apple of his Mama's eye, and when the Captain died – oh quite heartbroken, she was, stuck here in this place where she didn't belong, and her man dead less than two years since he was invalided home – so when the Captain died she had little to be doing but dote on the boy. Which she did. He sent his portrait home – one day I'll take you Upstairs and show you where it's hanging yet, in the dining-room – and oh, the thrilled she was with that picture! I'd be going Upstairs to lay the table, and there she'd be, in the dining-room, just standing there looking at that there picture. When she saw me she'd pretend she wasn't – pretend she'd come in there for something else – but I knew what she was doing. Oh, it was a sad state of things, indeed it was. Out there in India – those young fellows – chances are they'll never be coming home again. Though this one did, for better or worse, as you shall hear.

'When he did come at last he didn't stay long. As soon as his leave was over off he went away back to India again, leaving the mistress with . . . well, it seemed a selfish-like way of acting at the time, or so we were thinking. But maybe it was all for the best, after all. But the poor little waif – for so she was, back then – she had never a letter from him, barring the first year. But twice only he was writing that child a letter, and after that I reckon he forgot, for so far as I know she's never had word from him since. Now I'm not a letter-writing woman, but that Mr Wells – book-learning enough at him for half a dozen. He could have spared a few words for his own child, surely. But she never seemed too sad about *that*. I don't think he'd ever been much of a father to her, and that's a fact. It was the other life she was missing, poor little thing. Such a sad waif she was, when she came first. You'd hardly believe it now – she used to be feeling the cold so terrible hard – she'd come creeping down here like a li'l ghos', and I'd tuck her up in a shawl, in that rocking chair with the cat, just where you're sitting now, and there she'd sit by the chidlagh until she got warmed through. But the little she was; I reckon she soon forgot to be homesick. Anyway, she never really complained much, and soon enough she settled down.

'She's a pillar of society, Mrs Wells, and the Church, and all of that, but I'm telling you, until that little girl came, she was a lonely woman after the Captain died. And for all the shock it was to her, that child turning up was maybe the best thing that could have come on her; it was indeed. Though the shock must have been terrible. The young fellow never said a word about it, you understand. Never said he was married – if married he was – for whether it was a heathen ceremony or a proper church wedding no one is knowing for sure – but either way he never said. And there's no doubt but his Mama had plans for him, when he came home . . . He never told them he was married to a heathen, see. Not one word about any of it! Maybe you couldn't be blaming him for that. But the Indian lady died, seemingly, when the child was born, and still he was never writing home a word about it. So the Captain went to his grave not knowing he had a grandchild at all, and by that time the little girl would've been all of seven years old, and ourselves not even knowing she existed.'

'That's sad,' said Lucy. 'Would the Captain have minded so much?'

'That's what we'll never know,' said Aunt Annie sagely. 'The dead don't talk, and maybe that's just as well. His Mama would have forgiven him anything. She'd have forgiven him if there'd been a whole harem of foreign ladies at him, and babes too – but I shouldn't be speaking that way to your innocent ears, so we'll say nothing of that. The fact was she knew he was coming home all right – his leave was due – and – Jee bannee mee – the excited she was about that! She'd not seen the boy in fourteen years! That's what she kept telling us. Going around the house, half-laughing, half-crying she was: "I've not seen my boy for fourteen years!" she'd say, and wander on, from room to room, not able to settle to anything.

'And then the letter came. Don't you never trust an unexpected letter, Lucy veen. It's like letting a viper into your bosom. You're taking it in, easy as you please, and you're opening the thing, and just a few words on a bit of paper – and all of a sudden your whole life is shattered all through others. Oh, a letter is a powerful thing, and I thank my stars I don't get none, not being a writing kind of woman, and I reckon I never will be, either. I don't like letters.'

It was true, Lucy thought, as she lay staring at the ceiling. While she'd been thinking of Aunt Annie her eyes had been unconsciously drawn to the bright square of light framed by the window, and now when she looked at the ceiling it had a shining green square swimming across it. There was a fiery cross in the middle of the square the same shape as the window panes. Outside, the sound of the sea was strengthening; in her mind's eye she could see the swell getting up. There'd be white water breaking over Sker ny Rona by now. The wind was starting to whine around the house. The wuthering in the chimney meant it was shifting southerly. The *Betsey* wouldn't be able to land in this. Sure enough, when Lucy looked at the window again the sky was no longer blue but grey, and the clouds were scudding past. No good expecting Finn tomorrow then. The surveyors were stuck, and they all just had to thole it.

No, Aunt Annie would never write a letter, and that was a pity, because it meant they'd never hear from her again. How wonderful it would be if Aunt Annie were in Castletown now . . . but there was no point even imagining that. When Mrs Wells' household had broken up, less than a year after Lucy went to live in Castletown, Aunt Annie announced that she was marrying her Johnny and going off to America. Oh, if only Annie had stayed, and there'd been someone to turn to when Lucy had needed it! What would Aunt Annie have said to Lucy, in her great trouble, if she'd still been there, and there'd still been the safe kitchen to run to? But perhaps even that was just as well . . . Lucy had thought about it sometimes over the years: Aunt Annie had been a woman of the world. She knew much more than Lucy ever would. Would Aunt Annie have suggested a solution that might have meant there'd never have been Billy? Lucy didn't know; the thought, now, was impossible to contemplate. And what would Lucy have done if Aunt Annie had said . . . no, no, she didn't want to think about that!

And why had she started thinking about Aunt Annie, anyway? (Was that a spatter of rain against the window pane? The gulls were screaming of a change in the weather. Would that mean everyone would come back to the house, God forbid? Lucy could do without that if she was to get any sleep at all.) Aunt Annie, bless her, had gone cheerfully out of their lives eleven years ago, and never been heard of since. Oh yes, Lucy recollected, she'd been thinking about Diya. The day she'd first seen Diya.

It had been a Thursday afternoon, and Lucy had been crossing the market square on her way to see Aunt Annie. The front door of Mrs Wells' house was at the top of five stone steps that projected out into the square. Just as Lucy reached the house the front door opened and a tall girl came out. She was fashionably dressed in a green bonnet and pelisse, with matching kid boots, and she carried a reticule. The door closed after her, and she came down the steps into the square. She was a very smart young lady, and yet her face was as brown as peat. Lucy had never seen anyone that colour before. She knew at once that this must be Mrs Wells' granddaughter, whose arrival had caused such terrible consternation ten years ago. You'd never guess now that the young lady had arrived under such a shadow. She looked so confident and bright, so at home on the grand doorstep of her grandmother's house. She didn't see Lucy, of course. Lucy was just a common servant girl in a print gown and frieze cloak, part of the crowd in the square. Miss Wells wasn't looking at any of the people. She came down the steps, walked briskly through the crowd in the square, and disappeared down Arboury Street.

Lucy had never told Diya about that day. She'd seen Diya quite often after that, but she'd never spoken to her. Jim had seen Diya too, and he *had* spoken to her. In those days, when their Da was still looking after the light, Jim had been able to come into Castletown sometimes. He had friends there, which is more than Lucy ever did, though friends had been what she'd hoped for when she'd insisted on leaving home. But when she arrived in Castletown she'd realised it was quite different for a girl. Lucy wasn't allowed out for long enough to go into town, except on those precious alternate Thursdays. Jim had known Aunt Annie's kitchen long before Lucy ever set foot in Castletown. And though Lucy never met Diya in that kitchen, she knew from Aunt Annie that Diya still clung to her childhood habit of coming down to the kitchen to sit in the rocking chair with the cat, just as Lucy did, and chat to Annie. Lucy's brother had met Diya there more than once, but never, for some reason, on alternate Thursdays. Until Jim and Diya's extraordinary wedding day, Lucy had never seen the unlikely couple together. Probably no one had except Aunt Annie, and she – for Aunt Annie kept her secrets, in spite of all her talk – had never said a word about it.

The outside door opened, and a rush of cold air came in under the closed bedroom door. The kitchen was suddenly full of treble voices: it was only the children back again. Lucy had learned long ago to sleep through as much noise as three children could possibly make. So many rainy days, sleeping through the afternoon with the cries of the gulls on the one hand, and the shrilling of the bairns on the other . . . That was life as she knew it. If only it could always be like this . . . Lucy rolled on her side, and shut her eyes, listening to the sounds of the day, just as her father had before her, and his father before that. The children, the island, and the light – those had always been the things that mattered, down to the third generation. For the moment nothing had changed, if only Lucy could hold time still, and not have to wake up to a different day . . . not have to wake . . .

Chapter 20

ARCHIE AND BEN LOOKED DOWN ON THE LANDING PLACE FROM Gob y Vaatey. The tide was flooding across the mouth of the narrow giau. Sharp waves rose and jostled each other, throwing up spurts of white water. Two seals rolled in the surf, vanishing into the waves and bobbing up again on the far side.

'Sea's getting up,' remarked Ben. 'And we're no seeing England any more, either.' He pointed eastward towards a line of grey cloud. 'I reckon that'll be on us in an hour or two, sir.'

Archie folded his telescope and put it in his pocket. 'So long as the rain holds off . . .' He was studying the rocks down in Giau y Vaatey. 'I was right; it's the only place . . . if we build the jetty over that shelving rock – raise it by six or seven feet maybe – it's far enough out to give enough draft except at spring low water, though it canna be as sheltered as the present landing place. But if we build a sea wall on the south side the jetty'll provide its own shelter.'

'You'd get five or six hours at each tide if you built the jetty right in the giau,' objected Ben. 'You couldna come in as far in as Finn brought us, I grant you that, but' – Ben pointed – 'down there, say.'

'Five or six hours for a yawl like Watterson's. We canna bring all the men, *and* the supplies out here in a yawl. It'll need to be a smack – or something around that size anyway. We're talkin about a draft of five feet at the verra least, and we have to be able to use it for as many hours as possible.'

'So you'll no need Finn?'

'Oh ay, we'll be using Finn. We'll need him to pilot the smack – if we use a smack – to begin with, anyway. All right, let's get down there before the tide gets any higher.'

By the time the rain began, just over an hour later, they were both wet and breathless from scrambling over seaweed-covered rocks. Archie stopped writing, carefully wrapped his notebook in oilskin, and stowed it in his pocket. 'We canna do more in this. I can write it up indoors. I hope to God this weather passes through tonight.'

'There's a good wind behind it,' said Ben reassuringly. He hesitated. 'The gear'll be all right in the keeill, sir. Were you wanting me for anything more just now?'

'No.'

'Thank you, sir. I'll follow you later.'

'Verra well,' said Archie absently. He was frowning at the rain. 'I think it's only a shower. No matter – there's enough to do . . .'

Ben strolled away past the keeill. People didn't trouble him much, but he liked to be alone sometimes. He didn't mind the wet. It was only a shower, anyway – he could see the sky already brightening behind it – although there'd be more rain coming. The circling puffins were being blown about a bit, wheeling untidily as they rode the wind. Probably the rain would send all the children back to the house. Young Archibald wouldn't have planned on that. Ben grinned to himself. If Aunt Deer wanted her Breesha to have a Natural Philosophy lesson, he'd be willing to wager that a Natural Philosophy lesson was what she'd get. Though Young Archibald could be stubborn too. He'd get his plans drawn all right, even if he found himself doing them in the middle of a nursery. The kitchen would be full of people, snug no doubt, but stuffy – it must be getting on for supper time too. Well, they wouldn't be missing Ben for a bit.

This rain was just a shower; the drought-like weather would still be holding. Anyway, they'd done at least four hours since the other bairns had been sent off. He'd reminded Archie to dismiss Billy too, when they'd stopped levelling and gone to look at the harbour. Billy had run off somewhere. Ben looked out to sea. There was a fair bit of white water out there. The weather would decide what time they had; they wouldn't be seeing Finn tomorrow for sure.

Ben passed the keeill, and picked his way from tussock to tussock among the puffin burrows. The puffins turned their glossy heads to watch him pass. A brig, sails spread to the east wind, was making its way north-west; on that course it would pass less than quarter of a mile north of the cletts. It must be taking its chance on the channel between Ellan Bride and the Chickens; maybe it was bound for the Clyde. So there was someone else who'd be praying that the weather wasn't about to take a turn for the worse. Ben stood still, the rain blowing in his face, and watched the brig. White water rose and fell over the half-submerged cletts; he could hear the waves breaking harder on Gob Keyl. A brig like that – she could be going anywhere in the world . . . China, India, the Americas . . . Ay well, there had to be a first step on every journey, an irreversible moment when the ship pulled away from the quay, and the gap of water widened. For the time it took for a wave to break, you could still step over the gunwale, if you changed your mind, and get back on shore, but then the next wave would come, and the ship would slide away, and that was you – committed to the voyage and no going back at all.

The rain was getting harder. Ben stopped on Gob Keyl. He must be standing over the arch they'd seen from the *Betsey*. There were lush clumps of campion and mayweed at the edge where the cliff fell away; even a goat couldn't get down there. The cleft below was tightly packed with guillemots. The sea roared under Ben's feet, and he felt a faint tremor through the soles of his boots. He liked a rough sea – if everyone he cared about were safe ashore, that was – somehow it set a man's thoughts a-flowing, and cleared his mind.

On Gob Keyl it was hard to tell the difference between the sea and the rain. Ben's lips tasted salt. Black-backs had been feeding up on the headland; they'd left a scattering of whitened fishbones behind them. Ben pulled his hat hard down over his head, and headed south again down the rugged west coast.

The shower cleared, and once he was in the lee of Carn Vane the wind fell away. Suddenly it was like springtime again. It *was* springtime. He'd weathered the long winter and he wasn't even unhappy. Time was the great healer. His mother always said that. His mother was right at that. Time *had* healed. He'd not thought about Maisie once since he and Young Archibald had left Edinburgh. Or had he? Once or twice, maybe . . . not more. Last summer was a hundred years away – measuring it by how he felt, that was.

The eyebright was already out on this part of the hill, along with clumps of primroses around Towl Doo. The water in the pool was brackish from the birds, and unhealthily green around the edges. Perhaps he could begin to think about last summer without pain. If they'd only stop hurting, his memories were worth having, after all: those long summer nights in the green woods by Penicuik. At the time he'd thought himself lucky to be kept in Edinburgh, surveying new streets and terraces in the ever-expanding city for a whole season, though he'd have found it tame work after the Sutherland survey if it hadn't been for Maisie. It had been a long walk out from Edinburgh to see her every time, but he couldn't doubt, now the hurt was over, that it had been worth it. He'd known, of course, deep down. He'd known the first time they lay together that she couldn't be as innocent as she'd said. Ay well, he hadn't been the first, but he'd chosen to believe – well, she *had* protested as much, often enough – that whatever she'd done before, Ben Groat was the only one she cared for now.

He'd been gulled, of course. Looking back, he realised how much he'd chosen not to know. Otherwise why did they have to meet in secret? Why hadn't she taken him home? When the summer ended they'd had nowhere to go. Maisie hardly seemed to care; in fact she'd seized on the autumn weather as an excuse. And yet she had her own bedchamber, now that her sisters were wed, and a wee lattice window through which a man could easily creep, were he invited. Ben had reached the point – for he'd been besotted enough – when he'd have been quite willing to meet her parents anyway. There was no reason for them to disapprove of him. It was true he was no beauty, but he had a steady job and he earned a good wage – you'd expect that would matter more to her family than a handsome phiz.

The thing that hurt most – because it did hurt, even now – was her parting shot. 'No, Ben Groat!' she'd said. 'Not never! Not never! And that's all about it, see! And if ye want to know for why – if ye truly want to know for why – I'll tell ye. Ye're too damn *kind*. A lass wants more than that – a lass doesnae want a man to be so *kind*. It makes her feel bad. No – what she wants is a man that speaks for himself – ay, and fights for himself too – so she does – a proper man that isnae so peely-wally *kind*.'

Ben had been cut to the quick, though he hoped he'd not shown it – he'd had that much pride left. But when he thought about those scented summer nights, lying in the grassy hollow in the shelter of the blackthorns, maybe he'd not been a fool to take what Maisie gave, and ask no questions. No red-blooded man could have said no. Because Maisie . . . Ben stared unseeing at the white waves gently licking the feet of Stack ny Ineen – she'd been a bit on the plump side, it was true, but that was nothing, compared to the softness of her under his hands . . . and her own hands on him . . . oncoming, she'd been, to say the least . . . and she knew how . . . and as for . . . luscious, that was what Maisie had been . . . altogether luscious . . . and now it was eight starved months ago . . . a whole long winter . . .

'Hey! Did you see it, Mr Groat?'

Ben nearly jumped out of his skin. But by the time Billy

had slid down the grassy slope and landed beside him, he'd recovered himself, and said easily, 'Seen what, young Billy? The raree show?'

'The what?' Billy looked puzzled for a moment, then hurried on, 'There was a killer whale just off the stack. I saw the grey stripe behind its fin – that's what it was. I saw the fin roll over and then it went behind the stack. There might be a whole pod of them. There were last time! You didn't see? But you were looking that way. I saw you! I was watching you through the telescope from up there!' Billy pointed up towards Cronk Sheeant.

Somehow it was disconcerting to have been in the boy's sights, even though the telescope could hardly illuminate his private thoughts. 'No, I didna see it,' said Ben. 'But it'll maybe come back if we keep watching.'

They watched for a while, but there was no sign of anything like a whale. The sea was grey and yeasty. 'It's hard to see them when it's like this,' said Billy, disappointed. 'Last time they came the sea was calm and sort of white, and they showed up pretty well.'

'Ay well, I daresay they'll be back.'

'It was going south. If we went to the end of Kione Roauyr we might see it again.'

Ben hadn't the heart to refuse. It didn't surprise him, though, that when they stood at the end of the next headland there was no sign of any whale. 'No luck this time,' he said to Billy. 'It's a bit rough to see much, anyway.'

'Well, I'm going to watch for a bit. When they go round the island they do keep coming back if you wait long enough. There's a good place . . .' Billy led Ben along the edge of Giau yn Ooig, and showed him where the soil had eroded away to make a small sheltered platform at the top of the cliff. 'It's fine as long as it's not a southerly.' Billy jumped down the foot or so into the hollow. Ben didn't follow him, although there was plenty of room for two. There was a moment's pause. 'I'll see you later then, Mr Groat,' said Billy doggedly.

Ben would have liked to walk on, thinking his own thoughts: the rare chance of solitude was much more appealing than a passing whale, even supposing there were one. It was the hint of wistfulness in the child's voice . . . if Billy had *asked* him to stay Ben could easily have said no, but Billy would not ask. Ben hesitated, and was lost.

When Ben stepped into the hollow beside him, Billy's face lit up, but he didn't say a word. He moved up, and put his telescope to his eye, scanning the empty sea. Presently he looked round, and held out the telescope. 'Want a shot?'

Ben twisted the focus and saw a shifting swell flecked with white caps. Through the glass it looked close enough to touch, though the muffled crashing of water on rock two hundred feet below gave the lie to that.

'Is our lighthouse just like all the other ones?'

Ben still had the glass to his eye. He almost lowered it, and then grew still. There was an urgency about Billy's question he couldn't quite fathom. *Never look a wild creature in the eye.* Who'd told him that? He didn't know, and it didn't matter. Ben went on watching the waves through the glass without really seeing them, and said casually, 'Ilk lighthouse is different. Your lighthouse is the best-kept one I've ever seen. And the standard of our Scottish lights is very high.'

'But our lighthouse isn't any good any more. It's too old.'

Ben laid down the telescope, but kept his eyes on the sea. From here he could just see the waves break over – Creggyn Doo, was it? – in showers of foam. 'Not everybody would say your lighthouse was too old. Some lighthouses are much older than Ellan Bride, and any lighthouse is a lot better than nane. But the Commissioners of Northern Lights are wanting to make all the lights in Scotland as good as possible. They build more of them all the time, and – ay, it's true – they make the old ones better too.'

'And the Isle of Man as well,' Billy pointed out. Then he asked, 'Do you think everything they do is good?'

There was a pause. 'That's a hard question,' said Ben. 'My

mother might tell you "no". That's because, before I was born, Mr Stevenson was building the greatest lighthouse of all time – for that's what it is, without a doubt, and I reckon it always will be – a lighthouse that's already saved more lives than you can begin to guess at – at the Bell Rock. Have you no heard of the Bell Rock? It guards the Firth of Tay, and no one can begin to guess how many ships have been lost there since men first put to sea.'

'The Bell Rock goes under the water at high tide,' replied Billy. 'And before there was a lighthouse, the Abbot, who was a very holy man, put a bell on it, and it rang to warn the ships, only there was a wrecker who didn't want a bell because he didn't get any wrecks and so he took it off, and then he got wrecked on it himself and he was drowned, and that served him right.'

'Ay well, that was a long time ago. But the lighthouse I'm speaking about was finished in October of 1810. My father worked on it. He'd worked on lighthouses since he was a boy. His first job was on an island in the Pentland Firth – that's between Scotland and Orkney – and he got on so well that when Pentland Skerries was finished he stayed working for Mr Stevenson – him that built the lighthouse – and left Orkney. His sweetheart – that was my mother – waited for him ten years and then they were wed, and she went away sooth with him.

'My mother telt me my father was proud to be working on the Bell Rock. It was a terrible dangerous job, and he was there right from the beginning, working with the great blocks of granite. They had a sort of platform where they lived – it seemed like it could have been swept away any old time, but Mr Stevenson knew what he was doing, and it held. Then, when the tower got too high to raise the stones, they built a temporary tower with a pulley for getting the stones across, and a swinging bridge between it and the light.

'The lighthouse was nearly finished, and they were about to take the bridge down. Just before they did, twa-three fellows ran across – really for the sake of it just – in high spirits they were, see, with the lighthouse about to be finished. Only the bridge broke, and all three of them were killed. And one of them was my father. So my mother canna be glad of that lighthouse, for the way it blighted her own life. But would it no be worse if the Bell Rock light hadna been built, and those three men had had their lives out, while dozens more ships fell foul of the rock and hundreds more lives were lost to it? I dinna ken the answer to that myself, Billy, and that's a fact. It's a sum without an answer. So I dinna ken what's good or not. I canna tell you.'

'So was your Da dead before you were even born?'

'That's right. I was born twa months after.'

'So you didn't ever see your Da?'

'No. But my mother's telt me all she can about him, so I seem to ken him even though I didna.'

There was a long pause. Either Billy was trying to calculate how old he was, thought Ben, which wouldn't be too difficult, or he was working out something a good deal more complicated. He was a little apprehensive, but not altogether surprised, when Billy spoke again.

'I didn't ever see my Da either after I was born. But he *isn't* dead.'

'Is he no?'

'No,' said Billy positively. Instinctively he reached for his telescope, then realised Ben had it. Ben handed it back to him. 'My Da sailed away on a brig,' Billy told him, cradling the telescope.

'A brig, was it?'

'Yes.' The cloud had come lower so they could barely see the Creggyns. It was beginning to rain again. Billy turned up his collar and shifted round so he had his back to the wind. 'To the China Seas,' he informed Ben.

'Opium trade?'

'It might be.' Billy sounded uncertain.

'Tea, maybe?'

'Yes.' Billy knew about tea. 'And silk,' he offered. 'And spices and stuff. Things like that.'

'But whiles he must sail hame again?'

'No, not really.' Billy followed Ben's gaze out to sea. The shreds of passing cloud were already lifting. Beyond the rocks Billy caught sight of the smoke from a distant steamer, but the ship itself was lost in mist. 'He decided to stay in China,' said Billy presently. 'He's been getting very rich because of the China trade. That's why he hasn't come back yet.'

'That's tough for you,' remarked Ben. He hesitated, then decided to take a risk: 'You must have missed him all the more when your Uncle Jim was drowned.'

'Well . . .'

'You and your Mam,' said Ben.

'Well . . . you see . . . my Da might know about that.'

'About what?'

'About if Uncle Jim wasn't *really* drowned. Because you see . . .' Billy had stopped looking for the steamer and was watching Ben anxiously. Ben was quite aware of it, and so he kept his eyes resolutely on the distant tail of smoke. 'No one knows *for sure* that Uncle Jim got drowned. And if he'd been picked up by a ship, see, after he fell in the water – well, a lot of ships go past here on their way to the China Seas. And if my Uncle Jim is still alive: well, you see, my Da might even know about it.'

It wasn't Ben's business. He was sorry for them, of course, but none of the troubles of this small family were any of his business. *A lass doesnae want a man to be so kind* . . . But his mother wouldn't have said that. She was never one to hold back her hand, or her word either, if help were needed. *For what were we put on this earth for, Ben, if not to help one another?* That's what Mr Stevenson went by, too – if he'd not given a hand to a boy who had no claim on him, Ben wouldn't be on Ellan Bride today.

'Billy,' Ben laid his hand on the boy's damp sleeve. 'Billy, I've been working close to the sea all my life. If your Uncle

Jim was swept out to sea from Giau y Vaatey on a bad night, he was drowned. I'm sure that's what your Mam telt you, is it no? She wouldna lie to you about that, would she? Because you ken very well, do you no, that your Uncle Jim would never have stayed away without telling you all if he was still alive? Not that I kent him, of course, but if he was anything like you and your Mam he *couldna* have done that to you. *Never!* It's more important to ken that than to ken just exactly what happened to him. Believe me, it is!'

Ben glanced at Billy. The boy had gone quite white under his tan. He was hugging the telescope tightly to his chest. Ben didn't let go of his sleeve: there was a two-hundred-foot drop in front of them, and if the boy moved suddenly . . . but Billy was used to the cliffs. There was no need to fear for that – only he couldn't get himself out of this one, poor lad, not by himself, anyway.

'Talking of brigs,' said Ben, a few moments later, 'I saw one going north-west off Gob Keyl. It must've been steering a course between here and the Chickens. I doubt you'd be wanting to do that in rough weather. I'll wager you dinna see many ships take that route? No?

Billy made a small movement that might be a shake of the head.

'Mind you,' Ben went on cheerfully, 'I've been through narrower straits than that in my time. I've sailed through the Sound of Harris, for example – that was one of the tightest bits of sailing I ever saw. We were heading back to Eilean Glas: we'd been taking a look at the west coast of the Outer Isles. A wild, exposed coast, yon is. It's got the whole Atlantic battering against it, and no the glimmer of a light the entire length of it. Will I tell you about that?'

Billy gave an almost imperceptible nod.

'We'd been lying off the Monachs, see, west of Uist. That's a tricky group of islands if ever there was one. Just a few flat stretches of sand, that's all they are – in bad weather you'd be grounded without ever even seeing them at all, that's how hard they are to spot. There's no anchorage. We'd moored off to the north-east, but there was no shelter to speak of – just as well the weather stayed fair. Anyway, we beat back to the Sound next day in good time for the tide.

'We'd a local man to pilot us – a stranger couldna get through that place without – the channel's awful narrow at the beginning, with islands and cletts all around you. We were passing so close to the skerries you could see the barnacles on the rocks. The swell was nearly as deep as those waves on Creggyn Doo right now' – Ben noticed that Billy's eyes followed his pointing finger, so it must be worth blethering on like this – 'and we were barely a yard from white water, both port and starboard. The channel's that narrow – you can only get through on a high tide – and when the rocks are covered you canna tell where they are without a local man to show you. Even a light wouldn't help much with that passage, it twists and turns so much among the skerries. I'm telling you, it was a relief to get to Eilean Glas. No that there's much shelter there, either.'

'What's Eilean Glas?' Billy sounded subdued. He thought for a moment, then asked, 'Is it a grey island? That's what it would be here.'

'And so it is up there. But it's a lighthouse, too. Have you no heard of the Eilean Glas light?'

Billy slowly shook his head. He'd stopped hugging the telescope quite so hard.

'It's one of the first lights the Commissioners built in Scotland.' Ben stood up. 'It's going to rain again, Billy lad, and I'm cold. D'you think it might be getting on for supper-time?'

Billy fell into step beside him as they climbed up Cronk ny Mannanan. 'Is Eilean Glas a light like ours? Or is it different?'

'I telt you before: ilk lighthouse is different.'

The boy wasn't looking distressed any more, and he was back to asking his interminable questions. That was all right. Ben could deal with questions that had sensible answers. For a moment Billy had given Ben a glimpse into a more complicated world altogether. Ben reckoned the gap was safely closed again now, just in time for supper. That was what they were both needing, thought Ben: a good meal. He interrupted Billy with a serious question of his own: 'What would you guess Aunt Deer will be giving us for supper, then?'

CHAPTER 21

WHEN MANNANAN RIDES IN HIS CHARIOT OVER THE WAVES, HE looks down through the water at the lost lands lying at the bottom of the sea. In fair weather the rising sun shines through the water, and Mannanan can see all the sunken world which he created. But when Mannanan is angry he stirs the seas with his stick and makes the storms rise. When that happens the drowned lands are lost to sight, and if Mannanan stirs the sea hard enough it turns to blood.

Mannanan helped Bran to cross the sea by taking him in his own chariot. Very few mortals have ever ridden in the chariot of Mannanan. Hardly any have looked down through the waters at the sunken lands.

'The drowned lands are India,' said Breesha. 'But we have to look very quickly because we're going so fast, and any minute the weather might change.'

'Well, supposing it's *not* going to change,' argued Mally. 'Supposing we can go quite slow and the sun is keeping on shining. That's what it does in India.'

'But we're not *in* India. We're still in the chariot, and we're still going over the sea. We're still in *our* country. We're only looking *at* India, and it could change any minute.'

'Well, supposing we don't change it. Supposing we say it just keeps on being nice.'

'No. Otherwise it doesn't work. You can't just suppose it's nice all the time or there isn't any game. Anyway, we have to look over the edge.'

'I *am* looking. If I lean any more I'll fall out.'

'Well, hold on tight then. Because supposing it's getting a bit rough. What can you see?'

'Elephants,' said Mally promptly. 'I can see elephants.'

'Only one elephant,' corrected Breesha. 'With a young rajah in a howdah.'

'Supposing there are *lots* of elephants,' said Mally obstinately.

'I can only see one.'

'There are *lots*. Or else I won't play. Because I think supposing we could get down there and ride on one. And then this could be *our* howdah too.'

Breesha took a moment to weigh the advantages of such a transformation. The main disadvantage was that it was Mally's idea. Breesha preferred the ideas to be her own. Another disadvantage was that Mannanan couldn't come into India with them, because he was the god of the sea, not India. India had its own gods. The part of the game that Breesha always kept to herself was the vital presence of the sea god in his chariot. Mally tended to forget the god was there, and Breesha seldom reminded her. But for Breesha the god was the most important part. She'd never paused to wonder why, but she was aware it was to do with the fact that when she was falling asleep at night she always imagined herself in the chariot of the sea god, speeding over the water as the waves rose and fell, rushing towards some other country, which she longed and yet feared to reach. It was comforting, and yet also a little alarming, to feel the presence of the god with her in the chariot. He held the reins, and he always sat a little behind her, on her left. She was always asleep before they came anywhere near to sighting the other country. Breesha never felt like supposing that the chariot was actually arriving. But just now it was daytime, and she was awake, and with Mally. She had to decide. If they went down into India they couldn't take the sea god with them. Or could they? Supposing they did, would that be too great a confusion? There was a sea in India, wasn't there?

'Supposing all the elephants are by the sea,' said Breesha aloud. That was a good way of making a concession without saying so, and also providing the sea god with his own element so he could come too. She didn't need to tell Mally the rest of her thoughts.

'Bathing,' said Mally, pleased. 'The sea in India is so hot you can walk into it. That's what our elephant is doing now.'

'But *we're* not getting wet.'

'No, we're *much* too high up, even for the big waves.'

The first floor of the lighthouse was a good place when it was raining. They weren't allowed to play in the lantern; in fact they weren't supposed to go up there at all if no one was working. But they were allowed to go on the first floor. It was warmer than the ground floor because it had a wooden floor, and it was less full of things. It was rather dark, because the only light came down through the trapdoor from the lantern. They were allowed to go up and hook the trapdoor open so as to get some light. The first floor was really only a platform between the store-room at the bottom of the tower and the lantern at the top. There was a spiral stair made of stone down to the ground floor, and a wooden ladder leading from the platform up to the light. Stairs and steps took up most of the space inside the tower. The only things that the lightkeeper kept on this level were a bolster and a couple of blankets. There wasn't a proper bed because the lightkeeper must never sleep on watch, but she could sometimes make herself comfortable down on the platform. At night it was easier to see down here, because the light streamed through the trapdoor once the lamps were lit.

Breesha and Mally had brought up a few things of their own. They'd used driftwood to make the sides of the chariot. The seat was a heavy log, whitened by the sea, that had come ashore on the slabs a year or two back. The lightkeeper's blankets and bolster made the chariot comfortable inside. It had been very difficult getting the log for the seat up the stairs, but they'd managed it. There was no question of asking for help. This game was private. They didn't even play it with Billy. It wasn't a boy's game. Obviously the lightkeeper had noticed the presence of a chariot in the middle of the lighthouse, but Aunt Lucy could be trusted not to comment on that sort of thing if she felt it didn't matter. All she ever did was to pile the chariot away against the wall when they weren't using it, so it looked as tidy as everything else in the lighthouse. They had string for the reins, because sometimes Breesha or Mally took a turn at driving the magic horses, and an old tinder box for supplies. Mam almost always gave them provisions if they said they were going on a very long journey. Today they had ships' biscuit, which was satisfying because it made it seem more like a real voyage than ever.

'We're running out of provisions,' said Breesha presently. 'We'll have to forage.'

'Do you mean get off our elephant? But supposing there are tigers? Let's not get off.'

'No, we needn't get off. We can pick fresh coconuts from the trees as we pass.'

'Green coconuts?'

'Yes. In fact, supposing they're coconuts like they used to sell on the beach when Mam was little. And the seller is coming up to our elephant, and he's taken a big knife and sliced off the soft green flesh at the top, and we can drink the milk . . .'

'"Just like taking the top off a boiled egg."' They both knew the coconut story by heart, so Mally was quoting Mam verbatim. 'And first we can drink the lovely sweet milk, and then we eat the big moist chunks of coconut.'

'"And sometimes it's soft inside like butter and it all falls apart in your hand, and sometimes it's hard like cheese from the Island. You don't know until you open it."'

'Mine is all squishy and juicy.'

Silently they conjured up lush visions of imaginary coconuts.

'Are they as nice as the sugar plums that Mr Groat bought?' asked Mally presently. She sounded rather wistful.

'They're a lot nicer. *Everything* in India tastes better than it does here. All the sweets in India are much sweeter than any sugar plums!' Breesha's imagination swept ahead of her, and suddenly she found herself saying something she'd never thought of before. 'When I'm grown up I'm going to go to India – not just supposing but *really*. I'm going to go and find Ajoba. And Aji. That's what I'm going to do when I grow up.'

'Oh,' said Mally. The idea was so new she had to think hard about it for a moment. 'Can I come too?'

'I don't know. I don't know how I'm going to do it yet.'

'And if we did that, it would be easier supposing there were elephants because they'd be real ones.'

'If they were real we wouldn't *have* to do any supposing, silly.'

'The elephants went by as high as the garden wall where Mam was a little girl,' said Mally.

'And if we did go, we could *really* go in that very same garden too.'

'And the best sweets – sweeter sweets than any of Mr Groat's sugar plums, even – would come at Diwali. That's when all the children have sweets. As many sweets as they can eat without being sick. At Diwali all the houses would put out little lights and we'd see them shine, and it would seem just as though there were little lighthouses everywhere.'

'And we'd go from house to house and visit our friends,' put in Breesha. 'We wouldn't have to light just one little lamp in the keeill on an icy cold November night. We'd have lamps lit everywhere. And it would be *hot* even though it was winter. And we'd have other places to go to as well. And other people.' Breesha frowned with the effort of imagining it. 'We'd have cousins – more cousins than just Billy. Lots of cousins to go around with, and they'll take us everywhere we want to go.'

'But Breesha . . .'

'What?'

'It wouldn't be . . . we aren't supposing that India would be better than if we stayed on Ellan Bride?'

'I'm not talking about a game,' said Breesha. She sounded quite fierce about it. 'I'm talking about when I'm grown up, and then it won't be just a game. It'll be *real*. I'm going to make it real, one day! And anyway, we're not going to be allowed to stay on Ellan Bride any more, so that's that!'

Et in Arcadia ego . . . Archie absentmindedly drew a border, just like the ornamental scroll on the original carving, around the words he'd copied from over the door of the lighthouse. He was alone in the kitchen with the only person on the island who might conceivably be able to tell him what the Latin words meant, but nothing would have induced him to ask her. Having no Latin was one of the things that distinguished him from a gentleman. The enigmatic motto presumably represented some fancy of the deceased Duke of Atholl. It was hardly relevant, in any case, and by the end of the summer the old lighthouse, inscription and all, would be reduced to its constituent stones.

The only sounds in the kitchen were the wind in the chimney, the flames crackling round the logs on the hearth, and the occasional chink of crocks. Diya made no noise at all as she moved from dresser to table to hearth and back again. She'd kneaded the bread for the second time and set it to bake in the bread oven. As the afternoon waned the smell of new bread began to fill the room. She'd gone into the larder and hung the sour milk in a muslin cloth to make cheese. She'd brought a bowl of water to the table and peeled half a dozen wizened potatoes, chopped them up, and added them to the broth pot. She'd set the broth to boil and brought in fresh fuel for the fire. And now she was sitting at the other end of the table letting out the tucks in a child's nightgown. She hadn't said a word to Archie since he'd sat down to work. The kitchen was as clean and peaceful as a kitchen could well be.

When Archie had attended the school in Callander, he'd

often sat with his slate at the kitchen table in the evenings writing out his sums for the next day. His mother would work around him, just as Mrs Geddes was doing now. Unlike Mrs Geddes, his mother wouldn't have been able to read his work under any circumstances, but she'd protect his right to do it, even when his brothers scoffed at him and called him a sook. Both Archie's brothers were working in the mill back at Kilmahog, while he, Archie, was here on Ellan Bride. And in October he'd be sailing a good deal further than the Irish Sea, and you might say it was all because of those long-ago evenings at home spent writing numbers on a slate.

It didn't matter that they'd got rained off. They'd done a fair day's work, and there was enough material now to be able to make a start. Already Archie could see the map in his mind's eye. Ellan Bride was so small – barely half a mile long – that the whole island would fit easily onto foolscap, even at a scale of twelve inches to the mile. Archie had brought with him a dozen loose sheets of foolscap, as well as his drawing instruments and log book, and while he was waiting for the weather to clear, he began to adjust the chain measurements to the heights they'd logged this afternoon. As he did his calculations, he drew each triangle with compasses and ruler to the corrected dimensions. Before long he was able to look through the network of ruled lines, and, as if he were watching the fog clear on the other side of a barred window, he began to see the actual shape of Ellan Bride forming on the flat page. For over an hour he was absorbed, unaware of Mrs Geddes moving softly around the room. It was almost as if he were creating the island himself; certainly it had never been represented on paper before. There was more data to collect – another day's work – but he had enough material now to see pretty well what the island was going to look like.

He didn't become aware of his surroundings again until Diya took the loaves out of the bread oven, and laid them upside down to cool on a wire tray at the other end of the table. They looked as good as they smelt. He was hungry. It must be getting on for supper-time. It wasn't just the new bread; he could also smell the broth simmering in the pot. They'd been alone in the kitchen for a long time, he and Mrs Geddes. She certainly knew how to be silent. That was a rare blessing in a woman.

Diya must have noticed he was looking at her, and not at his work, because suddenly she spoke. 'Do you like the hot crust? I sometimes let the children have a bit as a treat. It's not good for the digestion, of course.'

'Ay. I mean: yes, I do.' His voice was hoarse after the long silence. Archie cleared his throat.

She picked up a much-sharpened, lethal-looking knife. It went through the fresh loaf as if it were butter. 'Here.'

'Thank you very much, ma'am.' No one had cut off a crust hot from the oven for him, and passed it to him in her fingers, since he was about ten years old. It was a little disconcerting to be treated as if he were her nephew Billy. The bread tasted very good. Archie watched Diya stirring the broth with a long wooden spoon.

He was tired, he realised as he chewed his bread. He'd slept very badly the previous night. He could hardly blame Ben for that; the man had been sound asleep, but he'd taken up a lot of room, and at one point he'd certainly been snoring. The last time Archie had woken, the dawn had been creeping in at the kitchen window. He'd given up at that stage, and got up. Besides, he'd had a bad dream. Unconscious that he was still staring at Diya as she stirred her broth, he gradually pieced together what the dream had been.

The brig was racing before the wind. The swell was piling up behind them, pushing them onto the lee shore. If they couldn't round the Cape they were done for. Sheets of spray shot up from the lethal skerries. They might get round, but there was no light . . . He couldn't draw the plan because the wind was too wild, gusting over the cliffs where the waves broke far below, and trying to blow him off his feet. He couldn't navigate; he couldn't take the papers from his knapsack, and because of that the ship . . . But he had been in the ship . . . No, that was in the dream . . . All of it had only been a dream.

It wasn't the first time Diya had moved softly around a kitchen, fully aware that a young man's eyes were fixed on her wherever she went. Mr Buchanan was not in the least like Jim, and the kitchen on Ellan Bride was not in the least like the high-ceilinged kitchen in Grandmother's house. Moreover, Diya herself was no longer the young girl she'd been back then. She was a widow, the mother of two growing daughters, and it hadn't crossed her mind in five years that there'd ever again be a man who'd be unable to take his eyes off her. Diya went on kneading the bread as if nothing unusual were happening, but she was very conscious of being watched.

When Jim had erupted into the basement of her Grandmother's genteel feminine household, Diya had been half-shocked, half-fascinated. She'd had very little knowledge to guide her; she'd discovered more about sexual matters in the years before she was eight than anything she'd learned since. What was normal in India was apparently non-existent in Castletown. As she grew older Diya had become aware, without being able to define her feelings precisely, that this was a lie. But a man like Jim was unthinkable, and so Diya obediently did not think. As she rolled the dough into soft round loaves, Diya wondered how she could possibly have remained so ignorant. But there'd been other ways of knowing than thinking. And now Diya was a widow, and not innocent at all; in fact she knew precisely what Mr Buchanan might be thinking about as he watched her leaning over the hearth, setting out the loaves to rise.

Diya was less sure what she thought about him. He came from a world that was closed to her for ever. Unless . . . but no, she wouldn't even think about that. Diya straightened up quickly, and hurried into the larder to hang up the sour milk to make cheese.

It was ironic, she thought as she unfolded the boiled muslin, that this man had, like Jim, suddenly appeared in the very heart of her house, bringing with him disturbing intimations of other ways of life, other possibilities . . . The difference was that Diya recognised the world Archie came from, whereas Jim's world had, when she first met him, been a complete mystery. But that might also be a delusion. What did she know about Mr Buchanan? That he was a Scotch surveyor who was interested in geology. That he had fine dark eyes, was a well set-up, athletic young man, although not very tall – exactly her own height, in fact. That he was polite when he chose to be, although often uncivil when his mind was engaged on other matters. That, as ever, she must always be aware of the boundaries of what he found acceptable, and take care not to transgress them. That he could hardly take his eyes off her. And that was about all.

It wasn't even worth thinking about. Diya poured the milk into the muslin, and hung it from a hook so the whey could drip slowly into the pot beneath. There was something else about Mr Buchanan: she didn't even dare formulate the notion. It was too dangerous. Diya took an enamel bowl and started to select usable potatoes from the bottom of the sack. But she couldn't help her thoughts: she knew she didn't want to stay on Ellan Bride for ever. She didn't want her daughters to grow up here, knowing nothing else. At the same time she was terrified – though no one must ever guess that – because she had no money and nowhere to go. Wasn't that the only thing that had driven her here in the first place?

No, that was a wicked thought. She'd loved Jim. Not true: she hadn't loved him when she'd married him. She'd been fascinated by his complete unlikeness to anyone else she'd known – by the way he didn't hide what he was, in the way that Grandmother's male friends seemed to do so adeptly – and, also, she'd been desperate. Diya scrabbled in the bottom of the sack. There weren't enough of last year's potatoes left to do another meal; she might as well finish them now . . . And then she'd married Jim, without proper consideration really, and sex had immediately ceased to be an unmentionable mystery. And what that had led to, in the end, was that she'd loved him.

But that was all over. Diya tumbled the potatoes into the enamel bowl, and came back to the table. Mr Buchanan was bent over his drawing and seemed not to notice her. Diya poured cold water over the potatoes, and picked up the knife. Jim was dead and Diya was a widow, and that was that. There'd been an aunt in India who'd been a widow. Diya didn't want to think about that; it wasn't the same on the Island. There hadn't been potatoes to peel in Aji's house either: this was another world altogether. But perhaps some sense of abasement had lingered. Diya recoiled from the memory of that resigned, white-clad figure, who'd drifted around the edges of Ajoba's household, with no place to call her own, tolerated but not respected, and certainly not welcomed. Diya dropped a peeled white potato into the pan. She couldn't even recall the woman's name. She didn't want to. There were more immediate things to think about. Potatoes, for example. She was having to cut big chunks out of them where they'd started to rot. This year's crop wouldn't be ready for a month or more. By that time they might all have left the island.

Diya didn't wish to remember anything bad about India. India was all sunlight and what seemed, in retrospect at least – for who could really see clearly through the long dark tunnel of the intervening years? – to have been a happy childhood. Only the brightness of the sun, as Diya recalled it, was certainly real and true. Sometimes, as in the present drought, there were rare golden days when that sun came as far north as Ellan Bride and Diya knew that her memories had not been playing her false. But as for the rest . . . there was no going back. She had lost her place in the other world long ago. And if a woman must be a widow, she was in a more compassionate country now, whatever happened to her and Breesha and Mally when they had to leave the sanctuary of Ellan Bride.

Only she hadn't expected that anyone would look at her

again as this man kept doing. She didn't flatter herself that Mr Buchanan was as interested in her as Jim had been, although when she came back into the kitchen again with a basket of logs he looked up, stared at her, and said nothing, just as Jim had once been used to do, when Diya would go down to Annie as usual, and find that Annie's young nephew from the remote island was once again visiting her in the kitchen.

Diya had recognised as soon as she'd arrived in Castletown, even at eight years old, how the class system worked. Aji would have understood it at once; in fact Aji would have found it very lax. Aji would have been horrified to think of an unwashed young man of low class, in sea-stained breeks and a tattered seaman's jacket, polluting the sacred centre of the house. In Aji's house no man, not even Ajoba himself, ever entered the kitchen. Aji's kitchen was not down in a basement, but right in the middle of the house, and the cook was not a menial, but Aji herself. Before Diya was permitted to enter that kitchen – which only happened when she was allowed to help – she had first to take off her shoes, then wash her hands and feet, and then put on clean clothes. There was a sacred niche in the wall just where you went into the kitchen, where Ganesha dwelt as a little jade image; the presence of the god blessed all the food that was prepared and eaten in the house. Aji wore a special silk sari when she cooked, and she worked alone in the kitchen for many quiet hours before each meal. Diya was never allowed to take food outside the kitchen. At meals Aji served everyone herself. When the men had eaten she would put Diya's food on her plate for her, along with any of the cousins who were in the house, and last of all, when everyone else had finished, Aji would serve herself. Diya had been taught, and she had never forgotten in spite of everything that had happened since, that the making and eating of food was a very sacred thing.

Diya was glad, therefore, that this man sitting in her kitchen was not trying to disturb her. He'd stopped looking at her now. He was absorbed in his drawing, and no longer seemed aware that Diya was there. As she passed close by his chair she could see that he was ruling a whole network of triangles on his paper. There must be a way of working out the chain measurements in relation to the heights to get the outline of the island to come out right. Mr Buchanan must have worked it out to his satisfaction, anyway, because at last he stopped drawing, and now he seemed to be thinking instead. While he thought, he kept his gaze fixed on Diya as she opened the bread oven and turned the brown loaves inside. He obviously didn't realise he was doing it.

On board ship she'd realised that English people had very different views about kitchens. On the voyage, the man who'd cooked Diya's rice for her in the galley had been roughly dressed, like Jim, and roughly spoken, also like Jim. He was more like a street seller than a cook. Diya had been slightly less shocked than she might have been, thanks to her cousins. Some of the young cousins were much less strict than Ajoba. There'd been a memorable occasion when one of the boys had bought them coconuts from a man who was selling them on the beach. The coconut man sliced off the top of each coconut, and handed them over in his bare hands. There hadn't even been a plate! The forbidden fruit had been so sweet, so deliciously green and juicy: afterwards they'd all had to walk right into the sea to wash off the tell-tale stains from their hands and clothes. If Ajoba had known about those coconuts the scene would have been truly terrible. Even now Diya felt a little frightened at the thought.

But all that was long ago. Both Aji and Ajoba – Diya had never known their ages – were probably dead by now. That was another terrible thought. Diya couldn't help worrying about it sometimes. If she were taken back to the white road that led along the shore next to Aji's house, she would know her way home at once. But she would never be there again. How could she go back: a woman without a husband, without caste? It was impossible. And perhaps 'there' no longer even existed. Grandmother in Castletown had made sure Diya was taught to read and write, and post a letter, but all that was in English, and nothing to do with Aji and Ajoba.

Diya's father had promised, when he went back to India . . . But that was long ago, and now her father was dead, without having written another word to her, even to say goodbye. The letter from the East India Company had been sent to Grandmother, at the Castletown address, where it had arrived six months after her father was buried in the English cemetery in Bombay. It had taken another three months for it to be forwarded to Mrs Geddes, on Ellan Bride. But there was no point dwelling on broken promises. If one did that, the past years would hold nothing but endless disappointment, and that was not true. Diya would not let a thought like that be true.

She could smell that the bread was ready. Diya raked back the ashes and pulled the bread oven to the front of the hearth. She lifted the cover with a cloth, and took another clean white cloth to handle the hot loaves. She brought them over to the table and laid them upside down on the wire rack to cool. When Mummig used to lay out the hot loaves, when Diya first came to the island, she'd cut off a slice of the hot crust and give it to whoever was there – Jim or Lucy or Jim's Da. She'd offer it to Diya as well, but with the shade of Aji standing over her, Diya found it impossible to accept. And yet she'd learned to continue this small domestic custom with the next generation of Ellan Bride children – but then, life was never logical. If it had been Billy watching her now, instead of Mr Buchanan, Diya would have known at this moment exactly what he was thinking.

'Do you like the hot crust?' she asked impulsively. 'I sometimes let the children have a bit as a treat. It's not good for the digestion, of course.'

'Ay. I mean: yes, I do.'

He sounded dazed, as if his thoughts had been very far away. He was quite forgetting to be formal; perhaps he didn't feel shy any more. 'Here,' said Diya, and passed him the piece she'd cut off, holding it in her fingers in exactly the way that Mummig would have done.

'Thank you very much, ma'am.'

Diya took her sewing box from the dresser, and sat down at the other end of the table. There was just time to take out the tucks in Mally's nightgown before supper. The children had no way of telling the time but somehow they always knew when the next meal was ready. Soon the long peace of the afternoon would be shattered. Diya caught herself up on the thought, and was surprised. This man had been in her kitchen all the time, and yet there had been peace. Lucy said Mr Buchanan was rude. Perhaps he was, sometimes. But the ability to be peacefully silent in another's company seemed to Diya the epitome of politeness.

Suddenly she broke the silence herself. Her own speech surprised her: it was just a passing thought, and there was no reason at all why she should be sharing it with this stranger, except that all of a sudden it seemed an ordinary thing to do. She stopped stitching and held the needle poised above the cloth. 'My grandfather in India used to sit drawing plans just as you do. Plans of streets and buildings. That was what he did for his work. He worked in a company in Bombay that was making new buildings for the city. An English company. Sometimes when he was at home he used to sit on the veranda drawing. And sometimes I would sit there with him. We didn't talk to each other. The garden outside was very hot, and everything was quiet. I had a parrot – a little green parrot called Mittu. Mittu could say his own name: *Mittu Mittu.* I would softly get Mittu to talk, and my grandfather would sit and draw, all through the long hot afternoon in the shade of the veranda. And my grandfather and I, we were at peace together.'

She'd taken him entirely by surprise and he forgot to be shy. 'I like that,' replied Archie without even hesitating. 'There isna enough peace in this world – or so it seems to me. When you do get a little bit of peace sometimes, it's worth remembering, anyway, if nothing else.'

Chapter 22

HAVING A CANDLE MADE ALL THE DIFFERENCE. ARCHIE dripped hot wax into the centre of the large green stone which sat in the middle of the floor, and stuck the candle down firmly. He squatted on the floor of the keeill and opened his knapsack. It would have been more comfortable to sit on the big stone at the east end, only some atavistic, half-acknowledged taboo prevented him. However, it seemed fair enough to use the altar as a writing desk. By no stretch of the imagination could the inside of the keeill be seen as relevant to his work, so Archie opened his notebook not at the next page of his survey notes, but at the back. The last pages were already filled with drawings: a basking shark, and a detailed sketch of the goniatite, drawn to scale. Archie turned the page backwards. He wrote a new title at the top of the fresh sheet: 'Celtic Chapel, Ellan Bride.' Then he laid the book open on the altar and took a measuring tape out of his pocket.

He could easily stand up in the centre of the chapel. From the top of his head to the slabbed roof was about three feet, as far as he could judge. He made a note: *Height c. 8' 6"*. The oblong chapel was roughly twelve feet long and five feet across at its widest points. The west door had a pointed arch, measuring two feet three inches from ground to apex. It was impossible to tell how far the floor had risen over the years. At the present ground level the door was nineteen inches across.

There was a small window, measuring six by nine inches, above the west door; there were signs that it might have been added later. The chapel walls had at one time been covered with lime mortar. There was an aumbry in the south wall close to the altar, ten inches across and nine inches high. In it lay an abandoned starlings' nest. The altar at the east end was a half-buried, almost rectangular, single stone. There were no signs of masonry above ground; evidently that was its natural shape. Archie noted its visible dimensions: *10½" x 25½" x 12"*.

He deliberately didn't study the objects in the chapel until he'd surveyed the building. Then he had a look at the cross. It was a rough, weather-worn thing, so crudely carved one could only infer that it was a cross from its obviously ecclesiastical context. There were faint carvings on its surface, so worn by the centuries that Archie could no longer trace the pattern. Altogether the cross was disappointingly primitive, and a closer inspection yielded nothing of significance.

Perhaps the most curious item in the chapel was the large green stone in the middle of the floor. It had been moved recently. He could still see the indentation to the right of the altar where the rock had lain for a long time. There was no indentation in its present position. That stone had never come from Ellan Bride. At a guess – Archie took notes so that he could look it up when he got back to Edinburgh – he'd describe it as green serpentine marble. Where could it possibly have come from? Ireland, he suspected, but he couldn't be sure; with any luck the answer would lie in the Advocates' Library.

When he'd finished with the stone, Archie sat down and began to make sketches, starting with the roof. The candle-light flickered in a breath of wind, and the five flat stones that constituted the ceiling seemed to quiver as if a wave had washed softly over them. As once it had: those slabs had originally been formed over long centuries at the bottom of a shallow sea. Over the aeons little particles of matter would have drifted down to the sea bed, slowly forming a layer of solid rock. And only in the last moment of time – in the mere flicker of an eyelid, as it were – if gods had eyelids – would those same stones have been taken and dressed, and laid over the corbelled walls to make a chapel roof.

As Archie sat drawing he gradually became aware of other things. Alongside the odour of damp earth, which was stronger than ever after the rain this afternoon, he caught a more subtle smell, musky but sweet, like old hay. The walls were no longer silent under the weight of the passing centuries; they were filled with little liquid rustling noises inside the stone. The sounds grew more insistent, and now it was not just rustling but curious twitterings. Mother Carey's chickens . . . now that the sun had set the stormy petrels were waking up. When it was fully dark they'd come out. It would be worth watching for that . . . later on, maybe, he'd come out again to see them. Archie's uncomfortable bed seemed a poor alternative. If he wasn't too sleepy he'd come back here later; now that the rain had passed he ought to be able to see well enough, even with no moon.

Aunt Diya had left a candle burning on the kitchen table because neither of the surveyors had come in. They'd both gone out after supper. It had stopped raining, and although there was a bit of wind Mam reckoned it was going to be a fine day again tomorrow. Aunt Diya said the rain hadn't been enough to do the garden much good. Billy didn't care about that. He wanted to go out with the surveyors again in the morning, and for that the weather needed to be fine.

Aunt Diya hadn't let Billy go out with the two men after supper; she said it was bedtime. Mally had gone to bed already. Billy had undressed unwillingly by the fire. It was odd getting ready for bed by himself. This was the second night Breesha had had to sleep with Aunt Diya because of the surveyors. She had to get undressed in the bedroom too, even though it must be colder than their usual place by the fire, and that was also because of the surveyors. Aunt Diya had taken away Billy's shirt when he took it off because somehow he'd ripped a hole in the elbow. Billy didn't remember how it had happened. Aunt Diya had laid out his other shirt, freshly washed and aired, for him to wear tomorrow, even though it would only be Saturday.

When Billy stood at the window in his nightshirt he could see the beam from the lighthouse shining on the sea. It never shone into the kitchen because the windows looked the wrong way. That didn't matter; you could almost always see the reflection of the light by looking at the sea. When Billy lay in bed he could look across to the window and tell by the colour of the window panes that the light was lit. The colour of the dark changed a lot with the weather and the moon, but there was a certain lightness inside even the thickest dark, which came from the lighthouse, right through the very worst storms of winter.

It wasn't as comfortable sleeping on a straw pallet as it was in his own bed. Also, there was that candle burning on the kitchen table, making the room too light. Billy lay wondering where Mr Groat and the Writing Man had gone. Surely they couldn't do any more work tonight because it was pretty well dark out there? Surely that would make the measuring much too difficult, and the Writing Man wouldn't be able to see to write?

There was a heaviness in Billy's chest which hadn't been there before. He was noticing it now that he was lying in bed with nothing else to do. At supper he'd forgotten about it, but now it had come back. In fact he felt sad. He even felt like crying, only Mr Groat might come back at any moment. Girls cried. Billy was emphatically not a girl. But even so he couldn't help feeling sad. Mr Groat had said that Uncle Jim was dead. Mam had said the same, long ago, but when Mr Groat said it there was something so true in his voice that Billy had no choice but to believe him. That meant there was no way of escaping it any more. For the rest of his life Billy would have to go on being quite certain, all the time, that Uncle Jim was dead.

In his mind Billy saw a bright vision of a far away island, white sands fringed with palm trees, a little hut, Friday's footprint . . . and in the middle of it all Uncle Jim, patiently waiting for the inevitable ship that would come to bring him home. But the picture had got very small and far away. It had gone all out of focus, and nothing Billy could do now would bring it back. Mr Groat's words had slammed the door on that other country, and Billy would never be able to look into it properly again.

Even though that made him feel like crying, Billy wasn't angry with Mr Groat. He liked him. It wasn't Mr Groat's fault if the things he said were true. Billy thought sleepily about Mr Groat. Mr Groat had started to be a chainman when he was fourteen. He'd grown up on an island, and he'd left it and gone all on his own to Edinburgh. Perhaps he, Billy, could be a chainman too. If he couldn't be the lightkeeper on Ellan Bride maybe being a chainman would be the next best thing. And then he could go wherever he liked, and stay up at night as late as he liked, with no Aunt Diya to tell him not to, just like Mr Groat . . .

The wind was growing stronger. There were huge whitecaps on the sea. The magic horses were pulling at the reins. They insisted on galloping much too fast. They were huge and white and reared their heads. They tossed their great necks in a shower of foam. She didn't want to go with them. It was dark at sea, and it was all right here because the lighthouse was lit and she could see. The spindrift caught the light and the horses were shining bright. But the dark was deep and frightening. She didn't want to go into it. It wasn't horses any more, it was elephants, and they were pulling so hard she couldn't hold them . . . she couldn't hold them back . . .

'Mally veen, what is it? Mally, wake up, wake up! Mally! It's all right, Mally veen, did you have a bad dream? It's all right now, Mam's here. Wake up, sweetheart, try to wake up!'

Ben was saying, 'But you ken, do you no, Miss Lucy, that men in offices in Liverpool and Castletown and Edinburgh and London are all arguing with each other about the harbour dues that ships should be paying for Ellan Bride?'

'No,' said Lucy obstinately. 'I'm not knowing and I'm not caring. All right, so you're telling me that the old Duke was making half a million pounds, while we're getting eighteen pounds a year. So what's that to do with anything? If the Ellan Bride light is saving a single man from drowning, or a single ship from foundering, then it's all been worth it. That's what the light is for. That's what it's *always* been for.'

'That's no true,' answered Ben. 'It's what it's for to *you*. It's what it was for to your father and your grandfather, I don't doubt. But 'tis no why it was built. There's no but one reason it was built. For money! If the Duke still owned the light I doubt you'd be any better off than you are now. He'd be doing whatever would make him richer. If that meant selling to the Commissioners of Northern Lights, and no keeping your family on here, then that's what he'd do. He wouldna stop to think about it for a moment. 'Tis what any rich man would do.'

'But it wasn't just the Duke! The Liverpool merchants were the ones petitioning to have the light here, so's to save people's lives! And it does! All these years it's done that!'

'Oh ay, all these years it has! And that's good – I didna say it wasna. Make no doubt of that! All I'm saying is, the lighthouse wasna put here out of charity, or loving-kindness, or because poor sailor-men value their own lives, God help them. It was done just because – and *only* because – rich men could make money! To hell with the sailors; 'twas their *property* those men were wanting to protect. What costs the most? A ship? A cargo? Or the scum of the earth who sail her to the four corners of the world for five pound each a year?'

'I never heard anyone speak so!' cried Lucy. 'I don't like it! Do you not believe in *anything*? Because if not, I'm wishing you'd go away and leave me in peace! I can't be arguing all night, but I *know* you're not right! Why, there's a rich man on the Island – a very rich man – who's doing all he can to save poor sailors, and he's not asking for anything back at all. He was leading the rescue of the sailors from the *George* last year.

And now he's trying to set up a boat which'll just be there to go out and save ships that are in trouble. Mr Hillary isn't never doing that for money! He's doing it out of . . . of what did you just say? Out of charity and loving-kindness. And that's the *truth*. And now I'm going up to check the light.'

Lucy picked up the oil can, which she'd put down on the bottom step of the spiral stair, and turned to go.

'I'll leave you in peace, if you like,' said Ben, suddenly humble. 'But I'd like to come up and look at the light. That's if you dinna mind.'

'You and Mr Buchanan were looking at it for long enough last night!'

'No. Mr Buchanan looked at it. I was just keeping out of your way, if you recall.'

'And you're thinking if you come up again tonight you won't be in my way?'

'I hope not.'

'Well, come if you like.' Lucy tossed her head, and went up the stair. 'I'm not caring. But I don't want to *argue*.'

'I winna argue,' promised Ben. 'It's just . . .' He followed her up to the platform. ''Tis just the way of it, see. Sometimes I do wonder . . . it's no just you, Miss Lucy. 'Tis everywhere. I'll tell you one thing: I'm glad I work for Mr Stevenson. And I'm glad Mr Stevenson works for the Commissioners of Northern Lights. We all have our living to make, and that's a fact, but I wouldna wish to be putting money in a rich man's pocket, just. No, I wouldna want only to be doing that. Will I help you with that?'

For some reason there were bits of driftwood arranged in a rough square in the middle of the floor, with a couple of blankets draped across the middle. Ben helped Lucy roll a large log against the wall.

'Thank you. Sometimes the children are playing here when it's wet . . . Mr Groat?'

'Ay?'

'Are you what they call a Radical?'

'I doubt it,' answered Ben. 'I'm a peaceable man myself. I just get to thinking sometimes that the world could be arranged a mite better than it is. These are supposed to be enlightened times, but in Edinburgh there're bairns younger than your Mally begging on the street. Peedie girls . . . I wouldna like to say what happens to them . . . But I said I wouldna argue. Will I leave you in peace now? D'you honestly want me to go, for I'd as lief stay? Missus Deer was putting the bairns to bed in the house, and I thought I was in the way. It's a little early to be turning in myself.'

'Mr Groat!'

'Ay?'

'When you tell me things like that it fairly makes my blood run cold. They're making us go away from here, you know that. We'll be leaving Ellan Bride before the summer's out. Sometimes I wonder what's going to become of *us*.'

Before he could reply to that Lucy quickly disappeared up the ladder. Ben hesitated for a moment, not sure what to do, and then he put his hand to the rail, and followed her up into the brightness of the light.

When Breesha woke suddenly she couldn't think where she was. It was dark, but she could feel the absence of walls around her. Of course, she wasn't with Billy in the kitchen bed. She was alone in Mam and Aunt Lucy's bed. There was some kind of commotion in the room. She heard Mam's voice, and Mally sobbing. Mam was hushing Mally . . . Mally had had a nightmare, that was it. Nothing to worry about after all.

Breesha felt wide awake now they'd woken her up. She couldn't even try to go back to sleep. Before she'd fallen asleep the first time, her thoughts had been racing around inside her head, and now they were roused again they wouldn't leave off. Her mind seemed to be full of anxious voices. Breesha tried telling the horrible thoughts to be quiet but they wouldn't. It would be easier if they were simply black or white, but they were all mixed together in a chaotic whirl of different colours.

Breesha didn't like not being able to decide at once what she thought about anything.

For example, there was the Writing Man – Mr Buchanan. Through the telescope she had seen him look, for one instant, like Ali Baba. Then this afternoon, when he'd shown her how to use the level, she'd almost felt as though she liked him. No – it wasn't liking exactly – she'd been able to forget for a moment that she didn't like him, because he'd been showing her how to use the level, and that had been interesting. Also, he'd treated her as if she were a proper person, just for that once. As if she were a boy. He hadn't been looking at her, of course. Perhaps he'd forgotten for a few minutes that she wasn't Billy. Hadn't he noticed that she was cleverer than Billy? No one ever mentioned the fact, but Breesha knew she was the cleverest at lessons. One could hardly help noticing a thing like that however much Mam never said so.

Then Mam had asked the Writing Man to show Breesha about the chaining and the triangles. It wasn't so much that Breesha wanted to do sums in the evening – that was Mam's idea, and even the cleverest of people would hardly want to spend their time doing that – but that Breesha had expected him not to forget. With Mam and Aunt Lucy, if they said they'd do something they always did it. Even if they forgot, you only had remind them they'd made a promise, and then they'd keep it. *Had* the Writing Man promised? Probably not exactly, but he *had* given his word, and Mam said that to give your word was as good as making a promise. Anyway, the Writing Man had ignored her completely for the whole of supper-time, and afterwards he'd got up and gone out without a word to anybody.

Mally wasn't crying so loudly now. It must have been a very bad nightmare . . . It wasn't quite true that the Writing Man hadn't said a word. He'd thanked Mam for the meal, and asked her for a candle. Mam had given him the candle without asking what it was for. And what *was* it for? What could the Writing Man be doing with a candle out of doors anyway? It was – Breesha listened to the waves and the wind through the window – a moderately windy night. The rain had gone past, but the wind was certainly rising. Where could the Writing Man possibly be using a candle? It couldn't be the lighthouse – you wouldn't need a candle inside the light, and anyway, Aunt Lucy would have a lamp there if she needed to go downstairs – and surely the Writing Man wouldn't ask for a candle if he was just needing the outhouse? The store shed, possibly? None of them were allowed to take lights in there because of the oil. Had the Writing Man designs on the oil store? No, that made no sense at all. There was only one place he could be going.

Breesha sat up in the dark in furious indignation. How *dare* he? The keeill was nothing to do with Mr Buchanan. Mally had told her how the Writing Man had suddenly stooped down, and without a by-your-leave to anybody, had crawled into the keeill, right in front of their eyes. But the keeill wasn't part of the survey. The keeill belonged to the Saint, and it was their own private place. And anyway, why on earth . . . But there wasn't anywhere else where he could possibly be using a candle.

Now Mam was softly singing Mally back to sleep. Breesha knew that chant almost better than she knew anything in the world. Mam had sung it to her since she was in her cradle, and then Mam had sung it to Mally too. Breesha lay down on her back, staring into the dark. The chant soothed her. Her unruly thoughts stopped whirling through her head and began to settle, one by one, like dragonflies on the murky waters of Towl Doo. Their strident colours were easier to bear when they stopped still. Breesha could almost see each thought properly, looking at them one by one, but the chant was making her sleepy, and she didn't feel like bothering any more. Mam sang:

Vakratunda Mahakaya
Suryakoti Samaprabha
Nirvighnam kuru me deva
Sarvakaryeshu
Sarvada

Mam chanted the same words over and over again. There was comfort in their sameness. Breesha knew every sound by heart although she couldn't understand the words. Mam said that when you sang that chant Ganesha would bring his light into your life, and that all the difficult things that frightened you would vanish away. And sure enough Breesha's horrible thoughts were beginning to dissolve away. They had no choice . . .

Diya listened in the dark. Mally's breaths were soft and even. Diya quietly eased her hand free, but Mally's fingers instantly tightened around her mother's thumb. When Diya tried to prise the small fingers away one by one, Mally gave a little gasp and clung even tighter. Diya gave up for the time being, and tried to make herself comfortable, sitting cross-legged on the cold floor beside Mally's truckle bed. At least she could lay her head on the pillow . . .

She'd once sat cross-legged like this before Aji on the cool floor. Aji had sat cross-legged too, combing Diya's hair with a fine ivory-toothed comb. Diya had just come out of her bath and her hair was still wet. Aji had scoured Diya's head with the sharp comb. 'Aji, don't! It hurts!'

'We have to get the horrible lice out of your hair, beti.'

'But Aji . . .!' Diya had jerked her head away. The beautiful ivory comb had snapped in two.

'I didn't mean to break it! I didn't mean it!' Aji had stood up slowly, and fetched another comb. The two pieces of ivory lay on the floor beside Diya. She'd picked them up, and pressed them back together.

In the centre of the carved comb there was a peacock. The ivory was hard and white and didn't seem to be alive, and yet the peacock was unmistakeably the same as the sapphire- and emerald-coloured peacocks that danced on the roof with their gorgeous tails in full display. The top of the comb was the peacock's extended plume. Its body swept down the sides.

'Aji, may I keep this comb?'

Aji had laughed. She'd sat crosslegged again, and gone on combing Diya's hair with a different comb. She'd rubbed in oil, and braided Diya's hair with a ribbon the colour of marigolds. 'That's it. You can go and play now.'

'Aji, may I keep that comb?

Aji had handed her the two broken pieces. As Diya ran out to the veranda, she'd heard Aji speak to herself: 'Silly child!' and then her soft laughter through the open door.

Diya had brought that broken comb with her on the ship to England, in her carved sandalwood treasure box with her beads and bangles. Those silver bangles didn't fit her any more; sometimes the children wore them, but bangles weren't really part of life on Ellan Bride. And the comb? Perhaps the pieces were still at the bottom of the box. They must be. She'd never taken them out, not for years. The box was at the bottom of Diya's clothes chest. She didn't often delve down to it, but always when she opened the chest there was a very faint whiff of sandalwood. Suddenly it seemed desperately important to know if the pieces of Aji's comb were still safely in the box. Diya controlled the urge to pull her hand away from Mally's and go to look. This was foolishness. She could perfectly well search in the daytime, when she was alone. She *had* had the broken comb on Ellan Bride though: she remembered now – one winter day when it was snowing – finding the bangles for Breesha, and seeing the comb still there. In fact she'd told Breesha the story. Surely she'd not given her the comb to play with? Breesha could only have been five or six years old. No, Diya wouldn't have done that. She was being nonsensical now; there were far more important things to worry about. But in the morning she would go and look.

Chapter 23

THE CANDLE ON THE KITCHEN TABLE BEGAN TO GUTTER, AND in the fitful light the shadows wavered on the walls like uncertain ghosts. When Archie came in at the door the light flickered and almost went out.

Archie took the candle he'd been using from his pocket, lit it at the dying flame, and stuck it in the hot candlestick. Light filled the kitchen. There was no sound beyond the wind in the chimney. Billy was sleeping by the hearth, huddled in his blanket. The bed curtain was closed. Presumably Ben had already turned in. Archie took out his watch and turned its face to the candlelight. Nine twenty-five. That was still too early for stormy petrels. The fire had not been smoored. Did that mean Mrs Geddes was still up? There was no sign of her. Archie found it hard to believe she'd forgotten to attend to the fire.

Luckily he'd left his book on the dresser, so he didn't have to disturb Ben. Archie stuck the candle on the mantelshelf so the light fell on his page, and made himself as comfortable as he could on the wooden settle. The fire was nearly out. He quietly picked some fresh coals from the bucket, one by one, so as not to wake Billy, and laid them on the glowing ashes.

Assuming, then, that man is, comparatively speaking, of modern origin, can his introduction be seen as one step in a progressive system by which, as some suppose, the organic world advanced slowly from a more simple to a more perfect state? To this question we may reply, that the superiority of man depends not on those faculties and attributes which he shares in common with the inferior animals, but on his reason by which he is distinguished from them . . .

The bedroom door opened with a little creak. Archie looked up. Mrs Geddes was standing there. She wasn't wearing her cap and her hair was coming loose. He'd not seen her without her cap before. Her hair was as black as night. She had an unguarded look about her, like someone roused from untimely sleep. Scheherazade . . . *Principles of Geology* nearly slid to the floor, but Archie clutched it just in time.

'Oh!' said Diya, when she saw him sitting there. 'I thought everyone was gone to bed.'

'So did I.' Archie swallowed. 'I mean, I think they all have. I was going to stay up. I heard the stormy petrels in the keeill. I thought I'd go out later to see them fly.' She might think that was ridiculous. He wanted to explain that he was acting in a spirit of objective scientific inquiry but he couldn't find the right words. 'There'll be sufficient visibility, I think,' added Archie.

'I don't know,' said Diya. She still sounded dazed. 'The wind's rising.'

'Well, I can wait and see. That's if you don't mind.'

'I don't mind what you do, sir.' Diya came over to the fire. 'Oh, thank you for doing that – I thought it might have gone out. I fell asleep . . . I had to sit with my daughter . . . she had a bad dream . . .'

'I'm sorry.'

'Oh, she'll be all right now.' Diya glanced at him. 'It's the uncertainty. About the future, I mean . . . It unsettles the children, naturally.'

Perhaps she shouldn't have said that. She was still sleepy and not thinking very clearly. Diya didn't want Mr Buchanan to think her importunate. She certainly intended to enlist his help, if he had any influence at all with the Commissioners, but it wouldn't help to be too direct. She knew what she wanted him to think, but it must seem like his own idea. Diya sat down in the rocking chair opposite him, pulling her blue shawl more tightly round her shoulders, and gazed into the fire, apparently quite abstracted.

'Mrs Geddes!'

'Sir? – but please – keep your voice low.' Diya pointed to the sleeping Billy.

'Of course. I'm sorry – I wanted to say: I was thinking about that. What I was going to say . . . I mean . . . I hope you understand: the policies of the Commissioners of Northern Lights regarding their employees are not . . . I don't necessarily endorse them, you understand. Mr Groat and I . . . we're not employed by the Commissioners. We're employed by Mr Stevenson. I'm just the surveyor. If the appointment were in my gift . . . the appointment of the Ellan Bride lightkeeper, that is . . . if I could, I would . . . What I mean to say, ma'am, is that Mr Stevenson is both a kind and a charitable man. I don't know if the lightkeeper has written . . . What I mean to say is, a personal letter to Mr Stevenson might draw his attention to your plight.'

'It's very kind of you to think of us, Mr Buchanan,' said Diya, with an air of surprise. 'I appreciate your concern.'

In spite of the fact that her hair was coming down and her eyes were still sleepy, she was as capable of standing on her dignity as ever. Archie, on the contrary, had been stammering like a bashful boy. He was annoyed with himself, but neither was he ready to abandon his point. 'If you wish, ma'am, I could speak personally to Mr Stevenson when I return to Edinburgh. As I say, I'm just the surveyor, but I shall be making a full report, and I shall certainly make your situation known to him.' Archie was aware of spoiling the effect of his measured sentences the moment he added abruptly. 'He's helped others before.'

She came straight to the point. 'You, sir?'

'Ay,' admitted Archie cautiously.

Diya moved the rocking chair in front of Billy's pallet, closer to the fire. 'Thank you, Mr Buchanan. It's most generous of you to desire to help us.'

'Anything I can do, of course. Not that I . . .'

'I thank you. That being the case – for which, as I say, I thank you – I would like to know a little more about Mr Stevenson. As you say, it would be as well if I – I mean if the lightkeeper – were to communicate with him personally. Would you mind telling me a little more about it?'

'About me, do you mean? How he helped me?'

'Only if you have no objection.'

'Why should I object? I just . . .' Archie collected his thoughts, and carried on, remembering to speak quietly. 'Very well: I wasn't a rich man's son, Mrs Geddes. My faither was a miller by a small town. I was a country lad, but from as far back as I can remember I was always interested in the natural world about me. I was always asking *why*. About so many things . . . my older brothers didna seem ever tae ask . . . And then I found at school that I had a natural bent for mathematics. And working in the mill, of course, I was interested in the mechanical properties. There seemed so many possibilities.

'When I left the school I took myself to the City of Glasgow. I walked fifty miles. It took me into a new country, the like of which I'd never seen before. I walked for two days. I had to keep asking the way. When I got there Glasgow seemed to me quite monstrous in its immensity . . . the sheer noise . . . and so much diversity within it I couldna begin to comprehend . . . such contrasts of affluence and beggary . . . such elegance and iniquity . . . all existin cheek by jowl in such a little space . . . I'd never imagined the like of it. To be frank with you, ma'am, I was terrified.' Archie wished as soon as the words were out that he hadn't said that; it struck entirely the wrong note.

'I'm not surprised, sir. I remember arriving at the port of Liverpool. I saw very little of it, but to be honest, I thought

– I was only a child at the time, you understand – that we had docked in hell.'

'Is that so, ma'am? Coming from so far away, it must have been a shock indeed.' Archie cleared his throat and carried on more rationally: 'I enrolled myself in the classes they held for working men. I had no money for the University so I attended classes at John Anderson's Institute – that's a place of *useful* learning – where a working man can attend evening lectures on the applications of Chemistry and Mechanical Science. But I liked my classes in Natural Philosophy and Mathematics much better. First I supported mysel by doing whatever jobs I could get' – he'd worked as pot boy in a tavern to begin with, but Archie stopped short of telling Mrs Geddes that – 'then one of my Professors gave me work helping him with some chemical experiments. When I wasna in the laboratory I had to make fair copies of his notes and drawings for him, and copy citations in the library. I did that for a year because I needed the money: I'd much rather have been reading Natural Philosophy. And then: Professor Ure had known another Glasgow man, Thomas Smith, who'd made his fortune designing street lighting for the city of Edinburgh. Mr Smith had died a few years before, but when I was ready to move on, Professor Ure gave me a letter of recommendation to his partner, Mr Stevenson, in Edinburgh.'

'So Mr Smith moved from street lighting to lighting up the sea? I know about Mr Stevenson, of course, because I remember them building the Calf lights. It was a great matter in Castletown when I was a girl. But please, go on. You went to Edinburgh to meet Mr Stevenson?'

'Ay – that is – indeed, yes, ma'am. I had high hopes, but of course I was nervous. I mind well arriving on the doorstep of Mr Stevenson's office in Baxter's Place and summoning up the courage to gie a chap at the door. In fact they just told me to come back when Mr Stevenson was there. When we did meet, he gave me a month's trial without wages. I wasna working with lights after all. I was sent off with Mr Ritson to work on harbour plans in Fife. I was very happy. I wanted to travel as much as possible.'

'Well, indeed, sir, in your employment you must have as much travel as a man could possibly desire.'

'Well . . . maybe . . . Anyway, Mr Ritson must have given me a good report. I'd only been back in Edinburgh two days when Mr Stevenson sent for me to go with him to the new lighthouse on the Isle of May. That's an island just a bit bigger than Ellan Bride which guards the entrance to the Firth of Forth – where Edinburgh is – do you know the geography of the country?'

'I've never been there, but I've studied the use of the globes. I know where you mean.'

'That was the first time I'd ever been to sea, Mrs Geddes. It was the first time I was ever inside a lighthouse. Mr Stevenson conducted me around the lighthouse himself. I realised later he'd been watching to see how I coped with the trip, because while we were still on the island, he offered to keep me on permanently – to join his staff. Mrs Geddes, that was one of the happiest moments of my life!'

Diya had learned the art of captivated attention in her Grandmother's house. She suspected that Mr Buchanan very seldom talked to anyone about himself, and she knew better than to interrupt him now.

'But all this is no to the purpose,' Archie continued. 'What I wanted to explain to you was that Mr Stevenson not only employed me as an apprentice surveyor, on the strength of what I'd achieved for myself – for my education was all got by myself – I told you I'm not a rich man's son – but he sent me to do more classes at the University in Edinburgh, to complete my education in Natural Philosophy and Mathematics. You might say – indeed, Mr Stevenson did say – that an educated man was of more use to the firm – but you might equally well say that he had no practical incentive to provide for my interest in Natural Philosophy, which is not a discipline which has any immediate application. He could tell, though, that I would do better with it than without it, and so it was that Mr Stevenson gave me what I wanted most in the world, which I was unable – certainly at that period in my life – to acquire for myself.'

There was a short pause. 'I'm grateful to you for telling me this,' said Diya. 'It gives me a good notion of how I should proceed.' She hesitated. 'I don't wish to be impertinent, sir, but your story interests me. I would like to ask: will you stay always with Mr Stevenson? For it seems to me that your real interest is in Natural Philosophy, rather than its mechanical applications. Do you think you will survey lighthouses all your life?'

It took Archie's breath away, how acutely this woman observed matters without appearing to do so. Was she equally aware that in her present state of déshabillé she was also intoxicating? Archie took a long breath before he answered her. 'You are very acute, ma'am. The truth is – if I may speak in confidence?'

'Your confidence is safe with me, sir.'

'Because' – Archie glanced towards the bed curtain, and lowered his voice a little further – 'Ben doesn't know this. No one at Stevenson's knows yet.'

'There's no need to speak unless you wish it. However, your confidence is safe with me.'

'I *do* wish it!' whispered Archie vehemently. 'I would like to tell someone. I have had to keep the maitter verra much to myself, until I tell Mr Stevenson. I shall do that when I return to Edinburgh. It won't be easy, of course. But here' – he took out his pocket book – 'I can show you the letter. The thing is, you see, ma'am, I was in London last year. I was sent to Greenwich, to look at chronometers . . . that's by-the-by. While I was in London I was invited to dine at a gentlemen's club, and I sat next to another guest, a Captain Fitzroy. We had a very interesting discussion. The long and the short of it, ma'am, is that in October of this year there is to be a scientific expedition to study Natural Philosophy in the remoter parts of the globe. And I have been invited to join it! We sail first for the Americas . . . Here, let me show you my letter.'

Archie watched Diya peruse his letter. As she did so, he was aware of a curious sense of relief. Naturally it was good, after so much pent-up excitement and imposed reticence about his appointment to the *Beagle*, to share the marvellous news of his good fortune. But it wasn't just that . . . Watching her, he found himself at last able to admit that he found her extraordinarily attractive. He had found women beautiful before, of course, but never quite like this . . . Mrs Geddes had a natural intelligence too, and a vast intuitive understanding. How easy it would be to fall in love with her! Impossible, of course, because he was leaving the country in October, and would probably be away for years. However, it was a relief to admit his feelings, even if only to himself. It was like being able to breathe out properly for the first time since he'd laid eyes on her. From the moment Archie had landed on Ellan Bride he'd been aware of an indefinable tension . . . at least now he knew what it was. If only he were not going away, he would be tempted to speak to her. The temptation was very great anyway. But impossible, of course – it would not be fair on her, even supposing she were willing to listen. It would be quite wrong of him to say a word, because in October he was going away.

Archie was not as inexperienced with women as his chainman suspected. It had been his ill-fortune, however, that every time he had fallen passionately in love it had been doomed from the start. If the lady were not inaccessible, through previous marriage or some other calamity, then she had been about to remove to some distant locality. Or she had been so superior to him socially that he could never make her an offer. Passionate liaisons, in Archie's life, had always been tempestuous, clandestine, desperate and necessarily all too brief.

'But this is excellent!' said Diya in a low voice, when she'd thoroughly read the letter. 'You must be delighted beyond words, sir! It will suit you excellently!'

'Ay well, so I think.'

'I remember you said before that you had never travelled beyond the British Isles. Now you will truly see how wide the world is, Mr Buchanan. I think that will please you very well.'

'So I think,' repeated Archie. 'But I wish . . .'

'Wish what, sir?'

'I wish I may do a little more to help your own situation, ma'am – the uncertainty that you and your family face – before I leave Edinburgh.'

'I won't deny that I'll be grateful for whatever you can do.'

It crossed his mind that there was one thing he could do, but must not. She looked so beautiful, sitting there with her hair as dishevelled as if someone had already run his fingers through it – and how desirable it would be to do that – yet it was not to be thought of. But he couldn't help but be aware that in her current predicament, he could offer her a hope – merely a hope, of course, because there was no guarantee whatsoever of his ultimate return. The voyage was not only long, but dangerous and uncertain. It would be unfair on any woman to speak now. He'd be away for years on end . . . Moreover – the recollection was like a sudden douche of cold water – she had two children. They wouldn't grow up for years, and no man could desire such a responsibility. This was absolutely not the moment to speak, and yet her predicament was so dire that she might have every reason to listen. Was the offer of years of uncertainty better than no hope at all? But another man's children . . . that was the last thing he wanted in his life. His thoughts were racing much too fast. He mustn't say anything he might regret.

'Did you speak to the Lieutenant Governor when you were in Castletown?'

The cool question brought him to his senses, which was just as well. Obviously she had no idea what he was thinking.

'No, ma'am,' replied Archie, recovering himself. 'I was instructed to speak to the Water Bailiff.'

'Mr Quirk?'

'You know him?'

'Of course. He used to visit my Grandmother. I expect when

he spoke to you he wanted the House of Keys to have some say in the appointment of a new lighthouse keeper for Ellan Bride.'

'There's no question of that, ma'am. The Commissioners appoint their own people.'

'Scotch?'

'Of course. We're a Scottish institution.'

'But this is a Manx island. Not that it signifies; it makes no difference to us.'

'Your father was Manx, I take it?'

'No, my father never even lived here. My grandparents settled here, as so many half-pay officers did, after the War. My mother-in-law – Lucy's mother – was Manx. The Duke of Atholl appointed Lucy's grandparents from his Scottish estates, and their son – my father-in-law – married a Manxwoman. Naturally he did so; by that time he belonged here.'

'So the original lightkeeper brought his wife from Scotland with him?'

'Exactly so. She was from the Highland country, I believe. Her name was Mcfarlane. What is it? That strikes a chord with you, sir?'

'My mother is a Mcfarlane.' Why the coincidence should fill him with consternation was beyond Archie. Even supposing that the lightkeeper were a remote cousin – which was highly unlikely – what of it? He'd hardly imagined her to be of a different species. But Archie's mother wouldn't have seen it like that. If his mother were to encounter a woman of her own name she'd think of her as kin. And if Lucy were kin, then Archie could no longer comfort himself that the lightkeeper's distress was no business of his. That dream he'd been having – the dream that had kept coming back ever since they started on this trip – his mother wouldn't have discounted that so easily either. *So why would all that come back to you now, Archie? What haunts you still?* Always in the dream the wind and the sea were overwhelming him, forcing him towards a perilous edge where he didn't wish to go. Archie hadn't been to see his parents since the letter from Captain Fitzroy had come. It wasn't going to be easy to tell his mother about it. There was no question of hiding anything; she'd know from the moment she set eyes on him that something was afoot. She'd probably guessed already, come to that. Archie's mother was as acute as this woman he was talking to now, who, in spite of her Scottish name, was as alien a creature as anyone he had encountered in his life. At least Mrs Geddes was no kin of his: that much was certain.

'So you too are of the Highland country?' said Diya. 'I've read about that. Yes, I can see it in you, I think. You take after your mother, do you not?'

'So they say.' It was time the conversation took a more rational turn. 'As far as the Commissioners of Northern Lights are concerned,' said Archie, 'there would be no point in petitioning the Water Bailiff, or the House of Keys. However, I don't know if Mr Quirk knows that your mother-in-law was a Manxwoman, but it might weigh with him.'

'I think what will weigh with him more,' said Diya drily, 'is that he knew my Grandmother.' She glanced at Archie. 'In a way I'm more concerned for Lucy than I am for myself, sir. I've lived in the world before, Mr Buchanan, and Lucy has not. She was born and bred to the lighthouse here, and I was not. Of course, you weren't aware until now that you might be connected to her by blood, but I've read enough about your people to know that this is a matter of great significance.'

'It would have been once,' admitted Archie. 'The world I come from is changing very fast.'

'So kinship is no longer important to you?'

A brief image of his parents and elder brothers flashed across Archie's mind. 'Maybe not in the way you're thinking. I have my family, of course. But as I say, things change.'

'For the better, sir?' said Diya sharply.

Archie was obscurely aware of having offended her, but he couldn't think why. He had no answer of his own to give. 'It's true my mother would say no.'

‘She sounds like a woman of great wisdom,’ said Diya. She stood up. ‘Do you mind if I cover the fire now, sir? Otherwise it won’t keep in until morning.’

Archie watched as Diya raked out the ashes. When she’d emptied the last of the coals, and laid damp turfs over the fire, she remarked, ‘Like you, sir, I was fortunate enough to be brought up by women who were very wise.’ She took the brush and started sweeping the hearthstone clean. ‘I’m sorry the fire is not so cheerful to sit by any more, but now I must go to bed. The children will be up early.’

‘It doesna matter. It’ll stay warm enough while I wait.’

Diya stood up and went to the window. ‘The wind is rising, sir, and there’s more cloud coming in. I doubt you’ll be lucky to see the *Kirreeyn varrey* tonight. But it isn’t raining.’

‘I’ll take my chance on it,’ said Archie. ‘I’ll see what it’s like out there in an hour or so. Goodnight, ma’am!’

‘Goodnight, Mr Buchanan. I hope the weather holds for you.’

Chapter 24

DIYA LAY WITH HER BACK TO BREESHA, KEEPING VERY STILL so as not to disturb her daughter. Breesha slept on her back, her arms flung out, diagonally across the bed. Even as a baby Breesha had managed to take most of the room. As an infant she'd not slept well. She'd had an uncanny knack of waking and crying whenever Jim came off his shift at the light. In her parents' bed she'd want to lie between them, and in her sleep she'd somehow manage to force them as far apart as she could, until they were each balanced on the cold edges, facing away from her. Mally, on the other hand, had slept contentedly in her own crib from the first, except on the rare occasions when she had nightmares. That had been a bad nightmare tonight.

Of course the children were upset, thought Diya. This was the only life they'd known. Jim hadn't worried about that. He'd known no other life either, but there'd been as much future for him on Ellan Bride as he'd ever hoped for. In his view his daughters were fortunate indeed to belong here. Once he'd brought Diya back to his island he was content. More than content: Jim had wanted a woman – and marriage was the only way to get a woman on Ellan Bride – but to capture Diya was far beyond his expectations. He'd thought himself so lucky, but at the same time he genuinely believed he'd rescued her from all that could possibly threaten her. That had been a little hard to accept, but Diya had never directly contradicted Jim. Aji had never contradicted Ajoba. Aji just thought her own thoughts, and when it was necessary she did things her own way.

Perhaps rescue was always another word for a kind of trap. There was always a price to be paid. But it had been done with love – whatever that was. Oh yes, there had been love. Grandmother had been married and had had a son, but she'd never mentioned married love to Diya. The closest anyone had come to an admission of the truth was a phrase that stayed in Diya's mind from her marriage service: 'With my body I thee worship'. That was so unlike anything else Diya had been taught about the Castletown sort of worship that she couldn't help noting it, even as she stood, outwardly unshakeable, before the priest at the austere St Malew altar, which was adorned only with its wooden symbol of the tortured god. The priest had intoned the words they had to say, draining them of meaning; Jim had repeated each of his phrases with husky hesitancy, as though he honestly believed in what he was saying, and over those particular words he'd stumbled a little. The phrase had immediately become entangled in Diya's mind with another image: herself standing with a wreath of marigolds, her hand in Aji's, in the noisy glory of the Temple; above their heads a stone image showed the smiling god and goddess sinuously entwined. The image had stirred her then; even now it was mixed up in her mind with the smell of heat and crushed petals, and the colours of kumkum and marigold.

That was the image she'd taken to Jim's bed with her, and that was the living source of the private life they'd once shared. That was why her unlikely marriage had not only been tolerable, but in its secret way a delight. In the dark of their bed in the kitchen there was nothing Diya had to hide, and nothing to be held back. *Et in Arcadia ego* – the inscription on the lighthouse had held its own kind of truth while Jim was alive. But it had not been true for Diya since he was drowned, and was certainly not true now.

So Mr Buchanan was going on a great voyage. How foolish

Diya had been ever to think . . . No, she never had thought . . . she'd not let herself, and that was just as well. He'd opened a door for her, that was all. He'd let her see that, in spite of all the very real things that she had to fear in the short term, a different sort of future, perhaps even a better future, was actually possible.

But Diya couldn't help thinking what it would be like to be Archie Buchanan, and to be able to take ship and sail away: to expand the horizons of the known world and of one's own thoughts at the same time. And on Mr Buchanan's ship there'd be the other scientists, the other scholars . . . the possibilities were infinite. One couldn't begin to imagine the ideas they might bring home with them. Mr Buchanan, being a man, and childless, had the chance to sail off, unencumbered, into the future, of his own free will.

Diya turned over cautiously. Breesha stirred, and muttered in her sleep. Diya was growing sleepy. Sometimes while she fell asleep she used to imagine herself on board ship again, feeling the lift and fall of the waves under the keel, like being rocked in a cradle, sometimes softly, sometimes so roughly you had to hold on or else be flung out onto the floor. Of course it had been terrible to leave India, but at the same time there was something new about the voyage . . . the idea of going somewhere else . . . sailing forward into the unknown, and not forever having to look back . . . She remembered very clearly the moment when the great ship began to slide away from the quay on Bombay. A sliver of space had appeared between the ship's rail and the shore, then a thin strip of clear water, then a widening gap that she could never cross over again. She'd wept out loud for what she was leaving, but hidden very deep in her heart there was also expectancy. Diya hadn't let anyone see that, because it seemed disloyal. She hadn't admitted, even to herself, that the emptiness of the future had not only been a terror, but also, even then, little as she was, a faint glimmer of possibility.

* * *

In Breesha's dream Saint Bride sat at the arched doorway of her cell. The Saint was eating her breakfast, a mug of milk and a plate of honeycakes, while she sat warming herself in the first hot sun of the year. The sky arched blue above her, and the far lands had come in so close that you could see the folded curves of the Mountains of Mourne. In the dream Breesha was partly herself, looking at the saint from the outside, and partly she was the Saint, because she was seeing with the Saint's eyes, right from the inside. Saint Bride came from Ireland, and when she looked west over the sea to the far lands she was looking home. It made her sad sometimes to see home from the outside, looking as if it were not quite real, but at other times she was content to be where she was, knowing that there was nothing more sacred on this earth than to be alone on Ellan Bride: no better way to serve the god who sent her than to live like this.

Suddenly, out of the still brightness of a May morning, she smelt danger. She – Breesha – Bride – whichever one of them it was, because there didn't seem to be a difference any more – stood up, and looked around in sudden fear. Because perhaps this was the end of her life here, this unknown thing that she could feel coming towards her. Perhaps the island would not always be lonely, or at peace. Perhaps one day the whole world would change, and no saint would be safe on a lonely island any more. And when that happened . . .

Breesha sat up in bed, wide awake in a moment. Had that really been a dream? There were dreams and there were also visions. Mam had explained that to them. Visions were when you saw something else . . . something outside your own head. Breesha caught her breath. There it was again – a sound, something moving outside the window. The window was in the wrong place. And it was open. She could hear the sea. That was it: an open window. She wasn't in her own bed. She was in the bedroom, and it wasn't Billy beside her. Breesha put out a cautious hand and felt the curve of another body under the blanket. It was Mam. She could hear Mam's quiet breathing. She was in Mam's bed, and the odd sound had come in through the bedroom window which was always kept open.

Another sound. A scraping noise, and a door closing. Light. A light outside the window, moving away.

Aunt Lucy? No. Breesha knew it wasn't Lucy. Lucy came into the kitchen at night when they were asleep, but nothing Aunt Lucy could do would have woken Breesha like this. This was different. The strangers . . . but it wouldn't be Mr Groat, because he was quite nice. The Writing Man? Billy and Mally said the Writing Man had gone into the keeill without stopping to ask anyone. Perhaps the Writing Man wasn't just an ordinary person. That could be a disguise. Mam said they had to be civil to him because he was a guest. But if Breesha's dream had been real, it was more important to obey a vision from a Saint than to obey Mam about something as dull as just being polite. And supposing it was really the Saint: the shreds of Breesha's dream – if it was a dream – still clung about her. Suppose that the Saint knew that something was wrong. That there was danger. Breesha stared at the dark with wide-open eyes. The fitful light at the window had vanished. Now there was only the steady beam of the lighthouse reflecting off the sea. But that other light *had* been there. That wasn't part of the dream. She hadn't imagined it. There *had* been a lantern, and it wasn't Aunt Lucy. Something *was* happening. Something real.

Breesha was terrified. If she went after the Writing Man he might be very angry with her, and then Mam would be cross too. But the dream . . . she'd had the dream. Nobody else had. If it wasn't just the Writing Man, but a ghost, or a demon . . . or supposing it *was* the Writing Man, then for all anyone knew he might be in league with the powers of darkness. No one could scold her if she'd had a real vision; a vision wasn't the sort of thing even Mam could argue about. If the Saint had known . . . Silently Breesha pushed the cover back, and slid out of bed.

It was cold. Breesha groped on the chair until she found Mam's shawl. She wrapped it tightly round her, then she turned the door handle, and opened the bedroom door, swiftly so it didn't creak. She closed it behind her the same way.

The kitchen fire was smoored so the room was dark. Breesha thought of waking Billy. But if either of those men were to wake up – if they were both asleep in the kitchen bed after all – Mr Groat would be there anyway – no, it was better not to try to wake Billy. Silent as a ghost, Breesha opened the outside door and closed it again behind her.

She saw the light of the lantern. It was going along the path by the Tullachan, towards the keeill. Breesha didn't know how she knew that, but she did, for certain. If it was the Writing Man, the Saint wouldn't want him doing anything to her keeill. After all, it was the Saint who'd called her, in the dream . . . There was an east wind blowing. It found its way through Mam's shawl and through Breesha's cotton nightgown, and touched her with icy fingers. She shuddered. The lantern vanished behind the Tullachan.

The Saint was in danger.

Breesha was trembling with fright and cold, but she knew what she had to do. The Saint had lived on Ellan Bride all alone. She'd had no Mam, no Aunt Lucy, no Billy . . . not even a little sister. If the Saint had no one in her hour of danger to call upon but Breesha, her namesake, then there was only one thing to be done.

Breesha was as familiar with the path to the well as with her Mam's face. Even so, in the dark it was different, and she had to feel where to put her feet. The light didn't shine down here because the path to the keeill was in the shadow of Hamarr; it was one of the darkest places on the island. She'd been to the well in the dark before, in winter, but not without Billy, and if it had been as dark as this they'd have had the lantern. But Breesha knew the dark well enough to realise that after a little while she'd start to see better. That was true: by the time she'd passed the Tullachan and saw the lantern again, she could see the shapes of the rocks several yards away. She had the profile of Hamarr to guide her, as the beam of the lighthouse shone over the cliff above her head. She couldn't see as far as the sea on her right, but she could hear it. It was telling her that she was in the right place. Breesha put one foot in front of the other, and the very mud between her toes told her exactly where to go.

The path grew fainter after it passed the well. But as Breesha felt each rock under her feet she recognised it. The rocks were showing her the way, telling her each step through the soles of her feet. And there was the lantern, darting about like a will o' the wisp – *was* it a will o' the wisp? If that were so, then she was in terrible danger, much worse danger than if it was just the Writing Man. Everything was different in the dark. Things you might not believe in daylight suddenly became much more real. Only the Saint would not have betrayed her to a demon. It was preferable to believe it was just the Writing Man after all. But supposing it *really* was something else . . .

Faith . . . Mam talked about having Faith. Faith in the Saint was what Breesha had to have. She stopped and took a deep breath, trying to summon up Faith. She felt Faith's reluctance, but Breesha had a strong will, and knew it. She forced Faith to come to her aid. The Saint would never let her down. This was *their* island. And *they* were in danger. Still trembling with fear, but utterly determined, Breesha crept towards the keeill, where, sure enough, the darting light had settled, like a bee on an unsuspecting flower.

It would have been better to do this last night, Archie thought. Last night the sky had been as clear as one could wish, but tonight the afternoon's rain had left a heavy cloud cover behind it. When he first stepped out, just after midnight, the dark had come in so thick he couldn't see across the yard. He waited until he could see the dim outline of the gable, and the water butt beneath it. But that was all. There was not a single star in the sky to give him a bearing, only the pale beam from the lighthouse, but that didn't shine directly into the yard, and it wouldn't help him on the path to the keeill either. Archie hesitated. If he lit the lantern his eyes wouldn't grow accustomed; on the other hand, the track to the keeill was rough and narrow, and he needed to see where he was putting his feet. Reluctantly he went back into the kitchen, took a taper from the mantelpiece, and lit the lantern from the fire. When he went back outside with the lantern, everything beyond his little sphere of light was blacked out entirely.

After Diya had gone to bed, he'd had another idea. It had been prompted by a late foray into the larder looking for some bread and cheese to stave off the midnight pangs. As he was cutting off a large hunk of Stilton, he'd noticed five puffin carcases, plucked and drawn, hanging from a hook. Sunday dinner, no doubt. So they did harvest the puffins. In which case . . .

Sure enough, when he'd taken a candle and looked in the outhouse, he'd found a fleyging net lying across the rafters, next to a well-sharpened scythe and a couple of fishing rods. It had been quite a job to extricate it; obviously no one had used it for a while. At this time of year it would be easier to take the puffins straight from the burrows. He'd examined the net in the lantern light. It had been mended more than once, and one of the poles that held the triangular net open had split and been roughly splinted with a sliver of driftwood. But it would do. He'd knocked over a metal bucket – luckily not the privy one – and a couple of flower pots trying to get the twelve-foot-long pole through the outhouse door, and that had made a fair bit of noise. The outhouse was only a few feet from the bedroom window. Archie had stood in the yard, listening. He'd heard no sounds of anyone stirring. Not that it would matter much if they were. He was sure Mrs Geddes wouldn't mind lending the fleyging net for an hour or two.

He was hampered by carrying the net and lantern as well as his haversack. The much-trodden path to the well was fairly easy going, but after that he had to avoid tripping over the rocks on the way to the keeill. The beam of the lighthouse threw the high edge of Hamarr into relief on his left, and the sound of the waves on his right kept him more or less straight when he lost the path. He wasn't quite sure where he'd got to when he suddenly stumbled over a pile of loose stones, and realised he'd reached the broken dyke behind the keeill. When he held up the lantern he could see the keeill a few yards away, a round black shape like a monstrous animal. Archie sat down on the small circular wall nearby, the one Mrs Geddes had called the Saint's cell, and drew the shutter over the lantern.

From the lighthouse tower it looked almost as bright as day along the summit of Dreeym Lang, as far as the white cairn on Carn Vane. The beam shone out to sea on all sides, catching the tops of the waves in its light, illuminating the stacks and skerries. The east side of the island, below Hamarr, was dark under the lee of the cliffs. The wind had shifted, and now they were looking the other way, west out to sea, where the thin beam of light disappeared into the night. Ben stared after it as he went on telling his story.

'Twa-tree years afore I was born they stopped using the lighthouse on North Ronaldsay and moved the lighthouse to Start Point on Sanday. The only other lighthouse in Orkney is the one at Pentland Skerries. That's where my father went to work when he was a boy, and that's where he met Mr Stevenson. There are more ships sailing round our coast now than there've ever been. The ships nowadays sail what they call the Great Circle – it's quicker to cross the Atlantic as far north as possible because of the world being round. Ships come out of the North Sea and head to North America past our coasts. So one day they'll build more lighthouses in Orkney. They're bound to. It'll be *necessary*; there's no question about that.'

'So you might be sent to survey new lighthouses in your own country one day?' asked Lucy.

'I might.'

'And would you like that?'

'A chainman doesna stay in one place for long,' said Ben. 'I like to see the world.'

'Well, I don't!' cried Lucy.

In spite of the east wind the night was still warm, and very dark. The stars, always dimmed by the presence of the light, had now gone out entirely. When Ben and Lucy had first come up to the lantern there'd been a new moon, a finger-nail crescent just dropping to the sea east of the Calf lights. The moon had long set, but the cloud was still high enough for the flash of the Calf lights to be visible in the north-east. It was quite sheltered on the west side of the parapet. From where Ben and Lucy sat they could see a steady pulse of white water where the waves crashed on Stac ny Ineen and caught the light.

'That's a shame,' said Ben. 'To dismiss the whole world. I doubt you can do that, Miss Lucy. It makes no sense.'

'I don't mean here. I mean the world outside.'

'I ken that. But for all that it makes no sense. There's a lot more in the world than you ken aboot – than either of us kens aboot, come to that. I grant you it's no all good. But good and bad – you canna say anywhere is one or the other. You like it here, but you canna say it's all been good. You've lived your life, like the rest of us – good and bad together – and that's all there is to it.'

'I think you just like to see the good in everything,' said Lucy. 'But that's as much a lie as the other.' She shivered, and pulled her shawl closer round her shoulders. 'It's almost low water. See – it's dark now on the Creggyns, where there was all that surf before. There's still quite a sea though – hark!' They were silent for a moment, listening to the crash of water on rock. 'Only we're not seeing it from here. Wind's easterly, and the tide's almost at the ebb, that's why.'

'When's low water? An hour after midnight?'

'An hour and sixteen minutes past. It must be about half past twelve now.'

'You dinna have a chronometer?'

'We have the sundial.'

'I'm thinking that's what Mr Buchanan would call a fairly abstract proposition just at the moment.'

'You mean because it's dark? What of it? It's often easier to tell the time at night; there's always *something* to go by.'

'But you must be using tables to tell you the exact times of the tides, and sunrise and sunset too? Yet you dinna have a chronometer?'

'Of course: and the moon too. The tides do different things anyway – you just have to watch them. But the times are all in the almanack. I get Finn to bring one over every year.'

'But without a chronometer you dinna ken what the time is anyway,' objected Ben. 'So I canna see what use the almanack can be to you.'

'I wish you wouldn't *argue* so, Mr Groat. You seem to look at everything backwards. Why would I be wanting a chronometer when it's the light and the tides that give me the time? I'm never needing a clock to tell me it's sunset, but when it's sunset I can read off the number in the almanack, and that way I always know what time it is.'

'But . . .'

'Well, I should have thought it was obvious, anyway,' said Lucy impatiently. 'Would you like to be doing something useful, Mr Groat?'

'Delighted to be of service, ma'am, in any way. But why do you no call me Ben?'

'Because I don't know you.'

'You ken me better than you did four hours ago – Lucy.'

Lucy said irritably, 'I don't know why you don't go and get a decent night's sleep like a sensible man. But since you *are* here—'

'Ay?'

'I usually go down to the house about now and make some tea. Do you like tea, Mr . . . Ben?'

'Ay. I didna ken you had any.'

'I only take it at night. There's a teapot on the dresser. It's got tea leaves in it already. Unless you'd like to put in fresh ones?' Lucy suddenly sounded uncertain. 'I mean . . . I usually make them last four nights – but this is only the second.'

'I'm no here to plunder your tea stores. Second brew is fine. You'd like me to fill the teapot?'

'There are tankards on the dresser . . . it's easier than cups. And there's bread and cheese; in fact there's that peculiar smelly cheese you were bringing with you. Take the lamp, and don't be waking Mr Buchanan. I can't deal with him up here as well.'

'Or Billy. No, I winna do that.'

'The children never wake when I'm in the kitchen at night.'

Ben ducked under the lintel, and disappeared behind the light. A gust of cold wind blew like a live creature across the empty space he'd left behind him. Lucy clutched her shawl round her, and gave a little shiver.

The stormy petrels were out. Archie stood with his hands spread flat against the keeill, as if he could hear through his palms. It felt like that: the walls were filled with a strange warbling chatter. The darkness all round him was filled with flittering shapes. When he tried to look at them the dark came in between. All he could see – or sense, rather – was the tantalising fluttering at the edges of his vision. It was no use unshuttering the lantern; that would only kill the little natural light he had to see by. He'd laid the lantern and his haversack at the door of the keeill. He'd have to wait until it started to get light. Supposing it were one o'clock now, there should be a bit of light in the sky in an hour – two hours perhaps, with this layer of cloud obliterating the stars.

Very little was known about stormy petrels. There were all sorts of legends, no doubt going back as far as people had inhabited these islands, concerning Mother Carey's chickens. Some said the birds never came to land at all, even to nest. He'd even heard someone say they nested at the bottom of the sea. In winter they vanished off the face of the earth – of the ocean rather, for it was on the sea that one saw them, gliding and fluttering over the waves with a confidence extraordinary in any creature so small and seemingly delicate. Certain it was that these little swallow-like sea birds were as elusive as the spirits of the deep. Archie knew it wasn't true about never coming to land. He'd been told about nesting places on far-flung islands, where these shy birds could breed as far from human habitation as any creature could hope for. He'd heard of remote colonies in rocks and ruins, where the stormy petrels could sometimes be heard singing from within the stones, although they only came out at night. He'd seen petrels at sea, almost always at dawn or dusk, dipping and darting alongside the boat, but never stopping long enough for him to focus on them through his telescope.

He'd once talked to a Shetland man he'd met at Kinnaird Head, who'd told him how the stormy petrels nested in an old Picts' castle on one of the islands. That fellow had said to him – and Archie had proved now that it was true – that what gave the elusive birds away was the smell. He'd said to watch for a musky smell, like old hay. That was the very smell Archie had noticed when he'd crawled into the keeill. When he laid his cheek against the keeill wall now, he could smell it again. As a boy he could remember climbing up into the hay barn, where it was always warm, even in winter. The hay barn had been a good place to hide. That was what the keeill smelt like now.

The stormy petrels fluttered around him in the dark. He'd never come so close to them before. He could hear them, smell them, and almost see them. Yet still they eluded him. Even now he had very little idea how big they were, whether they really were a sort of swallow, whether they were all one species, or two, or even many . . . There was so much to find out. The very air seemed to mock Archie with its twittering. They were here in their scores – it was all true – they did nest in the keeill, but he'd already discovered that short of dismantling the building stone by stone, which he was neither able nor willing to do, he couldn't get any nearer to the nests. He couldn't come near to touching one. Unless . . .

Archie felt his way to the keeill door and picked up the fleyging net. It seemed huge and much too clumsy for its present purpose. This was truly hunting in the dark. There was no chance of deliberately aiming it. All he could hope for was to get the net into the flight path of the birds, and hold it still and just hope that one bird – it only needed one – might fly into it. It was a very small chance, but better than none at all.

'You make a good mug of tea,' conceded Lucy. She'd settled in her usual place on the bolster, down on the platform below the light. Ben had set the tray on the floor between them, and was sitting on the big driftwood log the children had carried in for their game. Light streamed down the ladder from the open trapdoor. The dark lurked in every corner where the light couldn't reach.

'You should thank my mother for that.'

'Is your mother in Orkney still?' It didn't come naturally to Lucy to ask personal questions, but Ben Groat seemed to do it so easily, and apparently with such genuine interest in the answers, that Lucy found herself tempted to try this style of conversation herself. After all, she *was* beginning to be interested: she'd so seldom encountered strangers in her life that she'd never really thought before about enquiring into the different lives they must lead. Ben Groat, and even Mr Buchanan, came to Ellan Bride bearing intimations of other worlds. Everything they said, or did, was an unconscious revelation of something alien. Foreign though they were to Lucy, from their point of view, their way of seeing things must seem normal and familiar. For the first time in her life Lucy found herself trying to imagine what it was like to be somebody else. To do that, she was finding it necessary to ask questions – either aloud or just in her own mind – of a sort which hadn't occurred to her before. She was wondering now what it was like to be Ben Groat. To know the answer to that she had to know about his family and where he came from. She wanted to understand things he might not even have noticed about himself. These were new thoughts; in spite of herself Lucy was beginning to be intrigued by them.

'Indeed she is,' replied Ben. 'She's back in Evie where she was born. I doubt she'll ever leave the place again either. She's like you – she likes her own country best. Not but what there's more folk in Evie than there are on Ellan Bride. My mother would think this was a lonely place. But all her kin are in Evie. She went straight back to her family when her man was killed. They waited years to be wed, my parents. They'd grown up in the same parish – been sweethearts fairly much all their lives long – and then when my father was sixteen he went away to work on the lighthouses. They didna get married for another ten years. I dinna think I'd wait that long if I found the lass I wished to wed. But my parents did, and the only way it could be, in the end, was for my mother to follow him sooth. She hated it, for she no more wished to be in Dundee than . . . than in Bombay. But she left home to be with him, and twa years was all they had together – and him on the rock a lot of that time, too – when he was killed. And my mother's lived a widow ever since.'

'That's a sad story.'

'I'd no be too sorry for her, though, if I was you – at least, I wouldna show it if ever you meet her. My mother's made a life for herself, among her ain folk, and there isna a soul on this earth she'd envy. She's no made that way. Though' – Ben paused for a moment, and added more soberly – 'the truth is, she'd no be sorry if I were to go back home, or a bit nearer to it. But there's no way for that to happen, as matters stand, and she wouldna stand in my way by repining. She's no the sort to make a fuss. Lucy, there's more bread and cheese on this plate. Are you no going to eat it?'

'You made about twice as much as I usually do,' said Lucy, taking another piece.

'That's because there's twa of us.'

'I mean twice as much *each*.' Lucy smiled. 'My brother Jim

and I – we used to share the watches even in summer – half a night each – and he used to make a proper feast when we changed over. Not just bread and cheese, but bacon, sometimes, and pickled onion: that was his favourite. Pickled onions.' She chuckled at the memory. 'And always in winter we have broth.'

'But you do both watches yourself now?' Ben glanced at her. 'Even in winter? Sixteen hours? Surely not?' What a strange life she led, an extraordinary life for a woman. To be sure, all lightkeepers had to work at night, but for a young woman like Lucy . . . and even if Aunt Deer helped her sometimes, all the responsibility was on Lucy's shoulders. And her a mother too . . . she'd have had to sleep through half the day even when the boy was wee. Ben didn't think it right, but all he said aloud was, 'You live like one of the stormy petrels yourself, so you do.' And you're about as elusive too, he thought to himself, which is no wonder, seeing what your life has been like.

'No, no, Diya takes first watch in winter, and I take second, usually, though I always light the lamps for her. Because in the daytime we have the children. Though Billy and Breesha are big enough now to watch the light in the afternoon – they did it together this last midwinter. When Jim died they were still very little. Mally wasn't even two, but luckily she usually slept through the night by then. It would have been hard to manage else. Well, it was hard anyway. Diya hadn't ever worked with the light, you see. My Da was still the lightkeeper when Diya first came here, and he had Jim to help him. When Diya married Jim she didn't have to do anything with the light. My Mam was alive then too.'

'When did your parents die?' asked Ben diffidently.

She told him without reservation. 'My mother died six weeks before Billy was born, and my Da died two years after. I'd only been home three months when Mummig died. They'd not told me she was failing . . .' There was a little tremor in Lucy's voice. She cleared her throat fiercely and continued. 'I think – being with her every day as they had been – they didn't see what I saw at once, the moment I laid eyes on her again. If I'd *known*! If I'd known I'd have come home at once – months earlier. And if I had . . .' Lucy's voice trailed away, and she kept her face turned away from Ben.

'If you had, I don't suppose you could have cured her,' remarked Ben. He glanced at her sideways. 'And if you had come hame, you'd no have Billy now.'

The silence that followed filled Ben with trepidation. He'd taken a risk, and maybe he'd gone too far. He knew that he had when she pointedly changed the subject, but at least she didn't send him packing, which was what he'd feared.

Lucy was thinking that this asking of questions might be a dangerous game. It was intriguing to ask, and there was a certain pleasure in answering – a certain pleasure, indeed, in finding anyone who was interested in constructing the details of one's own life inside his head – because it was a novel, and slightly intoxicating, experience. She found herself wanting to say more. But now Ben Groat was venturing onto territory she'd guarded so long – and from her own family too – that her instant reaction was to repulse him. Lucy didn't want to be rude, however, because she wanted the conversation to continue. It was a shock to admit it, but she was enjoying herself, up to a point. So she changed the subject as politely as she knew how. Anyway, it was a chance to ask him something else that she had found curious. 'Does your Mr Buchanan *always* talk in . . . in abstract propositions?'

Ben accepted the rebuff at once. 'He's no "my" Mr Buchanan. But no. He's very shy with women. Your sister-in-law puts the fear of God into him, I'm thinking, which is hardly to be wondered at. Missus Deer is an unexpected kind of lady to be finding here, I have to say.'

'It's "Diya". D – I – Y – A. It's an Indian word for light. If she frightens you I'm surprised you call her "dear".'

'Di – *ya*. How came she to be married to your brother? If you don't mind telling me, that is.'

'How nice of you to ask. Perhaps later you'll ask if I mind

you stopping half the night and distracting me from my work,' said Lucy chattily. She was beginning to feel quite at ease with him; it was almost like talking to Jim. 'How did Jim get to marry Diya? A lot of people were asking that at the time. In fact it was a terrible scandal. Terrible for Castletown, that is. In fact it was almost – if you looked at it like that – *funny*. Because you see, I was hearing it all. Of course. The thing about being a serving maid – I don't know if I was telling you, but at the time I was a serving maid for one of the old Manx families near Castletown – they think you don't see or hear *anything*. They think you don't *think*. I had to wait on the ladies when it was the other girl's afternoon off. I was really only the under housemaid, but they didn't have a second parlour maid, so sometimes it had to be me. I was *bad* at it, Ben. Really bad. I wasn't never getting the idea of how to hand things, and which side of them to pass the plate. It was all so *silly*. But that's what I was having to do. And I was doing it, in the parlour on a Thursday afternoon – that was the Mistress's At Home day – when the news had just got out about Jim and Diya's wedding. Of course they'd no idea I was his sister. I don't suppose they were even noticing that I was in the room – apart from the cakes being handed somehow, you understand. You're just sort of turning into an arm with a plate on the end of it, and the rest of you's invisible. At least that's how it's supposed to be. *You'd* be finding it hard, Mr Groat. I don't think they could have missed *you*.'

'Ben,' corrected Ben. 'I've nivver been invited to a ladies' tea party. That would set the cat among the pigeons, would it no? I'd be terrified. So what did they say?'

'They were like this: "*Oh my dear!*"' said Lucy, simpering, '"have you not *heard*? About Mrs Wells' granddaughter? Have you not heard what she's *done*?"

'"Oh, I knew about the money, of course. I heard at *once*! Before the news was out, really, because the *lawyer* . . . oh yes, we heard . . ."

'"We heard that there was *nothing*! And that Mrs Wells – she lived as high as a coach horse . . ."

'"But she couldn't hold household. Indeed she could not! In fact, ever since the Captain died, I believe . . ."

'"She had not a *notion* . . ."

'"She could easily have ended up in the *jail*! There were debts going back *years*. I even heard that her dressmaker . . ."

'"And the girl . . . would you believe it? . . . the girl left *destitute*! Nothing but a pile of debts. Even the *rent* was in arrears. How Mrs Wells managed it . . ."

'"And that girl, who thought herself so high and mighty, giving herself airs . . ."

'"They were come-overs, that family, of course, and when all's said and done . . ."

'"Too much *pride*. Though goodness knows why. Her *mother* . . ."

'"A *native*. *Blood tells*. Mrs Wells made too much of her, but I could have told her. Sharper than a serpent's tooth . . ."

'"I don't think the girl was exactly *ungrateful*. But naturally she had heathen tendencies . . ."

'"Impossible to eradicate . . ."

'"But the *cook's* nephew!"

'"The grandmother would turn in her grave, and her scarce buried! The headstone not yet raised, even, and that girl goes off and . . ."

'"Hard to know what she *could* have done else. She inherits *nothing*."

'"But what about her father?"

'"Wells? He died in India – it would have been a year or two ago. But they'd not heard from him for ever . . ."

'"There's no saying but what he took another *native* wife. They get a taste for it, I believe. Having done it once . . ."

'"My *dear*, he probably had dozens! In a *heathen* country, after all . . . God *knows* how many children . . ."

'And so on,' finished Lucy. 'That's the sort of thing I had to listen to. I didn't know whether to laugh or cry.'

Ben had had no idea that Lucy could mimic so well. He'd thought of her as much too direct for satire. It crossed his mind that he and Mr Buchanan might be grist to her mill. That would be a joke indeed, but probably not one she'd ever share with him. Did Lucy and Aunt Deer – Di-*ya* – ever laugh together? It was hard to imagine. What was less hard to picture, though, was what Lucy might have been like when she'd had her brother with her. Being brought up together the way they'd been, they were bound to be close. No, that wasn't necessarily true. An only child himself, Ben was inclined to think that the possession of a brother or a sister was a welcome gift, but he'd known folk for whom that had hardly turned out to be the case. However, he had a strong notion that Lucy had been very attached to her brother Jim, and he to her. And her Da – she said very little about her Da – had she loved him too? Ben had no idea, but he thought it might well have been so. Perhaps those two children, growing up in mutual isolation on this island twenty-odd years ago, had made their own kind of fun. The way Lucy could take off those society ladies, Ben almost felt as if he was in the room with them. She'd learned to do that somewhere. Here, in fact: for Lucy there'd never been anywhere but here.

Ben laughed, 'Ay well, Lucy, I canna picture you handing cakes in a ladies' drawing room. I just canna. But you – what did you feel yersel when your brother married Miss Di-*ya*?'

'Me?' Lucy frowned, thinking about it. 'I was all a-mazed. It happened so quickly. They didn't read the banns – Jim went to the Bishop and got a special licence. He went right up to the Bishop's Palace away north beyond Peel, and asked for one – just walked up to the door, as bold as brass, and asked to see the Bishop. The Bishop wrote him a note to take to the Vicar General, and Jim walked on again, over the hills to Douglas. There wasn't any . . . any cause or just impediment, and because Jim lived on Ellan Bride, and couldn't take time away from the light, the Vicar General gave him the licence – sold it, rather, because it cost Jim a lot of money. Jim wasn't scared about getting his way when he needed to. Not at all. So then Jim walked all the way back to Castletown. He came to the back door of the house I worked at, and asked to see me. He told them it was urgent family news, so they *had* to let him talk to me, although I wasn't really allowed to see any visitors except on my day off. But Cook was nice – I don't think she ever told the mistress. So I went down to the back door, and then Jim and I were standing there in the yard, and Jim said, "Lucy, I'm going to be married tomorrow. I'm wanting you to come to my wedding!" And I was so surprised . . . Ben, I had no *idea*! I knew he liked Miss Diya because he'd told me so, but she was *Quality*. Our sort doesn't marry gentlefolks! I never *dreamed* . . .

'But Jim was explaining to me how Diya had been left with nothing at all – not a penny in the world – nothing but a pile of debts. And the rent was overdue . . . she had just one week to leave the house, and it was *full* of things. Everything was going to the auction, and Diya wasn't getting any of it, because it all had to pay the debts. Even the things that were supposed to be her very own were taken away. And everything was harder to sort out because there wasn't any will. Aunt Annie said it was all the most terrible muddle. But Diya stayed calm all the way through. Aunt Annie said that girl was a marvel, the way she was bearing it, and her only nineteen years old. She talked to the lawyers, and arranged the funeral just as her grandmother would have liked.

'She – the old lady – was buried at Malew Church. Everyone came to the funeral – all Castletown polite society. But were they there afterwards when the will was read? Or when Diya realised her situation? They were *not*. There was only one person sticking by her, and that was her friend Sally, but she was just a young girl like Diya. She couldn't *do* anything.

'So that's how it was that Jim was daring to ask. He was over in Castletown, and he heard the news as soon as he got there. He went straight away to see Aunt Annie, because obviously Aunt Annie would be out of a place too, unless the next tenants were wanting her with the house. He knocked, and Aunt Annie didn't come, so he let himself in at the back door, and there was Diya – that's what he told me – on her own in the kitchen, sitting by the chidlagh in the old rocking chair with the cat on her knee, not doing anything at all. I think she must have been there because she was upset, but Jim didn't talk about that. Aunt Annie was at market. So Jim said he had nothing to lose, and all to gain . . . well, of course he didn't tell *me* all about what happened then, but the long and the short of it was he was asking her to marry him, and she said yes. Don't ask me to explain it any more, because I can't. I wasn't there and I don't know.

'I got permission to go to the wedding. I probably wouldn't have – not from the Mistress – but Cook talked to the housekeeper privately, and I was allowed an hour to go over to the church and go to Jim's wedding and come straight back. They weren't never telling on me. So I was one of the witnesses. The only other people in the church were Miss Sally and Aunt Annie. The vicar was drunk. Diya said maybe that was just as well. The old vicar – Mr Harrison – he'd known Diya ever since she came, and he might have tried to stop Diya marrying Jim. But Mr Christian wasn't giving a damn, Jim said, so that was all right. There was no wedding breakfast. I had to go back to the house, and obviously Miss Sally wasn't sitting down at table with Aunt Annie and Jim. So we were saying goodbye at the church door. Jim had borrowed a gig, and he took Diya back to Ellan Bride the very same day. And the cat. The cat went too. Aunt Annie brought him to the church in a basket. We were hearing him yowling in the porch right through the service, but luckily the wedding didn't take very long. Diya couldn't leave the cat behind, you see. And the bailiffs certainly weren't wanting him. So he went back to Ellan Bride too.'

'That's no the cat you have now?'

'No, the old Smokey died, and Finn brought us this one – his full name is Smokey Two. T – O – O or T – W – O,' explained Lucy carefully. 'Diya says it's a pun. Anyway, that's one problem we're not getting here: kittens. My mother said we should be thankful. She grew up at Meayll, and they were always having to drown kittens.'

'Sad for the cat, though. But perhaps he doesna ken what he's missing.' Even sadder for the people, thought Ben, because they presumably did know that life might offer a little more. He wondered how often Lucy thought about that. 'So your brother and Diya came straight back to Ellan Bride?'

'The very same night. Jim had come over in our boat, you see. When Jim was alive we used the boat to go to the Isle of Man and back, and we went much more often – at least, Jim did. Mother never left Ellan Bride, not in thirty years. She was always saying she had everything and everyone she loved just where she was, so what was the point of going anywhere? There was plenty to do – that's what she used to say – plenty to do in the place where God was putting her, and that was enough.'

It was freezing, and she was terrified. Breesha was shaking all over: big, violent shakes that seemed to come from the pit of her stomach, and make her teeth rattle. If she clenched herself tight all over, she could stop her teeth chattering, but it was a strange kind of relief to hear the sound, like making sure she was still there, inside herself. She could go home. She knew she could just go home, and crawl back into bed and press herself against her Mam's warm body. That was the coward's way out. The Saint had woken her, on purpose, because the Saint herself needed her. Breesha didn't know why, or how, because nothing like this had ever happened before. It was like a game coming real. All the frightening games they'd ever played – and Breesha knew how to make games frightening all right – had been building up to this. She'd stepped over some invisible boundary, to a place where the unknown wasn't play any more, but real.

The *kirreeyn varrey* were out. That was good. Their presence sustained Breesha through her fearful watch. Breesha had once come here before at night to see the *kitty varrey*. Mam had brought her and Billy, very late, long after bedtime. They'd sat in the lee of the keeill. There'd been a full moon. Breesha had sat between Mam and Billy, feeling the warmth of them on either side, forgetting to feel sleepy, as she watched the hundreds of little dark birds flittering and twittering through the air before the round face of the moon. Mam had told Breesha and Billy how these were Saint Bride's own birds. Saint Bride, whose name Breesha shared, also used to sit outside the keeill listening to the *kirreeyn varrey* at night. She too had loved to watch them fly before the moon. The *kirreeyn varrey* were the Saint's friends, and ever since she'd gone away they'd stayed faithfully at her keeill, remembering. Even though Saint Bride had left so long ago, the *kirreeyn varrey* still returned to her each spring. The Saint could understand the languages of all the birds, and when she listened to the *kirreeyn varrey* at night, their mysterious twittering told her as plain as day what they had seen and where they had gone, far away across the sea.

The Writing Man had been standing by the keeill for a very long time. It felt like hours and hours. He held something long. Breesha couldn't see what it was. It looked like a spear but there was something big at the end of it. Occasionally he moved around the keeill. The spear thing moved too. Breesha could see the faint outline of the keeill. The Writing Man had gone round to the seaward side. She couldn't see him properly because he was hidden in the shadow of the keeill. The keeill itself looked different in the dark, big and round, like the way Mam drew elephants on the slate. Far overhead the sky was pale where the light beamed out to sea. The light was much too high and pale to help her now.

Then it happened. The spear leaped in the air. Breesha heard a sound – a gasp, or a flutter – a sudden movement. She didn't know what it was. The spear was gone.

The Writing Man was moving around in the dark. He was back at the door of the keeill. She could see him standing there, and then he shrank down, as if he were disappearing into the earth. There was a little click.

He'd unshuttered the lantern. That was why it had clicked. He was crouching over the sudden beam of light. He was holding something. The light shone on it. A net! He had a net, and in it . . .

In spite of the fearful thumping of her heart, Breesha had to see. She crept forward a pace or two, trusting the dark to cover her. Now he was looking into the lantern, he wouldn't be able to see her even if he did look up. He didn't. He was looking down at the thing he held in his hands. He wouldn't see her, and if he did – her heart gave a sickening jolt at the very thought – if he did, she could run better than he could, so long as it was dark, because her feet told her where the path was, whereas he had to have a light.

The struggling thing in the net was a bird. It was one of the *kirreeyn varrey*. He'd snared one of the Saint's own birds. It was the fleyging net he'd got there. *Their* fleyging net. And now he was doing something to the bird . . . pulling it . . . he was twisting it round inside the net. Was he *killing* it . . .?

The light went out.

'Damnation!'

What did he mean by that? What was he doing? He hadn't blown out the lantern. It had gone out by itself. He'd let the oil run out, leaving it shuttered all that time. The lantern *knew*.

The Writing Man stood up. She couldn't see what he was doing. Why had he taken the bird? Was he killing it? Was he murdering one of the Saint's own birds, under the cover of the dark? Breesha crept back to her hiding place behind the rock. He was moving . . . he was moving away from the keeill. He was coming towards her. Breesha scuttled backwards like a frightened mouse.

He'd not seen her. He was near the path. He was looking for the path. Of course he'd been looking at the lantern light. He couldn't see . . . If he was trying to find his way back . . .

He'd taken one of Saint Bride's birds. He still held it. She hadn't seen him let it go. Why? What demon drove him? She had no idea what the Writing Man meant to do. She knew in her bones that it was wrong. Even to *touch* one of Saint Bride's birds, let alone *capture* it, to *kill* it, if that's what he'd done . . .

As Breesha fled through the dark, her feet somehow finding the right way, she could see the beam from the light high in the sky above her. You couldn't see the lighthouse from here, so it didn't help . . . the light didn't help . . .

Terrified as she was, wrought up far beyond being able to think straight, Breesha suddenly *knew*. The dream . . . the spear . . . the kill . . . The Saint had *told* her . . .

She already had about twenty yards' start on him. Abandoning herself to sheer instinct, Breesha plunged into the dark, and ran.

Chapter 25

NOT LONG AFTER LOW TIDE, LUCY WENT ROUND WITH THE oil can checking the lamps. She carefully trimmed a couple of wicks which were beginning to smoke. It wouldn't be long now before it started to get light. There were no stars, only the thick darkness of cloud beyond the steady beam of light. Lucy opened the west window again, and sat down on the parapet.

'D'you think it'll be fair the morn?'

Lucy gave a start and swung round. 'I thought you'd fallen asleep down there! Don't stand in the beam, please, Mr Groat.'

Ben squatted down just behind her. 'I only dozed off for a moment. No enough time to become "Mr Groat" again, I hope.'

'All right, then: Ben. You've been sleeping above an hour. They'd better not be setting *you* to keep a light!' Lucy didn't say how, half an hour earlier, she'd stood looking down at Ben where he'd lain sprawled across the blankets on the platform, his mouth slightly open, snoring a little. She'd remembered that two days earlier – was it really only two days? – Mally had called Ben 'the ugly man', and no one had contradicted her. That seemed a long time ago already. Ben had looked younger when he was asleep. And if his face was unusual, there was nothing wrong with his body; in fact if he'd remember not to slouch he'd be a remarkably well set-up young man. When Lucy and Jim used to take the night watches together, Jim used to look very much the same when Lucy went to wake him up in the small hours. But that was long ago . . . In fact Ben Groat couldn't be so very many years older than Billy. Billy would soon start to grow up too. It took so few years for a boy to turn into a man, it frightened Lucy a little to think of it. Where would Billy be when he was Ben's age, and what would have happened to them all?

Up until that moment when she watched him sleeping, Lucy had felt slightly in awe of Ben Groat. He knew the world so much better than she did that she'd somehow taken a notion that he was a good deal older and wiser than she was. That no longer seemed to be quite true. If he'd been born the year the Bell Rock lighthouse was first lit – Lucy had done a quick calculation as she stood over the unconscious Ben, lamp in hand – why then, he was five years younger than she was. In a strange way that allayed a certain fear inside her head – a fear that she hadn't even been aware existed until that moment.

'Have I?' said Ben, looking rather put out. 'Ay but, *I* was working all of yesterday. If I had to keep a light I daresay I'd grow accustomed. Would you like me to go and make some more tea?'

'What, tea twice in one night! Oh, very well, then, if you want it.'

'I do,' said Ben, rubbing his head sleepily. 'This is thirsty work. And I'm hungry. How about some biscuit?'

'Why not indeed? And a sugar plum or two, perhaps!'

'Your children ate all the sugar plums, ma'am. I'll be back shortly.'

Of course he should have checked the oil in the lantern before he'd set out. Archie was annoyed with himself, but it could have been worse. He'd extricated the bird in time. In the lantern light it had been a lighter brown than he'd expected. Under its feathers it was just a little scrap of flesh, though it must be as tough as wire to fly far over the ocean the way it did. He'd taken great care not to hurt it. Anything that felt so delicate in his hands, and yet could do so much, must be fine-tuned to the highest pitch. The least dislocation might be fatal: he'd never have got the bird out of the net undamaged without the light. As it was, he'd already disentangled it, and was holding it safe in his cupped hands when the lantern went out.

It had taken him a moment to think what to do. He could feel the little creature light as thistledown in his hand. At first it was struggling, trying to flap its wings against his closed fingers. Then it lay still, but he could feel a quickening heart-beat against his palm.

The obvious thing to do now was to kill it. It was easy to study a dead bird. One could weigh it, measure it, and write a description of it, all at leisure and with no difficulty at all. He'd not seen a stuffed specimen of a stormy petrel. Archie had never attempted taxidermy. He could probably do a reasonable job if he set about it, but the conditions here were not ideal. All those children . . . he wouldn't get the peace to concentrate. And yet . . . there were hundreds of the birds flying about all round him: to take a single specimen would make no difference. For some reason he was preternaturally aware of the small pulse against his palm. He might as well let it go alive if he wasn't going to use the carcase. He could make notes and a drawing whether it were living or dead, anyway.

With some difficulty Archie used his left hand to pull his handkerchief from his right-hand pocket. He wrapped the live bird loosely inside it, as well as he could in the dark, placed it carefully in his pocket and tucked in the flap. He found his haversack and slung it over his shoulder. The useless lantern and the fleyging net could stay where they were until tomorrow.

It must be about one o'clock, nowhere near dawn yet. He'd have to feel his way back as best he could. If he kept the light-house beam on his right, and the sound of the sea on his left, he'd come to no harm. He didn't want to trip over, though, because of the bird in his pocket. Gingerly Archie set out, feeling for each step. He wasn't on the path, but that didn't matter. There was little chance of finding it anyway.

He'd hoped to get to the well by keeping close to the Hamarr cliff, but after a while he realised he must have missed it in the dark. He walked on for a bit. All of a sudden it got lighter: too light, in fact. He looked round, and saw a solid sphere of brightness high up, almost directly behind him. He'd gone too far seaward; he ought not to see the lighthouse from the path. Archie retraced his steps, and a moment later the light disappeared again.

A small, single light shone out just ahead. It must be a light from the house: the lightkeeper, perhaps, fetching refreshments from the kitchen. Relieved – because the simple walk was harder in these conditions than he'd expected – Archie took a step towards the little glimmer.

No.

That light was in the wrong place. The beam from the lighthouse coming over the Hamarr cliffs was too low. The angle from the well path to the top of Hamarr was in no place less than sixty degrees. From here it was more like forty. That would only make sense if he were passing east, not west, of the Tullachan. The Tullachan . . . From the Tullachan to the top of Cam Giau was thirty-three yards, and the bearing from the summit of the Tullachan to the end of the Cam Giau cliff was sixty-nine degrees. Which meant that if the Tullachan were on his right, and not on his left . . . Wait a minute . . . the fact was he oughtn't to be able to see the house lights at all. In fact, he'd *only* be able to see a light from the kitchen window if he were almost at the cliff edge. Which he wasn't, because the sea didn't sound close enough. And that could only mean that this glimmer of light was coming from the far side of Cam Giau, where quite certainly no light should be.

But why would anyone . . .? Unless they'd deliberately set a light, knowing he was coming back from the keeill. No, that was impossible! And yet . . . was there any other explanation? The light wasn't moving. Someone was staying quite still on the far side of Cam Giau. Impossible! But he needed to be sure . . .

Now that he'd stopped to work out exactly where he was, Archie moved forward cautiously, but with more confidence. He went very slowly, and in less than two minutes he heard the sound he'd been listening for: the swish of waves below, and with it a sudden awareness of emptiness. That was it. That dangerous twist at the top of Cam Giau . . . it was nineteen yards from the kink in the Giau to the declivity in the ground where the chasm ended. Archie paced it as well as he could in the dark, and sure enough the ground fell away into a small hollow exactly where he'd calculated.

From the foot of the hollow it was safe enough; if he was going uphill he had to be moving away from the precipice. On Gob ny Sker the vegetation changed from turf to heather. Yes, now he was in deep heather, having to pick his way. And there was the false light, not very far away now, above him on the height of Gob ny Sker, between the Tullachan and the sea.

The sound of the sea hid the rustling in the heather. Archie came up close to his quarry, close enough to see that the light was a makeshift lantern, a candle stuffed into a bottle with the bottom knocked out. He'd seen that very lantern on the kitchen dresser. As for the person holding the lantern up so it that was clearly visible across Cam Giau: all he could see of her was her black hair, and the corner of a blue shawl. He'd seen that shawl round Diya's shoulders less than two hours ago. He stopped, feeling cold inside. He'd been betrayed before – that feeling at least was familiar – but not since he was a child – not like this – no one had ever tried to do anything like *this* . . . And all this time he'd thought that she . . . He'd thought of her as . . . And all the while she was . . . what? Laughing at him? Or merely hating him? *Why?* She must be a devil incarnate . . . Or simply mad?

He didn't want to know. He could turn and run. It was too horrible; better not to know. But if he left now he'd never find out . . . He'd never face her again, knowing this, and that meant . . . no, he couldn't leave it like that. Something as bad as this

– whatever nightmare notion had brought her to do this – he *had* to know.

He'd been standing there, not knowing what to do, almost shivering from the shock of realising it was her. Suddenly he was aflame with rage. Was she *mad*? Not she – there was nothing mad about her whatsoever, he was sure of that – but if she were sane, then she was as wicked a woman as ever played with a man's feelings – not just his feelings: his *life*. Impossible to believe, but there she was – she wanted his *life*. He came softly up the slope towards her, to within a couple of yards.

She hadn't heard him. There was no doubt at all about what she was doing. She was holding up the bottle lantern so that it would shine across Cam Giau. From the keeill path it could easily be mistaken for a light from the house. She'd *known* he was going to the keeill to watch the stormy petrels – she was the only person who'd known. She'd sat so douce in the rocking chair across the hearth while he'd told her about it. She'd listened to him talk – oh, how civilly she'd listened! When he thought how much he'd told her about himself – more than he'd told anyone in all his adult life – he wanted to fling himself on top of her and throttle the life out of her. She'd seemed so *interested*. Was she deranged? He'd thought her kind, for all her manner was so cool – he'd thought she'd *liked* him.

The bottle lantern shifted. She was changing her grip on it. It must be hard on her arms, holding it up high like that. The blue shawl slipped. For a moment the light shone on her face. He was behind her: he couldn't see properly. The outline of her cheek was illuminated through a stray tendril of black hair. Her cheek, where the light shone on it, was softly rounded. But Diya wasn't . . . Diya's face rose vivid in his mind's eye; he'd had the chance to study it very well that evening. What he'd noticed the first time he'd laid eyes on her – what he'd thought about ever since – what was beautiful about her, in fact – was her clarity of feature – the fine shape of her bones beneath the skin – whereas this . . .

The lamp flickered, and flared up, as if a whisper of wind

had found its way inside the bottle. She was wearing something white. The same small breeze that had caught the flame made her skirts billow round her ankles. For the first time he saw that she was little. He hadn't realised. Because of the slope of the ground she was above him. That's why he'd thought she was tall. It wasn't . . . It was . . . It was the girl! It was only the girl! Thank God for that! The relief was so overwhelming he found himself shouting at her furiously.

'What the *devil* d'ye think you're doing?'

Breesha swung round. Her mouth was wide open in terror. But she didn't scream. She just stood there staring, all mouth and eyes. Then she took a step nearer, holding up the lantern, and stumbled over the heather. Of course, she'd been staring at the light. She couldn't see him. The light fell on his face, and he blinked. He opened his eyes and saw her looking at him aghast over the lantern light. For a second their eyes met. Then Breesha started, and flung away the bottle lantern. It shot into the giau, and the dark swallowed it.

He couldn't see. He'd been looking at the light, and now all he could was bright greenness against his eyes. Where was she? The sea echoed from below so he couldn't hear her either. He groped forward, and made out a dim shape, no longer silhouetted against the stars. That's why he'd not seen her: she'd backed away, down into the shadows between the height and the edge of the cliff. But that meant . . . they'd measured this ground only yesterday . . . It fell away steeply, crumbling down to the edge. She was much too near . . . She must be out of her wits, or else just blinded. He could see the faint outline of the edge behind her.

He slithered down the slippery space between them, and pounced, grabbing her by the arms. He caught a flash of white below: the surf funnelling into the giau. Then, still slipping, he pulled her down flat, holding her to the ground with all his weight on top of her. They weren't sliding, thank God. She was screaming. Archie was barely aware of it. There was no ground below his feet. Still forcing Breesha down with all his weight, he scrabbled for a purchase, found rock under his feet, and managed to push them up the slope. It was steep, but now he could crawl. He had to drag her with him. She did nothing to help herself; she didn't seem to *realise*. He got a grip round her middle. She was so slight he was feared she'd slip right out of his arm. Then he dragged her back, a safe two yards up the slippery grass. It was steep, and the ground was crumbly. He didn't loosen his hold until they were on solid grass. Then he managed to stand up shakily, pulling her upright with him.

Once she was on her feet she struggled like a demon. He still had her round the waist. She put her head down and bit his hand, hard. Furious, he slapped her head away with his left hand. She screamed, and twisted her elbow into his guts.

She was no match for him. He had her pinioned against his chest, holding her in his left arm. He remembered something else – if it wasn't already too late – and held his right hand over his pocket to protect the bird. He could feel his own heart hammering. Another step – if she'd pulled backwards when he caught her – Christ, it had been close . . . he was just beginning to register how close to the edge they'd been. He was trembling – with fear or fury or both at once. He jerked her roughly round to face him.

'What the *devil* . . .?'

She didn't scream again. Instead she fought wildly. She hadn't a chance. He was far stronger than she was. 'Stop that! Stop it at once, ye besom!' He was beside himself with rage, now that they were both safe. This bairn . . . this *monster* . . . she'd tried to *kill* him. 'Or I'll throw *you* over, you wee devil!'

She heard that. She suddenly went limp. It was like holding a dead thing. If she'd fainted . . . She was breathing all right. Whimpering. She was terrified . . . she thought that he . . .

His brothers . . . they had him, one at each end, holding him by the wrists and ankles. They swung him high, right over the edge of the mill race. White water surged below. The great wheel clanked. He dare not struggle, because if they let go he'd go flying . . . he dare not scream . . . they were laughing at him . . . laughing all the time

... and him swinging there between them ... helpless as a ... as a ...

A bairn. That's all she was. A bairn. And he'd said ... She was whimpering ... She'd believed that he would ...

'Don't be so bloody daft,' said Archie roughly. 'I'm not a damned murderer! But *you* ... ! What the *hell* did you do that for?'

Such a childish trick as it had been! But – suddenly it dawned on him – the reason he felt so furious – the reason he'd like to beat her black and blue until she screamed for mercy – was that it might have worked. It was so *stupid*, so *crude*. No one could have believed for a moment ... But to his eternal shame he *had* been duped. Oh, only for thirty seconds, it was true, but that was long enough. He'd been fooled, and not just about the false light in the bottle lantern. He'd thought that her mother ... What he'd thought was unforgivable. He wanted to bury it, deny even in his own heart that he'd ever imagined for one moment that it could have been Diya. Of course the very notion was preposterous. But he *had* believed it. It was that shawl ... she was wearing her mother's shawl. He'd never tell anyone, but *he* knew. He'd always know. Just for that space of time, Breesha had fooled him. The worst part she'd done unknowingly, but he felt none the better – she'd deceived him anyway. He couldn't forgive her, bairn as she was, for that.

'Very well, if ye've nothing to say to me, we'll see what your mother has to say about it!'

That brought her back to life with a vengeance. 'No! No! No! You can't make me! No! No! I hate you! I won't! I hate you!'

'Ay, ye've made that fairly evident.'

She refused to walk, and he couldn't make her. She just dragged her feet when he tried to pull her along. Without further ceremony he swung her over his left shoulder, where she couldn't kick the stormy petrel. She rained blows on his back with her fists, but they were so puny he barely felt them. It was harder to stop her wriggling off altogether. Twice, as they stumbled back, he'd had enough of it, and slapped her really hard. But she didn't stop fighting. God knew what demon possessed her, but she was a fighter. Never had Archie been so glad to reach the shelter of a house.

He had to find it in the dark, but by that time his eyes had grown accustomed again. There was no light in the window. The only light came from the lighthouse up above on Dreeym Lang. He had to face her mother now. Thank God he was so angry that he didn't care. He was beyond caring about any of them. The sooner he and Ben were off this accursed island the better it would be.

The baby was crying . . . No, not a baby; that was long ago . . . One of the children . . . Breesha! Diya was out of bed before she was properly awake. That was Breesha, sobbing desperately. Breesha never cried like that, not even when Jim . . . But then Breesha had never believed . . . This was something real. Over there. In the kitchen. Diya flung the door open.

It was too dark to see. 'Breesha? Where are you?'

'Mam! Oh, Mam!'

Breesha was in her arms. She was icy cold, and shaking violently. She clung to Diya, weeping wildly.

'It's all right, Breesha beti! It's all right, stop it now. Come on now, take a breath.' Diya could feel the hysteria rising through the child's body. 'Stop now, Breesha! Stop crying! Mam's here! You're not hurt. Try to stop.' Breesha's hair was damp, and the smell of wet grass hung about her. She'd been out! Outside . . . On the ground . . . Diya was shaken by a pang of terror. What . . .? Who . . .? 'Everything's all right now. Try to stop, Breesha veen. Then you can tell me what happened.' She heard her own voice sounding ordinary and calm. 'Come on now, beti! Mam's here.'

There were other voices in the room – there had been all the time – making a great deal of noise. Diya paid no attention to them. Only when someone lit a candle and placed it on the table did she look up. It was Mr Buchanan, looking scared and dishevelled. He'd been out too . . . He was still fully dressed. Of course . . . the stormy petrels . . . But what . . .? And how . . .? And someone else was crying too. Not crying: shouting, in a high, terrified treble. 'Breesha!' screamed Billy. 'He got Breesha! He got *Breesha*!'

'Mrs Geddes – ma'am – please, I can explain – something happened –'

'He got Breesha!' Billy yelled, drowning out Mr Buchanan. 'He did something to Breesha! He hurt Breesha!'

'Ma'am, if you'd just let me . . .'

Mr Buchanan came a step nearer Diya. Breesha screamed, and buried her face in her mother's nightgown.

'Stop it,' shouted Diya. 'Stop it *at once*! All of you! Billy, be quiet! Breesha, stop crying at once. You *must*! You, sir, be quiet! Now, then. All of you! Stop!' She'd shocked them into dazed silence. Billy, in his nightshirt, stood with his mouth still open, staring at her with frightened eyes. His hair was all standing up on end from the way he'd been lying on his pillow. Breesha clung to Diya, trembling all over, her teeth chattering, but she stopped making a noise. Over her head Diya met Archie's eyes. The look in her own was enough to make any man quail. 'Now, sir, an explanation, if you please!'

It was the way they looked at him: that woman looking at him as though he were a prisoner in the dock – and the boy too, for God's sake – the little boy, as if *he* . . . And that woman – how beautiful she was, and that made it so much worse – looking at him as if *he* – and all the while that devil's daughter – that little *demon* – yet they were looking at him as though *he* . . . It dawned on Archie why he stood accused, that they thought . . . at least, the woman was thinking, if not the boy . . . The *injustice*!

'How *dare* you!' Archie flung back at her. 'How dare *you* ask *me* to explain! Why dae ye no ask *her*? That's right, *her*! *Your* daughter! Ask her what *she* did – what she tried to do! And don't ye *dare* to look at me like that! Don't ye dare! As if I . . . as if I . . . as if I would *ever* hurt a bairn! Not even a damnable little demon like *that*!' He flung out his arm at the quivering Breesha, who began to sob afresh.

'Don't you call my daughter a demon! Don't *you* dare! Explain yourself, sir! Explain yourself at once!'

'You're no even going to speir what she did? What she tried tae dae to me?'

'Control yourself, sir. What could a little girl possibly do to *you*? You're a man grown: I hold *you* responsible! And don't you try to get out of it! I won't have you blame her!'

'I canna be responsible for your bairn, ma'am. If you like to teach her to murder – to aid and abet her to wander around the place *killing* people – then God help ye baith, that's all I can say! I want naethin whitever tae dae wi either of you. You can damn well explain to ain anither, for aw I care, God rot ye!'

Diya shoved Breesha aside, marched up to Archie, and slapped him across the face.

He raised his arm, as if to hit her back. She gasped. Just as Archie let his hand drop again, Billy threw himself against Archie's chest, battering him as hard as he could with his bare fists. 'No!' screamed Billy. 'No, you shan't! No, no, no!'

In the red-hot centre of his rage Archie suddenly remembered what was in his right pocket. His head cleared at once. He got Billy by the wrists and held him away from his body. 'Stop it, Billy!' He wasn't yelling any more; he was relieved to hear his own voice sounding cold and determined. 'Billy, dinna do that. You'll hurt the stormy petrel. It's in my pocket. Billy, you'll kill the petrel! Stop.'

Billy stopped. The voice of authority was back. This was the Writing Man he recognised. Billy had no idea what was happening. He just knew he didn't like it when everyone suddenly stopped being like themselves and turned into something else. But if the Writing Man said he had a bird in his pocket, then a bird in his pocket was what he had. He wouldn't tell a lie. It was all too muddling. Billy stood back, shivering, and sucked his skinned knuckle.

'Mammy!' It was Mally, in her nightgown, her hair flying

loose around her shoulders. She flung back the bedroom door and rushed to her mother. Diya picked her up and held her on her hip. With Mally clinging to her shoulder, Diya turned to face Archie.

'Now see what you've done!'

'That's no fair,' said Archie icily. 'If I'd had any choice in the matter I'd not have woken a soul, ma'am, except yourself. As it is . . .' He looked round, and realised who was missing. As soon as he thought of him, he found himself wishing, embarrassing though all this was, that Ben was there. 'Where's Mr Groat?'

'I should have thought that was *your* responsibility, sir. And now, perhaps you'll be good enough to tell me what upset my daughter?'

Diya sounded fiercer than she felt. Furious though she was, she had to admit – though never to him – that her worst fears were unjustified. He'd behaved unpardonably. *That damnable little demon* . . . She'd never forgive him that. But if the man truly had a live stormy petrel in his pocket, that had to prove his innocence. He hadn't intended violence, and he could hardly have perpetrated any, or the bird would be dead. That didn't exonerate him from the fact that *something* had happened. Only Breesha . . . An icy trickle of doubt was beginning to dampen Diya's wrath. Her own Breesha, whom naturally she'd defend with the last breath in her body, whatever happened . . . *What had she done*?

'Your daughter, ma'am, set a false light on the south side of Cam Giau. She hoped to lead me over the precipice when I was walking back from the keeill.'

'But that's *preposterous*!' Except that the moment he said it, Diya knew it was true. 'The child was in her bed! She didn't even know you'd gone out!'

'It can hardly have escaped your notice, ma'am, that the child was manifestly *not* in her bed, and' – Archie's cold formality suddenly failed him – 'the bairn kent damn well where I was. Because then she damn well tried to murder me!'

'Nonsense!'

'D'ye call it nonsense to set a light on the far side of Cam Giau, so I'd think it was a light from the house?'

'You must have known it wasn't!'

'Ay. That's why I'm alive now.'

'Nonsense! Of course she couldn't have killed you! I don't share your taste for melodrama, sir!'

'*Melodrama*!'

Mally didn't want the Writing Man to start shouting again. It was terrible to be suddenly woken in the night by angry voices and find Mam not there. And now all this crying, and shouting, when Mally had been fast asleep and then found herself suddenly and terrifyingly awake, was more than she could bear. Mally began to cry loudly. Sensing a way out, Breesha also began to sob, and clung to her mother. Archie, hard-pressed, instinctively looked at Billy. Billy looked back at him helplessly, with quivering lip.

'Och, s'truth!' cried Archie. 'Can we no leave this until the morn?' And take your appalling brats away – no, he couldn't say that out loud. 'Mrs Geddes, I havena muckle time. If I dinna set this bird free before dawn the gulls will get it. Can these bairns no go to their beds and be done wi it? I'll speak to you the morn, ma'am, if you're so set on it. But I've telt ye what happened, and that's that. It's up to you what you do with her. She's no mine, thank God, and I dinna want to give the matter anither thought. So, if you please: goodnight!'

What Diya wanted to do most was to hit him. But she wasn't in enough of a rage any more. Short of that, she wanted to tell him what she thought of him – after all, he'd flung enough insults at her, and hers. With two weeping children holding her down she couldn't do that either. The worst thing of all was knowing, deep down in her mind, that at least half her anger was with Breesha. Diya would never let Mr Buchanan know that. She'd never betray her own daughter. But Mr Buchanan was telling the truth. If only she could doubt him, she'd hate him less. As it was, his protestations of innocence were unforgivable, because in her heart she knew they were just. And there was Billy, standing there all by himself, not knowing what to think . . .

'I'd thank you, Mr Buchanan, to speak to us all more civilly. It's certainly true that I have nothing more to say to you tonight. I hope you manage to sleep well, sir, with all this lying upon your conscience. Goodnight!'

Diya swept herself and her daughters out of the kitchen in one magnificent gesture, and left Archie standing. What it had cost her to do it he never knew, because the bedroom door was closed firmly in his face, and he heard no more from them that night.

A thin light came creeping in before the dawn. Standing in the yard outside the kitchen door, they could begin to make out, as if they were looking through smoke, the low part of the island beyond the Tullachan, over Cam Giau to the corner of Gob y Vaatey. A chill west wind was bringing the smell of the sea in with it. The cloud had blown away, and the empty sky was turning grey. No birds were flying; the island lay as silent as if no living creature had ever inhabited it at all.

Billy was so tired it was like being in a dream. He'd never been up for so much of the night. At first, after everyone had gone into the bedroom and the kitchen had been mercifully quiet, it had been hard to stay awake. He'd felt so very sleepy. But he'd wanted to see what the Writing Man would do. He was very glad now that he'd managed not to fall asleep.

At first the Writing Man had been quite shy. Billy understood that. After all, the shouting and crying that had been going on were enough to make anyone feel shy. But then the Writing Man had looked Billy in the eye, and said, 'I think we deserve a nightcap after all that, don't you?' That had been puzzling, because in Billy's family they only wore nightcaps in winter. It turned out that what the Writing Man had meant was a drink. He'd asked Billy what was the strongest drink they had in the house? Billy had shown him the teapot. Mam must have been down from the light not very long ago, because the teapot was already by the hearth, and the tea was still hot.

Billy and the Writing Man had each had a cup of tea, sitting one on each side of the hearth. They didn't talk. Billy had enjoyed it in spite of all the horrible things that had happened earlier. He'd never been allowed to drink tea before, though naturally he didn't tell that to the Writing Man. The tea itself was bitter, and too hot. But it was like being a man grown, sitting there in the middle of the night with the Writing Man, and the others all gone to bed.

When they'd finished the tea, the Writing Man had said, 'D'you want to have a look at the stormy petrel?'

Billy had never seen one of Mother Carey's chickens close to. It was almost as small as a wren – which was why it was called a sea wren, of course – but more like a swallow. It was dark brown, with a broad white patch above its tail, and it smelt – the Writing Man told Billy to smell it, and asked him what the smell made him think of – like grass in autumn. Its feathers were smooth and very soft, and through them its flesh felt warm. It must have been frightened, but its eyes were expressionless, like black beads.

When they'd finished looking at the bird all over, the Writing Man asked Billy to hold it. Billy held the stormy petrel for a long time while the Writing Man did a drawing. When that was done, the Writing Man used a ruler to measure how long the bird was, and then he drew another picture of it as it lay in Billy's hand. The picture was very clever; it looked just like the real bird.

'Look at its beak,' he said to Billy. 'See how the nostrils are formed so it can dive.'

'They don't dive,' objected Billy. 'They just sort of hover and run over the water, and dip in when they're catching something. That's why they're called petrels. Aunt Diya told me that. Because of St Peter. He ran over the tops of the waves too. Only that was magic, like Mannanan in his chariot.'

'Magic?' The Writing Man sounded as if he was shocked.

He opened his mouth as if he was going to say something, and then closed it again. Then he wrote something in his notebook.

Next the Writing Man gently stretched out one of the petrel's wings. It was remarkably long for such a small bird. There was a thin white stripe under the wing, at the end of the inner row of feathers. The Writing Man made a note and measured the length of the wing. He wrote down *6.1″*. Then he made another drawing of the outstretched feathers.

'Very well,' said the Writing Man at last. He seemed to be speaking to the bird, not to Billy. 'I think that's enough, don't you?' He turned to Billy. 'Will we let it go now, d'ye think?'

'All right,' said Billy. He was sniffing his fingers. 'My hands smell like the bird. Like dead grass.'

So now they were standing in the yard, looking at the cold sky. 'Time enough,' said Archie. 'It'll find its way back to the keeill afore dawn.'

'Because at dawn the gulls will be out?' said Billy.

'That's right. But if we let it fly now, it'll get back safely.'

Archie was holding the bird in his cupped hands. It kept so still he was almost afraid it wouldn't recover. It would be in shock, if birds felt shock. Did birds suffer, or remember? It would know its own way home, one could be sure of that. He held the stormy petrel in the hollow of his hand. Then he threw it up. Even though it seemed to weigh nothing at all, he almost expected to see it fall like a stone, but the moment it was in the air, it spread its wings, fluttered skywards, and was gone.

Towards dawn the low cloud cleared. Much higher overhead, a great stripe of mackerel cloud slowly took shape in a pearl-pale sky. A few puffins began to circle the island. The birds on the cliffs were just beginning their daytime chorus. Ben and Lucy had moved round the parapet as the wind changed, so now they were facing due east. The ghost of a grey curve on the horizon might be the far hills of Cumberland; it wasn't yet light enough to tell.

About an hour, thought Ben. Sunrise was at four-fifteen. It must be past three now. He'd stayed up all night with the lightkeeper because he wanted to. He was a man grown, and if that's what he chose to do, his time was his own and there was no one on God's earth to stop him. Certainly the lightkeeper had not stopped him. That was her choice too. Ben was still not completely sure why he'd done it. Not sure in his mind, that was. Both his heart and his body knew damn well why he was here. In the east the sky was a delicate shade of yellow, just beginning to show a tinge of pink. He and the lightkeeper were sitting very close, side by side in the open window.

'There's still a bit of biscuit left,' said Ben. 'Will we finish it?' He unwrapped the napkin. 'And some of that cheese. I'll cut you a bit.' He unclasped his knife and tried to slice crumbly lumps of cheese onto the fragments of ships' biscuit. 'It's a bit of a mess, I'm afraid. Help yourself.'

'D'you ever stop eating, Ben?'

She was laughing at him as she leant over his knees, gathering up bits of broken biscuit. Her hair brushed his face. A quiver of delight ran through him. 'Ay,' he said, 'I do sometimes. Dinna take all the broken bits. Have the whole one.'

'It was me that broke it!' She brushed the crumbs off the cloth. Ben felt her fingers gently brush across his knee. Then she was licking her fingers, looking out to sea again.

At ten past four Lucy would stand up, ready to put out the lights. Ben glanced south, where the waves were breaking on Sker ny Rona. The tide was flooding in over stranded rock pools; another fifteen feet or so and it would have covered all the seaweed. Ben had calculated over an hour ago that mean tide must be at six minutes after half past three. It was now or never.

Ben put his arm around Lucy's shoulders. She was away in a dwam; when he touched her she gave a start, as if her thoughts had been very far away, and looked round at him. Now or never, thought Ben, and kissed her. He tasted biscuit crumbs on her lips.

To his surprise Lucy didn't resist him at all. Had she been expecting this all the time? Surely not? Then she suddenly pulled herself away. 'What do you think you're *doing*, Mr Groat?'

'I dinna think, I ken,' said Ben, and tried to do it again.

But this time Lucy pushed him off. 'No!' Clearly she was upset. 'I suppose you're thinking – *No*! – You're thinking just because my son must have had a father . . . you're thinking that I . . . that I . . . that I *know* about all this. But you're wrong. Mr Groat, you couldn't be more wrong!'

'No!' protested Ben. 'I wasna thinking anything of the sort! I was thinking that I . . . I was thinking about *now*. How we could be – now. Like this.'

This time Lucy didn't try to stop him. She knew that she ought to, and somewhere at the back of her mind a small voice whispered insistently that she would be sorry, that once again she was flinging herself headlong into a lifetime of regret, while he – this man whom she hardly knew – could, and would, walk away and never spare a thought for her again, if that's what he chose to do. But the voice of reason was drowned out by a rush of feeling that had been pent up so many years she'd forgotten even to acknowledge it was there. Taken by surprise, it wasn't Ben, it was her own body that betrayed her. There was no question in Lucy's mind, this time, that the choice was hers. She wasn't in the least afraid of Ben, or anything he might do to her. Too late, she realised that the sheer joy of not being afraid of him was her undoing.

Lucy stood up suddenly, took Ben's hand and pulled him to his feet. Then she turned away and disappeared down the ladder.

Ben was aghast. She'd *liked* it! She hadn't told him not to! He hadn't forced her! And now she'd got up and rushed off. Why? Where? A horrified vision rose in his mind of Lucy rushing back to the house, rousing them all with her screams, and making a formal complaint to Young Archibald . . . Even in his consternation it occurred to Ben that it must be the first case of a lightkeeper accusing one of Mr Stevenson's surveyors of assault. Only she'd *liked* it! Horrified and bewildered, Ben clattered down the ladder after her.

She was still there, on the platform. She was facing him, as though she was waiting for him. When he held his hands out to her she didn't run away. When he took her in his arms she twined her own round his neck and embraced him fervently. There was no mistaking that. He hadn't got it wrong.

Ben couldn't believe his luck. He'd have thought himself lucky to steal a kiss. But this . . . it was the kind of thing he'd dreamed of – in fact he'd been dreaming of it since he was ten – but never what he'd expected to happen, or, at least, not to him. Maisie hadn't been coy, it was true, but this . . . Lucy wasn't pretending anything. She never did pretend. She wanted him, Ben Groat. She didn't just let him kiss her passionately, she wanted – and she was completely honest about it – to kiss him back. She wanted to unfasten his clothes and caress his body. She wanted to make love with him, there and then. She wanted to do everything that was possible just as much as he did. She did nothing to stop him touching her, or taking her clothes off. She let him caress her as much as he liked. She wanted him as straightforwardly as he wanted her.

Lucy had thought she was strong, but Ben had found his way to the one place in her life where she had no defences. She'd never learned any. Life had cheated her once, and she'd been alone since then, and lonely, and her dreams too often left her burdened with unfulfilled desires. It was true what she'd said to Ben: to love this way was almost unknown to her, but her body knew what it wanted, and Ben seemed to know too. The voice saying she ought not was still whispering in her head, faint but insistent. She smothered it. The years of longing would get paid for, just once, and she didn't care what it cost.

For over an hour Lucy and Ben lay together on the platform below the light, with two blankets and a bolster for their bed. Delighting in one another, they forgot everything else in the world except the light. The moment a shaft of yellow sunshine leaped through the trapdoor Lucy pulled herself out of Ben's arms for the second time, and sat up. 'The light! I have to put out the lights!'

She grabbed her petticoat, pulled it over her head, and was up the ladder in a trice. Ben blinked and sat up. He had a glimpse of her going up the ladder. With the light above her, her petticoat was transparent and he could see her body quite plainly – the same body she'd just given to him. He still couldn't quite believe his luck. Ben groped for his shirt and breeks, whistling under his breath, as blithe as any man could be. Lucy was Lucy, and Lucy was his, and last summer would never cast its blight on him again. The dawning day was shining bright. That was all Ben cared to think about at the moment; the rest could take care of itself. He suddenly felt desperately sleepy. He recollected that it was Sunday, and breathed a quite genuine prayer of thanks that no one could ask him to do a serious day's work. If he curled up in the blankets, just as he was, and went to sleep, surely no one could object? Young Archibald would realise he hadn't slept in his bed anyway. No, he couldna really do that. But it was only four-fifteen. Surely she'd come back, just for an hour or so . . . surely no one else would be up until gone five. If he put on his shirt, in case anyone came . . . Ben sleepily put his shirt back on, did up one button, then rolled himself up in the blanket, and shut his eyes.

Something terrible had happened. Something that couldn't be mended. Jim. Jim was gone. The colourless future loomed, forcing its way in as it did every morning, and Diya struggled not to wake to it. Day succeeded day, and every morning the grey light came back inexorably, and every morning she shut her eyes against it, and did her best not to wake up. However late she slept, it could never be long enough . . . But all that was over. It was finished years ago, and now . . . Then what . . .? It wasn't Jim pressed against her side in a small tight heap . . . Breesha. It was Breesha. The last shreds of sleep fled away, and

Diya remembered. Mr Buchanan . . . the Writing Man – that's what the children had called him always – the Writing Man. And Breesha . . . Breesha had tried to lure the Writing Man over the cliff with a false light. And she, Diya, had slapped his face. Never, since they dragged her from Aji's clinging arms, had she so far forgotten herself in public. He could never forgive either of them now. Something more precious than she'd realised had been broken last night, and now it could never be mended.

'Mam?'

Reluctantly Diya opened her eyes. Mally was standing by the bed in her nightgown, looking down at her anxiously.

'What is it?' Diya felt so tired; she didn't want to face any of this.

'The sun's well up, Mam.'

No wonder Mally was disconcerted. She'd never been the first to wake before. 'Then we'd better get up too. No, don't wake Breesha. Let her have her sleep out.'

Diya slid out of bed and pulled the curtain back. It was long past dawn; the sky wasn't grey at all, but blue. It was going to be another lovely day. Where was Lucy? Diya hadn't heard her come in. Melodrama. That's what she'd accused Mr Buchanan of. And she'd slapped his face. She couldn't imagine how any man could forgive that. And after what Breesha had done to him, he'd surely never want to see any of them again. Diya felt so weary. Friendship was not so easily found if one lived on Ellan Bride. However fleeting it might be, one could hardly afford to snap it in two and fling it away. But that's what she'd done. Or rather, it was what Breesha had forced her to do. Diya glanced back to the humped up shape under the bedclothes. Breesha hadn't understood what any of it meant – either what she'd tried to do to Mr Buchanan, or what it would mean to her mother. Or had she? Mr Buchanan had called Breesha a demon. Diya had enough self-knowledge to understand why that had enraged her beyond the point of control: it was because she saw some truth in it. Oh yes, she'd been angry with him, indeed she had. What's more, she'd held back none of her rage. A demon, he'd said. Like daughter, like mother, he'd be thinking now.

He'd want to get away from them now as soon as he could. Diya looked out at the chickens foraging on the grass outside – they'd have had no breakfast either – and gave herself a little shake. What did it matter? He'd go off on his voyage and forget that any of them even existed. It was foolish to mind what he thought of her – of them. He'd have gone away anyway, and left them all behind without a backward look. Nothing had materially changed. However badly they'd behaved towards him – yes, mother and daughter both – he could hardly punish them for it.

'Mam!' Mally needed the buttons at the back of her pinafore done up. As Diya bent to do it, Mally said in a hushed whisper, eerily echoing her mother's thought, 'Is Breesha going to be punished?'

'I think Breesha's sorry already.'

'I don't mean sorry. I mean *punished*. Because she tried to kill the Writing Man, didn't she?'

Diya looked down at her daughter in consternation.

'I heard you last night. I couldn't *help* hearing you. And if you kill people,' said Mally, her brow wrinkled in anxiety, 'you get punished. I don't mean *scolded*. I mean *punished*. I know you do!'

'Dear God!' whispered Diya. 'Don't say that, Mally. Oh, dear God!'

Chapter 26

THE GOATS KNEW SOMETHING WAS WRONG. PERHAPS THEY smelt fear in the air, or felt it in the touch of Diya's hands. Mappy, with her swollen belly, gobbled her corn quickly and skittered away over the rocks before either of the humans could come near her. When Turk came to be milked, she tried to pull her head out of the yoke, and to kick away the bucket.

This wouldn't do. Diya took away the bucket, and made herself be calm, squatting on the ground beside the restless animal. If even the goats felt her anxiety, how unfit she must be to deal with the child. She gazed out to sea. The water was grey and wrinkled, with shadowy lines across it where the swell rose almost imperceptibly over the hidden cletts. So many mornings Diya had come out here, through so many summers when the goats were out on the hill. Not for much longer. Their days here were numbered. Indeed, all days were numbered, but it was not given to humankind, thank God, to know the exact figure until the numbers became small enough to count.

The days of Breesha's innocence had also been numbered. There was no going back to yesterday. Nothing on earth could change what had happened last night. If Diya could have known . . . But what had there been to know? Should Diya have known her child better, and recognised her danger? Had Breesha always been marked, or was this a terrible accident, a whim of fate that no one could have predicted or prevented? God knew. Diya had not known, but that didn't mean that she wasn't responsible. If she hadn't known, then she was also to blame for her own ignorance.

If only Breesha's father . . . But Jim had also vanished in a night, five years ago. How could he! How *dare* he! Irrational rage welled up inside her, not for the first time, but Diya was no less shaken by it. She was still furious with Jim for dying, for leaving her to . . . Oh yes, she'd done her best to be a mother to them, but she was a poor hand at being a father. If Jim hadn't gone out that night . . . If only Jim . . . then Diya wouldn't have had to . . . and then Breesha . . . Ah, if she'd had her father, perhaps none of this would have happened. If only Jim were here now, then at least . . .

'Mam, aren't you going to milk Turk?'

Breesha's voice was small and subdued, quite unlike her usual self. She knows how upset I am, thought Diya – at least she knows she's responsible for that – but does she know the worse part of what she's done? She stretched out her hands to Turk again, saw that they were trembling, and let them fall.

'I could milk her, if you'd rather.'

Breesha often came here with Diya, on the mornings when it was Billy's turn to do the light. Breesha was good at milking the goats. Her fingers were strong and deft. Breesha had a sure touch with all the animals. It was one of the things Diya loved about her.

'Very well. You milk her.'

Clearly it was a relief to Breesha to have something that she was able to do. Oddly enough, the moment she put her hands to Turk's udders, the goat calmed down. She didn't try to kick, and she didn't hold the milk back. In a moment two gleaming streams of milk were squirting into the bucket.

No child was irredeemable. And this child was Diya's own.

Punished, Mally had said. Diya should have thought of it herself. Breesha had attempted murder. She had come within a hand's breadth of deliberately killing another human being.

Diya watched her daughter's hands vigorously milking the goat. Breesha's small fingers confidently gripped and pulled, gripped and pulled. Turk knew that she was safe in Breesha's hands, and the milk flowed easily. Turk's udders were almost empty. Those same child's hands had held up the bottle lantern, with intent to kill a man.

To kill a man . . . Archibald Buchanan, a stranger. He could press charges. To set a false light was a capital offence. It was murder. A hanging matter.

There'd once been a hanging in Castletown while Diya was living with Grandmother. Diya remembered the crowd milling round the house, pushing its way through to Castle Rushen. Then she and Grandmother, alone in the big drawing-room, had watched the 95th Regiment march past, and presently they'd heard the dreadful dirge of the funeral psalm. A little while after that the black flag had risen slowly over the Castle keep, telling the world a man had died, just a few hundred yards from where they sat. If Breesha's case came to court . . . it must not come to court. A ten-year-old . . . If a ten-year-old committed murder then that ten-year-old was a murderer, and therefore justice demanded that same ten-year-old be hanged. That was the law. If Mr Buchanan chose to press charges, Breesha would be in the dock.

They might decide she was too young to hang. There'd been a ten-year-old sentenced when Diya was in Castletown – what was his name now? – Thomas something – the Deemsters had said he should hang, but in the end he'd only been transported. All he'd done was steal a little money and a pair of shoes. He'd been transported for seven years. Diya had heard Finn tell of others, since she came to Ellan Bride: little children shipped off to Botany Bay or God knew where, usually for the pettiest of thefts. But not one of them had attempted murder.

Breesha had had no provocation. She could plead nothing. Ignorance? Breesha was not ignorant of death. She knew what she was doing. Breesha in the dock . . . A hanging matter. Or, if the Deemsters were merciful, what then? Even if they did transport her instead . . . Those other cases had all been boys. Innocent as Breesha was, what would become of her? Her mother would never know, except that in her heart she would know all too well. They couldn't do that to a little girl as innocent as Breesha. Except that Breesha was not innocent. She'd attempted murder.

If they charged her, they'd take her away. Even though Castle Rushen had lain just across the square, Mrs Wells' granddaughter had never seen inside the great gates. She'd never entered the prison. If Mr Buchanan saw fit, this child in front of her, who was just raising the bar over the yoke to release the small brown goat, could be immured in Castle Rushen before the week was out. Did Breesha know that? No, her mother was certain she had not the remotest idea of it.

She'd been right to think Breesha would be better away from Ellan Bride. But already perhaps it was too late. It was a cruel irony to think of Castletown as a place of terror. It couldn't be true: surely if they were in Castletown now, everything would become simple and civilised. Breesha could have grown into – oh dear God, if she could still grow into – a normal little girl in an ordinary world. She could have found an outlet for her vivid imagination in the Circulating Library, and kept her wild fancies within the safe bounds of fiction. Diya had thought of Castletown as a civilised society all these years, and yet Castletown was also where the prison was, where people died, or were exiled for ever – punished, in fact – whoever they were, if they were found guilty. And who, thought Diya bitterly, is without guilt?

Breesha had not killed a man. She'd surely not even understood what she was doing. Perhaps Diya was letting her thoughts run out of control. *Punished*, Mally had said. But Mally hadn't meant this! Mally knew nothing about such things. Breesha had made a mistake, a silly childish mistake. She'd not killed anyone!

Only it was mere chance that she had not . . . But the man

lived, and now he held them in the hollow of his hand. When Diya thought about what he might do to them . . . but he had not done anything. It was Breesha who had done it . . .

Turk, free, ducked under Breesha's arm, and trotted away.

For a crazy moment Breesha thought of running after Turk. She knew lots of places where Mam could never reach her. With enough of a start she could climb down into Giau yn Stackey. She was fairly sure she could run faster than Mam, and she could certainly climb better. Not as well as a goat. Breesha was not a goat. The goats could stay out on the hill for ever. Breesha couldn't. Sooner or later she'd have to go back. There were thousands of safe places on the island, but not for her. She'd have to go back where the people were. That made her their prisoner, only she'd never realised it before.

She was terrified. Not when she'd been asleep: the terror hadn't followed her there. But the minute she'd woken this great weight had settled on her again, as if it knew her very well, and had just been sitting on the end of the bed, patiently waiting until she came back from sleep. The weight felt like a yoke. Like the yoke, its wood had worn slippery-smooth on the shoulders from much use. This imaginary yoke fitted Breesha exactly. She hadn't seen it before, but it had known her and been waiting for her all this time. Perhaps it would never go away again. The hours – though really they'd only been minutes – of long terror last night, when she'd held up the bottle lantern: the fear that had settled on her then hadn't been just for the present. Perhaps it would last for ever. The fear was not being able to see into the enclosing dark, not knowing what was happening out there . . . the fear was holding the little light in her hand and the dark swallowing it up as if she were in the belly of a monster . . . the fear was trying to keep Faith with herself, to call upon the Saint who suddenly seemed so very far away . . . the fear was being determined not to waver, because she was strong and would never give in. But all the time it had been a wrong thing to do. That was why it had been so fearful: Breesha realised now that the reason it had been so difficult was because she'd made a terrible mistake. But it couldn't be undone. Whatever she did now, yesterday would never come back. The Breesha of yesterday still seemed so close she seemed to be her own self, and yet she wasn't. Yesterday's Breesha had turned into a stranger. Breesha missed yesterday's Breesha so much she wanted to throw herself on the ground and howl.

That was impossible. She was being accused, and Mam, sitting there looking at her like that, was the cruel judge. Breesha could only hide what she felt, and stand up for herself as best she could. There was nothing left to do except brazen it out. That meant she had to carry this great weight. It meant knowing that Mam was her enemy: Mam was her judge, her accuser. But Breesha couldn't run away. There was nowhere to go.

'Breesha veen, sit down. I need to talk to you.'

Breesha hesitated. Diya had never seen her daughter look at her with so much fear in her eyes. 'Sit down, Breesha.'

Breesha sat down reluctantly about three feet away.

'Breesha, if Mr Buchanan had fallen into Cam Giau he'd have been killed.'

'I don't want to talk about it!'

'Breesha, we *must* talk about it. Do you understand what you tried to do?'

'I didn't mean it!'

'What do you mean, you didn't mean it?' Diya held her breath, and then said levelly, 'Breesha, if Mr Buchanan had fallen into Cam Giau because you set a false light, he'd have been killed. You tried to make him fall into Cam Giau.'

'I don't want you to say that!'

That was too much. 'You don't want me to say that! But you *did* it, Breesha. Don't you understand? Are you stupid? Don't you *realise* – you tried to *kill* him. If he hadn't realised where he was in time, that man would be *dead*! And it's no use crying. You can't get out of it that way. If you're old enough to try to kill a man, you're old enough to hear me say so!'

'Well, all right! But I can't help it *now*! What do you want me to say *now*? You can't just shout at me! What d'you expect me to do *now*?'

Never had Diya felt so helpless. Her own child was suddenly a stranger. It wasn't only what Breesha had done: it was the way she looked at her mother with such terror – perhaps even hatred – in her eyes, like a cornered animal. She wasn't even sorry. She almost seemed not human any more – a little demon, Mr Buchanan had said – but of course Breesha was human. Breesha was still herself, still the little girl she'd been yesterday, only suddenly Diya could see something else in her. The horror of it was, she was sure that this new aspect of Breesha had come to stay. The little girl of yesterday was dead, overlaid by this wild stranger with terror in her eyes. Mixed with her immediate fear Diya felt immense grief – but that couldn't be addressed yet.

'I expect you at least to be sorry,' said Diya coldly. 'I expect you at least to be aware of what you tried to do. And I would like to know why you did it.'

'Don't talk to me in that horrid voice!'

'Breesha, pull yourself together! You should thank God I'm here to talk to you in any voice at all. Don't you realise that it matters – that you tried to *kill* Mr Buchanan?'

'I didn't! I never touched him! I only had the light! I didn't *do* anything!'

'Breesha, you tried to kill Mr Buchanan.'

When Diya said it like that, Breesha did begin to cry. She wasn't cold and strange any more; she cried like a child, the way Mally would have cried if she'd done something bad and found herself in trouble. When Breesha cried in that way Diya was at last able to comfort her in the same way she'd comforted Mally the day before, when Mally had cried about leaving Ellan Bride.

'It'll be all right, Breesha veen. Mam's here. We'll think what to do. We'll find a way through this. Mam will do her best, Breesha.'

Yet behind the comforting words a cold fear remained in Diya's heart, embodied in the image of the prison in Castle Rushen: justice and retribution. Punished. A hanging matter. Mr Buchanan held them in the hollow of his hand. Diya would have to talk to him, and find out what he meant to do.

When Breesha was quiet, Diya said, 'Breeshaveen, can you try to explain it to me? What really did happen?'

She waited patiently for an answer. 'I dreamed about Saint Bride,' said Breesha shakily. 'She was frightened, and that made me frightened too. So I got up and he was there, and I followed him. He was at the keeill. And I saw him – he caught one of the *kirreeyn varrey*. And in the light – I saw him pulling at it. He pulled its wing.' She began to sob again. 'I don't know! I don't *know*! Mam, I didn't know what he was doing! But I'd had the dream – and I *knew* – he oughtn't to have done that – it was in the dream – and I thought – I don't *know*! – I just thought he oughtn't – and then I thought of . . . of that – and it *didn't* seem bad – it didn't – because of what he'd done – I don't know why he pulled its wing. But he pulled its wing and he oughtn't – it would hurt it!' Breesha could hardly speak for tears. 'I don't *know*! I'm sorry, I'm sorry, I'm sorry! But he was hurting it! And . . . I don't *know*!'

'Oh Breesha!' Diya didn't know what else to say. What Breesha said was the truth. Breesha always told the truth. Diya understood that, but she also knew with total clarity that it was the wrong kind of truth. It couldn't possibly satisfy the Deemsters in the court at Castletown. Seen in that light, what Breesha had to offer was no explanation at all. Diya had always known that Breesha lived in a world where dreams and facts flitted across unguarded boundaries. Did that make the child innocent? Innocent or guilty – what did that mean? Her own daughter had tried to kill a man. The one saving grace was that the man was not dead. He was alive, and on Ellan Bride, and he held them – the phrase was beginning to haunt her – in the hollow of his hand. Diya couldn't begin to explain to Mr Buchanan why Breesha had done it. She didn't even understand herself, but she understood what *kind* of thought had prompted her daughter. Diya would have to talk to Mr Buchanan, not as an equal any more, but as a suppliant. If he wasn't prepared to show them mercy, then there would certainly be no mercy in the world outside. Diya would do anything within her power to persuade him to be merciful, anything at all. Her little girl could never be wholly innocent again, but if Mr Buchanan chose – if she, Diya, could make him choose – her Breesha might still go free.

Chapter 27

WHEN ARCHIE WOKE HE HAD NO IDEA WHAT TIME IT WAS. That in itself was disconcerting. He was alone in the kitchen bed on Ellan Bride except for a grey cat, which had curled itself into the warm hollow behind his knees. A small circle of light showed at a gap in the closed curtain, just under the rail. Archie caught the tail of a dream; he closed his eyes again and tried to focus on it, but the last shreds were evaporating even as he tried to grasp them. Beltane night, and the fire on Ben Ledi . . . they'd been carrying wood up to the fire . . . he and his father, walking side by side, bearing the wood for the fire . . . They did that every year . . . But something had been wrong: there was something he didn't recognise in his father's face – an unspoken intent – it vanished even as he tried to remember . . . Danger. Archie had been in danger of his life. Yet all he could remember of the dream was walking up the ridge to the summit of Ben Ledi, he and his father: the two of them walking side by side, carrying the wood.

The dream was gone. Last night had been no dream, though it was hard to believe it now, in the broad light of day. Because it *was* daylight, although the kitchen seemed quite quiet. Archie reached out and pulled the curtain back so he could peep out. There was no one in the room but his chainman, who was sitting at the table eating porridge. One other place had been laid but it was empty. The rest of the table was bare. A large pot was simmering over the fire, and a savoury smell, which was certainly not porridge, permeated the kitchen.

'Ben?'

'Is that you, sir?'

'What time is it?'

'About nine, I think, sir.'

'*Nine*!'

'I think so, sir. But no matter: 'tis Sunday, if you recall.'

'*Nine*!' Archie was out of bed in a moment. He grabbed his breeks and began pulling them on. 'That's half the day gone!'

'Ay, but it's Sunday anyway, like I said. Will I get you some porridge, sir? She's left plenty in the pan.'

'She . . .? Where *is* everyone?'

'Well, sir, the lightkeeper had her breakfast and went to clean the light. She took the peedie girl with her – Mally. Pleased as Punch, she was, the peedie lass – seemingly she's no worked with the light before today. It should've been Billy, but he's still sleeping, if you look over there, sir. Dead to the world, that boy. I dinna ken what's been going on here, I'm sure.'

'And . . . the others? Mrs Geddes?'

'She had the dinner in the pot before I came in. We're having puffins to our Sunday dinner, sir. That's the stew simmering away just now – I had a look – you can surely smell it? Then she took the other lass and they went to milk the goats. That was maybe an hour since. *I* dinna ken why they're no back yet. 'Tis no matter, anyway: there's plenty o porridge in the pan. And it's Sunday, sir, so there's no need to be in a taking about the hour.'

Archie tucked in his shirt. It was none the fresher for having been slept in for two nights, but there was no one here who'd be caring much about that. He delved in his portmanteau for a clean cravat. 'Nine o'clock, Ben! I canna believe it! And where were *you* last night? For I surely didna see you here.'

'Out, sir,' said Ben stolidly. He ladled porridge into the other bowl. 'Here you are, sir. The fact of the matter was, I took a fancy to watch the light.'

'What, all night?' Archie hadn't meant to sound irritable, but realised he must have done when he got no answer. 'Ay well, it's nae matter. Thank you.' He hadn't realised how hungry he was until Ben put a bowl of steaming porridge in front of him. For a while the two of them ate in silence.

'Ben?'

'Ay, sir?' said Ben cautiously.

'Whit would ye say . . . I mean to say: would you object at all, Mr Groat, to doing a small amount of work this afternoon? I wouldn't ask you to act against your conscience, naturally, but if . . . if you did feel able to do so, why, I think we could be ready to leave tomorrow, in spite of yesterday's weather.'

Mr Stevenson had strong views about working on the Sabbath. Both Archie and Ben knew it. Only on the Bell Rock had Sabbath observance given way to the more imperative dictates of tide and weather. Ben didn't answer at once. Instead he got up, went over to the hearth, and helped himself to more porridge.

'The fact is,' said Archie, 'I'm anxious to get away as soon as possible. If Mr Watterson comes tomorrow, I'd want to be ready to go with him immediately.'

And you slept until nine, thought Ben. *Something*'s been going on here, and no mistake. Aunt Deer was in a right taking this morning too. When he'd come in from the light – for Ben had slept late himself, until nearly eight o'clock – he'd found the two wee girls silently finishing their breakfast, very late, and looking scared and anxious. Lucy and Aunt Deer had been in the bedroom, and when they came out it was obvious that something was amiss. He'd thought at first it might be him, but no one had said anything to his face; in fact they seemed to take him so much for granted that clearly whatever the matter was, it was nothing to do with him. It didn't seem a sensible moment to try to get a private word with Lucy. He'd contented himself with remaining in ignorance, and eating a substantial breakfast. And now here was Young Archibald suddenly so desperate to get away he was asking Ben to work on Sunday, which was dead against company rules. Young Archibald would know that Ben would never betray him, but it was quite unlike him, hasty though he was, to even dream of asking. Ben came back to the table, and sat down.

'But of course,' said Archie, 'if you have any objection at all, I won't mention it again.'

Ben suddenly realised he had a monumental objection. He hadn't thought about it – he hadn't thought about the future at all – until Young Archibald talked about being ready to leave tomorrow. Tomorrow! It struck Ben like a flash of lightning: he didn't want to leave one bit. He wanted to stay on Ellan Bride as long as possible. He wanted to lie with the lightkeeper, not just tonight – if she'd let him – she hadn't even said that much – but the next night as well. And the night after that. He wanted to make love to her every night, as far as he could see ahead. And if he couldn't see ahead, he still wanted to lie with her again, right over the horizon of possibility. He wanted that – he hadn't really thought it out, but he knew he wanted it – and the one certain thing he could say about the future was that he didn't want to leave Ellan Bride with tomorrow's tide.

'I'm no sure but what I do object,' said Ben.

'Ay well,' said Archie, looking haggard, 'in that case of course there's no more to be said.'

Mally carefully rubbed the south-facing reflector with a piece of tow. The reflector was very smeary where the lamp had burned all night long. She had to rub hard for a long time. Gradually the little mirrors began to shine again. When they got clean they started to wink in the sun. When Mally leaned forward she could see her face in them. Mally seldom saw her own face; the looking glass in the bedroom was too high. The dark-brown eyes that looked back at her now from all the little mirrors looked very responsible and serious. Mally wouldn't be eight for a long time yet, but here she was, working with

Aunt Lucy in the lantern. Breesha and Billy had each started after their eighth birthday, but Mally was starting much sooner than that.

Mally had entirely forgotten that this was not for ever. Lucy didn't remind her; what would be the point? Mally was happy this morning, and that was enough. Lucy needed time to think. She needed to think about Ben Groat, although when his image rose in her mind it was more a matter of remembered delight than sensible thought, and that was no use at all. She also needed to think about what Diya had told her when she came in from the light. Diya had hustled her into the bedroom and told her this appalling thing about Breesha . . . Breesha had set a false light for Mr Buchanan. Breesha had done that, while Lucy had been letting Ben Groat stay on watch, uninvited, in the lighthouse. Not that the two things could be connected in any way, except that they'd happened at about the same time. But what Diya told Lucy this morning had added itself to the growing heap of troubles at the back of Lucy's mind. If only none of this had happened! If only that letter had never come!

But Mally was happy this morning, even though she'd been woken in the night. She'd already forgotten to worry about Breesha. Mally was more pleased to be working in the lighthouse than either of the others had ever been. Lucy realised, watching Mally, that she loved her like one of her own. Mally had been so little when Jim died. The other thing Diya had said this morning, for the first time ever, was that the family might have to part . . . that perhaps it couldn't go on being all five of them together when they left Ellan Bride, especially now that Breesha had done this terrible thing. Diya said Mr Buchanan could charge Breesha with attempted murder. Surely not! Surely he wasn't as vile a man as that! In fact Lucy had stopped thinking he was vile at all. But Diya had told Lucy she'd been thinking about it all night. She said Lucy oughtn't to have anything to do with what might happen to Breesha. Diya had said that it was quite enough that Lucy had Billy without having – Diya had actually said this to her – 'yet another source of shame'. Diya had been more upset than Lucy had ever seen her, but Lucy still couldn't believe that she'd said that. Diya had been talking about Billy – their own Billy – when she'd said Lucy oughtn't to have 'yet another source of shame'. Had Diya always thought that about Billy? It would be unbearable to think that all these years . . . Lucy would not think it. She didn't want to think about any of it.

The way Mally set about her new task was typical. It had taken Billy a long time to learn to clean the lights thoroughly. At the beginning he used to leave smears all over the reflectors, and miss every corner when he did the windows. Breesha, to begin with, had done everything much too fast, and then had to be set to do it all again. She used to get angry about that, but doing the light was a step towards adulthood, and to be demoted would have brought shame on her, and so Breesha had obeyed. But Mally wasn't like either of the other two. She was working away at the south-facing reflector very slowly and carefully, with the utmost concentration. Mally would still be trying to make it perfect when Lucy had done all the other eleven reflectors and cleaned the windows. It didn't matter. Lucy hadn't expected any material help from Mally on her first day anyway, and they had all the time in the world. Also, Mally, unlike Breesha, was very quiet, absorbed in her own world. Lucy was glad of that. It gave her time to think.

Only she wouldn't think about what Diya had said. She wouldn't let herself keep remembering those words. There were much healthier things to think about than that. Benjamin Groat, for example. But that too was not so easy . . . 'Yet another source of shame.' What she and Ben had done last night meant that it could happen again: 'yet another source of shame'. Diya was upset beyond thinking clearly, because of Breesha. Lucy had no intention of telling Diya that she'd once again courted disgrace herself – had brought on them, perhaps, 'yet another source of shame' – another, and another . . . The family might have to part. Probably Diya wouldn't want to know Lucy any more anyway, if Ben Groat had fathered another child on her. Which – if that's what had happened last night – Lucy had willingly let him do. And now Ben could walk away, if that's what he chose, while Lucy and Billy would have to live with it. If there were another child now, as well as the retribution that might fall on Breesha . . . Breesha had tried to kill Mr Buchanan. Breesha too had become 'yet another source of shame'. But if Ben Groat came to Lucy again tonight she might fail to say no to him. Because – did she love him? She thought she did, but on the other hand, Lucy had also been convinced that what she'd felt for Billy's father had been love. She'd been wrong. Love was, in fact, what she felt for Billy. And for Mally. And for Breesha. Before that Lucy had loved Jim and Mummig and Da, so she should have known very well what love was all the time, but this other thing . . . She wanted Ben Groat. Her whole body wanted him, but it wasn't just her body. She didn't want to think about it. If those two men had never come, then there wouldn't have been all this confusion. If only they could all have been left in peace!

Lucy didn't send Mally to fetch the boiling water because she was too young to do that. When Lucy went down to the kitchen herself, she found Ben Groat standing at the table cleaning the porridge pan in a basin of hot water.

'You don't have to do that!'

'Someone has to do it,' said Ben. He wiped his wet hands on his breeks, came round the table, and put his arms round her.

Lucy pushed him off, but didn't make him let go her hands. 'No, no, not now – the children – where *is* everyone?'

'I dinna ken. At least, I ken Young Archibald had his breakfast, for I gave it him. He went oot after that. He's in a rare taking, Lucy. I don't ken what happened – maybe thu kens? But he's wanting to get this job done and be away from here the morn's morn if he possibly can. He was wanting me to work today – that shows he's in a bad way. He wants to be away from here as soon as maybe. At least, that seems to be the wy o't.'

'Oh!' So Ben was leaving tomorrow. And that was that. 'Oh,' said Lucy again. It was too much to take in. She had to get back to Mally, and the light. 'I must go.' She unhooked the kettle from the chain. 'So if Finn comes tomorrow, you'll be leaving at once?'

'No if the job's no done. If we're no finished when Finn comes back, he said he'd wait a day. Are thu taking yon kettle up to the light? Will I carry it for thee?'

'I carry things up to the light every day of my life!'

'Ay well, thu can have a day off doing it for once.' Ben took the kettle from her.

Lucy swept ungraciously out of the kitchen ahead of him, but when they were going up the path she said, 'Why wouldn't he be wanting you to work today anyway? Don't you have to, if he says so?'

''Tis Sunday.'

'Oh,' said Lucy again. 'I was forgetting. It doesn't make any difference to us: the light must still be lit. But he – what were you calling him just now – Young Archibald?'

'Ay. He's been ca'd that ever since he joined the company, so I believe. Not to his face, of course,' explained Ben.

'Oh. And now Young Archibald wants you to work today so you can go tomorrow?'

'Ay, that's what he asked me to do.' Ben followed Lucy into the lighthouse. 'I said no.'

'Oh,' said Lucy. She was a little surprised; it was hard to imagine Ben saying no. 'Thank you. You can put it there.' She called up the stairs, 'Mally! Mally! I'm needing you down here now.'

'I'm coming!' They heard the patter of light feet above. 'Thank you, Ben,' said Lucy dismissively.

'Ay well,' said Ben. 'I'm no going far.'

When Lucy and Mally had finished work, Mally had a turn at looking through the telescope. It was too heavy to hold still while she focused, so she balanced it on the top of the railings, which were just the right height. Mally twisted the focus, and studied the island carefully from the top of the tower while Lucy cleared away the cleaning things. Someone was on Gob Keyl, because the gulls had all risen. That would be Mam and Breesha milking the goats. There was also a cloud of kittiwakes over Gob y Vaatey; Mally moved round the parapet, and carefully focused the glass.

'The Writing Man is doing writing all on his own on Gob y Vaatey. Now he's put his notebook on the grass. He's got *his* telescope. He's looking at the rocks in Giau y Vaatey again. He was doing that yesterday. Yesterday he was watching the tide go out. Now he's watching it coming in. And now he's got his notebook again and he's writing in it.'

'The Writing Man?' repeated Aunt Lucy, suddenly paying attention. 'Can I have a look?' Mally waited patiently while Aunt Lucy focused the glass on Gob y Vaatey. 'Mally,' said Aunt Lucy presently, 'you've done a very good morning's work. I'm proud of you. Now I'm going down to Gob y Vaatey, so you can go and find the others, if you want.'

'I want to go on looking through the telescope.'

Aunt Lucy hesitated, then she said, 'Take great care of it, then. And don't take it away from the lighthouse. And don't lean over the parapet. Promise?'

Mally had never been alone at the top of the tower with the telescope all to herself. 'Promise.' She seized the telescope with alacrity, and was trying to focus on the circling puffins when Lucy disappeared quickly down the ladder.

In fact there was a lot of work that could be done without Ben's help. Archie now had a clear picture in his mind of what Giau y Vaatey was like at all stages of the tide. The rock where he and Ben had come ashore was useless for anything larger than Finn's yawl, and even a yawl could only float alongside for an hour each side of low tide. Archie was working out now how to build the jetty over the shelving rocks further out, in the place he'd pointed out to Ben. The jetty would need to have a protective curve that would act as a sea wall on the south side of the harbour, within which a boat twice the size of Finn's yawl could shelter from the prevailing south-westerlies. Ben was right when he said that it wouldn't be as sheltered as Finn's landing rock: in any serious weather a support vessel would be forced to run back to the Isle of Man to find an anchorage.

Archie was absorbed in working out a building plan in relation to the minimum underwater depth of his jetty, and the building hours available at each tide, when a shadow fell across the page. He looked up, still focused on his columns of figures, and saw the figure of a woman silhouetted against the bright sky. He blinked, and realised it was the lightkeeper. A twinge of disappointment mingled with intense relief. He'd forgotten about last night; as soon as he remembered, an undefined apprehension settled itself around his heart. He hadn't realised he'd shaken it off until it came creeping back.

'Good morning, sir,' said Lucy.

The first time Archie had seen the lightkeeper, she'd planted herself sturdily in front of him and shaken his hand. She'd given no trouble since, and so he hadn't given her much thought. It occurred to him now that if one had to do business with a woman, Lucy was about as uncomplicated as one could hope for. If she'd been a man he'd have heartily recommended that the Commissioners keep her on.

'Guid morning, Miss Geddes,' said Archie. 'Did you want me?' That was a singularly foolish question, as she had the whole island to walk in, and had chosen to come and stand within two feet of him, but at least with Lucy one didn't always feel at a disadvantage.

'Yes,' said Lucy. She looked down at him, frowning. 'D'you mind if I sit down? You're busy, aren't you?'

It was Sunday. Automatically Archie covered his page of notes with his hand, but this wasn't the Hebrides; she meant no more than she said.

'Well, I won't take long,' said Lucy. She sat on the grass beside him, her legs tucked under her. An image flashed through Archie's mind of a neighbour's daughter at Kilmahog.

They'd played together as children, hardly spoken to each other between the ages of eleven and fourteen, and then stopped to chat when they met on the hill, which they did sometimes because she often did the rounds of her father's sheep. There'd been a time when Archie had liked Jessie very much, but he'd forgotten all about her as soon as he'd left home. Waiting for Lucy to find words – she seemed to be having a little difficulty with that – the adjective that occurred to Archie, with just the faintest shadow of regret, was *wholesome*.

'It's about my niece,' said Lucy abruptly. 'Breesha. I was hearing what happened last night. It was very bad, and I'm sorry.'

'It wasna your fault!' Archie didn't know why he felt indignant. It wasn't merely that he didn't want the subject mentioned: he also couldn't help feeling that it wasn't in any way the lightkeeper's responsibility. He certainly didn't want to discuss it with her.

'Breesha's my niece,' said Lucy. 'You're our guest. It was very wrong, and I'm sorry.'

'Please, Miss Geddes, *you* don't have to apologise.'

'I do. But I also have to ask you something. Her mother's very upset, of course. And she's very worried.'

'She may well be!'

'Why, sir?' Lucy turned pale under her freckles. 'What are you going to do?'

'What am *I* going to do? I hardly think it's my responsibility!'

'What do you mean, please?'

'I'd have thought it was obvious! If I had a daughter and she tried tae kill a man I'd be more than worried! I'd . . . I'd . . . My God, I dinna ken what I'd do! All I can say is, I thank God I havena.'

'Haven't what, please, sir? You mean you haven't got a daughter?'

'Of course I havena! But that's not to the point.'

'Well, I wasn't to know that, sir. For all I know you might

have a dozen daughters, but that's no concern of mine. *My* concern is Breesha. Please, sir, her mother is so frightened – and I can tell you, honestly I can – it wasn't just bad, what she did – it was more *stupid*. Very very stupid. Breesha knows that now. She'd got herself into such a state – it wasn't your fault – but such a state about us having to leave Ellan Bride – she wasn't thinking straight. Truly, that was what it was. She knows now how bad it was. She won't *ever* do it – do anything like that, I mean – ever again. That I promise you, sir.'

'I should damn well hope she willna! But it's nae concern o mine. I hope I'll be away from here tomorrow, and frankly, I never want to see that girl again – or her mother either. For your sake, I hope you're right. I'm sorry for ye. You're left with this, but it's no your fault. In no way do I hold *you* responsible, Miss Geddes. But – to be honest – I dinna think there's much point you talking to *me* about it.'

'So you're not going to do anything?'

'Do anything? How d'ye mean?'

'Tell anybody?'

'Who the hell would I want to tell?'

'You're not going to try to get her punished?'

'If she was mine I'd give her a damn guid hiding, if that's what ye mean. I doubt her mother's capable of doing that, though, more's the pity. But 'tis naught to do wi me.'

Lucy drew a deep breath. 'Sir, you set my mind at rest, indeed you do! I'm heartily grateful to you, and I'll tell Diya so too. So when you go away from Ellan Bride you'll just please forget that it ever happened. Won't you?'

'No,' said Archie. 'I'll no forget an attempt on my life quite that easily. But I willna be losing any sleep over it, I promise you.'

'Sir,' said Lucy, 'my son was telling the truth: you're a right one! Indeed you are. And I thank you from the bottom of my heart!'

She held out her hand. She was the very spit of Jessie – odd how he'd never noticed – Jessie at sixteen – he'd been away from Kilmahog a long time. Archie shook Lucy's hand for the second time. Her hand was very firm: of course, she was used to hard work. She was like her boy too – a nice lad – he'd made himself useful in spite of being so wee – a proper, steady boy, not like that little demon – cousins, too – you'd never think it. For the first time since they'd met, it occurred to Archie to wonder who Billy's father might have been.

'I'll go and tell Diya,' said Lucy happily. 'Sir, I *thank* you.' She got up, and added, 'You'll remember to come for your dinner, sir, won't you? In about an hour? And that's a good thing too – I couldn't think how we were all going to sit through dinner together, indeed I could not! And it's puffins – my sister's making them with suet dumplings, and it would have been such a waste to have had no appetites. But *now* it'll be all right. I'll send one of the children . . . or indeed, you have your own watch, sir, so you're knowing when it's midday.' Relief had made Lucy quite garrulous. She made herself stop short, and turned away.

Archie had already gone back to his notes. He was vaguely aware of her speaking again, as she set off up the hill. 'Oh sir, I do *thank* you, indeed I do!'

Chapter 28

BREESHA SAT ON THE TOP OF THE TULLACHAN. THE DAY WAS getting hotter. The sky was deep blue all round, except to the south where the sun made the blue so bright that it was almost white. Even the puffins had stopped circling in the noonday heat, except for a few hardy stragglers. Breesha could feel the sweat running down her back. She felt sick. This was the most dreadful thing she'd ever had to do. She couldn't imagine it ever being over, or that normal life would ever go on again. Everyone else – Billy, Mally, Mam, Aunt Lucy and even Mr Groat – seemed to have retreated behind a dark glass. They lived in a world of sunshine and hope. Only Breesha was immured, all alone, in the shadow of what she had to do.

There was no choice. She couldn't go home until she'd done it. It was puffins for dinner with suet dumplings. Breesha loved suet dumplings. But she couldn't have any – in fact she could never sit down to dinner again – until this appalling trial was over. She glanced up at the sun. The time of horror was almost upon her. She swallowed. Her throat felt tight. Perhaps she really was going to be sick. The one saving grace was that Mam had finally agreed that she could do it on her own. Mam wouldn't have agreed if Aunt Lucy hadn't stood up for Breesha. Aunt Lucy had said Breesha could be trusted. Aunt Lucy had said that if Breesha said she'd do a thing, then she would do it. Breesha, Aunt Lucy had said, had never been known to lie.

Breesha loved Aunt Lucy better than anyone in the world. She hated Mam. Her hatred might not last for ever – though there was no need to admit that – but just now Breesha hated her.

He was coming.

She could see him coming up from Gob y Vaatey. He was skirting the bog. He'd reached the path by the well. He was coming towards the Tullachan, on his way back to dinner, just as Aunt Lucy had said he would. He'd taken off his coat and he was carrying it slung over his shoulder. He'd rolled up his shirtsleeves. He was feeling hot too. His canvas knapsack hung from his other shoulder.

Breesha was quite sure she was going to be sick.

The Writing Man was close enough to hear. Breesha caught her breath. She couldn't believe it: the Writing Man was whistling. He was whistling a cheerful little tune. Just like Da! She'd forgotten. She hadn't realised – in fact she'd never thought of it in all these years – but suddenly it came back to her as if her Da had never gone away. Da used to whistle. Whenever he'd been around, when Breesha had been little, they'd hear Da whistling. Whatever he was doing, he'd be whistling a cheerful little tune, just as the Writing Man was doing now.

Breesha stared at the Writing Man, open-mouthed. Part of her felt sick and cold. That part wished she could die. A different part of her was flooded with astonishing warmth. There wasn't a moment to work it all out, because the Writing Man had almost reached the Tullachan. In a way the whistling made it far, far worse. Breesha leaped to her feet, and jumped and slid down the grassy slope.

She landed at the feet of the Writing Man. He stopped whistling. He stood quite still on the path and looked at her. Clearly he was not in the least pleased to see her. Perhaps he hated her.

Breesha wasn't used to being hated. She looked straight past him, and said very fast, 'Sir I'm very sorry that I held up a false light. It was a very wrong thing to do to you sir and I didn't mean it and I hope you'll forgive me now please because I'm very very sorry. Honest.'

'Oh,' said the Writing Man. He didn't say it didn't matter. Instead he said, after thinking for a moment, 'Ay well, I wasna best pleased about it masel.'

'I'm very sorry,' said Breesha again, because she couldn't think what else to do.

'Ay well,' said the Writing Man again.

Breesha stole a glance at him. He didn't seem to be filled with fury, or an uncontrollable desire for revenge. In fact he looked puzzled, as if he couldn't quite think what to do next. It occurred to Breesha that he didn't know what he was supposed to say. She'd had time to rehearse this horrible conversation, and he hadn't.

Obscurely aware that she'd somehow gained an advantage, Breesha said, 'Please, sir, it would be very kind in you to forgive me before dinner because Aunt Lucy said I had to come and say sorry first or we can't all sit round the table in any comfort. And it's puffins,' added Breesha, 'and suet dumplings that my Mam made specially because you were here.'

'Ay well,' said the Writing Man for the third time. 'Ay well.' After a moment he added, 'Bygones should be bygones, I suppose.' He gave the glimmer of a smile. 'Especially if it's dinner time. But, lass . . .'

'Yes, sir?' asked Breesha breathlessly, when he hesitated.

'See, lass, if I'd no kent this island, I'd have walked to my death, followin that false light of yourn. Ye need to ken that – that would have been the end o ma life – o ma whole *life*, ye ken – and' – Archie was surprising himself: he hadn't thought he had anything at all to say to her, but even as he spoke he realised that he needed to tell her – 'and 'twould have blighted your own. If ye'd killed a man – a wee girl like you – your life wouldna ever have been the same again either. Ye ken that?'

Breesha hadn't expected him to talk to her. The trial she'd envisaged had been about exchanging a form of words – humble abasement on her part, and righteous justification on his. It had seemed to have no meaning other than being a huge ordeal that she somehow had to get through. In her eyes the Writing Man had always been cold and stiff and formal. Now she'd discovered, all in a minute, that not only could he whistle a tune, but he could also look her in the face and talk to her as if she were another person, equal to himself. That *really* hurt, because – it dawned on Breesha for the first time – it meant that she'd done him, the Writing Man, a great wrong. She'd thought it wouldn't matter if he were dead. But if he had been dead – if she *had* made that happen – why then he would never have whistled so cheerfully ever again: she would never have heard that little tune and he would never again have talked to anyone as he and she were talking now. Breesha hung her head. A moment later a large tear ran down her nose, and fell into the grass.

'Ay well,' said the Writing Man awkwardly. 'Maybe we'd better get tae our dinner, lass, seeing that, as it happens, there's no harm done.'

Diya had stewed the puffins in a rich broth. There were potatoes and carrots and onions in it, as well as the dumplings, which were a triumph of their art, and the whole was flavoured with rosemary and thyme from the garden. When the pot was scraped bare they all wiped their bowls clean with fresh bread. It was easy to believe that the silence in which they ate was entirely caused by the excellence of the food put before them.

It was Billy who finally broke the silence, after he'd eaten two helpings of stew and a quantity of bread and gravy. 'Please, sir, you said before that I could look at the map of the island.'

Archie had planned to go out again at once. He had plenty to do, and he didn't want company. However, he had indeed, in a misguided moment, given his word about the map, and with any luck tomorrow would be too late to keep his promise. 'Ay,' he said reluctantly. 'I did say that.' He hoped to God that this wasn't going to involve the whole family. He could hardly plead work as an excuse today.

'You can have the table when we've done the dishes,' Diya

said. 'Because then I'll be in the garden. Breesha, you can come with me, and I'll hear you do your reading while I work. Can you wait half an hour, sir?'

'Willingly,' said Archie, relieved.

When he came back half an hour later there was no one in the room except Billy and Ben Groat. Ben looked to be dozing in the rocking chair with the cat on his knee. Billy was unenthusiastically sweeping the floor. He put the broom away at once when he saw Archie. 'Are we going to look at the map now, sir?'

Ben watched through half-closed eyes as Young Archibald took out his sheets of foolscap. He could go out and lie in the sun, but that would mean disturbing the cat, and he couldn't be bothered to move. The lightkeeper had retired to bed ten minutes ago. Ben would have given much to be able to join her, but they didn't live in a world where such things were possible, which was a pity. Ben felt full of dinner and very sleepy. And there was Young Archibald explaining his map to Billy as if he really wanted Billy to be able to read it. What's more, he was actually finding the sort of words that Billy would understand. Ben hadn't thought Young Archibald had it in him.

Ben watched Archie turn over the page, and show Billy how to shade in a height of land. Archie even let Billy try to draw Dreeym Lang himself, with one of Archie's own drawing pencils. If Ben hadn't been feeling too sleepy to react to anything short of an earthquake, he'd not have been able to believe the evidence of his own eyes. What had come over Young Archibald? *Something* had happened. No one had said a word right through dinner. The stew had been as good as Ben had ever tasted, but the lack of drawing-room conversation had been distinctly noticeable. Not that Ben cared for that. He closed his eyes. When he opened them again, twenty minutes later, Billy and Young Archibald were still talking quietly at the table, and Young Archibald was putting his pencils back in their case,

'We've got a map too,' Billy was telling Archie. 'We've got a jigsaw puzzle map of Europe and Asia. It's all in little bits and you have to put it together. It's not as good as having a real map of Ellan Bride, of *course*. But it's a good one. Would you like to see?'

'If you want to show me.'

Billy dragged a wooden box from under the dresser. Both he and Young Archibald had apparently forgotten that Ben was there, or else they thought he was fast asleep. They seem to *ken* each other, thought Ben, as if they'd been in the same family all their lives, and yet only yesterday they'd not been able to speak a single word to one another without Ben's help. A lot had been going on, seemingly, while Ben and the light-keeper had been at the light. Ben watched under his eyelashes as Young Archibald and Billy laid out the wooden pieces of the jigsaw map. 'Usually we do the sea first,' Billy was explaining, 'because then you can start with the edges. You have to look for the straight bits.'

'I think I ken,' said Young Archibald meekly.

Billy *likes* him, thought Ben, surprised. He likes both of us. What that boy wants . . . No, he didn't want that thought! Ben felt a faint chill creep into the warm sleepiness of the afternoon. Billy was Lucy's son. They belonged to one another. Ben liked Billy: there was no difficulty about that. It was just the beginning of a fear, like a little touch of ice, that Ben might find himself needed in a way he hadn't reckoned on, and not be able to get away.

'I dinna think that piece fits,' said Young Archibald. 'It's the wrong sort of blue.'

'I think you're right.' Billy undid the piece of jigsaw he'd forced into place. 'You're very good at doing this jigsaw puzzle, sir. Have you been practising?'

'No,' said Archie. 'I canna say that I have.'

No, he hasna, thought Ben, and nor have I. Ben had refused to work for Young Archibald today, but tomorrow they'd probably be away in spite of that. It was likely, but by no means certain, that Ben would be sent back to work on Ellan Bride when they came to build. If he wasn't, he could ask for a week's leave before the year was out, and then he'd be able to come back on his own. He meant to tell Lucy before he left – he'd been thinking about it most of the morning – that he would come back. But supposing he did, then – this was what had suddenly dawned on him – it wouldn't just be Lucy. There was also Billy, who, young as he was, obviously had desires and fears of his own, and who would probably want to do jigsaw puzzles on Sunday afternoons, and look at maps, and other things, no doubt, that were all very well once in a way, but not as a permanent responsibility. Except that Ben liked Billy. He also liked Billy's mother very much indeed. This was beginning to feel like very deep water, but in spite of that, Ben was almost certain that he didn't plan simply to go away from Ellan Bride and never come back again.

Lucy was quite right: there was no point in keeping the garden going if they weren't even going to be here for the rest of the summer, let alone for all the seasons yet to come. Diya hadn't realised, until she'd known for certain that they were leaving, that she came to the garden not only because it was essential for the garden, but also because it was necessary for her. She squatted now between two rows, delicately thinning the carrots. Even if the family weren't here to enjoy the full-grown vegetables, they could still eat the thinnings and have the good of that. But she'd have thinned the carrots anyway. She did it because the garden demanded it.

This garden had seen her suffer greatly – for it wasn't like another person; Diya didn't have to hide the truth from it – and it had also seen her as happy as she'd ever been. The garden was one place where Diya never had to pretend. That was why she liked best to be alone in it. Plants came and went according to their nature, and unlike human beings they didn't make any fuss about it. The garden made it very clear to her – and this she found reassuring – that her own life, whether or not it seemed to her like suffering, would simply go on until it stopped, and that was all there was to it.

She had no idea where she'd be living in a month's time. At the moment that seemed a minor detail. Diya was feeling as the garden must feel after a great storm: scoured and exhausted. The most important thing was that Breesha was sorry. She'd apologised to Mr Buchanan, and he'd accepted her apology. Perhaps all Diya's anxieties had been for nothing. Perhaps *she* was the one who'd given herself over to melodrama. But no, a different kind of man might have wreaked havoc on them all. Mr Buchanan was kind. It was odd – that was how Lucy always judged people: by whether or not they were kind. Perhaps Lucy was right to make kindness so important. In any case, Mr Buchanan had been kind to Breesha, and Diya could tell that Breesha was genuinely sorry for what she'd done, now that she'd been made to understand.

In a day or two the surveyors would be gone. It seemed strange to think how she and Lucy had dreaded their arrival. The surveyors were nothing to the purpose. They'd only come to draw their plans, and the fact that their job was almost done didn't really change anything. She and Lucy had already known perfectly well that they had to leave. Perhaps Mr Buchanan would still be kind enough to mention their predicament to Mr Stevenson, who might bring it to the attention of the Commissioners. Whatever happened, it was stupid – melodramatic, even – to think that they'd be left destitute. Once they were on the Island, Diya knew enough people who could be asked to speak for them. For the Commissioners, or the Governor, or Tynwald, to cast the whole family into beggary would make far too great a scandal. Lucy might not believe that; that meant it was Diya's sole responsibility to make sure they were provided for.

In any case, the surveyors were of no importance, and would soon be forgotten. And yet they seemed to have lived through so much together in the last three days. It was not true to say that the encounter with Mr Buchanan had not been important. It mattered, in the same way as it mattered to thin the carrots. It was important to leave everything right and civilised between

Mr Buchanan and herself – and her family too, of course. It would be insulting to both of them to part in disorder. Also, Diya had some new ideas to thank him for, and it would be unjust not to acknowledge it. Just because there was no future, it didn't mean there hadn't been any point.

Diya was sorry that she wouldn't see Mr Buchanan again. For one thing, she was curious about his voyage. If she had a great voyage like that to look forward to, how different the future would look . . . As it was, she was disappointed that she'd never hear the end of the story. Even if it were ten years before he came back, she'd still be interested to know what he'd discovered. She was sure of that, even though she had no idea who or what she would be, in ten years' time, or even in ten months' time. Because in ten years . . . Whatever happened, in ten years' time she would *not* be living like this. Mr Buchanan had made her realise that. It meant losing too much.

In more ways than one, Jim Geddes' widow was living half a life. Oh, she'd keep faith with Jim. She'd hold him dear in her memory all her life, and she'd do her very best to bring up his children well, and to make up to them for what they had lost. Nor would she desert Lucy and Billy while they needed her. After all, they were her family too. She'd known Billy all his life – had she not been the first to hold him, when he was born? She'd been so frightened – Mummig was dead and Diya had had to help Lucy all by herself. Having her own children had not been nearly so frightening. Perhaps that was because Diya had always been sure she could look after herself. But in childbirth that was nonsense, and when she thought now how much she and Lucy had had to help each other – how close they'd *had* to become – she felt disloyal for even imagining that they might one day be separated. And Billy . . . when she'd cradled that slippery scrap of a child in her arms – alive, a boy, and whole – she'd registered all those things in a flash, but definitely in that order – she'd felt a great wave of relief. And love too: from the moment of his birth he'd felt like one of her own. Billy and Breesha, through all their lives until now, might as well have been brother and sister. That was how Jim had wanted it – and how delighted he'd been when Diya had unhesitatingly agreed with him – and that's how it had been, from the day Billy was born.

But that hadn't stopped Breesha last night. The children – the whole family – would always have each other – Diya didn't deny that for a moment – but that didn't mean it was enough. Surely that was no reason why they couldn't also have something more? Surely it wasn't wrong to prepare – that was only common sense, after all – for other possibilities?

Diya straightened up as she finished the row. The newly-thinned carrots looked straggly and naked, too weak to hold themselves up in their unaccustomed isolation. They'd want more nourishment too, when they started to swell. Diya fetched a bucket from the shed, and, carefully closing the gate behind her because of the goats, she strode downhill towards the shore, swinging the empty bucket.

Billy had said it was possible to get onto Creggyn Mooar at low water. Archie didn't say, when he went out, that this was what he was intending to do, because Billy would certainly have offered to come too. Archie kept out of sight of the garden by keeping to the west coast of Gob Glas. There was a pleasant westerly breeze, quite cool, and high overhead the sky was streaked with mackerel cloud. Once Archie was on the slabs he was safely out of anyone's sights unless they were deliberately watching from the top of the lighthouse. That felt better. The slabs fell away to the sea in a series of giant steps. Archie jumped from one to the next, feeling like Gulliver in Brobdingnag. The sun glanced over the dancing waves so brightly it almost hurt to look. The Creggyns were marooned in fields of gleaming seaweed. Seals basked in the sun on the dry skerries, and a colony of shags stood sentinel on Creggyn Doo. Archie didn't realise he was whistling out loud, but the same tune kept on running through his head:

There's nought but care on ev'ry han
In ev'ry hour that passes, O:
What signifies the life o' man
An 'twere na . . .

He jumped down the last dry rock into a field of gleaming seaweed. Someone was in front of him, a pillar of darkness against the blazing brightness of the sea.

'Mr Buchanan,' said Diya.

Archie slipped, and almost fell headlong. Once he'd got his footing again in the slippery seaweed, he could see Diya without the sun behind her. She looked as startled as he felt. She was wearing the old gardening pinafore she'd had on when they first met. The mischievous breeze tugged at her skirt, showing her bare ankles. Her hair fell down her back in a long braid, and she'd tied a red scarf round her forehead. The gold studs in her ears winked in the sun. Her feet were buried in golden weed. There was a wooden bucket on the rock beside her, half-full of fresh seaweed. Without her cap she looked like a young girl. She certainly didn't look like anyone's mother.

'Mrs Geddes!'

'I'm sorry. Did I startle you?' Perhaps Diya felt the apology was inappropriate, because she added at once, '*You* certainly startled *me*.'

'I'm sorry.'

She was immediately repentant. 'No, no, sir, you mustn't say that to me! Lucy told me she'd spoken to you this morning.' Diya stood up very straight and looked Archie in the eye. 'I must apologise to *you*, sir. I apologise for my daughter's behaviour, and for the fact that I didn't listen to you last night. In short, sir, I was distraught.' In spite of the garden soil on her cheek, Diya looked very far from distraught now. 'But Lucy has told me that you don't intend to pursue the matter, and all I can say to you now, sir, is that I'm very sorry for any way in which I or my family have wronged you, and I thank you for your generous response.'

She could have been dismissing an imperial embassy at the conclusion of a peace treaty. Archie couldn't help smiling at the thought. Two days ago her self-command would have reduced him to incoherent stammering. Had he learned so much in her company? 'Not at all, ma'am. She did me no harm, as it happened. I spoke to the lass myself. Least said soonest mended' – he realised as he spoke that he was quoting his mother – 'that's what I always say.' Why had he said that? He'd never used the phrase before in his life. His mother was always used to say it when his brothers had been particularly cruel; he'd never thought the words could rise so naturally to his own lips.

'I know you spoke to her. She told me. Sir, I can only thank you for your kindness. We remain forever in your debt.'

He'd told her about the *Beagle*. Why Archie should recollect that when she said she'd remain forever in his debt he couldn't think, but so it was. Only last night he'd shown her his letter from Captain Fitzroy, and she'd said that it was excellent, and he must be delighted beyond words. At the time he'd been thinking that of course he was delighted, but at the same time there was just the smallest twinge of regret, because he was speaking to a sympathetic and very beautiful woman who was unattached to any other man. She'd said then that it was excellent that he was going away, and that he must be delighted beyond words. She'd said it without a trace of self-consciousness: if she'd thought that there were any reason why it might not be excellent, or that his delight might not be entirely unmitigated, she'd given no sign of it. But then – Archie hadn't fully realised this before – she was more adept at hiding her true feelings than any other woman he'd encountered. Most of the time, that was. Last night she'd slapped his face. How could he have forgotten that, even for a moment?

Perhaps she'd remembered too, because her eyes dropped as if she were embarrassed, or confused. Perhaps she was just waiting for him to answer.

'I don't think you need,' said Archie awkwardly. 'Remain

forever in my debt, I mean. I'm leaving the country soon anyway. I wouldn't want you to feel indebted to me.'

'I don't think your whereabouts will alter my feelings, sir.'

What the hell did she mean by that? What she certainly couldn't mean was that she was preparing to forget all about him. The sea shone so blue behind her, and the seaweed sparkled so brilliantly at her feet that Archie felt as if he couldn't quite see straight. He could almost have said to her . . . But what had he said to her last night? Had he called her child a devil's daughter to her face? He'd certainly thought it. Surely he'd not said that to her out loud? Five minutes ago he'd never wanted to see her again. Last night he'd shown her his letter about the *Beagle*. She'd said it was excellent. His whereabouts would not alter her feelings, and he must be delighted beyond words.

'That's kind of you,' stammered Archie. Why did she do this to him every time? Five minutes ago he'd been as free as the bright May air, with a tune running through his head. But wherever he was – he knew this for certain, as he stood in the slippery weed, looking at her with the dancing ripples behind her – he would always remember how he'd spoken to the light-keeper's widow, down below the tide mark by the Creggyns, before he went away on the longest voyage of his life. Would he be sorry he'd never said anything? 'I . . . I'm not sorry that I came. I won't forget, either.' It occurred to him she might be thinking he was going to hold a grudge. 'Meeting you, I mean, ma'am. I won't forget that.'

'Thank you, sir.' Diya turned away and looked out over the Creggyns. 'It's a fine day again, sir. I think Finn will be able to come for you tomorrow. I hope you've managed to do all the work you needed.'

'Ma'am,' said Archie, 'I shall be gone for a good few years, I believe. It'll be a long voyage, and I hope I'll return from it. If ever I find myself in Castletown – if that's where you are – I hope I might have the pleasure of visiting you again.'

'I have no idea where I shall be,' said Diya. 'If we're at home

– if we have a home – you would of course be welcome to call on us. I hope you have a very fruitful voyage, sir. I think it will be a most important journey of discovery. You may be about to change the course of human thought: a privileged position indeed. Perhaps one day we shall be reading all about you in the newspapers.' Diya hesitated, and just for a moment her eyes dropped. 'And naturally I would be most interested, if you did happen to return to the Island, to hear about your explorations from your own lips.' She looked up and coolly met his eyes again. 'However that may be, I wish you well. And I must repeat: I remain forever in your debt.'

Diya picked up her bucket. It was only half-full, but evidently she'd decided not to collect any more seaweed that day. 'I won't keep you from your researches any longer, sir. If Finn is to come tomorrow, I'm sure you have much to attend to.'

Archie watched her climb lightly up the slabs, bare feet stepping easily into the footholds over the rocky steps, the wooden bucket swinging. Then he picked his way cautiously down to sea level over the clumps of weed. He was just too late: already the tide was swirling back through the channel between the slabs and Creggyn Mooar. It was still narrow enough to step across, but there were all the treacherous banks of seaweed to negotiate on the far side. By the time he'd got onto the skerry it might be too late to get back. He'd look worse than a fool if he got himself marooned, and came back soaking.

And after all, what did it matter? What difference did it make, in all the years that lay ahead, if he'd once stepped onto a little outcrop of grey rock that no one had ever heard of, or if he hadn't? Archie turned away, and began to walk back up Gob Glas instead. By the time he got to Giau yn Ooig he was whistling under his breath again:

For you sae douse ye sneer at this
Ye're nought but senseless asses, O . . .
What signifies the life o' man
An 'twere na for the lasses, O . . .

Chapter 29

THE BREEZE OFF THE SEA HAD GROWN CHILLY. LUCY PULLED her shawl tightly round her shoulders. In the north-east there was a thin crescent moon, pale against the still-daylit sky. The sinking sun had set the sky aglow behind the Irish hills. It would be fine again tomorrow. The water butt by the house was almost empty, and between the rocks the lighthouse path had turned to dust. The well had never failed them, but they couldn't waste well water on the garden. If life had been ordinary they'd have been taking the handcart over to Towl Doo tomorrow, and filling up two big barrels of water for the garden. Towl Doo itself might be getting low. As things were, it didn't matter if the garden dried out completely. Lucy had a sudden vision of her mother in the garden at twilight, watering her precious seedlings. Diya was right, Lucy thought: as long as we're here we have to look after the garden. In spite of every thing we'll take the cart to Towl Doo tomorrow. In spite of everything.

Up in the lantern, Lucy prepared to light the lamps as usual. Then she stood watching the sun slowly sink below the horizon. A ship, bigger than a brig, was sailing southwards between the Calf and Ireland. Lucy looked at it through the telescope. It flew the White Ensign: a Royal Navy frigate. Beyond it were two other sails, invisible to the naked eye, off the coast of Ireland.

Lucy lowered the telescope. In spite of everything . . . What if Ben Groat had fathered a child on her? What then? Had she been mad last night? If so, she was mad still, because she didn't in the least regret what she'd done. She knew that she ought to feel great guilt because in the eyes of the world she'd once again been very wicked. There was also that shadowy God that her Da used to teach them about whenever it occurred to him that she and Jim weren't learning enough Scripture. Da had said that God was watching them all the time. Lucy, at six, had thought that was rude of God, and that he might at least avert his eyes when she went to the outhouse. But she'd felt far more aware of being watched in Castletown than ever she had on Ellan Bride.

Lucy and Ben had committed what people called fornication. Lucy's Da had taught Lucy and Jim to recite the Ten Commandments by heart. Fornication was not one of the Ten Commandments. Adultery was different: that was the seventh commandment, and as a child Lucy had thought that one must be the easiest to keep, because you either did or didn't do it, and it would be quite easy not to. But in Castletown the punishment for fornication was just the same as for adultery, so really it made very little difference. The punishment was being forever cast out, and being called a fallen woman. The punishment for Billy, whose fault it wasn't, was a much worse thing to think about. And now there might be another child, who would also get punished. It was not a person's own sin to be a bastard, but in Castletown it might as well be. In any place at all, out there in the world, it might as well be. One day, Lucy knew, she might be sorry for what she'd done last night, but at the moment her heart was filled with joy because of it, and her whole body tingled with life in a way it hadn't done since she was very young. She could not make herself believe, while those feelings lasted, that she had done anything wrong.

In fact, if Ben Groat came again tonight . . . Lucy felt a sharp pang of apprehension – supposing he didn't? Oh, that would hurt! She wanted him. She wanted his body more than she wanted anything. And maybe she wanted something else as well – but that was deep water and she didn't dare to think about that. Had she put herself in his power so much? When she'd lain with him she'd felt so strong herself, so sure it was her own choice, but now she was suddenly assailed by doubt. Suppose he didn't come? He hadn't said he would. But he'd looked at her across the table at each meal that day as if he wanted her, as if he were only waiting for a chance to be alone with her again. She hadn't said anything to him either. Had she looked at him the way he'd looked at her? She didn't know. Had anyone else noticed? She didn't know that either. But she wanted Ben to come back again tonight. And after that? There was no point wanting anything more, or even thinking about it. It never occurred to Lucy that she could do anything to change what happened next.

The sun was almost gone. Only a little sliver of bright orange light touched the horizon. Lucy knelt over the tinderbox, and lit the taper.

Outside the dark quickened into life as soon as the lamps were lit. Lucy sat on the parapet looking out to sea. She could see Ben's body so clearly in her mind; she could still feel how her hands had touched him; she remembered every detail of what they had done together last night. She didn't want to lose any of it: it might be all she'd ever have. She could have told him she wanted him to come back tonight. It was too late now. This morning he'd come to the light when she and Mally were cleaning, and she'd sent him away. She'd had every chance to speak to him again since, but she hadn't done it. And now perhaps he'd never come back again.

'Lucy?'

What Lucy had forgotten to think of was any strategy for if he did come. She jumped up joyfully and flung herself into Ben's arms. Then she said, 'The light! Ben, we have to keep out of the light!'

They sat on the parapet below the beam. There was no

point in pretending she wasn't pleased to see him, and anyway, thought Lucy, Finn might come tomorrow, and pretending was a waste of time. Meanwhile they had one more night, and that was riches enough for a lifetime, while it lasted.

'If you'll excuse me, sir, I have letters to write,' said Diya.

'Of course, ma'am.'

Diya took a bottle of ink from the dresser shelf and blew the dust off it. She tried to twist open the top, but it had stuck hard. She got a cloth and tried to get a grip with that. Then she put it in a bowl and fetched the kettle. She was about to pour a little boiling water over the recalcitrant lid when the Writing Man said, 'Will you allow me, ma'am? If you do that, the glass may crack first.'

Reluctantly Diya handed over the ink bottle. The Writing Man twisted it hard, and the lid came off almost at once. The Writing Man laid the open bottle down carefully at her end of the table, beside her leather writing case.

'Thank you, sir.' Diya sounded more annoyed than grateful.

'Not at all, ma'am.'

It was impossible to go to sleep with Aunt Diya and the Writing Man in the room. Billy wished he could have his own bed back. He'd always liked it when he and Breesha had drawn their curtain, so they could still hear Aunt Diya moving around, but they were safe together in their private enclosed world. Billy missed having Breesha beside him, and he didn't like lying on the pallet by the hearth, down on the floor where he might get trodden on, and where the grown-ups could see him without him seeing them, if he had his eyes shut and fell asleep right there in the kitchen where anyone could look at him. For the first time Billy found himself wishing the surveyors would go away soon, but that was only because he wanted his own bed back.

The kitchen felt unrestful. The room was quite dim, lit only by two pools of candlelight above Billy's head. Neither reached into his corner by the hearth. One pool of light was at the far end of the table by the door, where the Writing Man sat reading *Principles of Geology* with one candle, and the other was at the near end of the table where Aunt Diya sat writing her letters. Lying with his eyes half shut, Billy tried to work out where the two lots of candlelight overlapped. But light wasn't like that. It didn't have any firm edges, yet at the same time there was definitely a circle of more brightness round each candle.

Aunt Diya's pen went scratch-scratch-scratch across the paper. The noise set Billy's teeth on edge. He wished Aunt Diya would stop. Aunt Diya never liked it when Billy's slate pencil squeaked. Sometimes if you licked your slate pencil you could make it squeak more on purpose. Aunt Diya wrote fast and fluently. Billy couldn't write like that. Sometimes Aunt Diya sat writing in her notebook when he and Breesha had gone to bed. They'd occasionally peeped through their bed curtain and seen her doing it, sitting all alone at the kitchen table. The Writing Man also wrote a lot in his notebook, not just at night when he was alone but also in the daytime when everyone was working. But tonight Aunt Diya was not on her own, and she was writing on separate sheets of paper. She folded the first sheet in three, sealed it with a wafer, and wrote a few words on the front. That would be the direction. Billy knew about letters, because Finn sometimes brought a letter for them to Ellan Bride.

Last night Aunt Diya had hit the Writing Man. It was hard to believe it had happened, now that they were both being so polite and quiet with each other. It had all been because of Breesha. Billy missed Breesha. He didn't see why he couldn't have moved into the bedroom with her while the surveyors were here. Then he needn't have had to witness that horrible scene last night. In fact Breesha wouldn't have followed the Writing Man without Billy in the first place, if Billy had been sleeping beside her as usual. Everything would have been different, because Billy would have had more sense.

But today he'd betrayed Breesha. He hadn't meant to do it. When the Writing Man and he had finished the jigsaw puzzle this afternoon, and the Writing Man had gone out, Mr Groat, who'd been asleep in the rocking chair, had opened his eyes and said to Billy, 'What happened here last night then, Billy?'

It was hard with grown-ups to know what they already knew and what they didn't. Billy hadn't meant to be the one who told Mr Groat what Breesha had done, but he'd been taken by surprise, and he had told Mr Groat about it. He felt bad about that now. He and Mally were always getting into trouble with Breesha for telling secrets, but no secret in the past had ever been as important as this one.

Mr Groat hadn't said much. It was all right telling him about the stormy petrel, of course. That hadn't been any sort of secret. Oddly enough Billy hadn't worried about being indiscreet until he'd said to Mr Groat, 'Where were *you* then, anyway? Because you weren't here in bed. Everyone was wondering what had happened to *you*.'

For the first time in their acquaintance Mr Groat hadn't met Billy's eyes. 'I went to help your mother with the light.'

Billy had been puzzled by that. 'Why?' he'd asked. 'Mam never wants us to help.' That wasn't quite true, and it might make Mr Groat think the family were no use to Mam, so Billy quickly added, 'Except in winter, I mean. In winter Breesha and I do the afternoon together, up until supper-time. We started doing it on our own last year. And when the nights are long Mam and Aunt Diya split the watches between them. But this is summer. So why did Mam need help *now*?'

'Ay well,' Mr Groat had said. 'Maybe it was more just the company.'

That was even odder. 'But Mam *never* . . .'

'So what was the stormy petrel like then, close to?' Mr Groat had asked.

Lying on his pallet, Billy closed his eyes and thought about the stormy petrel. He wondered if it had got home all right. Maybe it had slept all day on its secret nest inside the keeill. Maybe, now that the night had come again, it was waking up and getting ready to fly. Maybe it had forgotten about being a prisoner last night. The Writing Man said that a bird's brain was very small and not big enough to remember things. The Writing Man said no one knew how many years a stormy petrel could live. As long as *he* lived, Billy would remember last night. Some of it, like the stormy petrel, had been good, and some he would much rather forget. But there it was: he was a boy, not a bird, and he couldn't forget, any more than he could fly away, and that was that.

Just before the dawn came, Ben whispered in Lucy's ear, 'I *love* thee, Lucy. I love thee.'

Billy's father had said that too. When Ben said it, Lucy was silent. It was too much to have to think what it might mean, when all she wanted to do was lie naked against him, like this, and make the most of him for the little time that they had left.

But Ben propped himself up on his elbow so he could look into her eyes. 'Lucy, I *love* thee. I have to go back to Edinburgh. The morn's morn, maybe. But if they dinna send me back to Ellan Bride this summer I'll ask for leave anyway. I'll come back and find thee. Will I no?' There must have been something in her expression, for he sounded suddenly doubtful.

'Why?'

'*Why?* Because . . . because . . . Lucy, marry me. Will thu marry me?'

Lucy gazed into his eyes. They looked frightened. Frightened of her saying no, maybe, or maybe Ben was even more frightened that she might say yes. Lucy felt scared herself. Deep water . . . She'd never thought of anything except how she'd manage on her own: herself and Billy, as it had always been, and a future she dared not think too much about. She hadn't expected to keep anything but memories. Memories of remembered delights with Ben Groat, memories of the island – no other riches but these – which she could hoard away and possess for ever. But that wasn't what Ben was offering now; no wonder he looked afraid.

'I don't know,' whispered Lucy. All of a sudden she was trembling, and realised he must be able to feel it. 'I mean . . . I'm much older than you, Ben.' That was a foolish thing to say, nothing to do with anything, but the words came out instead of whatever it was she'd meant to say.

'Five years,' said Ben at once. 'What difference does that make to anything? I *love* thee.'

Lucy saw in a flash what that might mean, and gasped aloud. Was *that* it? Could *Ben* be the solution to everything? Could *Ben* be lightkeeper on Ellan Bride? The Commissioners would employ *him*, if he applied to them. They'd employ Ben, just as they'd have employed Jim, if he'd been alive, or Billy, if he'd been old enough. If Lucy had *Ben* . . . if *that* were the case, they wouldn't make her leave the one place on earth where she belonged. They wouldn't cast her out, not if she had *Ben*.

'Lucy!' Ben gave her a little shake. 'Lucy, will thu no answer me? I asked thee to *marry* me! Thu has to say something to that!'

Lucy put her arms round him and held him tight. He wasn't aroused by her this time, not now he'd said that about marrying her. He was too scared. Even as they clung to one another, Lucy knew she couldn't say what she was thinking . . . not even suggest it. Of course it wasn't possible. Not for Ben, who liked other people so much, who liked to travel and see the world, and had friends in Edinburgh and acquaintances in every lighthouse in Scotland, and a mother in Orkney, and a good wage, and pleasures of his own out there in the wide world that Lucy knew nothing about and probably never would. So if he meant what he said – she was sure he hadn't really thought about it until the moment he'd spoken it aloud – then he was inviting her to come back with him into his own life, in which case *she* would have to change, and face new things, and become someone else altogether. She wasn't sure that she could.

'Ben,' said Lucy. She pushed him away again so she could look into his eyes and tell him the honest truth. 'I might love you. I don't know. I love Billy best, of course, and I have to think about Billy first of all. You couldn't just have me. You'd have me and Billy. And maybe another one now, of course. Have you thought of that?'

No. She could see it in his face. Of course he hadn't. He might have thought of one of those possibilities, but not both at once . . . Or if he had, he hadn't wanted her to mention it, or not quite so directly. But Lucy didn't see how else she could have made it all quite clear.

'Lucy,' said Ben, after a moment. 'I love thee. And if . . . if . . . I'd no leave thee with my bairn, thu kens that, surely? And Billy . . .' Ben swallowed. 'Lucy, I'll *marry* thee, I tell thee. And where thu goes, Billy goes. I ken that.'

'Ben,' said Lucy, hugging him hard. 'I think I might love you. I might love you very much. I think you're the third-kindest man I ever met, and that makes me *want* to love you. And . . . and . . . and I think I have to think. And' – she looked over his head – 'it's starting to get light, and I have to check the lamps again anyway.' Lucy stood up, and reached for her petticoat. 'I'm sorry not to know better what to say,'

Ben knelt at her feet, groping for his shirt. 'Thu needna be sorry.' He watched her go up the ladder in her thin petticoat through which the light shone so revealingly. 'Lucy!'

She stopped halfway up the ladder. 'Yes?'

'I'd rather thu told me the truth than anything else at all,' said Ben. 'I'm hoping it'll be what I want to hear, that's all. But thu never needs to be sorry for that, Lucy. No to me.'

Chapter 30

ABOUT HALFWAY THROUGH THE MORNING MR BUCHANAN SAID to Billy, 'That's fine. We don't need you now. You can go, if you want.'

Billy didn't mind. It was a great thing to do a man's work for a man's pay, but it involved quite a lot of standing still and doing what he was told. When Mr Buchanan sent him off, Billy went running and leaping as fast as he could all the way over to the keeill. From there he saw Breesha and Mally down on the beach, digging. Billy slid down the dunes, and ran across the sand to see what they were doing.

'This is our boat,' said Breesha. Billy could see that it was: they'd built up the gunwales out of sand, and hollowed out the inside. The boat was the same shape as Finn's yawl. It was shipping quite a bit of water, but as the tide was going out the sand would soon be dry enough to sit in.

'We're going on a long voyage,' said Breesha. She showed him a bottle and a small package done up in brown paper. 'We've got supplies. Water and ships' biscuit. Are you coming?'

'I might. Where're you sailing to? Why aren't you doing the light?'

'Far off oceans,' said Breesha. 'We don't know what's there yet. Aunt Lucy and I finished the light a long time ago. Soon we'll be hull down over the horizon.'

'The surveyors have nearly finished too,' said Billy. 'They

don't need me any more. Is Mam still up at the lighthouse?'

'That's fine,' said Breesha. 'Soon the surveyors'll go sailing off too. They'll go in a completely opposite direction to us. Yes, I think so. She was checking oil in the storeroom.'

'I tell you what,' said Billy.

'What?'

'I'll be back in a minute. And then I'll come too.' Billy left them suddenly. He ran the length of the beach, and scrambled up the rocks. He didn't go round by the keeill, but climbed straight up Hamarr behind the well, clinging with the ease of much practice from one foothold to the next.

Lucy was in the storeroom opening a new barrel of oil when Billy came to the door.

'Don't stand in the light, Billy. Come in, if you want.'

'Mam?'

'Yes?' Lucy was examining the new oil as well as she could in the dim light.

'I had a Da too, didn't I, Mam?'

Lucy went very still. She stopped looking at the oil and looked at Billy. She couldn't see his face because the light was behind him. He was just a dark figure standing there: bigger, she realised, than he used to be not so very long ago.

'Yes,' said Lucy, 'You had a Da. Everyone has a Da. Do you want me to tell you about him?'

'Yes.'

'Then come outside where we can sit down.'

Sitting on the doorstep of the storeroom they could see the high rock of Hamarr, and the sea behind it. The sea was a delicate blue, silvery-pale on the horizon where it met the sky. At this hour of the morning the clouds of circling puffins were thin and straggly. The doorstep of the storeroom was quite small so Lucy and Billy had to sit close together, shoulders touching, looking out to sea.

Lucy knew exactly what to say because she'd been preparing her answer to this question for the last eleven years. Billy was the only person she'd ever intended to tell, because he was the only one who had any right to ask.

'Your father,' said Lucy, speaking very clearly, 'is what they call an antiquarian. His name is Michael Elliott. He came to the Isle of Man eleven years ago because he was writing a book. He was coming here to collect stories from people: stories and songs and charms and legends about the past. He was coming from the part of Scotland we can see from here, from Galloway. Are you wanting me to tell you more?'

'Yes.' A bumble bee buzzed among the silverweed at their feet. The shadow of the storeroom fell across the ground in a straight line. The grass was yellowy-gold on one side of the line, and blueish-green on the other. From where they sat Billy could see the kittiwakes like specks of silver against the sky, circling over their nests in Cam Giau.

'He began writing his book in Galloway,' said Lucy. 'That's where he was coming from, but he was a gentleman, so he went away to Edinburgh to get his book-learning, and when he'd got a lot of that he began to think about his own country, the place where he came from. And he was thinking that all the stories and songs and everything were going to get lost if no one was writing them down, so he went back to Galloway and he started collecting them from people and writing them down.'

The day was so clear that if Billy got up and walked round to the other side of the storeroom he'd be able to see Galloway. Galloway was a pale line on the horizon north-west of the Island, so far away that it very seldom had any visible shape. 'So why did he come to the Island?'

'All his life long, from when he was very small, he used to look at the Island across the sea from where he was living in Galloway. Sometimes the Island was looking close enough to throw a stone across to it, and sometimes it was far away on the horizon, and sometimes it was lost in mist so that for all anyone could tell it mightn't have been there at all. But in fact the Isle of Man isn't very far from Galloway. And on the Island people still speak the same language that they stopped speaking a long time ago in Galloway, so your father decided to come over here and start collecting stories and everything here too. D'you want me to go on?'

'Yes.' The bumble bee had stopped buzzing over the silverweed. It was delving deep into a red clover just beyond Billy's bare toes, its hinder end quivering. On afternoons like this it was hard to imagine that anything could ever change. Billy had never thought of that before, never quite realised until this moment how great the difference was between one long summer day and for ever. It was a new and complicated thought, and he couldn't quite grasp it, not at the same time as listening to Mam, anyway.

'Well, the way it is with gentlefolks they're mostly knowing one another, or else they know people who know each other. You know how I went to be a serving maid near Castletown when I was young? I've told you stories about that. Well, your father came to stay with the gentlefolks I worked for. He was staying for a few months. He'd go travelling round the Island, but he used to come back and stay at the house. My Mistress gave him the blue bedchamber. They moved a big desk in there and while he was staying he used it as a study. He kept it full of papers and books. And it was my job to go in there every day and clean and tidy the room. It was quite difficult because there were papers in piles everywhere and I wasn't supposed to disturb anything and at the same time I was supposed to tidy up and do the dusting. Do you want me to go on?'

'Yes,' said Billy, imagining a roomful of green foolscap notebooks filled with drawings of birds and animals.

'I never got much book-learning,' said Lucy. 'But I can read a bit. And I couldn't help seeing that some of the printed books had stories in. I had to clean the room while the gentlefolks were at breakfast. And then one day there was a book lying open on the desk. There was writing in it I couldn't read – in fact it wasn't English – and next to it someone had been writing on a bit of paper. The letters had been written almost as good as print, and I saw – I couldn't help seeing – a word I recognised. The word was *Mannanan.*'

'You mean *our* Mannanan?'

'Yes indeed. So I started to spell out the rest of the writing on the paper, and I forgot about the time, and I was still trying to read the words when Mr Elliott came upstairs.

'I thought he would be angry with me but he wasn't. He asked me what I was looking at and I told him. He asked me if I knew about Mannanan, and I said of course I did, because my mother had told me the stories about him, and lots more stories as well. I'd known them all my life. He was interested, and he told me the poem I'd been looking at. It was in Manx – your Gammer would have understood it, of course – but Mr Elliott was writing it out again in English, and that's what he read out to me. Afterwards I learned it by heart. The bit about the Island goes like this:

I will with my mouth
Give you notice of the enchanted Island:

Little Mannanan was son of Leirr,
He was the first that ever had it;
But as I can conceive
He himself was a heathen.

It was not with his sword he kept it,
Neither with arrows or bow;
But when he would see ships sailing,
He would cover it round with fog.

'There's more, but I can't remember the next bit. Anyway, Mr Elliott said the poem came from an ancient legend, and the poem was the first place anyone had ever written the story down. I told him how it wasn't an ancient legend because I came from an island where all these things were still true. And so he asked me about Ellan Bride, and I began to tell him Mummig's stories, and he started to write them down. After that he wanted me to come every day and tell him stories. The Mistress said that was all right, but it wasn't very easy with the other servants, because of the work – not very easy for me, I mean – but he was a gentleman, so he wasn't knowing anything about that. So that's who your father was, Billy, and that's how I met him.'

That was Lucy's story, the exact truth as she'd planned all these years to tell it, as soon as Billy should ask. The part of the story she didn't tell Billy, and never would, was as vivid in her mind as the day it had happened. Lucy had no intention of ever telling anyone how, during the story-telling sessions, Mr Elliott began to touch her sometimes, and how his caresses, so unlike anything that had ever happened to her before, had filled her with desire, which was so enticingly unfamiliar, even though it seemed to come from deep inside herself, and how she'd longed and yet dreaded that the touching might go on. She'd felt like a bird in a net, hating her own helplessness, and yet she'd liked it far too much. But she'd not wanted to lie with Mr Elliott; at least, she *had* wanted to, but that had seemed so far over the horizon of anything she knew about that she'd let herself think it was utterly impossible. But it had happened, and to this day she couldn't say for sure if at the last moment he'd forced her, or whether, just in that very moment, she'd been willing. All she could say – but no one would ever ask, and if they did she'd never tell – was that she'd never meant to do it. But it was no good saying that: whether she'd known what she was doing or not, she'd paid the price, and would go on paying it for the rest of her life.

'Where is he now?' asked Billy.

Lucy caught her breath. She hadn't expected Billy to ask that. She should have done, of course: she realised that at once. 'I don't know,' she said. 'He left and went back to Scotland. I suppose that's where he is still.' She added, 'Perhaps he finished the book. I don't know that either.'

'If he was a writing man,' said Billy slowly, 'does that mean he was very old?'

'I don't think you need to be very old to write a book,' said Lucy doubtfully, unsure of her ground. 'He was older than me. But then I'd only just turned sixteen.' Billy was asking all the wrong questions. Lucy searched for a satisfactory reply. 'I'm thinking he was older than Mr Buchanan is now. But I'm not sure.' Lucy added anxiously, 'Am I telling you what you want to know?'

'I'm glad I've got a Da too.' Billy stood up, and remarked, 'We've got a sand boat on Baie yn Traie Vane. Breesha and Mally made it.'

'So you're going back there now?'

'Yes.'

'Remind them to come back in time for dinner then.' Lucy had to call after him, as he was already on his way, tearing full-tilt back along Dreeym Lang. Lucy stood at the storeroom door for a minute, watching him running across the island under the noonday sun, among the ever-circling birds.

When Finn's yawl sailed past Traie Vane only Mally was still at the sand boat, which was now high and dry. They'd all three come back to it after dinner, and then Breesha had told Mally to stay and guard the stranded boat against hostile natives while she and Billy went to explore the undiscovered country. Mally had spent some time decorating the sand thwarts with lines of shells, but the others had vanished over the horizon a long time ago, and she was beginning to get tired of standing sentinel against nothing at all. When she saw the *Betsey* she forgot the game entirely, and ran as fast as she could to Giau y Vaatey.

It was sheltered in the giau because the wind was westerly, but the landing rock was still half-underwater. There was another man in the *Betsey* as well as Finn and Juan. Mally watched Finn bring the yawl right up to where the rocks were uncovered. Juan leapt ashore, and the stranger, with his knapsack on his shoulder, stepped easily onto the gunwale and followed him. Juan waved to Mally briefly, and ran to fetch a big stone from the beach. Mally came closer to watch. She'd seen Finn do this before when he'd arrived before the tide was out. Finn fastened a rope round the stone, tying it like a parcel so it couldn't escape, and balanced it on the bow. The other end of the rope was tied to the *Betsey*. Finn stepped ashore, holding the painter. Juan pushed the boat away from the rocks, stern first. When it was a couple of yards out Finn yanked the painter, and the stone splashed into the water. Mally watched Finn make the painter fast.

Finn straightened up and looked up at Mally. 'Well now, Mally,' he said. 'Here we are then, anyway.' He saw Mally was eyeing the stranger doubtfully. 'I'm bringing you another visitor, you see. This is Mr Scott.'

Mr Scott was a big hefty man wearing a fisherman's smock with the sleeves rolled up. His forearms were large and hairy with blue pictures on. Mally could see an anchor on one arm, and a heart up above it. She couldn't see what was on the other arm. At first she thought Mr Scott was alarming, but when she looked at his face he gave her a broad lopsided grin. He didn't have any front teeth, but his eyes were blue like Billy's, and twinkled in a friendly way, not in the least like a hostile native.

'Mr Scott is one of the surveyors,' said Finn. 'He was left behind last time, but here he is now.'

'Oh,' said Mally to Finn. 'That's why Billy had to do the measuring instead.'

'Ay, that's right,' said Mr Scott. 'And here's me hoping your brother made a good job of it, miss, and saved me a hard day's work.'

Mally wanted to put Mr Scott right, but he was too much a stranger to address directly. She hoped Finn would explain that Billy was her cousin, not her brother, but he didn't.

'Would you ken where Mr Buchanan might be just now?' asked the strange Mr Scott.

Mally pointed south towards Gob Keyl.

'In that case,' said Finn easily, 'we could be walking up to the house together. Juan, you're watching the boat just now, but we'll not be leaving you to starve when there's food on the table. Mally, I'm needing to talk to Lucy and your mother. Will they be up at the house just now?'

Mally led the way up to the path. 'But you'll have to wake Aunt Lucy up, if you want to talk to her now.'

'I'm thinking that's what I'll have to be doing. Juan and I, we'll need to go back with the tide in a couple of hours.'

Mam wasn't in the kitchen, so Mally had to wake Aunt Lucy herself. Aunt Lucy leapt out of bed in a flash when she heard that Finn and another surveyor had come. She pulled on her clothes, ran a brush quickly through her hair, and came into the kitchen. Mr Scott wasn't in such a hurry to find the Writing Man that he didn't accept a bowl of broth after the voyage. Mally was sent down to Gob y Vaatey with bread and the small milk churn with broth in it for Juan. She sat beside him on the rocks for company, and shared his bread with him. They didn't talk. Juan never talked. Presently Mally remembered something else she ought to do.

'Billy and Breesha went exploring. They won't know you've come. D'you think I'd better go and find them?'

'If you like,' said Juan. He held the churn to his lips, tipped back his head, and sucked up the last of his broth.

'It isn't *like*,' said Mally. 'Just whether they'd be cross if I don't.'

'I wouldn't be bothering then,' said Juan, wiping the inside of the churn with the last bit of bread. He settled himself on his sheltered rock, still chewing, stretched himself out in the sun, and shut his eyes.

'If you've got your eyes shut you won't see if the mooring doesn't hold.'

'You be watching her then.'

'All right,' said Mally seriously. She sat down next to Juan on the warm rock, and settled down to watch, keeping her eyes fixed firmly on the boat. The *Betsey* swayed gently in the swell, her stern to seaward as the tide tugged at her. The painter still had some slack in it, but you could see the anchor rope was pulled tight. It would stay like that until slack water. The landing rock was already almost out of the water. The shags were settling back on their nests since everyone had gone. There were no waves, just a gentle surge and fall over the flat rock. Juan seemed to be asleep. It was entirely Mally's responsibility now to keep watch. That meant she couldn't go and find the others however much they might say later that she ought to have. The *Betsey* would be safe with her.

Lucy, Diya and Finn sat in the sheltered corner of the garden facing south. Bees buzzed in the lavender, and the puffins flew to and fro overhead against a blaze of blue. Lucy and Finn sat on the driftwood bench under the apple blossom, their backs to the warm wall, and their faces to the sun. Diya sat on the grass in front of them, still wearing her gardening pinafore. As they talked she absentmindedly worked the dandelion roots in the grass loose with her knife, and carefully extricated them one by one. But presently she laid down her knife, and listened intently to Finn, as if she couldn't quite believe her ears.

'What it is that I'm telling you,' Finn was saying, 'is that when I was leaving those surveyors here on Friday, I was going away home and I was worrying about you all. For I was knowing what it all meant, you see. I was knowing ever since you were getting that letter a couple of months back. In fact I was knowing that you were having to leave Ellan Bride before that, because they were speaking of it away in Castletown, and the news was coming into Port St Mary – just bits of talk and none of it entirely certain – but I was knowing that behind it all there were great changes on the way that would be forcing you away from Ellan Bride. So when this Mr Buchanan came and was asking me to bring them over to the island, I was knowing at once that this was what we'd been hearing about, truly coming to pass. And I was thinking as well that your own family on the Island was all dead or gone away to America – for Annie Christian was the last one to be leaving, and that was twelve years back – there is none of them brothers and sisters left on the Island now, and if maybe you've far-off cousins, why then I'm thinking they're maybe too far off to be counting on now. It wouldn't always have been like that, indeed it would not, but the world is changing very fast, even in the Island. I thought maybe you wouldn't be knowing about that, and maybe were counting on a kinship that might be there no longer.'

'No,' said Lucy. 'I was knowing I had no kin to count on any more.'

'Well, sad to say you're right to be thinking that. So then I was thinking too that you were away here on Ellan Bride, and not able to be speaking up for yourselves, and maybe there was no one on the Island thinking of what was to become of you, and able to be speaking for you. And I was thinking to myself, "Finn Watterson, there is one man that's knowing them all these years, that was a friend to Jim Geddes, and Jim Geddes would have done the like for him, and that man is yourself: Finn Watterson." For I'd been seeing the surveyors by then, Lucy, and it was very clear to me that this Mr Buchanan, though he may be a great man at the surveying, is not the man for you to be relying upon if you're thinking of your own futures. Because he wouldn't be the man to be thinking over-much about that.'

'No,' said Lucy. 'I was knowing that too.'

'Well, again, you're right to be thinking that. So I was speaking to Mary about it on Friday night when I was getting home, and she was saying, "You're right, Finn. There's no one will be thinking about Jim's family but ourselves, and if anyone's to be speaking for them, as well you as another, Finn, and that's what you'd best be doing before another day goes past. For Jim was a good friend to you, Finn" – that's what my Mary was saying to me, and right she was – "and now this is him needing you to do a small thing for him." And once Mary has an idea in her head, there's no two ways about it: the thing must be done at once. And so she was seeing me on my way the very next morning, and I was at Castle Rushen before the Governor had full finished his breakfast.'

'You went to the *Governor*?'

Finn was addressing himself entirely to Lucy. That was fair enough: Lucy was the lightkeeper. Diya knew quite well that Finn had never felt comfortable with her, whereas he'd known Lucy since she was a baby. Diya didn't mind Finn ignoring her now; in fact it was a relief. She was already beginning to guess what was coming, and her thoughts were so complicated that she'd have been hard put to respond if she'd tried.

'Indeed I did, Lucy,' said Finn. 'And by ten o'clock on Saturday morning he was seeing me in his library. And a great grand room that is – I never saw the like. But I wasn't letting that put me off what I was having to say to him. For he's not a man to be fearing: I knew that for the way he was dealing with the riots in Castletown two years back. I knew he was a man I could be speaking to, for I was hearing much about him at the time of the riots, and all good. And so I was telling him about you all, Lucy. He was knowing about the new lighthouse, of course, and that the surveyors were already on the island – he was knowing that, too, already – and I think it was knowing all that made him willing to let me speak in the first place.

'But what were you *saying* to him, Finn? Oh, that was so brave of you, to be thinking of doing that for us!' Lucy's face was alight with hope. She hadn't looked so happy since the day Billy was born. Yes, thought Diya, Lucy had had that look in her eyes when she'd first laid eyes on her son. But she was wrong: Finn wasn't about to say the words that Lucy longed to hear. Even the Governor couldn't make the Commissioners of Northern Lights agree to *that*.

'It wasn't exactly courage I was needing,' said Finn. 'For the Governor's not but a man, when it comes to it. It was more – as Mary was saying – just seeing quite clearly that this was what any man – any man's friend – should do. So I was just telling Governor Smelt about how it was that Jim was drowned, and how you were the fourth Geddes to be the lightkeeper, and how your own mother was a Christian from the Island,

and how you and Mrs Geddes had the three little ones to think of, and no living at all but the light, which had been kept burning here, for the good of all, especially the fishermen of the Island, for fifty years and over it. And now the Duke, him that employed your family, was gone, should it not be the Island government that was giving you a home, and a pension, so that you could go on living comfortable enough after all the work you had done for the Island by keeping the light on Ellan Bride?'

'Oh, Finn.'

Obtuse Finn might be, thought Diya, but he couldn't help noticing Lucy's face fall. He looked startled, and then dismayed. Stupid man! He should have realised – none better – what Lucy had hoped for against all hope. He must have known there was only one thing in the world that she wanted. Hadn't it occurred to him how she'd interpret his story? A home! A pension! As if Lucy cared about that! Diya might have been worried to death all these months because they had no money and nowhere to go, but if they had to leave Ellan Bride, it was all the same to Lucy whether the Governor offered her his own castle, or they were reduced to begging in the streets. Finn should have addressed himself to Diya after all: at least she had some notion of the reality of the situation.

'Finn,' said Diya firmly, so that he had to turn and face her where she sat on the grass. 'That is truly kind of you, and a very practical thing to do. You're the only one who's done anything to help us. We're very grateful. God knows what would have become of us if you'd not gone to the Governor like that. We thank you with all our hearts. Don't we, Lucy?'

'What?' Lucy was looking dazed.

'I'm saying how kind it was of Finn to do this for us,' said Diya sternly. 'Was it not?' She fixed her eyes on Lucy, conveying not so much a message as a command.

'Kind?' Lucy seemed to recollect herself, for she turned to Finn, and gave him a thin, unhappy smile. 'Finn, yes, what you did was *kind*. I knew that; I was always knowing you were the second-kindest man in the world, and indeed you are! You mean the very best for us. I know that!'

'What did Governor Smelt say?' asked Diya.

'He said yes,' said Finn. 'What else could the man say? It would be rank injustice to be saying anything else. Indeed, Colonel Smelt was saying himself that it was a shameful thing he'd had no word of the matter before, for he would have been dealing with it at once, if he had known. But no one told him. But once he was knowing, he was calling his secretary in and getting out his pen and paper, and dealing with the matter then and there. What's twenty pound a year to a man like himself, or to Tynwald either? Twenty pound a year, and a fisherman's cottage at Port St Mary. Why, nothing at all! They'll be spending more than that on one breakfast, I'm thinking, those grand gentlemen.'

'Twenty pound a year and a cottage?' repeated Lucy numbly. 'Do you mean it, Finn? At Port St Mary? I mean, is that what he actually *said*?'

'That's what he was ending up saying,' said Finn. He reached inside his smock. 'Here, the letter's in my pocket.' He took out a sealed paper and handed it to Lucy. 'This is what the Governor was writing to you – he was just sitting down and writing it, in his own hand – he did it before I went away.'

With trembling fingers Lucy broke the Governor's seal, and smoothed out the paper. The letter was quite short, and written in big straggly script. Lucy glanced at it and handed it to Diya. 'You read it, Diya.'

Diya read aloud:

Dear Miss Geddes,

It has come to my notice that the Commissioners of Northern Lights will no longer require you to fulfil your duties as lightkeeper at the Ellan Bride lighthouse. I understand that you and your family have faithfully served the light on Ellan Bride for fifty years, to the great benefit of all shipping in these waters, and particularly to the fishing fleet on this Island.

The government of this Island will therefore grant you a pension of £20 per annum for your lifetime, further payable, if so be she survives you, to the former lightkeeper's widow, and also to any dependents whom you may leave who have not yet attained their majority, and will in addition provide you with a suitable cottage, on the same conditions, at Port St Mary or Castletown, whichever you shall desire.

Yours &c
Cornelius Smelt (Governor, Isle of Man)

'And the date,' added Diya, and paused. There was no need to say so – she hadn't had time to reflect anyway – but already she began to see possibilities. Of course this wasn't what she desired, any more than Lucy. She certainly didn't intend to spend the rest of her life in what amounted to an almshouse, along with Jim's sister and nephew, tarnished by – for the fact had to be faced – their undoubtedly dubious status. Diya would never openly acknowledge such an uncharitable thought – that would be disloyal – but inevitably it lurked in the recesses of her mind. How could it not? Lucy must not have the faintest inkling of it, but for Breesha and Mally's sakes, this cottage could only be the first step.

But as a first step it was – literally – an answer to prayer. It paved their way back to the Island, independently, respectably, and not beholden to anyone. Once on the Island, there would be opportunity to think, to plan, to make gradual changes . . . But the excellent thing – the thing that filled Diya's heart with gratitude towards their unlikely saviour – was that it meant she did not have to be afraid. For Diya was aware that, unlike Lucy, she had never dared to hope for the very best, because she knew so much more than Lucy did about despair. Finn couldn't give Lucy back her island, but he could rescue Diya from the greater terror of losing absolutely everything. 'Oh *Finn*!' said Diya, her voice warm with genuine gratitude. 'You've been a true friend to us – and to Jim – a true friend. Indeed you have. Oh Finn!' Diya drew a great breath of relief. 'How can we ever thank you?'

Finn looked embarrassed. 'I'm telling you, Jim Geddes would have done the same for me. I'm not needing you to be thanking me at all. That will suit you then, Lucy? I was telling Colonel Smelt what I was thinking you'd be wanting mostly. I'm hoping I was telling him right, Lucy?'

Finn didn't care what Diya thought – of course he did not: she realised her thanks were nothing to him. He was watching Lucy anxiously, trying to read the conflicting emotions that flitted across her face. Lucy, for all her stoicism, had never learned to guard her expression. Diya willed her not to disappoint Finn. Of course the man had got it wrong – he was but a man, after all – but the truth was he'd saved them, in the immediate term. They had somewhere to go, and they would not starve. Surely Lucy would see that? Or, even if she did not, surely she had the innate courtesy to thank Finn Watterson for doing his very best for them according to his lights? He couldn't have done more. He couldn't have reprieved Lucy from losing Ellan Bride, any more than he could give back to Diya her own lost past, about which he knew less than nothing. Surely Lucy would not be so uncivil as to hurt him, just because he could not give the impossible?

Diya needn't have worried. Lucy set too much store by kindness to deal out cruelty herself. 'Indeed you were, Finn,' she said firmly. 'No man could have done more. I thank you with all my heart; indeed I do.'

Chapter 31

TWO RAZORBILLS WERE MATING IN GIAU YN OOIG. THE NOISE they made was like the creaking door into Lucy and Diya's bedroom being opened and shut very slowly. The female was opening her beak very wide and shutting it again. The male, his beak wide open, in ecstasy perhaps, clambered on her back, wings flapping, thrusting and shoving hard, so that through the telescope it looked as if the two birds might go hurtling off their ledge. There was a final triumphant flapping of wings, then the male slid off wagging his tail feathers, and the two birds stood side by side on their ledge again, eyes expressionless, looking out to sea.

'That's it,' said Breesha, lowering the telescope. 'They've finished again.'

'All right, now it's my turn to look.'

Breesha handed Billy the telescope, and scanned the serried ranks of birds. 'I can't see anybody else doing it just now.'

It was mostly guillemots on this part of the cliff, with just a few patches of razorbills crowded in between. A low growling noise arose from the colony. 'They might not be,' remarked Billy, scanning the ledges through the telescope. 'Most of them have gone onto eggs already.'

Down in the sea a few seals were rocking lazily in the swell, floating upright with their heads just above water. One rolled forward in a single graceful movement, and dived. Through the telescope Billy watched it swim down and down until it merged with the deep shadows under the cliff. He looked out to sea, where big rafts of guillemots and gulls were floating in the sun.

'There's another pair!' said Breesha.

'Where?' Billy looked round to see where she was pointing.

'Down there. See their wings flapping? There!'

Breesha waited patiently while Billy took his turn. Without the telescope, all she could see of the brief ritual was a distant flapping of wings. 'I suppose they must enjoy it, to keep on doing it like that.'

'It's just instinct,' said Billy. 'They have to be made that way – so as to want to keep on doing it, I mean – to be sure of getting chicks.'

'And then the gulls eat most of them. The chicks, I mean. But if you're a razorbill I suppose you can't decide not to bother because of that.'

Billy stood up. 'Let's go down Gob Glas and look there.'

They were just coming over the hill to the slabs when Breesha suddenly threw herself flat on the ground. 'Get down!'

Billy flopped down beside her. 'What? Where?'

'*There*!'

'That's only the Writing . . . *Who's that?*'

'Three of them,' breathed Breesha. '*Three!* Let me look!'

'No, wait. I'm looking.'

In fact the surveyors were close enough for Breesha to see quite well with the naked eye. *Three* men were working on the grassy slope between the slabs and the garden wall. Ben Groat had the levelling pole down at the slabs. The Writing Man was setting up the level close to the painted mark on the garden wall. The third man had another pole set up nearer to Gob Glas. He was barely forty yards away from where Billy and Breesha were lying.

'What does he look like?' whispered Breesha.

'Ordinary, really. Quite big.'

'Let *me* look.' Breesha seized the telescope as soon as Billy reluctantly handed it over. 'Oh Billy! This one really *is* a pirate. He looks *much* fiercer than Mr Groat. And all muscly. I bet he's even stronger than Finn.'

'Well, that doesn't matter. The point is, Finn must have come, and if he's still here, we want to find him. Now, before he goes off again.'

Breesha thought for a moment. 'If we go back to Giau yn Ooig so we're under the skyline, then we can get across to Giau y Vaatey without anyone seeing us. If the boat's still there it means Finn is.'

'Oh, the boat'll still be there.'

'How do you know?'

Billy was looking at the Creggyns. 'It's not slack water yet. If he went away on the ebb he'd have gone south round the island, and that means we'd see him now. And the breeze is westerly. He'll stay in Gob y Vaatey till the flood. In fact the landing rock won't even be uncovered – he'd have to . . . Hey, Breesha, we left Mally to guard the sand boat! That was *hours* ago!'

'Never mind Mally. I think we should get over to Giau y Vaatey *now* without letting them see us.'

'Mr Groat's coming back up the hill! If they're coming this way . . .'

'We need to get over the skyline!'

'Follow me.' Billy began to crawl towards the rocky slope above them. As soon as they were off the bare hill they ran, crouching low, until they could see the chimney of the house below them, and the hill sheltered them.

'That means you won't need to take the letters I wrote last night,' Diya was saying. 'In fact I should write different ones before you go if there's time. And we must answer Governor Smelt's letter. How long can you stay, Finn?'

'Ah, there's no hurry on us. We'll need to be away three hours before high water to get back on the flood. I was telling Mr Buchanan just now I could be giving him four hours to be finishing his work here, so you've plenty of time yet. I'm sure you're a quick writer, Mrs Geddes. But there is another thing I was wanting to tell you, which is not so important to you now, perhaps, but about the surveyors.'

'Oh yes, what *had* happened to the other surveyor?'

Diya suspected that Lucy's renewed cheerfulness was put on so as not to disappoint Finn. The light hadn't come back into her eyes since she'd realised that it hadn't even crossed Finn's mind to ask the Governor to let her keep her job on Ellan Bride. It was possible, however, that the concrete offer of a cottage and an income might have begun to move her thoughts in a new direction. They wouldn't be able to talk freely until Finn had gone. By that time the surveyors would have gone too. Diya felt an unexpected little jerk of the heart. Too much was happening too quickly. But farewells were always like that. After all the fearful anticipation, there was always the one moment – painfully awaited and then gone in a flash – when the last tie was severed, and after which there was no going back.

'That's it, Lucy. I was just taking my leave of the Governor – I had the letter safe in my pocket to bring to you – and the servant came in and was saying that Mr Quirk was there. And the Governor said, "Excellent, the very man we want in this case" – Mr Quirk being the Water Bailiff as you'll know. So Governor Smelt was telling Mr Quirk all about what he and I had been saying together, and telling him to be taking the matter of your pension to the House of Keys, and Mr Quirk was saying, yes, indeed he'd be doing that.

'And then Mr Quirk was saying – and there's me standing there mum, for I was thinking I wished to hear, and not wanting to be sent away, as they might be doing if I brought the gentlemen's attention upon myself – that he was awful angry about this young surveyor you have here, this fellow Buchanan who's on the island now. For Mr Quirk was saying how he'd been speaking to Buchanan himself, on Thursday morning at the George, and this matter of what was to become of the lightkeepers hadn't been mentioned, and Mr Quirk was thinking how naturally the Commissioners of Northern Lights would be looking after the matter themselves, them having such revenues from the Ellan Bride light as there may be from this time on.

'Governor Smelt was telling Quirk how it was no matter: the point was that we were speaking of a Manx family – broadly speaking – who'd done the Island good service, and that was all there was about it. But it turns out – or so I was understanding, listening to the pair of them – that it wasn't so much that Mr Quirk was grudging you the money at all, but that he was wishing to complain – in fact 'twas the very reason he'd come that morning to the castle – about this very man Buchanan. Because the day before – that was on the Friday while I was bringing the other two out to you – there was this other fellow – this Mr Scott – who'd been in the jail the last couple of nights. He'd got himself into a fight at the Harbourside, and knocked a fellow out. I know who the man was myself, and I'd give my oath that this man Scott gave the fellow no more than what he was asking for.

'They were releasing Scott that morning without a charge, and the Deemster was informing the Water Bailiff about it – it being a maritime matter, so to speak, because the fellow was supposed to be working at the lighthouse – and this is when Mr Quirk discovered that Mr Buchanan had gone off to Ellan Bride leaving his man in the town jail, and making no provision for him, and not even bothering to inform anyone. And Mr Quirk was saying that if this was how these Edinburgh engineers were behaving we were wishing to see no more of them on the Island.

'So Governor Smelt was saying that the Edinburgh lighthouse men were here to stay, and that was the fact of the matter, but if Mr Quirk felt so strongly about it he could be writing to Edinburgh himself and making his views known. Which is what he'll be doing I make no doubt, because he was awful angry about it. But the Governor was cutting him short, saying

"Where's this fellow now, then? For here's Finn Watterson who can be taking him back to Port St Mary this very day, and be getting him out to Ellan Bride which is where he ought to be." And there was Mr Quirk saying "So who's going to pay for that?", and there's the Governor reaching into his own pocket then and there and giving me a florin, and saying "Enough, sir" – to Mr Quirk – and then to me – "Here, Watterson. Go into Castletown and find this man Scott, and get him out to Ellan Bride so he can get back to work. This is too much ado about very little" – that's what the Governor said – "Watterson will deal with it, and I wish no hear no more about it."'

'It sounds as if Mr Buchanan's going to be in trouble,' said Lucy listlessly. She had quite enough to think about without starting to worry about what would happen to Archie. 'What's this new one like? I hope he's not going to start fighting *here*.'

'Ah, he's all right,' said Finn. 'He can row a boat pretty well, which is what we were having to do to get out of the bay this morning. I'm thinking myself he was hard done by, for I was speaking to a fellow who was in the Harbourside that night, and he was saying this Mr Scott was not the only one drinking – not by a long shot – and they were making game of the two Scotchmen something awful, speaking Manx, of course, but making it pretty clear what they might be saying of them. This Scott, he was maybe a bit too ready with his fists – his friend was trying to hold him back, so they were telling me – and so the landlord sent a fellow to rouse a constable, but none could be found. So a couple of strong fellows hauled him over the road to the prison, and that's really all there was about it. There's no harm in the fellow, or I'd not have been bringing him out to you, you can be sure of that.'

'Well,' said Diya, 'at least it means they can get on and finish their job, and go away and leave us in peace.' Even in her own ears she sounded dismissive. That was good: Diya didn't wish either Lucy or Finn to guess at the turmoil of her thoughts. The Water Bailiff was an influential man in the government, and related to half the old Manx families. It augured ill for

Archie that he'd alienated Mr Quirk. Should she warn him? No, thought Diya, thinking quickly: there was no need. Although Mr Quirk was an important man in Castletown, his opinion would carry little weight in Edinburgh. And in October Archie would leave both Castletown and Edinburgh behind, perhaps for ever. When – if – he came back he would be far beyond caring for a bad word from Mr Quirk the Water Bailiff. Once the *Beagle* had her castors away, and her course set for the southern hemisphere, Archie would be free of all this . . . free of his whole past, as no woman – especially a mother of daughters – could ever hope to be.

Three hours before high water . . . Lucy relapsed into silence. Finn and Diya were still talking, but she wasn't hearing what they said. In four hours Ben Groat would have gone away. He'd said he'd come back before the year was out. But that was the future, and at the moment Lucy had no picture of the future in her mind, just a jumbled mass of fears and possibilities. Now – at this very moment – Ben was here, on the island. He'd be working until it was time to leave. That was what Mr Buchanan had said: the three surveyors would work right up to the minute when they had to go. Four hours and five minutes from now Ben would be gone. The *Betsey* would pull away from the landing rock, and that would be that. Lucy might not have a chance even to speak to Ben before he left.

'So that was it,' said Drew. 'He let me off with a warning, and I tell you, Ben, I'm no wanting to see the inside of that Castle Rushen again in a hurry. And then I hung around for a bit – just getting used to the light like, Ben, and a bit o clean air in me lungs – and I was swithering about what to do next, for I'd no a penny to bless mysel with, after I'd bought a bit o pie to be going on with, for a man must keep body and soul agither. I could've done with a pint of heavy, but I had naught in my purse but twa farthings, and what can a man do wi that? So I was just thinking to myself maybe I should set oot on the road to this Port St Mary and wait for ye there, and see what was doin, but I was in twa minds about that, ye ken, thinkin I'd no chance of a lodgin wherever I might find myself come nightfall. So there I was, crossing the market square again, no sure what to do or where to go, and this cully comes up to me and says the Governor of the Island, for God's sake, has telt him to take me out to Ellan Bride. And that was Finn Watterson, and the rest ye ken, for I telt ye. But I'm tellin ye now, Ben: Young Archibald will be findin himself in hot water when we get back again, and I'm no sorry. I telt ye he should have bailed me out the very next day – and now, see: the Governor of the Island is with me all the way, and that's a fact.'

Ben knelt on Dreeym Lang, tying the metal arrows into a bundle. He was too tired to think straight, let alone listen to Drew. He'd barely slept for three days now, and so much had happened his mind was still reeling. The turf of Dreeym Lang was studded with flowers: milkwort, eyebright, thrift and tormentil, just the same flowers as in Orkney. As Ben had walked around the island, pulling up the surveying arrows from each station, it had felt like plucking up tentative roots of his own. For seven years he'd been happy to move on, free as a bird – only even the birds were not free, thought Ben bitterly, driven as they were to come back to the same island every year, and wear themselves to a shadow every spring by the call to nest and breed. Only man was free to choose. Free too, to change his mind.

Not that Lucy had given him an answer. She'd eluded him all morning, and then she'd gone to her bed, only to be roused again when Finn arrived with the *Betsey*. And Finn had brought Drew. As soon as Young Archibald laid eyes on Drew he'd set them to work. Four hours, Finn had said, and Young Archibald had kept them to it for every minute. The job was done. Trust Young Archibald for that. Oh yes, he'd get his survey out of it, whatever happened. As for the lave of it . . . what were men, but cogs in the wheel of enterprise, and Young Archibald would keep the wheels grinding to the end, you could be sure of that.

Not that it was entirely fair to blame Young Archibald, for

he had no notion of what was in Ben's heart. He'd had eyes for nothing but the job in hand. Young Archibald hadn't noticed when Billy and Breesha had appeared above the slabs, watched them through the telescope, and then crept away again on hands and knees, just as if the surveyors were their sworn enemies. Just a game, no doubt, and it was foolish to worry about it . . . foolish to think for a moment that Billy might know, and judge, matters that had probably never entered the boy's head for a moment. Billy was Lucy's son. *Just because my son must have had a father you're thinking that I know about this* . . . That's what she'd said, but it hadn't been what Ben was thinking about at the time. But now . . . she'd still not told him anything more than that. Perhaps it was all she'd ever say. Did that matter? Ben wasn't sure. And now . . . he'd not heeded the risk they'd been taking, but now . . . *You're the third-kindest man I've ever met* . . . Ben couldn't stop thinking about that, either, and he was still no nearer working out exactly what she'd meant.

Before the tide turned he had to leave Ellan Bride. Even if they sent him back this summer Lucy wouldn't be on the island. He'd have to ask for leave if he wanted to find her. If he gave her his direction at his lodgings in Edinburgh, would she write a letter, if she needed to? Ben knew Lucy could write: he'd seen the lighthouse records. He wasn't sure she'd know how to send a letter.

And so Ben tramped round the island for the last time, collecting the metal arrows, his thoughts going round and round in circles, until he met Drew up on Dreeym Lang, and they put together their two sets of arrows into one bundle. At least, Ben fastened the bundle, while Drew went on talking.

'Ay,' said Ben, when Drew paused. 'Young Archibald shouldna have left ye, maybe, but if this Mr Quirk is truly going to write to Mr Stevenson, it winna just be Young Archibald that's in hot water. I'm hoping for both your sakes we never hear another word about it.' He stood up, and glanced at the sun. 'Time to be on our way, I think.' He wearily swung the bundle over his shoulder, and Drew fell into step beside him.

'So these folk here,' Drew was saying. 'The lightkeeper's wife. How comes it about she's a blackamoor?'

'Same way as any of us come about, nae doubt. But 'tis true I didna ask her.'

'Ach, Ben, ye ken what I mean. Was the lightkeeper a sailor mebbe, and was bringing her back from foreign parts?'

'No. She's fae Castletown.'

'Away ye go! And I'm a Dutchman! So how many weans has she? I ken there's the boy – I've no seen him yet – if Young Archibald was gettin him tae work he must be older than the wee girl I saw?'

'The boy is the lightkeeper's son. There's another lass, sister to Mally.'

'I thought the lightkeeper wiznae married?'

'Neither she is,' said Ben shortly.

Drew gave a low whistle. 'Is that the way o't? Ye're after tellin me that lass we saw has a bastard wean? Ay well, 'tis a gey lonely life out here tae be sure, and a rerr treat for the passing trade, nae doubt. And there cannae be much o that.' He chuckled. 'If there were, nae doubt she'd have a sight more weans at her tail than just the one.'

If Drew had rained blows down on Ben with his mighty fists it would have been a lot easier. It hurt, but Ben was feeling so weary he couldn't seem to do anything to stop it. Anything he said would make things worse anyway. He'd just give himself away, and that would betray Lucy too.

'Ken what I mean, Ben?'

'Ay well,' said Ben, and felt like Judas.

They passed the lighthouse. There was no one up at the lantern, and the door to the tower was closed.

'I widnae mind a look at the old light,' said Drew.

'Go and look, if you like,' said Ben, without stopping. 'I've seen it.'

'Ay well, maybe I'll no bother. A light's a light, just, and that's all there is tae it.'

'Ay.' Ben led the way down the well-trodden path.

The handcart was in the yard where they'd left it already loaded with their gear. Chickens were foraging over the slops in the ditch beside it. Through the open door of the house came the sound of voices. Ben hesitated for a moment on the threshold, then ducked under the lintel.

When Archie came into the kitchen, he found Lucy and Diya at the table, deep in discussion. As soon as they saw him he was vaguely aware of a change in the conversation. Archie stacked his precious notebooks at the other end of the table, loaded with all the data he'd collected on Ellan Bride, and packed them into his leather case. He reached into the kitchen bed and stuffed his few belongings into his portmanteau. Everything else was already loaded onto the handcart. Presently Ben and Drew came back with the last of the gear. Diya offered them refreshment, but time was running out, so as soon as they'd had a drink of water Ben grabbed his haversack, and Archie sent them to manhandle the cart down to Giau y Vaatey. Finn had already gone ahead to the giau. He was worried about keeping the *Betsey* off the rocks now the tide had turned. Billy and Breesha had gone with him. Diya had been writing letters. She hurriedly drew the last one to a close, and sealed it with a wafer.

'There,' said Diya to Lucy, putting the last letter with the others. 'That's Governor Smelt, the Reverend Gill at Malew, Mr Quirk, and this one for Sally.'

'That's very well done,' said Lucy. 'I never saw anyone write so quick.'

'Well, they're not as polished as I'd like, but they'll serve.' Diya screwed the top on the ink bottle and got up. 'We must go!'

The path to the well was churned to mud by heavy bootmarks. Diya's bare footprints were firmly imprinted on top. Lucy, following Diya, was aware of her own footsteps doing just the same. She avoided treading where Diya had trod, so as to leave both patterns separate and clear.

The children were standing in a row at the top of Giau y Vaatey next to the empty handcart. Mr Buchanan had arrived just a moment before Diya and Lucy. Billy had the telescope slung over his shoulder, so he and Breesha and Mally could run straight to Gob Keyl and watch the *Betsey* on her voyage home. The *Betsey* was already alongside the landing rock. Ben and Drew were swinging the last of the gear aboard. Diya jumped lightly down the rocks, and handed her packet of letters across to Finn, who stowed them in an inner pocket.

Ben scrambled up the rocks to the watching family. 'Mr Buchanan, sir!'

'Ay?'

'Billy's wages, sir! We owe Billy a sixpence!'

Archie was furious with himself for forgetting. It was exactly what a gentleman would never do. He took his purse from his pocket, found a sixpenny piece, and handed it to Billy. 'Thank you for your services, Master Geddes.' Archie looked down at Billy, and an image of a stormy petrel, flying back to freedom, flitted across his mind. This wasn't just any boy; this was Billy. 'Ye did a fine job, Billy. I'll tell Mr Stevenson, and ask him to speak for you if you ever need him to. I won't be in the country myself.'

Archie held out his hand. Billy looked at it. Then he remembered about shaking hands, and held out his own. He and the Writing Man shook hands. Then the Writing Man shook hands with Mam and Aunt Diya, and thanked them for having him and Mr Groat in the house. 'Come on, Ben,' the Writing Man said then, and hurried down to the waiting boat.

Ben Groat shook hands with Billy too. He turned to Breesha and held out his hand. It was the first time in Breesha's life that a stranger had ever offered her his hand. Mr Groat was treating her the same as he'd treat Mam, or Aunt Lucy. Breesha's face lit up. Ben had never seen her look like that before: it was like the sun coming out. Breesha smiled at him for the first time, and shook his hand.

Then Ben shook Mally's hand, and Diya's. 'Thank you,

ma'am. You've been very good to us. Thank you all.' Ben turned to Lucy. Everyone was watching him. 'Thank you, ma'am,' said Ben. He pressed a scrap of paper into her hand. 'I said I'd give thee this. And I'll be writing thee a letter.'

'Will you write it in print, please?' said Lucy.

'Ay, I'll do that.' Ben squeezed her hand between both of his, then turned and leapt down the rocks to the waiting boat.

Chapter 32

NEITHER DIYA NOR LUCY FOLLOWED THE CHILDREN UP TO Dreeym Lang. There was no point watching the *Betsey* until she was out of sight, but if that occupied the children for the next little while at least they'd have some time to themselves. The moment of parting was over, and that was that.

'So,' said Lucy, as soon as Mally, running after the others, was out of earshot. 'What do you think about all *that*?'

'Which bit?' asked Diya cautiously.

'What Finn was saying, of course. What else is there to think about?'

I could be thinking about that scrap of paper that Mr Groat pressed into your hand, thought Diya, and what you said to each other then. I could certainly be asking you about that, only I know you wouldn't tell me. Aloud she said, 'What Finn said? About Mr Buchanan, do you mean? Or about us?'

'Us, of course! That's what matters! But Diya . . .'

'What?'

'Why d'you think Finn wasn't asking the Governor about the light? About whether we could stay? Surely he'd *know* that's what we were wanting? You don't think he's not telling us everything?'

'Of course not. What wouldn't Finn be telling us?'

'What I mean is,' went on Lucy, as if Diya had not spoken, 'Finn's our *friend*. He'd *know* what to ask for – what we were wanting. And that leaves me thinking maybe he *was* asking the

Governor about us staying, and the Governor said no – at least, when Finn was asking him, he said no. Finn might not have explained properly how important it was to us. That's the only explanation I can think of. And maybe Finn wasn't wanting to tell us that bit in case it was too painful.'

Either Diya could tell the truth, or, which would be easier, she could let Lucy believe what she liked. They had a long way to go together yet: it had better be the truth. 'I'm sure Finn didn't ask at all,' said Diya. 'He knew already there was no hope. The Governor can't tell the Commissioners of Northern Lights what to do. That's the whole point of the 1815 Act. I'm sure Finn and Mary talked about it. I'd hazard a guess that Mary told Finn the best thing to say. If you haven't much time to make someone listen, you have to talk sense right from the beginning. It's much better just to ask one thing, and make it something you've some hope of getting. I'm sure Finn and Mary decided not to waste Finn's chance with the Governor asking if we could all stay on Ellan Bride. Because, Lucy – I've *told* you, over and over – it wouldn't have been the slightest use. There was no hope we'd be allowed to carry on here. No hope at all.'

They'd been walking slowly back along the foot of Hamarr. Lucy had gone ahead on the narrow path, but now she suddenly swung round and faced Diya. 'I know what it is! You're *wanting* there to be no hope! You're *wanting* to leave! And I *trusted* you. Right up until I saw you talking to that man, I trusted you! And then – the way you were going on with him – that man – I *realised*. You're not caring, are you? You're not even *wanting* us to stay here! You don't care about the light!'

Lucy was scarlet in the face, and shouting. Diya flinched. This had never happened before. 'Lucy, be reasonable . . .'

'That's what you're always saying! All it really means is *you're* wanting to go back to your old life in Castletown!'

Diya suddenly lost patience, and forgot to be afraid. 'Well, want must be my master then! Because I'll never have that life again! And if you think I have any influence with the Commissioners of Northern Lights – or anyone else come to that

– you must be all about in your head! I've thought about what to do as much as anyone can – and I've *done* a lot more than you have. Who wrote the letters? Who even *knew* who to write to? But we can't change the way things are. And just because *I* don't choose to act like a spoiled child because I can't have my own way it doesn't mean you can't trust me. Because that's *nonsense*!'

'It's not *my own way*! It's what we do – what all my family do – it's who we are! It's what happens to us! All of us! Because we're the lightkeepers!'

'No,' said Diya. 'It's what *you* want. Jim's dead.'

The brutal words hung between them.

'I'm sorry,' said Diya. 'I shouldn't have said that.'

Lucy regarded her stonily. 'Jim's dead,' she repeated. 'And you're not caring. That's it, isn't it? And Billy's not Jim's son. He's just his nephew. Not your blood. Mine. So you're not caring.'

'Don't you bring Billy into this!' flashed Diya. 'Don't you *dare* say I don't care for Billy! Are you going to deny *everything* we've been through – because that *would* be disloyal!'

'If Billy was your son,' pursued Lucy inexorably, 'you'd be doing your – your – your *damnedest* not to let them evict us – just for such a few years – because it's *Billy* you're betraying, and you know it! Because *he'd* be the next lightkeeper. And it's only a few years! And you were never mentioning *that* in your letters, were you?'

'That's unfair! I never thought of it – and neither did you! You never said a word about putting that to them! Ever! And anyway' – Diya looked Lucy steadily in the eye, although she quailed inside – 'is that what Billy wants? Has he ever said so? Because as far as I know you've never mentioned it to him. It's what *you* want, Lucy, and you don't want it because of the Gaffer, or Jim, or Billy. You want it because you don't dare face anything else. That's the truth, isn't it? Billy's just an excuse.'

'That's not *true*!'

'Well,' said Diya, 'you know what you think. I don't. But I think it's time you admitted that other ways of life are possible.

You might even begin to think that they might not be so bad. But you've never let yourself think about that for a moment, since that letter came. Have you?'

To her astonishment Lucy's face suddenly softened. She even gave a small, far away smile. 'Oh yes,' said Lucy. 'I have thought about it. More than you know.' She stopped smiling and gave Diya a hard stare. 'And I might not want to stay with you for ever, any more than you're wanting to stay with me. Because you aren't. Are you?'

'Benjamin Groat!' exclaimed Diya.

Perhaps Diya was more astute than Lucy had expected, because she recoiled at once. Then she recovered herself and said coldly, 'Answer my question. You *don't* want to live with me and Billy, do you? Because we're another source of shame. Are we not? Isn't that what you said?'

'That's not fair! You know I was worried to death about Breesha . . .' Diya was suddenly seized with remorse. 'Oh Lucy, please don't let's quarrel. We never have! Don't let them do this to us! It was you that made it all right about Breesha. *You* talked to Mr Buchanan. I was quite wrong to say you didn't do anything to help. Haven't we always helped each other, ever since . . .?'

'Since Jim died,' supplied Lucy grudgingly. She met Diya's pleading gaze dispassionately. 'We had to, didn't we? No one else was going to help us.'

'Please, Lucy. We can talk about the future. We can decide what we each want, and we can try to make it happen. But let's not be like this with each other. I think those surveyors have bewitched us, for we never quarrelled before. And I don't want to start now, indeed I don't! Please, Lucy!'

Lucy didn't meet Diya's eyes. 'I need time to think,' she mumbled, and slipped past Diya, heading back towards the shore. 'I'll come back later,' she called over her shoulder, as she broke into a run, leaving Diya standing there gazing anxiously after her.

* * *

Breesha, Billy and Mally stood on the arch at Gob Keyl watching the *Betsey*. She was running east before the wind, so they could see Finn in the stern at the tiller with the white sails behind him. It was getting harder to make out the other figures, even through the telescope, but Billy and Mally went on waving until it was impossible to see whether anyone was signalling back or not.

When at last they stood still, Breesha said accusingly, 'You're sorry they're not here any more, aren't you?'

'Well, yes,' said Billy, surprised. 'They weren't enemies after all. That was a mistake.'

'Mr Groat was nice,' said Mally. 'And I quite liked the new one.' She thought for a moment. 'Even the Writing Man wasn't horrible in the end.'

'We still have to leave the island because of them. And they caused us a lot of trouble.'

'No,' said Billy. 'We're having to leave anyway. It's not their fault. You *know* it's not their fault.' He thought of saying something about who'd caused the most trouble, but thought better of it.

'I know *you* liked them.'

'Well, yes, so I did like them. And so did you, some of the time. You liked working the level!'

'Well,' conceded Breesha, 'I suppose that part was all right. But I wasn't allowed to do much of it, was I?' she flung at Billy. '*I* wasn't their favourite, was I? *I* didn't get the chance to follow them about everywhere like a tantony pig, did I? *I* didn't get a sixpence!'

'I couldn't help it! It wasn't my fault!'

'It's because he's a boy,' explained Mally helpfully. 'He can't help it. They didn't want girls.'

Breesha swung round and swiped Mally hard across the ear. '*You* keep out of it! You don't know anything about it!'

Mally's face went tight. She pressed her lips together, and flung herself on her sister, pinching her as hard as she could.

'You can't fight here! Stop it, you two!' Billy pulled Mally off and held her arms down by her sides. 'Not on Gob Keyl! Go and fight somewhere else, if that's what you want to do. Mally, stop it!'

'Don't hold me then!'

'Will you keep off her if I let go?'

'Oh stop it, you two!' said Breesha, as if she'd had nothing to do with the quarrel at all. '*We* shouldn't be fighting. We should be . . . what we should be is united against our common enemy.'

'Our what?' said Billy. 'I haven't got any enemies. And even if we had, they're not here now.'

Breesha stared at him, frustrated, then all of a sudden her mood changed. She looked away from them, out to sea at the diminishing white sails of the *Betsey*. 'Oh let's not fight. It's boring. They've gone away and they're not coming back. Let's not think about them any more. I hope we never see any of them again.'

'I'd *like* to see them again,' said Mally defiantly, wriggling in Billy's hold. 'I hope we do. Especially Mr Groat.' A new thought occurred to her. 'I liked having them here. It was fun. And now . . .' – she searched for words – 'now it feels more empty.'

Breesha stared at her, frowning. Billy let Mally go. Mally didn't move.

'It's—' began Billy.

'No, wait,' cut in Breesha. 'She's right. That's the trouble – I said those men brought trouble, didn't I? What they've done is . . . It means nothing's going to be quite the same any more. I mean, we've not actually gone yet, and maybe it's not their fault that we must, but what is their fault is that it's all changed, even without us going anywhere. I mean – look at us now. What we're doing – right this very moment – already we're being all different.'

'What?' said Billy. 'Oh don't go on – who cares? It's ages until supper time. Let's stop wasting time and *do* something.'

'Billy,' said Breesha.

'What?' Billy was letting his impatience show.

'How much do you mind going away? I mean, seeing that anyway we're going to have to. Are you sad about it?'

'Of course I am!'

'No, I didn't mean anything bad. I mean, are you *completely* sad?'

'Of course. What's the point of talking about it?'

'Because you mightn't be. Because . . . because . . . because although this is the best place in the world, you liked being with those men, didn't you? No, please, Billy, listen. I'm not being angry. I'm just saying.'

Billy looked at her, puzzled, wishing she wouldn't keep changing her moods so fast. 'Can't I like more than one thing at a time?'

'Of course you can! That's what I'm *saying*. I'm saying *that's* what's difficult – more difficult than it was before. Oh, I can't –' Breesha made an impatient movement, then she said, 'Did you know the Writing Man could whistle?'

'*Whistle?*' If Breesha had gone out of her mind they weren't going to be able to do anything interesting with the rest of the afternoon.

'I heard him whistle a tune. Like this.' Breesha pursed up her mouth, and, concentrating hard, tried to reproduce the first two lines of the Writing Man's tune. She'd been practising as much as she could earlier in the day, but even in her own ears her whistling sounded very feeble.

'That's not a tune. That's all one note.'

'I have to practise more,' said Breesha with dignity. 'But that doesn't matter. What I'm saying is our Da used to whistle. Do you realise,' said Breesha, laying a peculiar emphasis on every word, 'we haven't none of us ever heard anyone whistle – not tunes, not like that – not since Da was drowned?'

She'd never said those words before. In fact it was Breesha who'd refused to hear it all these years. It was Breesha, when she and Billy were alone together in their bed at night, who'd started thinking up all the stories about what might have happened to her Da. When Ben Groat had told Billy that

Uncle Jim was truly dead, it had crossed Billy's mind afterwards that the one person he could never tell was Breesha. And now . . .

'But you mustn't whistle at sea,' said Mally. 'Finn says so.'

'We're not at sea.'

'But it might be . . . like the long-tails,' said Mally nervously. '*You* know.'

Breesha looked stubborn. She stared out to sea. The *Betsey*'s sail was a tiny splash of white, hard to see amidst the sparkling waves. From the *Betsey* Ellan Bride would be a small blue hump on the horizon, the same colour as the far lands. One day soon they too would be out there, sailing away, and watching Ellan Bride disappearing behind them. After that Ellan Bride would only be a memory, and not quite real.

'That's the whole point,' Breesha said, suddenly reverting back to what Billy had said. 'You can like two things at once. You can be thinking two quite different things at the same time, even if they don't make sense next to each other. And you can't do anything about it, that's the trouble.'

'It's all right to whistle tunes on land,' remarked Billy. 'It must be or Uncle Jim wouldn't have done it, and nor would the Writing Man. In fact' – Billy grinned suddenly – 'let's see if we could do it now. Whistle tunes, I mean. Now *that's* something useful we could be doing meanwhile.'

The island was still shining and peaceful, but inside herself Lucy could find no peace at all. The turmoil that she felt instead was horribly familiar, but she'd never noticed how it had gradually faded away, first after she'd come home from Castletown, and later after Jim had been swept away. Now that the feeling was back she recognised it all too well: a kind of queasy tightness just under her ribs that made her feel shaky all over. If only they could have been left in peace, as they had always been!

All through her childhood there had been peace on Ellan Bride. Why had she ever wanted to go away? It had been entirely her own idea. Da and Mummig had tried very hard to persuade her not to go. In fact her Da had been very angry with her, and . . . no, no, she didn't want to remember all that. She'd been fifteen . . . The truth was that if she really tried to bring it all back, she was forced to admit there had *not* always been peace when she was young. Those early golden years when nothing had come to disturb them, and Death had not yet made his presence felt on Ellan Bride, were partly – she had to face it – just a trick of her memory. Memories were like that: they made the past seem better than it was, or, sometimes, much worse. Memory made the past look simpler than it had actually been.

Looking at the island now, from the white cairn on Cronk Sheeant, Lucy was conscious in a new way of how well she knew this place. From the cletts beyond Gob Keyl, fully exposed now with their shelves of shining seaweed where the seals were basking, the white beaches, the soft green turf of Dreeym Lang, studded with daisies and eyebright, thrift and tormentil . . . the screams and smells from the nesting birds in the western giaus, right down to the shelving slabs and the Creggyns . . . Lucy knew every inch of Ellan Bride. She very seldom saw it at this hour on a spring afternoon, because usually at this hour she was in bed and asleep. Which was what she ought to be doing now . . . she'd be exhausted tonight. That was something else that was going to be different: there weren't going to be any more solitary nights, alone up at the light. She'd turn back into a daytime person, just like everyone else. She wouldn't have the long summer dawns to herself any more; she wouldn't be the first one to see all the different birds returning in the spring. The puffins that came back every April, and circled and circled the island, as they were doing now, round and round her where she sat . . . in three months they'd be gone again, wherever they went when their nesting was done, and so would Lucy be gone. She'd never see the puffins come back to Ellan Bride again.

But sometimes when Lucy had been growing up she'd felt

restless and angry. She found it hard now to remember what it had all been about, but then she'd never tried to remember before. She wasn't much given to trying to work out what she thought about herself, or anyone else, come to that. She'd preferred to be left in peace to get on with the things that needed to be done.

Only now it seemed as if there was very little to be done, and far too much to think about. Lucy wasn't used to so many things happening at once. In the last three days three complete strangers had come for the first time in five years, and one of them had turned out to be Ben Groat. She'd lain with Ben for two nights. Last night, in fact . . . the memory of his touch, the feel of his skin under her searching hands, the smell of him . . . all that was so recent that it almost seemed as if Ben was really still here, and not just an image inside her head. That image would fade, of course, as time passed. Memories, even of people you truly loved, didn't stay properly alive for ever. Lucy might even truly love Ben Groat. She'd never expected that sort of love to happen since she'd come home from Castletown.

And now she'd quarrelled with Diya. They'd argued sometimes before, but they'd never had an actual quarrel. They both hated that kind of thing too much. Diya thought the family might have to separate. More than that – Lucy realised that what she'd shouted at Diya was actually true – she'd known it, deep down, all along – Diya didn't *want* the family to stay together. *Another source of shame* . . . Supposing they were forced to stay together, was it going to be possible to forgive Diya that?

What mattered more was that while all these things were going on, Lucy had told Billy who his father was. She'd waited ten years for him to say something, and, in the middle of all this upheaval, he'd finally asked. What a moment to choose! Except that, when Lucy thought about it, he must have asked at such a time *because* the surveyors were here. That might be because they'd made him notice that he didn't know any men

– didn't know his own father, in fact. Billy had asked several things, and she hadn't had time to think properly about any of them – had that whole conversation only been this morning? So much seemed to have happened since. She'd had no chance to notice how Billy was feeling now. Had he been thinking about it too? He'd asked where his father was *now*. Did that mean . . . A chilling thought struck Lucy: Billy might not see that the whole story was actually *over*. It had never crossed Lucy's mind that her encounter with Billy's father belonged anywhere but in the remote past, something that had once happened, and could not be forgotten, but would certainly never reappear to trouble their peace in the present. But Billy had asked where Michael Elliott was *now*. Why? Could that mean that, in addition to all the other unknown terrors of the future, they were also to be haunted by a ghost that had long, in Lucy's mind anyway, been laid tidily to rest?

The last three days had been like a landslide. Sometimes a handful of soil would get loosened from the top of a cliff after heavy rain, and it would start to slide a little. And then the crumbly rock beneath would start to move. It would reach a certain point, and suddenly a whole slice of cliff would fall away and crash into the sea. It had happened four years ago at Giau yn Stackey. What might start with one tuft of thrift dislodged from its crumbling ledge, might end as a cataclysm, sweeping away plants, birds, nests, paths, beaches – people too, if they happened to be in the way. Little movements of rock and earth were happening all the time. Ellan Bride was imperceptibly getting smaller and smaller. Before the end of the world the whole island might have vanished into the sea.

Well, at least Lucy wouldn't live to see that. But since the surveyors had come, everything had got so much more complicated than it had been before. Perhaps in the middle of all the complexity there was something good. She missed Ben Groat. There was a part of her that would, for two pins, have leapt aboard the *Betsey* beside Ben Groat, and sailed away with him there and then. She couldn't say she'd have done it without a backward look – even if she'd been free to do it, her feelings would have been very mixed – but if it hadn't been for the light, and Billy – maybe she could have done it. Well, it was just the light really. If it hadn't been for the light, she and Billy could have gone with Ben together. If he'd asked them, of course. He hadn't asked. But then he couldn't have, could he, because he knew they had to stay with the light? He'd said he'd come back. But he might change his mind, because when he went back to his own world he might forget all about Ellan Bride, or it wouldn't seem particularly important any more. There was no point counting on Ben Groat. She had to take it as fate really: either he'd come back, or he wouldn't. She wouldn't think about it unless it happened. Except – Lucy couldn't help being honest with herself – the truth was she *was* thinking about it a good deal.

And what would Billy have said to sailing off with Ben Groat? Would he have left the island so easily? It occurred to Lucy for the first time that he might have been more willing to leave the island than to leave his cousins – to leave Breesha. Billy and Breesha had been brought up as if they were twins. Had that been wise? It had never occurred to Lucy to question it; in any case there'd been no choice. If she'd thought about it at all, she'd been glad that Billy had never had to be alone.

Diya had accused Lucy of never asking Billy what he wanted to do. Now, sitting alone on Cronk Sheeant, with no one to confront her, Lucy had to admit that it had never crossed her mind that Billy might not want to live all his days on Ellan Bride. But it had never crossed her mind either that he might ask her where Michael Elliott was now, and he *had* asked. Billy was thinking things that Lucy didn't know about. He must always have done, of course, because he and his mother were not the same person, and never had been, even before he was born. But now he was growing older, and soon he'd be able to do what he wanted whatever Lucy thought. He might even choose to do things that destroyed her peace of mind.

There was no peace now anyway. All these things that had

started to happen would not suddenly stop just because the men had gone. They had to think about what to do. Finn had got them a cottage and twenty pounds a year. That was the fact of the matter. It would be far more sensible to think about this cottage than to ask imponderable questions that had no answers. The cottage had to be faced.

It would be better to be in Port St Mary than in Castletown. Finn and Mary were in Port St Mary. Da and Mummig were buried in Rushen church. Nothing horrible had happened to her in Port St Mary. You couldn't see Ellan Bride from anywhere very close to Port St Mary because the Calf was in the way. It was a longer walk to Scarlett Point from Port St Mary than it was from Castletown. It wouldn't be a good idea to live too near Scarlett Point because it had too much past attached to it. Diya would want to go to Castletown, but it was up to the lightkeeper, whose cottage and pension it was after all, to decide. Everything would be less terrifying and more possible if she faced it now and made a decision.

The lightkeeper, sitting by the white cairn on Cronk Sheeant, took her courage in her hands and took a long hard look at the future for the first time. Four people depended on her entirely: she couldn't evade it any longer. Lucy gave a little shudder, and made up her mind. She would accept a cottage in Port St Mary and a pension of twenty pounds a year. A great weight of uncertainty fell from her mind. She should be glad – indeed the immediate relief was greater than anything she could have imagined – but all of a sudden she found herself crying. Big tears were pouring down her face and dripping off her chin. Lucy put out her tongue and tasted salt. It was oddly pleasant to taste her own tears. Her tears were making little circles of wetness on her skirt, dark against the faded blue, like drops of rain on parched soil. She watched, fascinated, as they went on falling. She'd always thought of crying as painful, but this didn't hurt. It hurt less than anything that had happened in a long time. She'd never seen so many tears before, or such big ones. It astonished her. She was sad – of course she was sad – because of what she was losing, but at least she didn't have to hold on to it any more. At last she could let go of the old life and look ahead. At last she knew exactly what to do.

Diya sat at the kitchen table with her pen poised over a blank sheet of paper. She'd wedged the door open so she could see the sunlit yard. The sun never shone into the kitchen in the afternoon so it was rare for her to stay in after dinner if the day was fine. But now there was work to be done. She was feeling so many conflicting emotions all at once – but that would have to wait. She urgently needed to sort things out with Lucy. The children must never know that Lucy and Diya had disagreed: all that must be resolved before they came in for supper. It had to wait, though, until Lucy chose to come back. Lucy would be exhausted, too, which wouldn't help. She ought to be sleeping at this very minute, but there was nothing Diya could do about that either. But making plans – that was something useful she could be getting on with, and it stopped her unruly emotions from swirling around so chaotically, which was all to the good.

Someone had to think about what to do. The quarrel with Lucy had shaken Diya more than she cared to admit. Neither in Grandmother's house nor in Aji's had people stood shouting at one another like that. There were more subtle ways of making one's feelings known. It was the second time in three days that Diya had been confronted by another adult saying unpleasant things directly to her face in far too loud a voice. The sooner she could remove Breesha and Mally to a civilised society the better it would be. Ellan Bride had been all very well for their infancy; in many ways it had been ideal – she couldn't deny that – but the last three days had brought so many shocks upon them that the one thing that emerged clearly was that the sooner Diya and her daughters were away from here the better it would be.

But there was much to be done. No one else seemed to have

any idea of that. At least now there was something definite to plan for. This cottage that Finn had arranged would only be temporary, but for now it meant security, and a practical beginning. Diya would always be grateful to Finn for that. In the letter for the Governor she'd given to Finn to deliver, she'd said that they would prefer to go to Castletown. She hadn't told Lucy she'd written that. It might be very difficult, especially now that they'd quarrelled, to explain that there just hadn't been time to discuss the matter. Someone had had to make the decision. She'd also asked the Governor in her letter when they might expect to be able to move. Obviously they couldn't leave the light until the next lightkeepers arrived. They'd actually have to meet them, of course, to hand everything over. Diya doubted whether Lucy had thought of that. She doubted if Lucy had thought of *anything*.

There were the animals too . . . would this cottage have land with it? If they were close to the town they wouldn't need goats, or pigs, or even chickens. If they'd known sooner they wouldn't have needed to buy the piglets, but now that they were here they might as well be fattened up for sale. That would bring in a little money at a time when every penny was going to be needed. There were bound to be expenses over the move. The goats must certainly go. Diya would miss the daily routine, only there were going to be so many other things to do in the new life she couldn't possibly be milking goats twice a day. It would be ridiculous anyway. Goats were a menace when they could stray onto other people's land – anyway, they probably wouldn't have any pasture of their own at all. There was no doubt about it, the goats must go. And that would bring in a little more cash. Mappy had her kid as well – two nannies, one with a kid. A shilling or two, perhaps? It would all help.

Diya wrote a heading on her paper: *Things to Do*, and underlined it neatly. Underneath she wrote: *Sell piglets. Sell goats. Chickens?* A moment later she wrote: *Smokey*. If they still had the lidded basket in which the first Smokey had travelled from Castletown twelve years ago it must be in the outhouse somewhere. It might have perished long ago, but Diya couldn't recall that it had ever been used for anything else. All of a sudden Diya felt tears welling up inside her. That was ridiculous: she'd only been thinking about the cat. It was just that she'd come here bringing almost nothing except a cat in a basket, and she'd be leaving still carrying a cat in a basket. But taking with her so much else . . . Breesha, Mally . . . and more memories than she dared to think of at the moment. She was determined not to think about any of that yet. Meanwhile, why would anyone weep because of a cat in a basket? It was ridiculous.

'Aji, what about Mittu? Can I take Mittu with me as well?'

'Diya beti, Mittu wouldn't be happy on a long journey. England would be much too cold for him. No, no, beti, leave Mittu here in the place he knows. Ajoba and I will look after Mittu, you can be sure of that.'

'But will you talk to him, Aji? He likes talking. You won't let him forget all his words, will you, Aji?'

'No, no, beti. We'll talk to the parrot, if you wish it. There, there, I promise you, beti. We won't let him forget the words you taught him.'

But it was not Mittu who had forgotten the words. Diya was quite alone in the kitchen. The whole house was empty. Suddenly she dropped the pen, pushed her list away, laid her head down on her arms and began to weep bitterly. She hardly made a sound. She'd learned the art of silent weeping long ago on a heaving ship, where the sound of the wind and the waves slapping against the hull would conspire with her to hide any small unhappy noises. Diya knew how to keep quiet while her whole body was shuddering with an overwhelming grief that seemed to come out of the very depths of her soul. She didn't ask herself why: all she was aware of as she wept was loss. She was weeping for everyone and everything that she had ever loved, all the people and places that had gone, all the things that she'd tried so hard to remember and keep alive, all the while knowing that, whatever she did and whatever happened to her, not one of those moments that had been so violently swept away from her could ever be brought back.

Chapter 33

ARCHIE FOCUSED HIS TELESCOPE ON THE CHICKENS. HE WAS sitting in the stern next to Finn, just out of the way of the tiller. The swell was heavy, and as the *Betsey* went down into each trough the Chickens would vanish, and then come back into his sights as they reached the crest of each wave. He'd have liked to get a proper look at the Chickens. The tide was right: the reef was well exposed now, with its shelving platforms of seaweed. But there was too much sea, and the wind wasn't favourable, so he hadn't even suggested it to Finn, and now the Chickens, like Ellan Bride itself, were rapidly diminishing astern. It was disappointing that they were keeping so well out to sea, on a direct course for Scarlett Point, but with this northerly wind it was the obvious thing to do. They'd only need to go about once, to head north-west, close-hauled on the starboard tack into Port St Mary Bay. That dashed Archie's hopes of getting a closer look at the Calf, and the fascinating cliffs of Spanish Head. Already they were far enough out to sea for all the lands around to have turned themselves into hazy shapes in the blue distance. Archie glanced back to Ellan Bride and saw a two-dimensional hump on the horizon, a shade darker than the sky.

Archie had done all the work he was supposed to do, and done it well, but still he was plagued by a vague feeling of dissatisfaction. He had his measurements and his reports, and the map of the island would be finished in a day, back at his desk in Edinburgh. But there was something nagging at him – as if the job had somehow not been concluded properly. He'd like to have circumnavigated the island, and studied the coast from the sea. Finn had given him the choice of sailing round the island or finishing the work on land, and of course the survey had had to take precedence. But it would have been helpful to see the west side of Ellan Bride from the sea.

'Mr Watterson!'

'Ay?'

'Suppose we wanted to get to the Calf before we left? If we stayed the night in Port St Mary? We could walk over to the Sound, maybe, if you weren't able to sail us out there. Would anyone be able to take us over?'

'That would be depending on the wind and the tide, I'm thinking. If you're not minding a wait – a day or two, maybe – indeed myself or another could be taking you across.'

Archie frowned. 'A day or two? We ought to be on our way. But still . . . If maybe it could be done tomorrow?'

No! Ben was amidships, sprawled among the gear, where he'd managed to make himself moderately comfortable, with his oilskin-clad back to the gouts of spray that came flying over the gunwale. He strained his ears to hear what Archie and Finn were saying. Archie's latest notion filled him with dismay, but of course it wasn't up to him. Hadn't Young Archibald had enough? The last thing Ben wanted to do was to look across at Ellan Bride from the Calf, knowing that it might as well be as far away as the moon. One hard parting was plenty to be going on with. But Young Archibald wouldn't be thinking of that; he'd be thinking about the job in hand. Well, then, maybe he was a better man than Ben. Or just not so lucky.

'What it is though,' said Finn to Archie, 'is that I was also having a message for you. There wasn't the chance to be speaking of it on the island. I was thinking there'd be plenty of time later, as there is indeed just now.'

'A message?'

'From the Governor indeed. He was wishing to see you before you're leaving Castletown. I was saying to him that as soon as I was fetching you off Ellan Bride you could be going straight to him in Castle Rushen. I'm hoping I was not inconveniencing you, Master Buchanan, but from what you were saying before, I was thinking this arrangement would be suiting you quite well.'

'The *Governor*! What does he want to see *me* for?' Archie was so startled he forgot to be aloof. He didn't want any more dreary interviews in Castletown; surely these Manxmen hadn't thought up any more difficulties?

'I'm thinking – I'm knowing, in fact – that the Water Bailiff was speaking to him.'

The mention of the Water Bailiff brought Archie to his senses: he should never be discussing this kind of business with the boatman. Still less should he let Finn Watterson see that the mention of the Water Bailiff filled him with an ill-defined apprehension. It was the feeling he'd had as a schoolboy when he'd forgotten to prepare his lessons. But he was a man grown, and the Governor – let alone the Water Bailiff – was hardly likely to give him the belt. 'Thank you, Mr Watterson,' said Archie stiffly.

Finn was silent, his eyes on Scarlett Point. It looked closer now than Ellan Bride did when he looked astern. He had a fair idea of what might be going through this young man's head. He'd not seen much of him, but he reckoned he'd got his measure. The more arrogant Master Buchanan's manner, the more frightened he was inside; Finn had met others often enough who were made the same way. Master Buchanan was the sort who got into trouble because they were too confused about who they were themselves to think clearly about the effect they might be having on everybody else. Either Finn could give him a little help in spite of himself, or he could accept the rebuff at face value, and let the poor fellow be getting on with it in his own way.

They were half a mile nearer Scarlett Point when Finn spoke again, quietly so that Ben couldn't hear. He didn't need to worry about Drew or Juan; they were away in the bows. Drew had pulled his sou'wester over his face and appeared to be sleeping, using the coiled anchor rope as a pillow. Juan was perched on the gunwale, gazing moodily ahead. That was just his shyness: the change that came over the boy when there were foreigners present was remarkable indeed. He was seeming quite a stranger to his own father when these surveyors were around. But he'd grow out of that sort of thing when he got to an age to be more comfortable with himself. It wasn't worrying Finn.

'Master Buchanan.'

'Ay?' said Archie absently. He had his telescope to his eye, trained on Spanish Head.

'Perhaps you should be knowing that the Water Bailiff was speaking to the Governor about you. It just so happened I was there in the room at the time, for I was visiting the Governor myself about another matter.' Finn lowered his voice so even Archie could scarcely hear him. 'It was about your man there. Master Scott. The Water Bailiff was not very pleased about Master Scott being left behind in the jail, and no one knowing a word about it until you were gone away to Ellan Bride. And I think you should be knowing that there may be a little trouble brewing about the matter.'

Archie slowly folded his telescope and put it in his pocket. He mustn't let Finn see what he was thinking. That was his first concern. But inside himself he was furious: furious with Drew, furious with the Water Bailiff, furious with these gossiping, prying Manxmen who couldn't mind their own business and took it into their heads to go around concerning themselves with everyone else's. He was also, just for a moment, panic-stricken. The very mention of seeing the Governor had left him with a shaky feeling that was half guilt – not that there was any reason for that – and half alarm. And now this . . . But he hadn't done anything! Drew had brought it all on himself! It wasn't Archie's job to chaperone his men whenever they had time off! What did all these busybodies think he should have done?

We kinna leave Drew to rot. That's what Ben had said, when they were leading that damned flea-bitten horse out to pasture. Archie hadn't listened. And now Ben, not for the first time, damn him, was apparently in the right of it. At least, there seemed to be all these other people who thought so. *We kinna leave Drew to rot.* But that's just what Archie had done. Ben wouldn't have done it. Mr Stevenson wouldn't have done it. This Finn Watterson certainly wouldn't have done it, Archie could tell. Already Drew had made it all too plain that he was holding a grudge, although he'd said very little, and been far less truculent than usual, while they'd been working on Ellan Bride this afternoon. In fact Drew's forbearance had been a bad sign. Archie had been dimly aware of that ever since Drew had turned up on the island, but there'd been so much work to do there'd been no time to waste on what was going on in Drew's mind.

We kinna leave Drew to rot. Three days ago, before it was all too late, Archie could so easily have listened to Ben. If he'd known at the time, he could so easily have dealt with it all differently. But he hadn't had any idea . . . *We kinna leave Drew to rot.* Oh God, he should have known that. And now everyone knew . . . Archie said nothing to Finn. He didn't care a whit for any of these God-forsaken Manxmen, but at the same time he felt utterly exposed.

It was infuriating to have to deal with all this just when the job he'd been sent to do was reaching a satisfactory conclusion. He ought to be cynical enough by now to realise that life was never like that. You did a good piece of work; you made sure everything was neatly tied up at the end and nothing forgotten, and just when you were going over the last paragraph of your report in your mind, a whole new set of problems would suddenly loom over the horizon. He'd finished his survey, the map was almost drawn, and all Archie wanted to do now was close the door on Ellan Bride, go home, and forget all about it. But even before Finn had mentioned the Governor he'd had that nagging feeling that there should be more to come.

In any case, he hadn't planned to go home and forget all about it. He'd half-promised – at least, he'd mentioned the possibility – that one day he might come back. Not that he'd committed himself, of course. He was in no position to do that. Maybe the desire to do so would fade away in time, but at the moment the memory of the lightkeeper's widow was still so fresh in his mind it didn't feel like a memory at all. It still seemed like part of the present, even though the chances were that they'd never meet again.

And now there was this other trouble waiting for him in Castletown: that made it all even more complicated. Diya knew the Water Bailiff. She certainly knew Finn very well. Possibly she even knew the Governor. When she came across to Castletown she'd hear all about Drew, and what Archie had done about it. She'd hear him discredited by all the gossips, male and female, of this benighted island. She'd realise that he wasn't what she'd call a gentleman.

What the hell did it matter, anyway? He'd probably never see her again. All he'd said was that he might call on her one day. Meanwhile, as soon as the *Beagle* left Tilbury dock, all these small affairs would fade into total insignificance. No one on the *Beagle* was going to know if he'd failed in any way; he wouldn't carry the past aboard with him – or only such private memories as he chose to take. If ever he came back to the Isle of Man, in five years, ten years maybe, even supposing he took his courage in his hands and went to call on Mrs Geddes – supposing she was still here – so much would have happened in between that he'd be free of anything that had gone before. Or, if that turned out not to be the case, he could just keep away altogether, and that would be that.

'Ready about,' Finn called, and Archie ducked as the boom swung over.

* * *

Ben sat up and looked round. On this new course he could see straight ahead into Port St Mary Bay. There was a big schooner at anchor, and fishing boats moored against the quay. He could see a row of buildings above the shore. They were getting more distinct every moment. Presently he could see the catch being unloaded, the piled up herring barrels, and the busy warehouses with the row of houses behind all looking out over the water. He'd only been gone three days. It felt like much longer. After the green and blue distances of Ellan Bride, this bustling village – for it was no more than a village really – looked so foreign, and so full of people, that it almost frightened him. But that was nonsensical; Ben had seen plenty of new places, and plenty of strangers; it was a very long time since he'd approached anywhere new with anything more than easy curiosity.

He'd been half-dozing most of the way from Ellan Bride. He'd waved his handkerchief at the three children on Gob Keyl for as long as they could see it, because it would have been unkind not to do that, but the moment they were out of sight he'd turned his back on the island, wriggled down into the bottom of the boat, shut his eyes, and tried not to think about anything. Into this half-comatose state – he might even have been dreaming – a voice had intruded itself. It was a persistent, irritating voice, and it was telling him a story. After a while it came to him: the old man on the quay at Castletown. He'd told Ben some story about the big castle in Castletown. But the story Ben found himself thinking of now hadn't come from the old man. His mother used to tell it when Ben was just a bairn. In the dream – if it was a dream – the movement of the boat was like being rocked in a cradle, the way it sent a man to sleep when there was nothing else to do – it was the old man's voice, but definitely his mother's story. Now that he was properly awake, and they were coming right into Port St Mary Bay, he couldn't help recalling it, even though he didn't want to in the least.

It was about an elf-woman who fell in love with a young

man from Evie. The elf-woman used to watch this young man when he went to the hill to mind his sheep or cut his peats, and one day when she saw he was thirsty she came boldly up to him with a brimming churn of milk, and offered him a drink. He'd never seen her before, but to his eyes that day she looked very young and beautiful – for she had him bewitched, that was the truth of it – and he was glad of the milk, for he'd been working hard, so he never thought to ask who she was, or why he'd never seen her before in all his life. So he drank the milk, and as soon as he'd done that he forgot who he was, and where he came from, and his family waiting for him at home. So away he went with her. She took him to her own green howe, and there he stayed three nights. Ben's mother never used to say just what the young man and the elf-woman did together – Ben had only been a peedie boy when she used to tell him the story – but certain it was that the young man fell so deep in love with the elf-woman there was no chance in the world he'd ever get over it. On the third day, though, he found himself lying alone out on the bare hill, with no memory at all of how he'd got there. He looked for the green howe but he never found it again, so all he could do was make his way home. And when he got there he found he'd been gone for seven years, and everyone thought he was the ghost of himself come back to haunt them. Whether it was the shock of that, or the sorrow of losing the elf-woman, no one knew, but certain it was that he was never the same man after, but just grieving all his life for what was gone for ever.

Coming away from Ellan Bride was the hardest parting Ben had ever made, even though he'd only been there three days. It felt so much longer because so much had happened. He'd met Lucy. He'd lain with her two nights. He'd wanted her so much he'd asked her to marry him, because that was the only way he could see of keeping her. Already he missed her so much it hurt. The worst part about missing her was that Lucy had nothing to do with the life he was going back to. Just seeing all the ordinary life going on in Port St Mary made Ellan Bride seem very far away. In a few minutes they'd come alongside the fishing boats. Juan was standing by the sail, ready to haul in the sheet. Drew, in the bows, had stirred himself at last, and held the painter coiled in his hand, ready to throw ashore. In five minutes Ben would be back in the world he knew. Already it felt almost as if Lucy didn't exist any more. Ben didn't like that feeling at all. He had nothing to remind him of her – he could so easily have asked for something – a keepsake – anything – but he hadn't. All he had to hold on to were his memories. But that would be enough, if he willed it. That would just have to be enough, until he was able to come back.

And then what? By that time Lucy would have left Ellan Bride. Would that change her? Would it change how she felt about him? By that time she'd be living in Port St Mary, or Castletown. Would she want to face anything more?

At fourteen years old, Ben had docked in the port of Leith for the first time, and followed the busy road south. The first thing he'd seen of the great city ahead was a pall of grimy smoke. When the open fields gave way to rows of houses, and the dusty road turned to cobbled streets, he'd had to walk right into the reek. The fume and the smell had made him choke. The noise was awful: hooves and iron-bound wheels on cobbles, people everywhere, making such a din it was a wonder they could hear themselves speak. Ben had felt as if he were being swallowed into the belly of a monster. It was the sheer size of the place that had frightened him; the monster itself hadn't been wholly unrecognisable. Edinburgh had rows of houses along streets and wynds just like in Stromness, only in Stromness you came out on the hill at the top end, or the shore at the bottom end, and it never took more than five minutes if you wanted to feel the wind and get a bit more space around you. In Stromness there were houses two storeys high; in Edinburgh the buildings were so tall it was like finding yourself in a maze of chasms at the bottom of the sea. Stromness on market day could be left behind when evening came, and you could walk away from it into the quiet gold of a summer night. In Edinburgh you couldn't get away. The smells and the din had once kept Ben awake at night, and when he had fallen asleep at last he'd had dreams about getting lost in endless dark wynds between towering faceless houses, and not being able to see out.

But Ben was at home in Edinburgh now. He hadn't had dreams like that for years. He'd served his apprenticeship to the city for seven years, and it no longer had the power to frighten him. In that time he'd travelled all over Scotland, by land and sea; he'd seen more new places in seven years than most men saw in a lifetime. And yet, as Juan lowered the sail, and they slid neatly alongside the fishing boats moored three-deep against the jetty, Ben wished he could just turn tail and head straight back to Ellan Bride.

It almost felt as if it wasn't his own thoughts he was thinking, but someone else's. Had she bewitched him, making him suddenly see the world through her eyes? If only he could have taken her with him now, it would have been so much easier than having to wait, and think, and wonder . . . He couldn't have done, of course, because of the light. If it wasn't for the light, for two pins he'd just have persuaded her to come home with him now, just like that. Would she have come? Billy would have come – Ben was pretty sure of that – and that might have helped her make up her mind. It was an odd thought that Billy, whom Ben didn't particularly want, would be no trouble at all, while his mother, whom Ben wanted more than he could begin to think about at the moment, would probably give Ben as hard a time as she was likely to give herself. Would any of this ever happen, or was he dreaming? However hard it might be for him to have Lucy, it would be better than this aching sense of loss. Or would it? Ben didn't know; he was tired of even thinking about it. There hadn't been any choice anyway, because of the light.

Chapter 34

'DIYA?'

Diya stopped slicing bread, and looked up, with the knife still poised over the loaf. She regarded Lucy warily. Lucy stood in the doorway, blinking, as her eyes adjusted to the dim kitchen after the golden light outside. Diya looked gaunt and hollow-eyed. Perhaps it wasn't just the light: Diya looked as though a layer had been stripped off her, leaving her skeletal and defenceless. Perhaps she'd been crying. Lucy couldn't read anything in her face except exhaustion.

One of them had to begin. That was one of the things about Ellan Bride. You had to go on being with people. There wasn't any choice. Lucy had learned that when she was younger than Mally. You could rush out of the house, hating them all, vowing never to speak to any of them again. But, especially if it was raining, there was nowhere else to go. You had to swallow your fury, or resentment, or pride, or whatever had driven you away, and just come back. In winter particularly you had to do it within minutes. It had been useful training in a way. Nothing less extreme could have taught Lucy to say things she didn't mean.

'I'm sorry,' said Lucy.

She'd guessed right. Diya had been crying. That wooden look wasn't indifference. Diya just didn't want Lucy to see how hurt she was. Lucy could understand that. Was this how Jim had seen Diya, when he came upon her unexpectedly in the Castletown kitchen, alone in the deserted house except for the grey cat on her knee? Lucy had never felt so strong in Diya's company before.

'It's all right,' said Lucy. 'We don't need to fight any more. We have to stop now anyway, because the children will be coming back.'

'I never wanted to fight.'

'No.' Lucy considered her sister-in-law. Diya had never had a brother. She didn't even know what fighting was. As far as Lucy knew, Jim had never been tough with Diya. He'd never even argued with her. Diya would have beaten him at that anyway, because Jim was a man of few words, and Diya, when she first came, had bewildered them all by her ability to find things to say about everything, and quite often – so Lucy's Da used to say – about nothing much at all. 'Well, then, let's not fight,' said Lucy. 'I said I'm sorry.' She waited.

'Sorry?' said Diya, considering the word. 'Oh that, yes. But that doesn't mean we can go back to where we were before.'

Lucy had never seen Diya in this mood before. 'Of course we can't go backwards. Time doesn't. So we go on.'

'Do we?'

'You're thinking we have a choice about it?' asked Lucy. Diya was being hopelessly unfathomable. It was very irritating, but the children would be back in a minute, so something had to be done. Perhaps Jim had had to put up with this sort of thing when he and Diya were alone together. Diya had sometimes been uncharacteristically quiet when she first came to Ellan Bride. Mummig used to complain – behind Diya's back, of course – that Diya sulked. And Jim – Lucy remembered it all now – had quarrelled with Mummig. He'd shouted at Mummig as she stood there kneading her dough with her mouth set in a hard line, saying it was hardly surprising that Diya should be unhappy when no one tried to understand what it was like for her. In fact, now that Lucy thought about it, when she first came home there'd been other trouble afoot in the house besides her own. Perhaps – it had never crossed her mind before – that was partly why Mummig had been so forgiving to her erring daughter. It might explain why, although Lucy had come home expecting a storm of anger to break around her ears, it never had.

'Diya,' said Lucy. 'I'm sorry about what I said. It's true that I believe you're wanting to get away from here. But maybe I can understand why.'

Diya looked up. 'Can you?' She sounded oddly wistful.

'Yes,' said Lucy. 'And what you were saying – it's a long time we've been together. And there was Jim, too. We'll be going on together – for a while, anyway. And maybe that'll be ending some time too. But even if we're parting, it doesn't mean –' Lucy hesitated, trying words that would fit what she wanted to say. 'Parting doesn't have to mean *breaking* anything.'

'Does it not?'

Lucy had never heard Diya sound so like Mally. Mally was one of the people Lucy loved, and certainly Lucy had never been in the least in awe of her small niece. It didn't come naturally to her – not with Diya – but Lucy made herself cross the empty space between the doorway and where Diya was standing by the table. She put her arm clumsily around Diya's shoulders. 'Whatever happens,' said Lucy sturdily. 'We're not breaking anything. We can't. Not with Billy and Breesha and Mally to be thinking of. This family is where they're *belonging*. That's how it's been all their lives – you and I had to make ourselves belong to each other on purpose, and that was harder – but we're not breaking it now. Whatever happens.'

Diya's face quivered. Lucy managed to stand her ground all the same. Diya laid her hand over Lucy's where it lay on her shoulder. There were sounds outside, coming nearer: treble voices calling to one another. Diya pressed Lucy's hand and let it go. 'Here they come,' she said. 'I'm sorry, Lucy. I never meant to say that about Billy. It wasn't true. I'm not . . . I'm *proud* of him, Lucy. Of all of them.'

'Of course we are.' Lucy stepped back, relieved that there were to be no more tears or heartsearchings. 'We ought to be telling them, Diya. About the letter and everything. About the cottage, and going to Port St Mary.'

Diya's eyes suddenly dropped. The children's voices were almost at the door. There was a little pause, and then she said, 'We'll tell them at supper. And then – what we've not done, Lucy – we should write another letter. We'd better do it together. We should write and say exactly where we want to go, and that we've both decided to go to Port St Mary. And then Finn can take it next time he comes. Otherwise the Governor might be assuming . . . he might have the wrong idea.'

'Hush, here they come!'

It seemed odd to have so much space round the table. They were back in their old places, with Lucy at one end of the table and Diya at the other, and Breesha and Mally on the bench on one side, and Billy, with his back to the fire, on the other. It was poached eggs on toast, which was a favourite, but when they first sat down everyone was so subdued that it might as well have been watered-down fish soup. Soup from dried fish was what they had quite often in the hungry gap of early spring, when there was sometimes very little to eat.

'Is Mr Groat having his supper too?' asked Mally wistfully, after she'd been trying for a while to cut her toast into strips with the bread knife.

'Mally, do you want me to help with that?'

'No, I can do it myself. Is Mr Groat having his supper too?'

'I expect so.'

'In Castletown, I expect,' said Breesha. 'They might be in Castletown by now.'

'The Pirate Man was left behind in Castletown before,' said Mally. She reached for the butter dish. 'Why was he left behind, Mam?'

'Not with the bread knife, Mally! Use this. And you don't need that much butter.'

'Why was the Pirate Man left behind in Castletown before?' asked Mally, carefully spreading butter into all the corners of her toast.

'I expect he killed someone,' said Breesha, with her mouth full.

'Nonsense, Breesha. You mustn't make up ridiculous stories about real people!'

'No, but I expect he did. Being a pirate. Perhaps supposing they were going to hang him, but he leapt off the – the whatever it is they hang you from – is it a sort of platform? – and fought his way through the crowd, and—'

'Breesha, that will do! We don't want to hear—'

'Anyway he didn't,' said Billy. 'Because Finn would have told us about it. Can I have some more toast?'

'You'll have to toast it yourself.'

Billy slid off his chair, while Aunt Diya cut another slice of bread. He squatted before the fire, watching his bread slowly brown, and holding the toasting fork at arm's length because the coals were still very hot from the cooking.

'I'll tell you what Finn *was* saying to us today, though,' said Lucy suddenly. She took a hunk of bread and began to wipe the egg from her plate. 'Much more important than about the Pirate . . . I mean Mr Scott. It's about us.'

Breesha and Mally stopped eating and looked at her with enquiring eyes. Billy looked round from his toasting.

'It's all because of Finn,' explained Lucy. 'Finn was doing everything he could to help us, after he went away from here last time. Because he was knowing that we had to be leaving very soon, now that the surveyors were here. And he was knowing that we had no money, and nowhere to go. So Finn went to the Governor himself. The Governor is the most powerful man on the Island, and he's living in Castle Rushen, right inside the walls of the Castle in a grand house that's looking over the harbour. And Finn went there for us, and was talking to the Governor. He was telling him how we were not knowing where to go or what was to become of us. And the Governor was very sorry that no one had been thinking of that. And because of Finn he arranged it all, there and then. The Governor is giving us enough money to be living on – all of us – and a cottage at Port St Mary. So that's where we'll be going to live, just as soon as the new lightkeeper comes to Ellan Bride.'

There was a short silence. Mally looked at Breesha with frightened eyes, to see what the three of them were going to say to that.

Billy looked up from the hearth. 'Can we live on the same bit of hill as Finn and Juan? Can we live right near *their* house?'

'We can ask,' said Lucy doubtfully. 'I'm not sure how it'll be arranged for us. But surely we can say what we're most wanting. And anyway, everywhere in Port St Mary is quite close to everywhere else.' She looked directly into Billy's face. 'Is this what you—'

'Billy, you've dropped your toast!'

'Hell!' Billy raked in the ashes with the toasting fork.

'*What* did you say?'

'He said "hell",' said Breesha with peculiar satisfaction. 'Like the surveyors. "Hell and damnation."' She let the juicy words roll off her tongue. 'You'll never get it out now, Billy. It'll be all burnt.'

'What I'd like to know,' said Diya, with her eyes on Breesha, 'is what you all think.'

'What about?' asked Mally, still looking frightened. She wanted Breesha to storm and rage, and say this couldn't be happening. But Breesha wasn't doing anything of the sort. But Mam *knew* what Mally thought. Did no one care about Ellan Bride any more?

'Billy,' said Lucy. 'Stop raking about there and listen, please. Then you can have another slice. Are you happy about that, then, to be going to Port St Mary?' She fixed her eyes on Billy.

Billy fiddled with the toasting fork, and nearly burned his fingers on the hot prongs. He wanted to wriggle away from such a complicated question but there was nowhere to go. It was like lessons. At other times his family were usually too busy voicing their own opinions to try to pin him down.

'Do you want to go to Port St Mary?' Diya asked him straightly.

Billy countered with a question of his own. 'Are we going to see Mr Groat again one day?'

His Mam suddenly went very still, but it was Aunt Diya who answered him. She was smiling a little, as if she thought Billy had said something he didn't mean. 'Do you want to see Mr Groat again?'

Billy stopped staring at the toasting fork and looked defiantly at Breesha instead. 'If we went to Port St Mary,' he said, 'maybe I could do some more measuring. I could get money for that. The Writing Man said so. I could do work like Mr Groat.'

'You could,' said Aunt Diya. 'But perhaps before that you could go to school – oh, not to do boring lessons like the ones I give you – but learn about measuring and other things like that. With other boys. And if you've been to school you'll be qualified – you'll know enough – to learn to do really interesting work. Maybe even the sort that Mr Groat does.'

'But doesn't he want to be a lightkeeper?' Mally's question sounded more like a cry of anguish.

'Boys!' exploded Breesha. 'Hell and damnation!'

'That will do, Breesha! We'll come to you in a minute. Billy,' said Aunt Diya gently, 'what Mally asked you – do you want to be a lightkeeper?'

Billy wriggled. The fire was getting very hot. He glanced at Mam. Then he stood holding the toasting fork across his chest, and looking at Mally, because she was the easiest. 'I could maybe *measure* for lighthouses,' he offered. 'I could maybe work for Mr Stevenson. I could maybe go to lots of *different* lighthouses. And that would be *like* being the lightkeeper on Ellan Bride, but maybe just not exactly the same.' His glanced at Lucy again. 'Couldn't I, Mam?'

To his astonishment Mam wasn't looking upset at all. She was red in the face and very bright-eyed. 'I don't know, Billy,' she said softly. 'I don't know, but if you're wanting it to happen it may well be possible. The Writing Man said he'd speak for you. We all heard that. But if we go to Port St Mary, maybe you could be going to school like Aunt Diya said, and be learning about the measuring. And maybe you could be going in the boat with Finn and Juan and learning more about the sea and everything too. And maybe – I can't be sure, mind – maybe Mr Groat will be turning up again too, and you can be asking him about it.'

Billy was grinning, but at that moment Mally burst into tears. 'You don't *care*! You don't none of you care! Breesha, *you* care! Breesha, tell them you care about staying on Ellan Bride!'

Diya went to pick Mally up, but Mally pushed her off, sobbing. 'You don't none of you *care*!'

'Mally,' said Diya. 'I told you before, beti, we don't have any choice.'

'Of course we care!' said Breesha suddenly. 'You know that! We'll never stop caring. I swear it! In fact' – a gleam came into her eye – 'maybe we could *all* have a swearing. A solemn vow – I know how we could . . . That we'll always go on remembering . . . Maybe in the keeill . . . And then every year, wherever we were, we could . . . But anyway' – Breesha suddenly became brisk – 'Mam's right, we don't have any choice. And – and – Mam, why is the school all boys? Why can't *I* go to school too?'

'Why do you want to go to school, Breesha beti?'

'Because, because . . . you said he'd have other boys. Well, I *hate* boys. I want to have other *girls*.'

'You don't hate Billy!' screamed Mally.

Diya glanced anxiously at Billy. Billy was looking at Lucy, who raised her eyebrows at him and pointed to the half-cut loaf. Billy nodded, and came over with the toasting fork while Lucy cut another slice. When she handed it to him she winked at him. Billy winked back, and returned to his toasting, turning his face to the warm fire, and his back to his family.

'That's nothing to do with it, stupid. I just hate *boys*. I want there to be *girls*.'

Mally wiped her nose on the back of her hand and said defiantly. 'Well, *I'm* a girl, so you don't hate *me*.'

'You! You're so small no one cares *what* you are!'

'Breesha, don't be unkind!'

'I'm not unkind. It's true! Anyway, it doesn't matter. Can I go to school too, Mam? Is there a school that just has girls?'

'We'll have to see about the school, beti,' said Diya, looking doubtful. 'There might not be one. But there will be other girls, I promise.'

Mally looked up. She'd smeared snot from her nose all across her cheek, and her eyes were puffy from weeping, but she'd stopped crying. 'Can I have a girl too?' she asked, suddenly eager. 'Can I have one the same age as me?'

Mally was remembering a story Mam had told her long ago, about a little girl in a red frock and a frilled pinafore who'd bowled an iron hoop across the market square outside Great-Grandmother's house in Castletown. Mam had heard the sound of the hoop and looked out of the window. Mam had been all on her own in the big cold house, looking out, and it turned out later that the girl in the red frock was called Sally, and she was the daughter of Great-Grandmother's friend and so Sally and Mam had been allowed to play together. Mally had never seen Sally, and it didn't occur to her that by now Sally must be quite grown up, but she had a very clear picture of her in her mind. She leaned over and pulled Mam's sleeve to get her attention: 'Can I have a girl? Can I have a girl too? A girl the same age as me?'

'I could put the horse to yon bit of pasture,' said Ben. 'Where we put the other one before.'

'If you like,' said Archie absently. He checked over their gear where it lay in the gig. 'We'll leave all that there. It's as safe as anywhere.' He looked bleakly at the other two men. 'We'll be off as early as we can the morn. I've an appointment here first, but with any luck I'll be finished quite early. I'm hoping we can be away by noon, or maybe even earlier. We'll wait for the next steam packet in Douglas, not here. And' – he glanced at Drew, as if he'd been about to say something, but thought better of it. 'Ay well,' Archie sighed. 'I'll be seeing you the morn.'

'We'll be getting a bite to eat then.' Ben added suddenly, 'Will ye no join us, sir?'

Drew jumped as if a wasp had stung him, and looked at Ben in horror.

'That is,' pursued Ben, 'if you're maybe no wanting to eat all alone in yon grand dining-room place. But maybe you are, and I'm meaning no offence. But when I've put this horse to grass, Drew and me'll be looking for a bite of supper, and you'd be welcome to join us.'

'That's kind of you, Mr Groat. I don't know that . . . I don't know but what . . . well, then,' said Archie, flushing. 'Maybe I will.'

'For Chrissake, Ben . . .' muttered Drew, as he followed Ben and the piebald mare along the muddy lane past the cottages. 'Whit the hell are ye thinking o? Are we takin Young Archibald all roon the toon – ken whit I mean? – for the rest o the night, for God's sake?'

'I'm no staying out late,' said Ben. 'And no more are you, Drew. We'll keep our heads down an our noses clean until we're all of us well out of this toon. And we're no going to yon Harbourside tavern again either. We'll just go along to that inn we passed on our way – I noted it specially – and we'll get a pint and some supper there. And that'll do for tonight. We'll be turning in early.'

'For Chrissake. Keep our noses clean, but! And me just oot o jail! Have a hairt, man!'

'Ay, a heart is just what I'm having! Do you no realise you've got Young Archibald into a fair bit o trouble? That's what's worrying him. Can you no tell?'

'*Me* get *him* intae trouble? Are ye oot o yer mind?'

They stopped on the threadbare turf, and Ben bent down

to fasten the hobble. 'There you go, lass.' He patted the mare on the rump. 'Mak the most of it while you can. Come on, Drew.'

'But . . .'

The taproom of Ben's chosen inn was half full, mostly with respectable travellers who'd stopped for a meal at the end of a long day. There was a low buzz of conversation, and although it was a fine summer evening a generous log fire blazed in the hearth at the gable end. The fireside seats were all taken up, but there were places at the other end of the long table. The three men sat down. Drew was openly disgruntled, and Young Archibald was shy and awkward. Ben left the two of them sitting in frozen silence, not meeting one another's eyes, and strolled over to the bar. Two minutes later he was back.

'It's fish stew and potatoes. The boy'll bring it over. Will I get you a pint, sir?'

Archie hesitated. Ben earned less than half of what he did. Archie should have thought of that sooner. It would be insulting to say anything now. If they had another round later he'd be ready to get in first. Two rounds . . . Then they could go back . . . Surely Drew wouldn't offer . . . Now that they were here Archie was wishing to God he'd said no in the first place. He couldn't think why he hadn't. 'Ay,' mumbled Archie. 'Thank you, Ben.'

'Drew?'

Drew glared at Ben. He was still furious. 'Ay, might as well.'

Ben came back with three tankards, apparently quite at ease. 'Ay, ay,' he said, sitting down opposite his companions. 'It's a bit of a change, this. Is it no, sir? They fed us pretty well on Ellan Bride. Mrs Geddes did all our cooking for us, Drew, and a good cook she was too. Was she no, sir?'

'Ay,' said Archie, and, making an effort, he added, 'indeed she was.'

'Ay, they were good to us,' went on Ben, 'seeing we canna have been exactly welcome. Strange though. I'm no used to working with women and bairns at a lighthouse. Barring the peedie boy, that is. But they've managed to keep the place running very well. Have they no, sir?'

'Ay,' said Archie, then added, 'they have.'

Drew was curious enough to forget his grudge. 'Ay, and whit's gaen to happen to them a' noo? When they send oot the new lightkeeper? They'll need to be awa when that happens, will they no?'

'I don't know,' said Archie stiffly, not looking at him. 'I promised I'd speak to Mr Stevenson about it. They weren't actually employed by the Commissioners, of course, but – I don't know.'

'We'll be back here anyway,' remarked Ben. 'We'll mak sure and see for ourselves. Finn will tell us where they're staying if they're no on the island.'

'D'ye ken where Finn stays then?' asked Drew.

'Ay, for I asked him. He stays on the hill above the port, in a peedie place ca'd Fistard. He has a bit of land up there too. He said anybody would show me the way, when I'm here again. And he'll ken where the lightkeepers have gone, wherever they are.'

'Well, *well*,' said Drew. 'That's all verra charitable of ye, Ben. Verra charitable indeed. So you'll be seeking them oot, will ye? Ye were maybe thinking o setting up an orphanage then, were ye?'

Ben flushed, but before he could speak again a sweating pot boy appeared with a laden tray. He set the steaming plates in front of them. Archie glanced up at him, and gave him a brief unhappy smile. 'Thank you,' he said.

The pot boy gave him a cheerful grin, and Drew looked up in surprise. It wasn't like Young Archibald to spare a good word for anyone, or so Drew had thought.

'I doubt we'll be back,' said Archie, suddenly entering the conversation. 'It's more likely we'll be back to Dunnett Head after this, I reckon.'

'Ay well,' said Ben.

Drew was watching them curiously. This was intriguing, and he'd quite forgotten how angry he was to be dragged here at all. 'Ye could ask the old man for leave though,' he said to Ben. 'Could ye no? Ye've no been hame to yer mither this year, have ye? Nor last year neither, if I mind correctly. He'd give ye a week or twa, nae doot. Ye'd no need to say whether ye were heading north or sooth.'

Archie looked from one to the other of them, startled into completely forgetting his own embarrassment. Ben Groat was looking unusually red in the face, but then it was very hot in here. Scott was grinning at Ben with a knowing look in his eyes. Archie had never seen Scott look less than truculent before; for the first time he saw that the man had a positive twinkle. The pot boy's face had lit up the same way when he'd smiled because Archie thanked him. Archie never forgot to be civil to the pot boy, however low the tavern: so many people just treated them like dirt. But for these people it wasn't a case of remembering on purpose. These men – Drew, Ben, the pot boy – they didn't seem to have to think at all. They found it so easy to be friendly with each other, and yet they didn't have much in common. Maybe when he, Archie, was away from all this – maybe when he was on the *Beagle* – he could start off by being easy too. No one there need know he'd ever been different. And there was Ben too, looking confused, but somehow pleased with himself at the same time – what was all that about? And how could Scott possibly know? Scott had only been on the island a matter of hours. Archie had been there all the time, and hadn't noticed a thing. Surely there'd been nothing to notice? Maybe it was just some nonsense of Scott's.

Drew winked at Ben, and raised his half-empty tankard. 'Ay Ben, so ye're the fast worker, are ye no? And is that no' – he chuckled as he found the word he was looking for – a word that would really make Ben blush, if anything did – 'is that no *romantic*? The wee lightkeeper, eh? Ay well, I wish ye luck! And a wean too, a wee boy all ready-made for ye. I'll get us a round and we'll drink to yer luck. Will we no, sir?' Drew swung his leg over the bench to get out.

Archie stood up suddenly, looking dazed, and almost knocked the bench over in his haste. 'No, no, I'll get this one.' Without meeting Drew's eyes he quickly pressed Drew's shoulder down, so that he sat down heavily on the bench again. 'This one's on me, Scott,' he said hurriedly. 'It's me . . . it's my round. This one's on me.'

Chapter 35

Lucy sat on the lighthouse parapet in the cool of the evening waiting for the sun to set. A fleet of Cornish herring smacks had gathered to the west of the Chickens, their sails catching the last of the sunlight. The cliffs of the Calf gleamed in the westering sun. Beyond them rose the blue summit of Cronk ny Arrey Laa, and away to the north-east, Snaefell. The far lands were blue and distant this evening, insubstantial as ghosts. Only Ellan Bride was green, the one solid thing in the middle of a world made of nothing more real than the colours of light and water.

Soon Ellan Bride would be gone. Or rather, they would be gone – herself and Billy, Diya, Breesha and Mally – they'd be the ones who'd go, and Ellan Bride would be left. Lucy would carry Ellan Bride away with her, inside her head, and no one could take one detail of it from her. She had it all recorded: every rock, every giau, every skerry, every name . . . But even that . . . one day Lucy herself would grow old and she might start to forget. She could remind Billy, and they could talk about it together for the rest of her life, but he was bound to forget more than she did, and after that – if Billy had children of his own – the island would only be a story, and a faint blue line, perhaps, sometimes seen on the horizon. But the actual island – this island, made of solid rock, inhabited by its own plants and birds and animals – Ellan Bride itself would still be there when all of them had gone for ever. It would be there after the last human being had landed and gone away again. It was like it said in the scroll over the door of the lighthouse, the way her Da had explained it to her so many years ago: *Et in Arcadia ego*. Even this must pass.

But at least now they had somewhere to go. In the pot on the kitchen dresser there was the letter in Governor Smelt's own hand, promising them a future. That was certain. And in Lucy's sea chest, hidden under her petticoat, there was a scrap of paper torn out of a notebook, with an address in Edinburgh printed on it in pencil. That was less certain. Wherever they went, she and Billy would have each other, and that was the most important thing in the world. If there were another child it would be difficult, but Lucy knew already that, whatever happened, she could be strong enough for all of them. At least she'd know if another child was on the way before they had to leave the island.

Finn had brought Lucy the best gift of all today: the chance to choose. Maybe that was why she felt strong again. There was no power out there in heaven or earth that could make game of her. Governor Smelt's letter offered one possibility. Ben might offer another. Even Governor Smelt's letter offered them its own element of choice.

And then there was Diya . . . Maybe she and Diya had understood each other better today than they ever had before. Diya didn't know everything that had happened since the surveyors came, but Lucy and Diya had stood by one another so long neither of them would break faith now, whatever lay in store. They'd stay together as long as they needed to. At least until something else happened.

Lucy picked up the log book, which she'd brought up to the lantern with her. She put in the date, and ruled a new line. She carefully recorded another day of drought, very warm and clear, with a light westerly breeze, turning northerly in the afternoon. Lucy ruled one more line and added a note: '*Betsey* 2 h to l.w. – 2 h past l.w.'. There was nothing else to put in about today.